S0-AEO-166

Introducing Discworld...

The Discworld is a world not totally unlike our own, except that it is flat, and magic is as integral as gravity to the way it works. Though some of its inhabitants are witches, dwarfs, wizards and even policemen, their stories are fundamentally about people being people.

The Discworld novels can be read in any order, but the Wizards series is a good place to start.

Discworld novels starring the Wizards

The Colour of Magic
The Light Fantastic
Sourcery
Eric
Interesting Times
The Last Continent
Unseen Academicals

A full list of the Discworld novels in order can be found at the end of this book

Terry Pratchett was the acclaimed creator of the global bestselling Discworld series, the first of which, *The Colour of Magic*, was published in 1983. In all, he was the author of over fifty bestselling books which have sold over 100 million copies worldwide. His novels have been widely adapted for stage and screen, and he was the winner of multiple prizes, including the Carnegie Medal. He was awarded a knighthood for services to literature in 2009, although he always wryly maintained that his greatest service to literature was to avoid writing any.

THE LAST CONTINENT

Discworld®: A Wizards Novel

TERRY PRATCHETT

PENGUIN BOOKS

TRANSWORLD PUBLISHERS
Penguin Random House, One Embassy Gardens,
8 Viaduct Gardens, London SW11 7BW
www.penguin.co.uk

Transworld is part of the Penguin Random House group of companies
whose addresses can be found at global.penguinrandomhouse.com

Penguin
Random House
UK

First published in Great Britain in 1998 by Doubleday
an imprint of Transworld Publishers
Corgi edition published 1999
Corgi edition reissued 2006
Corgi edition reissued 2013
Penguin paperback edition published 2022

Copyright © Dunmanifestin 1998
Discworld™ is a trademark registered by Dunmanifestin Ltd
The book titles, character names and the content of Terry Pratchett's
works are protected as trademarks and/or by copyright

Terry Pratchett has asserted his right under the Copyright,
Designs and Patents Act 1988 to be identified as the author of this work.

This book is a work of fiction and, except in the case of historical fact,
any resemblance to actual persons, living or dead, is purely coincidental.

Every effort has been made to obtain the necessary permissions with
reference to copyright material, both illustrative and quoted. We apologize
for any omissions in this respect and will be pleased to make
the appropriate acknowledgements in any future edition.

A CIP catalogue record for this book
is available from the British Library.

ISBNs
9781804990230 (B format)
9781804990223 (A format)

Typeset in Minion by Jouve (UK), Milton Keynes.
Printed and bound in Great Britain by Clays Ltd, Elcograf S.p.A.

The authorized representative in the EEA is Penguin Random House Ireland,
Morrison Chambers, 32 Nassau Street, Dublin D02 YH68.

Penguin Random House is committed to a sustainable future for
our business, our readers and our planet. This book is made
from Forest Stewardship Council® certified paper.

Discworld is a world and a mirror of worlds.

This is not a book about Australia. No, it's about somewhere entirely different which just happens to be, here and there, a bit . . . australian.

Still . . . no worries, right?

THE
LAST
CONTINENT

Against the stars a turtle passes, carrying four elephants on its shell.

Both turtle and elephants are bigger than people might expect, but out between the stars the difference between huge and tiny is, comparatively speaking, very small.

But this turtle and these elephants are, by turtle and elephant standards, big. They carry the Discworld, with its vast lands, cloudscapes, and oceans.

People don't *live* on the Disc any more than, in less hand-crafted parts of the multiverse, they live on balls. Oh, planets may be the place where their body eats its tea, but they *live* elsewhere, in worlds of their own which orbit very handily around the centre of their heads.

When gods get together they tell the story of one particular planet whose inhabitants watched, with mild interest, huge continent-wrecking slabs of ice slap into another world which was, in astronomical terms, right next door – *and then did nothing about it* because that sort of thing only happens in Outer Space. An *intelligent* species would at least have found someone to complain to. Anyway, no one seriously believes in that story, because a race quite that stupid would never even have discovered slood.*

People believe in all sorts of other things, though. For example, there are some people who have a legend that the whole universe is carried in a leather bag by an old man.

They're right, too.

Other people say: hold on, if he's carrying the entire universe in a sack, right, that means he's carrying himself and the sack *inside* the sack, because the universe contains everything. Including him. And the sack, of course. Which contains him and the sack already. As it were.

To which the reply is: well?

All tribal myths are true, for a given value of 'true'.

It is a general test of the omnipotence of a god that they can see the fall of a tiny bird. But only one god makes notes, and a few adjustments, so that next time it can fall faster and further.

We may find out why.

We might find out why mankind is here, although that is more complicated and begs the question 'Where else should we be?' It would be terrible to think that some impatient deity might part the clouds and say, 'Damn, are you lot still here? I thought you discovered slood ten thousand years ago! I've got ten trillion tons of ice arriving on Monday!'

---

* Much easier to discover than fire, and only slightly harder to discover than water.

We may even find out why the duck-billed platypus.*

Snow, thick and wet, tumbled on to the lawns and roofs of Unseen University, the Discworld's premier college of magic.

It was sticky snow, which made the place look like some sort of expensive yet tasteless ornament, and it caked around the boots of McAbre, the Head Bledlow, as he trudged through the cold, wild night.

Two other bledlows† stepped out of the lee of a buttress and fell in behind him on a solemn march towards the main gates.

It was an old custom, centuries old, and in the summer a few tourists would hang around to watch it, but the Ceremony of the Keys went on every night in every season. Mere ice, wind and snow had never stopped it. Bledlows in times gone past had clambered over tentacled monstrosities to do the Ceremony; they'd waded through floodwater, flailed with their bowler hats at errant pigeons, harpies and dragons, and ignored mere faculty members who'd thrown open their bedroom windows and screamed imprecations on the lines of 'Stop that damn racket, will you? What's the *point*?' They'd never stopped, or even thought of stopping. You couldn't stop Tradition. You could only add to it.

The three men reached the shadows by the main

---

*Not why is it *anything*. Just why it is.

† A cross between a porter and a proctor. A bledlow is not chosen for his imagination, because he usually doesn't have any.

gate, almost blotted out in the whirling snow. The bledlow on duty was waiting for them.

'Halt! Who Goes There?' he shouted.

McAbre saluted. 'The Archchancellor's Keys!'

'Pass, The Archchancellor's Keys!'

The Head Bledlow took a step forward, extended both arms in front of him with his palms bent back towards him, and patted his chest at the place where some bledlow long buried had once had two breast pockets. Pat, pat. Then he extended his arms by his sides and stiffly patted the sides of his jacket. Pat, pat.

'Damn! Could Have Sworn I Had Them A Moment Ago!' he bellowed, enunciating each word with a sort of bulldog carefulness.

The gatekeeper saluted. McAbre saluted.

'Have You Looked In All Your Pockets?'

McAbre saluted. The gatekeeper saluted. A small pyramid of snow was building up on his bowler hat.

'I Think I Must Have Left Them On The Dresser. It's Always The Same, Isn't It?'

'You Should Remember Where You Put Them Down!'

'Hang On, Perhaps They're In My Other Jacket!'

The young bledlow who was this week's Keeper of the Other Jacket stepped forward. Each man saluted the other two. The youngest cleared his throat and managed to say:

'No, I Looked In . . . There This . . . Morning!'

McAbre gave him a slight nod to acknowledge a difficult job done well, and patted his pockets again.

'Hold On, Stone The Crows, They Were In This Pocket After All! What A Muggins I Am!'

'Don't Worry, I Do The Same Myself!'

'Is My Face Red! Forget My Own Head Next!'

Somewhere in the darkness a window creaked up.

'Er, excuse me, gentlemen—'

'Here's The Keys, Then!' said McAbre, raising his voice.

'Much Obliged!'

'I wonder if you could—' the querulous voice went on, apologizing for even thinking of complaining.

'All Safe And Secure!' shouted the gatekeeper, handing the keys back.

'—perhaps keep it down a *little*—'

'Gods Bless All Present!' screamed McAbre, veins standing out on his thick crimson neck.

'Careful Where You Put Them This Time. Ha! Ha! Ha!'

'Ho! Ho! Ho!' yelled McAbre, beside himself with fury. He saluted stiffly, went About Turn with an unnecessarily large amount of foot stamping and, the ancient exchange completed, marched back to the bledlows' lodge muttering under his breath.

The window of the University's little sanatorium shut again.

'That man really makes me want to swear,' said the Bursar. He fumbled in his pocket and produced his little green box of dried frog pills, spilling a few as he fumbled with the lid. 'I've sent him no end of memos. He says it's traditional but, I don't know, he's so . . .

boisterous about it . . .' He blew his nose. 'How's he doing?'

'Not good,' said the Dean.

The Librarian was very, very ill.

Snow plastered itself against the closed window.

There was a heap of blankets in front of the roaring fire. Occasionally it shuddered a bit. The wizards watched it with concern.

The Lecturer in Recent Runes was feverishly turning over the pages of a book.

'I mean, how do we know if it's old age or not?' he said. 'What's old age for an orang-utan? *And* he's a wizard. *And* he spends all his time in the Library. All that magic radiation the whole time. Somehow the flu is attacking his morphic field, but it could be caused by *anything.*'

The Librarian sneezed.

And changed shape.

The wizards looked sadly at what appeared very much like a comfortable armchair which someone had, for some reason, upholstered in red fur.

'What can we do for him?' said Ponder Stibbons, the Faculty's youngest member.

'He might feel happier with some cushions,' said Ridcully.

'Slightly bad taste, Archchancellor, I feel.'

'What? Everyone likes some comfy cushions when they're feeling a little under the weather, don't they?' said the man to whom sickness was a mystery.

'He was a table this morning. Mahogany, I believe. He seems to be able to retain his colour, at least.'

The Lecturer in Recent Runes closed the book with a sigh. 'He's certainly lost control of his morphic function,' he said. 'It's not surprising, I suppose. Once it's been changed, it'll change again much more easily, I'm afraid. A well known fact.'

He looked at the Archchancellor's frozen grin and sighed. Mustrum Ridcully was notorious for not trying to understand things if there was anyone around to do it for him.

'It's quite hard to change the shape of a living thing but once it's been done it's a lot easier to do it next time,' he translated.

'Say again?'

'He was a human before he was an ape, Archchancellor. Remember?'

'Oh. Yes,' said Ridcully. 'Funny, really, the way you get used to things. Apes and humans are related, accordin' to young Ponder here.'

The other wizards looked blank. Ponder screwed up his face.

'He's been showing me some of the invisible writings,' said Ridcully. 'Fascinatin' stuff.'

The other wizards scowled at Ponder Stibbons, as you would at a man who'd been caught smoking in a firework factory. So *now* they knew who to blame. As usual . . .

'Is that entirely *wise*, sir?' said the Dean.

'Well, I do happen to be the Archchancellor in these parts, Dean,' said Ridcully calmly.

'A blindly obvious fact, Archchancellor,' said the Dean. You could have cut cheese with his tone.

17

'Must take an interest. Morale, you know,' said Ridcully. 'My door is always open. I see myself as a member of the team.' Ponder winced again.

'I don't think I'm related to any apes,' said the Senior Wrangler thoughtfully. 'I mean, I'd know, wouldn't I? I'd get invited to their weddings and so on. My parents would have said something like, "Don't worry about Uncle Charlie, he's *supposed* to smell like that," wouldn't they? And there'd be portraits in—'

The chair sneezed. There was an unpleasant moment of morphic uncertainty, and then the Librarian was sprawling in his old shape again. The wizards watched him carefully to see what'd happen next.

It *was* hard to remember the time when the Librarian had been a human being. Certainly no one could remember what he'd looked like, or even what his name had been.

A magical explosion, always a possibility in somewhere like the Library where so many unstable books of magic are pressed dangerously together, had introduced him to unexpected apehood years before. Since then he'd never looked back, and often hadn't looked down either. His big hairy shape, swinging by one arm from a top shelf while he rearranged books with his feet, had become a popular one among the whole University body; his devotion to duty had been an example to everyone.

Archchancellor Ridcully, into whose head that last sentence had treacherously arranged itself, realized that he was unconsciously drafting an obituary.

'Anyone called in a doctor?' he said.

'We got Doughnut Jimmy* here this afternoon,' said the Dean. 'He tried to take his temperature but I'm afraid the Librarian bit him.'

'He bit him? With a thermometer in his mouth?'

'Ah. Not exactly. There, in fact, you have rather discovered the reason for his biting.'

There was a moment of solemn silence. The Senior Wrangler picked up a limp black-leather paw and patted it vaguely.

'Does that book say if monkeys have pulses?' he said. 'Is his nose supposed to be cold, or what?'

There was a little sound, such as might be made by half a dozen people all sharply drawing in their breath at once. The other wizards began to edge away from their Senior Wrangler.

There was, for a few seconds, no other sound but the crackling of the fire and the howl of the wind outside.

The wizards shuffled back.

The Senior Wrangler, in the astonished tones of someone still possessing all known limbs, very slowly took off his pointy hat. This was something a wizard would normally do only in the most sombre of circumstances.

'Well, that's it, then,' he said. 'Poor chap's on his way home. Back to the big desert in the sky.'

---

* Ankh-Morpork's leading vet, generally called in by people faced with ailments too serious to be trusted to the general medical profession. Doughnut's one blind spot was his tendency to assume that every patient was, to a greater or lesser extent, a racehorse.

'Er, rainforest, possibly,' said Ponder Stibbons.

'Maybe Mrs Whitlow could make him some hot nourishing soup?' said the Lecturer in Recent Runes.

Archchancellor Ridcully thought about the housekeeper's hot nourishing soup. 'Kill or cure, I suppose,' he murmured. He patted the Librarian carefully. 'Buck up, old chap,' he said. 'Soon have you back on your feet and continuing to make a valued contribution.'

'Knuckles,' said the Dean helpfully.

'Say again?'

'Knuckles, rather than feet.'

'Castors,' said the Lecturer in Recent Runes.

'Bad taste, that man,' said the Archchancellor.

They wandered out of the room. From the corridor came their retreating voices:

'Looked very pale around the antimacassar, I thought.'

'Surely there's some sort of a cure?'

'The old place won't be the same without him.'

'Definitely one of a kind.'

When they'd gone the Librarian reached up cautiously, pulled a piece of blanket over his head, cuddled his hot-water bottle and sneezed.

Now there were *two* hot-water bottles, one of them a lot bigger than the other and with a teddy bear cover in red fur.

* * *

Light travels slowly on the Disc and is slightly heavy, with a tendency to pile up against high mountain ranges. Research wizards have speculated that there is another, much speedier type of light which allows the slower light to be seen, but since this moves too fast to see they have been unable to find a use for it.

This *does* mean that, despite the Disc being flat, everywhere does not experience the same time at, for want of a better term, the same time. When it was so late at night in Ankh-Morpork that it was early in the morning, elsewhere it was . . .

. . . but there were no hours here. There was dawn and dusk, morning and afternoon, and presumably there was midnight and midday, but mainly there was heat. And redness. Something as artificial and human as an hour wouldn't last five minutes here. It would be dried out and shrivelled up in seconds.

Above all, there was silence. It was not the chilly, bleak silence of endless space, but the burning organic silence you get when, across a thousand miles of shimmering red horizons, everything is too tired to make a sound.

But, as the ear of observation panned across the desert, it picked up something like a chant, a reedy little litany that beat against the all-embracing silence like a fly bumping against the windowpane of the universe.

The rather breathless chanter was lost to view because he was standing in a hole dug in the red earth; occasionally some earth was thrown up on the heap behind him. A stained and battered pointy hat bobbed about in time with the tuneless tune. The word 'Wizzard' had, perhaps, once been embroidered on it in sequins. They had fallen off, but the word was still there in brighter red where the hat's original colour showed through. Several dozen small flies orbited it.

The words went something like this:

'Grubs! That's what we're going to eat! That's why they call it grub! And what're we doing to get the grub? Why, we're grubbing for it! Hooray!' Another shovelful of earth arced on to the heap, and the voice said, rather more quietly: 'I wonder if you can eat flies?'

They say the heat and the flies here can drive a man insane. But you don't have to believe that, and nor does that bright mauve elephant that just cycled past.

Strangely enough, the madman in the hole was the only person currently on the continent who might throw any kind of light on a small drama being enacted a thousand miles away and several metres below, where the opal miner known only to his mates as Strewth was about to make the most valuable yet dangerous discovery of his career.

Strewth's pick knocked aside the rock and dust of millennia, and something gleamed in the candlelight.

It was green, like frosty green fire.

Carefully, his mind suddenly as frozen as the light under his fingers, he picked away at the loose rock. The opal picked up and reflected more and more light on to his face as the debris fell away. There seemed to be no end to the glow.

Finally, he let his breath out in one go.

'Strewth!'

If he'd found a little piece of green opal, say about

the size of a bean, he'd have called his mates over and they'd have knocked off for a few beers. A piece the size of his fist would have had him pounding the floor. But with this . . . He was still standing there, brushing it gently with his fingers, when the other miners noticed the light and hurried over.

At least . . . they started out hurrying. As they came closer, they slowed to a kind of reverential walk.

No one said anything for a moment. The green light shone on their faces.

Then one of the men whispered: 'Good on yer, Strewth.'

'There isn't enough money in all the world, mate.'

'Watch out, it might just be a glaze . . .'

'Still worth a mint. Go on, Strewth . . . get it out.'

They watched like cats as the pick pried loose more and more rock, and found an edge. And another edge.

Now Strewth's fingers began to shake.

'Careful, mate . . . there's a side of it . . .'

The men took a step back as the last of the obscuring earth was knocked away. The thing *was* oblong, although the bottom edge was a confusion of twisted opal and dirt.

Strewth reversed his pick and laid the wooden handle against the glowing crystal.

'Strewth, it's no good,' he said. 'I just *gots* to know . . .'

He tapped the rock.

It echoed.

'Can't be hollow, can it?' said one of the miners. 'Never heard of that.'

Strewth picked up a crowbar. 'Right! Let's—'

There was a faint *plink*. A large piece of opal broke away near the bottom. It turned out to be no thicker than a plate.

It revealed a couple of toes, which moved very slowly inside their iridescent shell.

'Oh, *strewth*,' said a miner, as they backed further away. 'It's *alive*.'

Ponder *knew* he should never have let Ridcully look at the invisible writings. Wasn't it a basic principle never to let your employer know what it is you actually *do* all day?

But no matter what precautions you took, sooner or later the boss was bound to come in and poke around and say things like, 'Is this where you work, then?' and 'I thought I sent a memo out about people bringing in potted plants,' and 'What d'you call that thing with the keyboard?'

And this had been particularly problematical for Ponder, because reading the invisible writings was a delicate and meticulous job, suited to the kind of temperament that follows Grand Prix Continental Drift and keeps bonsai mountains as a hobby or even drives a Volvo. It needed painstaking care. It needed a mind that could enjoy doing jigsaw puzzles in a dark room. It did not need Mustrum Ridcully.

The hypothesis behind invisible writings was laughably complicated. All books are tenuously connected through L-space and, therefore, the content of any book ever written *or yet to be written* may, in the right circumstances, be deduced from a sufficiently close study of books already in existence. Future books exist *in potentia*, as it were, in the same way that a sufficiently detailed study of a handful of primal ooze will eventually hint at the future existence of prawn crackers.

But the primitive techniques used hitherto, based on ancient spells like Weezencake's Unreliable Algorithm, had meant that it took years to put together even the ghost of a page of an unwritten book.

It was Ponder's particular genius that he had found a way around this by considering the phrase, 'How do you know it's not possible until you've tried?' And experiments with Hex, the University's thinking engine, had found that, indeed, many things are not impossible *until* they have been tried.

Like a busy government which only passes expensive laws prohibiting some new and interesting thing when people have actually found a way of doing it, the universe relied a great deal on things *not* being tried at all.

When something *is* tried, Ponder found, it often does turn out to be impossible very quickly, but takes a little while for this to really be the case* – in effect, for the overworked laws of causality to hurry to the scene and pretend it has been impossible all along. Using Hex to remake the attempt in minutely different ways at very high speed had resulted in a high success rate, and

---

* In the case of cold fusion, this was longer than usual.

he was now assembling whole paragraphs in a matter of hours.

'It's like a conjurin' trick, then,' Ridcully had said. 'You're pullin' the tablecloth away before all the crockery has time to remember to fall over.'

And Ponder had winced and said, 'Yes, exactly like that, Archchancellor. Well done.'

And that had led to all the trouble with *How to Dynamically Manage People for Dynamic Results in a Caring Empowering Way in Quite a Short Time Dynamically*. Ponder didn't know when this book would be written, or even in which world it might be published, but it was obviously going to be popular because random trawls in the depths of L-space often turned up fragments. Perhaps it wasn't even just one book.

And the fragments had been on Ponder's desk when Ridcully had been poking around.

Unfortunately, like many people who are instinctively bad at something, the Archchancellor prided himself on how good at it he was. Ridcully was to management what King Herod was to the Bethlehem Playgroup Association.

His mental approach to it could be visualized as a sort of business flowchart with, at the top, a circle entitled 'Me, who does the telling' and, connected below it by a line, a large circle entitled 'Everyone else'.

Until now this had worked quite well, because, although Ridcully was an impossible manager, the University was impossible to manage and so everything worked seamlessly.

And it would have continued to do so if he hadn't suddenly started to see the point in preparing career development packages and, worst of all, job descriptions.

As the Lecturer in Recent Runes put it: 'He called me in and asked me what I did, exactly. Have you ever heard of such a thing? What sort of question is that? This is a *university*!'

'He asked *me* whether I had any personal worries,' said the Senior Wrangler. 'I don't see why I have to stand for that sort of thing.'

'And did you see that sign on his desk?' the Dean had said.

'You mean the one that says, "The Buck Starts Here"?'

'No, the other one. The one which says, "When You're Up to Your Ass in Alligators, Today Is the First Day of the Rest of Your Life."'

'And that means . . . ?'

'I don't think it's supposed to *mean* anything. I think it's just supposed to *be*.'

'Be what?'

'Pro-active, I think. It's a word he's using a lot.'

'What does that mean?'

'Well . . . in favour of activity, I suppose.'

'Really? Dangerous. In my experience, inactivity sees you through.'

Altogether, it was not a happy university at the moment, and mealtimes were the worst. Ponder tended to be isolated at one end of the High Table as the unwilling architect of this sudden tendency on the part of the Archchancellor to try to Weld Them Into A Lean Mean Team. The wizards had no intention of being lean, but were getting as mean as anything.

On top of that, Ridcully's sudden interest in taking an interest meant that Ponder had to explain something about his own current project, and one aspect of Ridcully that had not changed was his horrible habit of, Ponder suspected, deliberately misunderstanding things.

Ponder had long been struck by the fact that the Librarian, an ape – at least generally an ape, although this evening he seemed to have settled on being a small table set with a red-furred tea service – was, well, so human shaped. In fact, so many things were pretty much the *same* shape. Nearly everything you met was really a sort of complicated tube with two eyes and four arms or legs or wings. Oh, or they were fish. Or insects. All right, spiders as well. And a few odd things like starfish and whelks. But still there was a remarkably unimaginative range of designs. Where were the six-armed, six-eyed monkeys pinwheeling through the jungle canopy?

Oh, yes, octopussies too, but that was the point, they were really only a kind of underwater spider . . .

Ponder had poked around among the University's more or less abandoned Museum of Quite Unusual Things, and noticed something rather odd. Whoever had designed the skeletons of creatures had even less imagination than whoever had done the outsides. At least the outside-designer had tried a few novelties in the spots, wool and stripes department, but the bone-builder had generally just put a skull on a ribcage, shoved a pelvis in further along, stuck on some arms and legs and had the rest of the day off. Some ribcages were longer, some legs were shorter, some hands became wings, but they all seemed to be based on one design, one size stretched or shrunk to fit all.

Not to his very great surprise, Ponder seemed to be the only one around who found this at all interesting. He'd point out to people that fish were amazingly fish-shaped, and they'd look at him as if he'd gone mad.

Palaeontology and archaeology and other skulduggery were not subjects that interested wizards. Things are buried for a reason, they considered. There's no point in wondering what it was. Don't go digging things up in case they won't let you bury them again.

The most coherent theory was one he recalled from his nurse when he was small. Monkeys, she'd averred, were bad little boys who hadn't come in when called, and seals were bad little boys who'd lazed around on the beach instead of attending to their lessons. She hadn't said that birds were bad little boys who'd gone too close to the cliff edge, and in any case jellyfish would be more likely, but Ponder couldn't help thinking that, harmlessly insane though the woman had been, she might have had just the glimmerings of a point . . .

He was spending most nights now watching Hex trawl the invisible writings for any hints. In theory, because of the nature of L-space, absolutely every-thing was available to him, but that only meant that it was more or less impossible to find whatever it was you were looking for, which is the purpose of computers.

Ponder Stibbons was one of those unfortunate people cursed with the belief that if only he found out enough things about the universe it would all, somehow, make sense. The goal is the Theory of Everything, but Ponder would settle for the Theory of Something and, late at night, when Hex appeared to be sulking, he despaired of even a Theory of Anything.

And it might have surprised Ponder to learn that the senior wizards had come to approve of Hex, despite all the comments on the lines of 'In *my* day we used to do our *own* thinking.' Wizardry was tradition-ally competitive, and, while UU was currently going through an extended period of peace and quiet, with none of the informal murders that had once made it such a terminally exciting place, a senior wizard always distrusted a young man who was going places since traditionally his route might be via your jugular.

Therefore there's something comforting in know-ing that some of the best brains in the University, who a generation ago would be coming up with some really exciting plans involving trick floorboards and exploding wallpaper, were spending all night in the High Energy Magic Building, trying to teach Hex to sing 'Lydia the Tattooed Lady', exulting at getting a machine to do after six hours' work something that any human off the street would do for tuppence, then sending out for banana-and-sushi pizza and falling asleep at the keyboard. Their seniors called it technomancy, and slept a little easier in their beds in the knowledge that Ponder and his students weren't sleeping in *theirs*.

Ponder must have nodded off, because he was awakened just before 2 a.m. by a scream and realized he was face down in half of his supper. He pulled a piece of banana-flavoured mackerel off his cheek, left Hex quietly clicking through its routine and followed the noises.

The commotion led him to the hall in front of the big doors leading to the Library. The Bursar was lying on the floor, being fanned with the Senior Wrangler's hat.

'As far as we can gather, Archchancellor,' said the Dean, 'the poor chap couldn't sleep and came down for a book—'

Ponder looked at the Library doors. A big strip of black and yellow tape had been stuck across them, along with a sign saying: Danger, Do Notte Enter in Any Circumſtances. It was now hanging off, and the doors were ajar. This was no surprise. Any true wizard, faced with a sign like 'Do not open this door. Really. We mean it. We're not kidding. Opening this door will mean the end of the universe,' would *automatically* open the door in order to see what all the fuss was about. This made signs rather a waste of time, but at least it meant that when you handed what was left of the wizard to his grieving relatives you could say, as they grasped the jar, 'We *told* him not to.'

There was silence from the darkness on the other side of the doorway.

Ridcully extended a finger and pushed one door slightly.

Behind it something made a fluttering noise and the doors were slammed shut. The wizards jumped back.

'Don't risk it, Archchancellor!' said the Chair of Indefinite Studies. 'I tried to go in earlier and the whole section of Critical Essays had gone critical!'

Blue light flickered under the doors.

Elsewhere, someone might have said, 'It's just books! Books aren't dangerous!' But even *ordinary* books are dangerous, and not only the ones like *Make Gelignite the Professional Way*. A man sits in some museum somewhere and writes a harmless book about political economy and suddenly thousands of people who haven't even read it are dying because the ones who did haven't got the joke. Knowledge is dangerous, which is why governments often clamp down on people who can think thoughts above a certain calibre.

And the Unseen University Library was a magical library, built on a very thin patch of space-time. There were books on distant shelves that hadn't been written yet, books that never *would* be written. At least, not here. It had a circumference of a few hundred yards, but there was no known limit to its radius.

And in a magical library the books leak, and learn from one another . . .

'They've started attacking anyone who goes in,' moaned the Dean. 'No one can control them when the Librarian's not here!'

'But we're a university! We *have* to have a library!' said Ridcully. 'It adds *tone*. What sort of people would we be if we didn't go into the Library?'

'Students,' said the Senior Wrangler morosely.

'Hah, I remember when I was a student,' said the Lecturer in Recent Runes. 'Old "Bogeyboy" Swallett took us on an expedition to find the Lost Reading Room. Three weeks we were wandering around. Had to eat our own boots.'

'Did you find it?' said the Dean.

'No, but we found the remains of the previous year's expedition.'

'What did you do?'

'We ate their boots, too.'

From beyond the door came a flapping, as of leather covers.

'There's some pretty vicious grimoires in there,' said the Senior Wrangler. 'They can take a man's arm right off.'

'Yes, but at least they don't know about door-handles,' said the Dean.

'They do if there's a book in there somewhere called *Doorknobs for Beginners*,' said the Senior Wrangler. 'They *read* each other.'

The Archchancellor glanced at Ponder. 'There likely to be a book like that in there, Stibbons?'

'According to L-space theory, it's practically certain, sir.'

As one man, the wizards backed away from the doors.

'We can't let this nonsense go on,' said Ridcully. 'We've got to cure the Librarian. It's a magical illness, so we ought to be able to cook up a magical cure, oughtn't we?'

'That would be exceedingly dangerous, Archchancellor,' said the Dean. 'His whole system is a mess of conflicting magical influences. There's no knowing what adding more magic would do. He's already got a freewheeling temporal gland.* Any more magic and . . . well, I don't know what'll happen.'

'We'll find out,' said Ridcully brusquely. 'We *need* to be able to go into the Library. We'd be doing this for the college, Dean. And Unseen University is bigger than one man—'

'—ape—'

'—thank you, *ape*, and we must always remember that "I" is the smallest letter in the alphabet.'

There was another thud from beyond the doors.

'Actually,' said the Senior Wrangler, 'I think you'll find that, depending on the font, "c" or even "u"

---

* Wizards are certain of the existence of the temporal gland, although not even the most invasive alchemist has ever found where it is located and current theory is that it has a non-corporeal existence, like a sort of ethereal appendix. It keeps track of how old your body is, and is so susceptible to the influence of a high magical field that it might even work in reverse, absorbing the body's normal supplies of chrononine. The alchemists say it is the key to immortality, but they say that about orange juice, crusty bread and drinking your own urine. An alchemist would cut his own head off if he thought it'd make him live longer.

are, in fact, even smaller. Well, shorter, anyw—'

'Of course,' Ridcully went on, ignoring this as part of the University's usual background logic, 'I suppose I *could* appoint another librarian . . . got to be a senior chap who knows his way around . . . hmm . . . now let me see, do any names spring to mind? Dean?'

'All right, all *right*!' said the Dean. 'Have it your own way. As usual.'

'Er . . . we can't do it, sir,' Ponder ventured.

'Oh?' said Ridcully. 'Volunteering for a bit of book-shelf tidying yourself, are you?'

'I mean we *really* can't use magic to change him, sir. There's a huge problem in the way.'

'There are no problems, Mister Stibbons, there are only opportunities.'

'Yes, sir. And the opportunity here is to find out the Librarian's name.'

There was a buzz of agreement from the other wizards.

'The lad's right,' said the Lecturer in Recent Runes. 'Can't magic a wizard without knowing his name. Basic rule.'

'Well, we call him the Librarian,' said Ridcully. 'Everyone calls him the Librarian. Won't that do?'

'That's just a job description, sir.'

Ridcully looked at his wizards. 'One of us must know his name, surely? Good grief, I should hope we at least know our colleagues' *names*. Isn't that so . . .' He looked at the Dean, hesitated, and then said, 'Dean?'

'He's been an ape for quite a while . . .

35

Archchancellor,' said the Dean. 'Most of his original colleagues have ... passed on. Gone to the great Big Dinner in the Sky. We were going through one of those periods of droit de mortis.*'

'Yes, but he's got to be in the records *somewhere*.'

The wizards thought about the great cliffs of stacked paper that constituted the University's records.

'The archivist has never found him,' said the Lecturer in Recent Runes.

'Who's the archivist?'

'The Librarian, Archchancellor.'

'Then at least he ought to be in the Year Book for the year he graduated.'

'It's a very funny thing,' said the Dean, 'but a freak accident appears to have happened to every single copy of the Year Book for that year.'

Ridcully noted his wooden expression. 'Would it be an accident like a particular page being torn out leaving only a lingering bananary aroma?'

'Lucky guess, Archchancellor.'

Ridcully scratched his chin. 'A pattern emerges,' he said.

'You see, he's *always* been dead set against anyone finding out his name,' said the Senior Wrangler. 'He's

---

* Broadly speaking, the acceleration of a wizard through the ranks of wizardry by killing off more senior wizards. It is a practice currently in abeyance, since a few enthusiastic attempts to remove Mustrum Ridcully resulted in one wizard being unable to hear properly for two weeks. Ridcully felt that there was indeed room at the top, and he was occupying all of it.

afraid we'll try to turn him back into a human.' He looked meaningfully at the Dean, who put on an offended expression. '*Some* people have been going around saying that an ape as Librarian is *unsuitable.*'

'I merely expressed the view that it is against the traditions of the University—' the Dean began.

'Which consist largely of niggling, big dinners and shouting damnfool things about keys in the middle of the night,' said Ridcully. 'So I don't think we—'

The expressions on the faces of the other wizards made him turn around.

The Librarian had entered the hall. He walked very slowly, because of the amount of clothing he'd put on; the sheer volume of coats and sweaters meant that his arms, instead of being used as extra feet, were sticking out very nearly horizontally on either side of his body. But the most horrifying aspect of the shuffling apparition was the red woolly hat.

It was jolly. It had a bobble on it. It had been knitted by Mrs Whitlow, who was technically an extremely good needlewoman, but if she had a fault it lay in failing to take into account the precise dimensions of the intended recipient. Several wizards had on occasion been presented with one of her creations, which often assumed they had three ankles or a neck two metres across. Most of the things were surreptitiously given away to charitable institutions. You can say this about Ankh-Morpork – no matter how misshapen a garment, there will always be someone somewhere it would fit.

Mrs Whitlow's mistake here was the assumption

that the Librarian, for whom she had considerable respect, would like a red bobble hat with side flaps that tied under his chin. Given that this would technically require that they be tied under his groin, he'd opted to let them flap loose.

He turned a sad face towards the wizards as he stopped outside the Library door. He reached for the handle. He said, in a very weak voice, "k," and then sneezed.

The pile of clothing settled. When the wizards pulled it away, they found underneath a very large, thick book bound in hairy red leather.

'Says *Ook* on the cover,' said the Senior Wrangler after a while, in a rather strained voice.

'Does it say who it's by?' said the Dean.

'Bad taste, that man.'

'I *meant* that maybe it'd be his real name.'

'Can we look inside?' said the Chair of Indefinite Studies. 'There may be an index.'

'Any volunteers to look inside the Librarian?' said Ridcully. 'Don't all shout.'

'The morphic instability responds to the environment,' said Ponder. 'Isn't that interesting? He's near the Library, so it turns him into a book. Sort of . . . protective camouflage, you could say. It's as if he evolves to fit in with—'

'Thank you, Mister Stibbons. And is there a point to this?'

'Well, I assume we *can* look inside,' said Ponder. 'A book is meant to be opened. There's even a black leather bookmark, see?'

'Oh, that's a *bookmark*, is it?' said the Chair of Indefinite Studies, who had been watching it nervously.

Ponder touched the book. It was warm. And it opened easily enough.

Every page was covered with 'ook'.

'Good dialogue, but the plot is a little dull.'

'Dean! I'd be obliged if you'd take this seriously, please!' said Ridcully. He tapped his foot once or twice. 'Anyone got any more ideas?'

The wizards stared at one another and shrugged.

'I suppose . . .' said the Lecturer in Recent Runes.

'Yes, Runes . . . Arnold, isn't it?'

'No, Archchancellor . . .'

'Well, out with it anyway.'

'I suppose . . . I know this sounds ridiculous, but . . .'

'Go on, man. We're almost all agog.'

'I suppose there's always . . . Rincewind.'

Ridcully stared at him for a moment. 'Skinny fella? Scruffy beard? Bloody useless wizard? Got that box on legs thingy?'

'That's right, Archchancellor. Well done. Er . . . he *was* the Deputy Librarian for a while, as I expect you remember.'

'Not really, but do go on,' he said.

'In fact he was here when the Librarian . . . became the Librarian. And I remember once, when we were watching the Librarian stamping four books all at the same time, he said, "Amazing, really, when you think he was born in Ankh-Morpork." I'm sure if anyone knows the name of the Librarian it's Rincewind.'

'Well, go and fetch him, then! I suppose you *do* know where he is, do you?'

'Technically, yes, Archchancellor,' said Ponder quickly. 'But we're not sure quite where the place where he is *is*, if you follow me.'

Ridcully gave him another stare.

'You see, we think he's on EcksEcksEcksEcks, Archchancellor,' said Ponder.

'EcksEcks—'

'—EcksEcks, Archchancellor.'

'I thought no one knew where that place was,' said Ridcully.

'*Exactly*, Archchancellor,' said Ponder. Sometimes you had to turn facts in several directions until you found the right way to fit them into Ridcully's head.*

'What's he doing there?'

'We don't really know, Archchancellor. If you remember, we believe he ended up there after that Agatean business . . .'

'What did he want to go there for?'

'I don't think he exactly *wanted* to,' said Ponder. 'Er . . . we sent him. It was a trivial error in bi-locational thaumaturgy that anyone could make.'

'But *you* made it, as I recall,' said Ridcully, whose memory could spring nasty surprises like that.

---

* Sometimes Ponder thought his skill with Hex was because Hex was very clever and very stupid at the same time. If you wanted it to understand something, you had to break the idea down into bite-sized pieces and make absolutely sure there was no room for any misunderstanding. The quiet hours with Hex were often a picnic after five minutes with the senior wizards.

'I *am* a member of the team, sir,' said Ponder, pointedly.

'Well, if he doesn't want to be there, and we need him here, let's bring him b—'

The rest of the sentence was drowned out not by a noise but by a sort of bloom of quietness, which rolled over the wizards and was so oppressive and soft that they couldn't even hear their own heartbeats. Old Tom, the University's magical and tongueless bell, tolled out 2 a.m. by striking the silences.

'Er—' said Ponder. 'It's not as simple as that.'

Ridcully blinked. 'Why not?' he said. 'Bring him back by magic. We sent him there, we can bring him back.'

'Er . . . it'd take months to set it up properly, if you want him back right here,' said Ponder. 'If we get it wrong he'll end up arriving in a circle fifty feet wide.'

'That's not a problem, is it? If we keep out of it he can land anywhere.'

'I don't think you quite understand, sir. The signal to noise ratio of any thaumic transfer over an uncertain distance, coupled with the Disc's own spin, will almost certainly result in a practical averaging of the arriving subject over an area of a couple of thousand square feet at least, sir.'

'Say again?'

Ponder took a deep breath. 'I mean he'll end up arriving *as* a circle. Fifty feet wide.'

'Ah. So he probably wouldn't be very good in the Library after that, then.'

'Only as a very large bookmark, sir.'

41

'All right, then, it's down to sheer geography. Who've we got who knows anything about geography?'

The miners emerged from the vertical shaft like ants leaving a burning nest. There were thumps and thuds from below, and at one point Strewth's hat shot up into the air, turned over a few times and dropped back.

There was silence for a while and then, bits cracking off it like errant pieces of shell on a newly hatched chick, the thing pulled itself out of the shaft and . . .

. . . looked around it.

The miners, crouched behind various bushes and sheds, were quite certain of this, even though the monster had no visible eyes.

It turned, its hundreds of little legs moving rather stiffly, as if they'd spent too much time buried in the ground.

Then, weaving slightly, it set off.

And far away in the shimmering red desert, the man in the pointy hat climbed carefully out of his hole. He held in both hands a bowl made of bark. It contained . . . lots of vitamins, valuable protein and essential fats. See? No mention of wriggling *at all*.

A fire was smouldering a little way away. He put the bowl down carefully and picked up a large stick, stood quietly for a moment and then suddenly began to hop around the fire, smacking the ground with the stick and shouting, 'Hah!' When the ground had been subdued to his apparent satisfaction he whacked at the bushes as if they had personally offended him, and bashed a couple of trees as well.

Finally he advanced on a couple of flat rocks, lifted up each one in turn, averted his eyes, shouted, 'Hah!' again and flailed blindly at the ground beneath.

The landscape having been acceptably pacified, he sat down to eat his supper before it escaped.

It tasted a little like chicken. When you are hungry enough, practically anything can.

And eyes watched him from the nearby waterhole. They were not the tiny eyes of the swarming beetles and tadpoles that made a careful examination of every handful he drank, a vital gastronomic precaution. These were far older eyes, and currently without any physical component.

For weeks a man whose ability to find water was limited to checking if his feet were wet had survived in this oven-ready country by falling into waterholes. A man who thought of spiders as harmless little creatures had experienced only a couple of nasty shocks when, by now, this approach should have left him with arms the size of beer barrels that glowed in the dark. The man had even hit the seashore once and paddled in a little way to look at the pretty blue jellyfish, and it was all the watcher could do to see that he got a mere light sting which ceased to be agonizing after only a few days.

The waterhole bubbled and the ground trembled as if, despite the cloudless sky, there was a storm somewhere.

* * *

Now it was three o'clock in the morning. Ridcully was good at doing without other people's sleep.

Unseen University was much bigger on the inside. Thousands of years as the leading establishment of practical magic in a world where dimensions were largely a matter of chance in any case had left it bulging in places where it shouldn't have places. There were rooms containing rooms which, if you entered them, turned out to contain the room you'd started with, which can be a problem if you are in a conga line.

And because it was so big it could afford to have an almost unlimited number of staff on the premises. Tenure was automatic or, more accurately, non-existent. You found an empty room, turned up for meals as usual, and generally no one noticed, although if you were unfortunate you might attract students. And if you looked hard enough in some of the outlying regions of the University, you could find an expert on *anything*.

You could even find an expert on finding an expert. The Professor of Recondite Architecture and Origami Map Folding had been woken up, been introduced to the Archchancellor, who had never set eyes on him before, and had produced a map of the University which would probably be accurate for the next few days and looked rather like a chrysanthemum in the act of exploding.

Finally, the wizards reached a door and Ridcully

glared at the brass plate on it as if it had just been cheeky to him.

' "Egregious Professor of Cruel and Unusual Geography",' he said. 'This looks like the one.'

'We must have walked *miles*,' said the Dean, leaning against the wall. 'I don't recognize any of this.'

Ridcully glanced around. The walls were stone but had at some time been painted in that very special institutional green that you get when an almost-finished cup of coffee is left standing for a couple of weeks. There was a board covered in balding and darker green felt on which had been optimistically thumbtacked the word 'Notices'. But from the looks of it there had never been any notices and never would be, ever. There was a smell of ancient dinners.

Ridcully shrugged, and knocked on the door.

'I don't remember him,' said the Lecturer in Recent Runes.

'I think I do,' said the Dean. 'Not a very promising boy. Had ears. Don't often see him around, though. Always has a suntan. Odd, that.'

'He's on the staff. If anyone knows anything about geography, he's our man.' Ridcully knocked again.

'Perhaps he's out,' said the Dean. 'That's where you mostly get geography, outside.'

Ridcully pointed to a little wooden device by the door. There was one outside every wizard's study. It consisted of a little sliding panel in a frame. Currently it was revealing the word 'IN' and, presumably, was covering the word 'OUT', although you could never be sure with some wizards.*

The Dean tried to slide the panel. It refused to budge.

'He must come out *sometimes*,' said the Senior Wrangler. 'Besides, sensible men should be in bed at three a.m.'

'Yes, indeed,' said the Dean meaningfully.

Ridcully thumped on the door. 'I demand that you open up!' he shouted. 'I am the Master of this College!'

The door moved under the blow, but not very much. It was blocked by what turned out to be, after some strenuous shoving by all the wizards, an enormous pile of paperwork. The Dean picked up a yellowing piece of paper.

'This is the memo saying I've been appointed as Dean!' he said. 'That was years ago!'

'Surely he must come out somet—' said the Senior Wrangler. 'Oh dear . . .'

The same thought had occurred to the other wizards, too.

'Remember poor old Wally Sluvver?' murmured the Chair of Indefinite Studies, looking around in some trepidation. 'Three years of tutorials *post mortem*.'

'Well, the students *did* say he was a bit quiet,' said

---

* The Lecturer in Creative Uncertainty, for example, held rather smugly that he was in a state of both in-ness and out-ness until such time as anyone knocked on his door and collapsed the field, and that it was impossible to be categorical before that event. Logic is a wonderful thing but doesn't always beat actual thought.

Ridcully. He sniffed. 'Doesn't smell bad in *here*. Quite fresh, really. Pleasantly salty. Aha . . .'

There was bright light under a door at the other end of the crowded and dusty room, and the wizards could hear a gentle splashing.

'Bath night. Good man,' said Ridcully. 'Well, we don't have to disturb him.'

He peered at the titles of the books that lined the room.

'Bound to be a lot about EcksEcksEcksEcks somewhere here,' he added, pulling out a volume at random. 'Come along. One man, one book each.'

'Can we at least send out for some breakfast?' grumbled the Dean.

'Far too early for breakfast,' said Ridcully.

'Well, some supper, then?'

'Too late for supper.'

The Chair of Indefinite Studies took in the rest of the room. A lizard scuttled across the wall and disappeared.

'Bit of a mess in here, isn't there?' he said, glaring at the place where the lizard had been. 'Everything's very dusty. What's in all those boxes?'

'Says "Rocks" on this side,' said the Dean. 'Makes sense. If you're going to study the outdoors, do it in the warm.'

'But what about all the fishing nets and coconuts?'

The Dean had to agree the point. The study *was* a mess, even by the extremely expansive standards of wizardry. Boxes of dusty rocks occupied the little space that wasn't covered with books and paper. They had been variously labelled, with inscriptions like 'Rocks from Lower Down', 'Other Rocks', 'Curious Rocks' and 'Probably Not Rocks'. Further boxes, to Ponder's rising interest, were marked 'Remarkable Bones', 'Bones' and 'Dull Bones'.

'One of those people who pokes his nose where it doesn't belong, I fancy,' said the Lecturer in Recent Runes, and sniffed. He sniffed again, and looked down at the book he'd picked at random.

'This is a pressed squid collection,' he said.

'Oh, is it any good? I used to collect starfish when I was a boy,' said Ponder.

The Lecturer in Recent Runes shut the book and frowned at him over the top of it. 'I daresay you did, young man. And old fossils too, I expect.'

'I always thought that old fossils might have a lot to teach us,' said Ponder. 'Perhaps I was wrong,' he added darkly.

'Well, I for one have never believed all that business about dead animals turning into stone,' said the Lecturer in Recent Runes. 'It's against all reason. What's in it for them?'

'So how do you explain fossils, then?' said Ponder.

'Ah, you see, I don't,' said the Lecturer in Recent Runes, with a triumphant smile. 'It saves so much trouble in the long run. How do skinless sausages hold together, Mister Stibbons?'

'What? Eh? How should I know something like that?'

'Really? You don't know *that* but you think you're entirely qualified to know how the whole universe was put together, do you? Anyway, you don't have to *explain* fossils. They're *there*. Why try to turn everything into a big mystery? If you go around asking questions the whole time you'll never get *anything* done.'

'Well, what are we put here for?' said Ponder.

'There you go again,' said the Lecturer in Recent Runes.

'Says here it's girt by sea,' said the Senior Wrangler.

He looked up at their stares.

'This continent EcksEcksEcksEcks,' he added, pointing at a page. 'Says here "Little is known about it save that it is girt by sea."'

'I'm glad to see *someone* has their mind on the task in hand,' said Ridcully. 'You two get on with some studyin', please. Right, then, Senior Wrangler . . . girt by sea, is it?'

'Apparently.'

'Well . . . it would be, wouldn't it,' said Ridcully. 'Anything else?'

'I used to know a Gert,' said the Bursar. The terror of the Library had sent his somewhat erratic sanity on a downward slide into the calm pink clouds again.

'Not . . . very much,' said the Senior Wrangler, flicking through the pages. 'Sir Roderick Purdeigh spent many years looking for the alleged continent and was very emphatic that it didn't exist.'

'Quite a jolly gel. Gertrude Plusher, I think her name was. Face like a brick.'

'Yes, but he once got lost in his own bedroom,' said the Dean, thumbing through another book. 'They found him in the wardrobe.'

'I wonder if it's the same Gert?' said the Bursar.

'Could be, Bursar,' said Ridcully. He nodded at the other wizards. 'No one's to let him have any sugar or fruit.'

For a while there was no sound but the splash of water behind the door, the turning of pages and the Bursar's randomized humming.

'According to this note in Wasport's *Lives of the Very Dull People*,' said the Senior Wrangler, squinting at the tiny script, 'he met an old fisherman who said in that country the bark fell off the trees in the winter and the leaves stayed on.'

'Yes, but they always make up that sort of thing,' said Ridcully. 'Otherwise it's too boring. It's no good coming home and just saying you were shipwrecked for two years and ate winkles, is it? You have to put in a lot of daft stuff about men who go around on one big foot and The Land of Giant Plum Puddings and nursery rubbish like that.'

'My word!' said the Lecturer in Recent Runes, who had been engrossed in a volume at the other end of the table. 'It says here that the people on the island of Slakki wear no clothes at all and the women are of unsurpassed beauty.'

'That sounds quite dreadful,' said the Chair of Indefinite Studies primly.

'There are several woodcuts.'

'I'm sure none of us wish to know that,' said Ridcully. He looked around at the rest of the wizards and repeated, in a louder voice, 'I *said* I'm sure *none* of us wish to know *that*.

Dean? Come right back here and pick up your chair!'

'There's a mention of EcksEcksEcksEcks in Wrencher's *Snakes of All Nations*,' said the Chair of Indefinite Studies. 'It says the continent has very few poisonous snakes ... Oh, there's a footnote.' His finger went down the page. 'It says, "Most of them have been killed by the spiders." How very odd.'

'Oh,' said the Lecturer in Recent Runes. 'It *also* says here that "*The denizens of Purdee Island also existeth inne a State of Nature*"' – he struggled with the ancient handwriting – '"*yette is in Fine Healthe & of Good Bearing & Stature & is Trulee a ... knobbly Savage ...*"'

'Let me have a look at that,' said Ridcully. The book was passed down the table. The Archchancellor scowled.

'It's written "knoble",' he said. '*Noble* savage. Means you ... act like a gentleman, don'tcherknow ...'

'What ... go fox-hunting, bow to ladies, don't pay your tailor ... That sort of thing?'

'Shouldn't think that chap owes his tailor very much,' said Ridcully, looking at the accompanying illustration. 'All right, chaps, let's see what else we can find ...'

'He's having rather a *long* bath, isn't he?' said the Dean, after a while. 'I mean, I like to be as well scrubbed as the next man, but we're talking serious prunes here.'

'Sounds like he's sloshing about,' said the Senior Wrangler.

'Sounds like the seaside,' said the Bursar happily.

'Try to keep up, will you, Bursar?' said Ridcully wearily.

'Actually . . .' said the Senior Wrangler, 'there is a certain seagully component, now that you mention it . . .'

Ridcully stood up, strode over to the bathroom door and held up his fist to knock.

'I *am* the Archchancellor,' he grumbled, lowering it. 'I can open any doors I damn well please.' And he turned the handle.

'There,' he said, as the door swung back. 'See, gentlemen? A perfectly ordinary bathroom. Stone bath, brass taps, bath cap, humorous scrubbin' brush in the shape of a duck . . . a perfectly ordinary bathroom. It is not, let me make myself quite clear, some kind of tropical beach. It doesn't look remotely like a tropical beach.'

He pointed out of the bathroom's open window, to where waves lapped languorously against a tree-fringed strand under a brilliant blue sky. The bathroom curtains flapped on a warm breeze.

'*That*'s a tropical beach,' he said. 'See? No similarity at all.'

After his nourishing meal that contained masses of essential vitamins and minerals and unfortunately quite a lot of taste as well, the man with 'Wizzard' on his hat settled down for some housekeeping, or as much as was possible in the absence of a house.

It consisted of chipping away at a piece of wood with a stone axe. He appeared to be making a very short plank, and the speed with which he was working suggested that he'd done this before.

A cockatoo settled in the tree above him to watch. Rincewind glared at it suspiciously.

When the plank had apparently been smoothed to his satisfaction he stood on it with one foot and, swaying, drew around the foot with a piece of charcoal from the fire. He did the same with the other foot, and then settled down to hack at the wood again.

The watcher in the waterhole realized that the man was making two foot-shaped boards.

Rincewind took a length of twine from his pocket. He'd found a particular creeper which, if you carefully peeled the bark off, would give you a terrible spotted rash. What he'd actually been *looking* for was a creeper which, if you carefully peeled off the bark, would give you a serviceable twine, and it had taken several more goes and various different rashes to find out which one this was.

If you made a hole in the soles and fed a loop of twine through it, into which a toe could be inserted, you ended up with some Ur-footwear. It made you shuffle like the Ascent of Man but, nevertheless, had some unexpected benefits. First, the steady flop-flop as you walked made you sound like *two* people to any dangerous creatures you were about to encounter, which, in Rincewind's recent experience, was any creature at all. Second, although they were impossible to run *in* they were easy to run *out* of, so that you were a smoking dot on the burning horizon while the enraged caterpillar or beetle was still looking at your shoes and wondering where the other person was.

He'd had to run away a lot. Every night he made a new pair of thonged sandals, and every day he left them somewhere in the desert.

When he'd finished them to his satisfaction he took a roll of thin bark from his pocket. Attached to it by a length of twine was a very precious small stub of pencil. He'd decided to keep a journal in the hope that this might help. He looked at the recent entries.

Probably Tuesday: hot, flies. Dinner: honey ants. Attacked by honey ants. Fell into waterhole.

Wednesday, with any luck: hot, flies. Dinner: either bush raisins or kangaroo droppings. Chased by hunters, don't know why. Fell into waterhole.

Thursday (could be): hot, flies. Dinner: blue-tongued lizard. Savaged by blue-tongued lizard. Chased by different hunters. Fell off cliff, bounced into tree, pissed on by small grey incontinent teddy bear, landed in a waterhole.

Friday: hot, flies. Dinner: some kind of roots which tasted like sick. This saved time.

Saturday: hotter than yesterday, extra flies. V. thirsty.

Sunday: hot. Delirious with thirst and flies. Nothing but nothing as far as the eye can see, with bushes in it. Decided to die, collapsed, fell down sand dune into waterhole.

He wrote very carefully and as small as possible: 'Monday: hot, flies. Dinner: moth grubs.' He stared at the writing. It said it all, really.

Why didn't people here like him? He'd meet some small tribe, everything'd be friendly, he'd pick up a few tips, get to know a few names, he'd build up a vocabulary, enough to chat about ordinary everyday things like the weather – and then suddenly they'd be chasing him away. After all, *everyone* talked about the weather, didn't they?

Rincewind had always been happy to think of himself as a racist. The One Hundred Metres, the Mile, the Marathon – he'd run them all. Later, when he'd learned with some surprise what the word actually *meant*, he'd been equally certain he wasn't one. He was a person who divided the world quite simply into people who were trying to kill him and people who weren't. That didn't leave much room for fine details like what colour anyone was. But he'd be sitting by the campfire, trying out a simple conversation, and suddenly people would get upset over nothing at all and drive him off. You didn't expect people to get nasty just because you'd said something like, 'My word, when did it last rain here?' did you?

Rincewind sighed, picked up his stick, beat the hell out of a patch of ground, lay down and went to sleep.

Occasionally he screamed under his breath and his legs made running motions, which just showed that he was dreaming.

The waterhole rippled. It wasn't large, a mere puddle deep in a bush-filled gully between some rocks, and the liquid it contained could only be called water because geographers refuse to countenance words like 'souphole'.

55

Nevertheless it rippled, as though something had dropped into the centre. And what was odd about the ripples was that they didn't stop when they reached the edge of the water but continued outwards over the land as expanding circles of dim white light. When they reached Rincewind they broke up and flowed around him, so that now he was the centre of concentric lines of white dots, like strings of pearls.

The waterhole erupted. *Something* climbed up into the air and sped away across the night.

It zigzagged from rock to mountain to waterhole. And as the eye of observation rises, the travelling streak briefly illuminates other dim lines, hanging above the ground like smoke, so from above the whole land appears to have a circulatory system, or nerves . . .

A thousand miles from the sleeping wizard the line struck ground again, emerged in a cave, and passed across the walls like a searchlight.

It hovered in front of a huge, pointed rock for a moment and then, as if reaching a decision, shot up again into the sky.

The continent rolled below it as it returned. The light hit the waterhole without a splash but, once again, three or four ripples in *something* spread out across the turbid water and the surrounding sand.

Night rolled in again. But there was a distant thumping under the ground. Bushes trembled. In the trees, birds awoke and flew away.

After a while, on a rock face near the waterhole, pale white lines began to form a picture.

* * *

Rincewind had attracted the attention of at least one other watcher apart from whatever it was that dwelt in the waterhole.

Death had taken to keeping Rincewind's lifetimer on a special shelf in his study, in much the way that a zoologist would want to keep an eye on a particularly intriguing specimen.

The lifetimers of most people were the classic shape that Death thought was right and proper for the task. They appeared to be large eggtimers, although, since the sands they measured were the living seconds of someone's life, all the eggs were in one basket.

Rincewind's hourglass looked like something created by a glassblower who'd had the hiccups in a time machine. According to the amount of actual sand it contained – and Death was pretty good at making this kind of estimate – he should have died long ago. But strange curves and bends and extrusions of glass had developed over the years, and quite often the sand was flowing backwards, or diagonally. Clearly, Rincewind had been hit by so much magic, had been thrust reluctantly through time and space so often that he'd nearly bumped into himself coming the other way, that the precise end of his life was now as hard to find as the starting point on a roll of really sticky transparent tape.

Death was familiar with the concept of the eternal, ever-renewed hero, the champion with a thousand faces. He'd refrained from commenting. He met heroes frequently, generally surrounded by, and this was important, the dead bodies of *very nearly* all their enemies and saying, 'Vot the hell shust happened?' Whether there was some arrangement that allowed them to come back again afterwards was not something he would be drawn on.

But he pondered whether, if this creature *did* exist, it was somehow balanced by the eternal coward. The hero with a thousand retreating backs, perhaps. Many cultures had a legend of an undying hero who would one day rise again, so perhaps the balance of nature called for one who wouldn't.

Whatever the ultimate truth of the matter, the fact now was that Death did not have the slightest idea of when Rincewind was going to die. This was very vexing to a creature who prided himself on his punctuality.

Death glided across the velvet emptiness of his study until he reached the model of the Discworld, if indeed it was a model.

Eyeless sockets looked down.

SHOW, he said.

The precious metals and stones faded. Death saw ocean currents, deserts, forests, drifting cloudscapes like albino buffalo herds . . .

SHOW.

The eye of observation curved and dived into the living map, and a reddish splash grew in an expanse of turbulent sea. Ancient mountain ranges slipped past, deserts of rock and sand glided away.

SHOW.

Death watched the sleeping figure of Rincewind. Occasionally its legs would jerk.

HMM.

Death felt something crawling up the back of his robe, pause for a minute on his shoulder, and leap. A small rodent skeleton in a black robe landed in the middle of the image and started flailing madly at it with his tiny scythe, squeaking excitedly.

Death picked up the Death of Rats by his cowl and held him up for inspection.

NO, WE DON'T DO IT THAT WAY.

The Death of Rats struggled madly. SQUEAK?

BECAUSE IT'S AGAINST THE RULES, said Death. NATURE MUST TAKE ITS COURSE.

He glanced down at the image again as if a thought had struck him, and lowered the Death of Rats to the floor. Then he went to the wall and pulled a cord. Far away, a bell tolled.

After a while an elderly man entered, carrying a tray.

'Sorry about that, master. I was cleaning the bath.'

I BEG YOUR PARDON, ALBERT?

'I mean, that's why I was late with your tea, sir,' said Albert.

THAT IS OF NO CONSEQUENCE. TELL ME, WHAT DO YOU KNOW OF THIS PLACE?

Death's finger tapped the red continent. His manservant looked closely.

'Oh, *there*,' he said. '"Terror Incognita" we called it when I was alive, master. Never went there myself. It's the currents, you know. Many a poor sailorman has washed up on them fatal shores rather than get carried right over the Rim, and regretted it, I expect. Dry as a statue's ti— Very dry, master, or so they say. And hotter'n a demon's joc— Very hot, too. But you must've been there yourself?'

OH, YES. BUT YOU KNOW HOW IT IS WHEN YOU'RE THERE ON BUSINESS AND THERE'S HARDLY ANY TIME TO SEE THE COUNTRY . . .

Death pointed to the great spiral of clouds that turned slowly around the continent, like jackals warily circling a dying lion which looked done for but which might yet be capable of one last bite.

VERY STRANGE, he said. A PERMANENT ANTI-CYCLONE. AND INSIDE, A HUGE, CALM LAND, THAT NEVER SEES A STORM. AND NEVER HAS A DROP OF RAIN.

'Good place for a holiday, then.'

COME WITH ME.

The two of them, trailed by the Death of Rats, walked into Death's huge library. There were clouds here, up near the ceiling.

Death held out a hand. I WANT, he said, A BOOK ABOUT THE DANGEROUS CREATURES OF FOURECKS—

Albert looked up and dived for cover, receiving only mild bruising because he had the foresight to curl into a ball.

After a while Death, his voice a little muffled, said: ALBERT, I WOULD BE SO GRATEFUL IF YOU COULD GIVE ME A HAND HERE.

Albert scrambled up and pulled at some of the huge volumes, finally dislodging enough of them to allow his master to clamber free.

HMM ... Death picked up a book at random and read the cover.

DANGEROUS MAMMALS, REPTILES, AMPHIBIANS, BIRDS, FISH, JELLYFISH, INSECTS, SPIDERS, CRUSTACEANS, GRASSES, TREES, MOSSES, AND LICHENS OF TERROR INCOGNITA, he read. His gaze moved down the spine. VOLUME 29C, he added. OH. PART THREE, I SEE.

He glanced up at the listening shelves. POSSIBLY IT WOULD BE SIMPLER IF I ASKED FOR A LIST OF THE HARMLESS CREATURES OF THE AFORESAID CONTINENT?

They waited.

IT WOULD APPEAR THAT—

'No, wait, master. Here it comes.'

Albert pointed to something white zigzagging lazily through the air. Finally Death reached up and caught the single sheet of paper.

He read it carefully and then turned it over briefly just in case anything was written on the other side.

'May I?' said Albert. Death handed him the paper.

' "Some of the sheep," ' Albert read aloud. 'Oh, well. Maybe a week at the seaside'd be better, then.'

WHAT AN INTRIGUING PLACE, said Death. SADDLE UP THE HORSE, ALBERT. I FEEL SURE I'M GOING TO BE NEEDED.

SQUEAK, said the Death of Rats.

PARDON?

'He said, "No worries," master,' said Albert.

I CAN'T IMAGINE WHY.

Four huge blooms of silence rolled over the city as Old Tom so emphatically did not strike the hour.

Several servants rumbled a trolley along the

corridor. The Archchancellor had given in. An early breakfast was on the way.

Ridcully lowered his tape measure.

'Let's try that again, shall we?' he said. He stepped out of the window and picked a seashell out of the sand. It was warm from the sun. Then he pulled himself back into the bathroom and walked around to a door beside the window.

It led to a dank, moss-grown light well, which allowed second-hand and grubby daylight into these dismal floors. Even the snow hadn't managed to get more than a brushing of flakes down this far.

The window on this side glimmered in the light from the doorway like a pool of very black oil.

'Okay, Dean,' he said. 'Push your staff through. Now waggle it about.'

The wizards looked at the gently rippling surface. There should have been several feet of solid wood sticking out of it.

'Well, well, well,' said the Archchancellor, going back in out of the cold air. 'Do you know, I've never actually seen one of these?'

'Anyone remember Archchancellor Bewdley's boots?' said the Senior Wrangler, helping himself to some cold mutton from the trolley. 'He made a mistake and got one of the things opened up in the left boot. Very tricky. You can't go walking around with one foot in another dimension.'

'Well, no . . .' said Ridcully, staring at the tropical scene and tapping his chin thoughtfully with the seashell.

'Can't see what you're treading in, for one thing,' said the Senior Wrangler.

'One opened up in one of the cellars once, all by itself,' said the Dean. 'Just a round black hole. Anything you put in it just disappeared. So old Archchancellor Weatherwax had a privy built over it.'

'Very sensible idea,' said Ridcully, still looking thoughtful.

'We thought so too, until we found the other one that had opened in the attic. Turned out to be the other side of the same hole. I'm sure I don't need to draw you a picture.'

'I've never *heard* of these!' said Ponder Stibbons. 'The possibilities are amazing!'

'Everyone *says* that when they first hear about them,' said the Senior Wrangler. 'But when you've been a wizard as long as I have, my boy, you'll learn that as soon as you find anything that offers amazing possibilities for the improvement of the human condition it's best to put the lid back on and pretend it never happened.'

'But if you could get one to open above another you could drop something through the bottom hole and it'd come out of the top hole and fall through the bottom hole again . . . It'd reach meteoritic speed and the amount of power you could generate would be—'

'That's pretty much what happened between the attic and the cellar,' said the Dean, taking a cold chicken leg. 'Thank goodness for air friction, that's all I'll say.'

Ponder waved his hand gingerly through the window and felt the sun's heat.

'And no one's ever *studied* them?' he said.

The Senior Wrangler shrugged. 'Studied what? They're just holes. You get a lot of magic in one place, it kind of drops through the world like a hot steel ball through pork dripping. If it comes to the edge of something, it kind of fills it in.'

'Stress points in the space-time continuin-uinuum . . .' said Ponder. 'There must be hundreds of uses—'

'Hah, yes, no wonder our Egregious Professor is always so suntanned,' said the Dean. 'I feel he's been cheating. Geography should be hard to get to. It shouldn't be in your windowbox, is what I'm saying. You shouldn't get at it just by sneaking out of the University.'

'Well, he hasn't, really, has he?' said the Senior Wrangler. 'He's really just extended his study a bit.'

'Do you think that *is* EcksEcksEcksEcks, by any chance?' said the Dean. 'It certainly looks foreign.'

'Well, there *is* sea,' said the Senior Wrangler. 'But would you say that it looks as if it is actually *girting*?'

'It's just . . . you know . . . sloshing.'

'One would somehow imagine that sea that was girting something would look more, well . . . defiant,' said the Lecturer in Recent Runes. 'You know? Thundering waves and so on. Definitely sending a message to outsiders that it was girting this coast and they'd better be jolly respectful.'

'Perhaps we could go right through and investigate,' said Ponder.

'Something dreadful'll happen if we do,' said the Senior Wrangler gloomily.

'It hasn't happened to the Bursar,' said Ridcully.

The wizards crowded around. There was a figure standing in the surf. Its robe was rolled up above the knees. A few birds wheeled overhead. Palm trees waved in the background.

'My word, he must have snuck out while we weren't looking,' said the Senior Wrangler.

'Bursaar!' Ridcully yelled.

The figure didn't look round.

'I don't want to, you know, make *trouble*,' said the Chair of Indefinite Studies, looking wistfully at the sundrenched beach, 'but it's freezing cold in my bedroom and last night there was frost on my eiderdown. I don't see any harm in a quick stroll in the warm.'

'We're here to help the Librarian!' snapped Ridcully. Faint snorcs were coming from the volume entitled *Ook*.

'My point exactly. The poor chap'd be a lot happier in those trees there.'

'You mean we could wedge him in the branches?' said the Archchancellor. 'He's still *The Story of Ook*.'

'You *know* what I mean, Mustrum. A day at the seaside for him would be better than a . . . a day at the seaside, as it were. Let's get out there, I'm freezing.'

'Are you mad? There could be terrible monsters! Look at the poor chap standing there in the surf! That sea's probably teeming with—'

'Sharks,' said the Senior Wrangler.

'Right!' said Ridcully. 'And—'

'Barracudas,' said the Senior Wrangler. 'Marlins. Swordfish. Looks like somewhere out near the Rim to me. Fishermen say there's fish there that'd take your arm off.'

'Right,' said Ridcully. 'Right . . .' There was a small but significant change in his tone. Everyone knew about the stuffed fish on his walls. Archchancellor Ridcully would hunt *anything*. The only cockerel still crowing within two hundred yards of the University these days stood under a cart to do it.

'And that jungle,' said the Senior Wrangler, sniffing. 'Looks pretty damn dangerous to me. Could be anything in it. Fatal. Could be tigers and gorillas and elephants and pineapples. I wouldn't go near it. I'm with you, Archchancellor. Better to freeze here than look some rabid man-eater in the eye.'

Ridcully's own eyes were burning bright. He stroked his beard thoughtfully. 'Tigers, eh?' he said. Then his expression changed. '*Pineapples?*'

'Deadly,' said the Senior Wrangler firmly. 'One of them got my aunt. We couldn't get it off her. I *told* her that's not the way you're supposed to eat them, but would she listen?'

The Dean looked sidelong at his Archchancellor. It was the glance of a man who also didn't want another night in a frigid bedroom and had suddenly worked out where the levers were.

'That gets my vote, Mustrum,' he said. 'Catch me going through some hole in space on to some warm beach with a sea teeming with huge fish and a jungle full of hunting trophies.' He yawned like a bad poker player. 'No, it's me for my nice freezing bed, I don't know about you. Archchancellor?'

'I think—' Ridcully began.

'Yes?'

'Clams,' said the Senior Wrangler, shaking his head. 'Looks just the beach for the devils. You just ask my cousin. You'll have to find a good medium first, though. They shouldn't ooze green, I said. They shouldn't bubble, I told him. But would he listen?'

The Archchancellor was currently amongst those who wouldn't. 'You think that taking him out there would be just the thing for the Librarian, do you?' he said. 'Just the tonic for the poor old chap, an hour or two under that sun?'

'But I expect we ought to be ready to protect him, eh, Archchancellor?' the Dean said, innocently.

'Why, yes, I really hadn't thought of that,' said Ridcully. 'Hmm, yes. Important point. Better get them to bring down my 500-pound crossbow with the armour-piercing arrows and my home taxidermy out-fit. And all ten fishing rods. And all four tackle boxes. And the big set of scales.'

'Good thinking, Archchancellor,' said the Dean. 'He may want to take a swim when he's feeling better.'

'In that case,' said Ponder, 'I think I'll get my thaumodalite and my notebooks. It's vital to work out where we are. It *could* be EcksEcksEcksEcks, I suppose. It looks very foreign.'

'I suppose I'd better fetch my reptile press and my

herbarium,' said the Chair of Indefinite Studies, who had got there eventually. 'Much may be learned from the plants here, I'll wager.'

'I shall certainly endeavour to make a study of any primitive grass-skirted peoples hereabouts,' added the Dean, with a lawnmower look in his eyes.

'What about you, Runes?' said Ridcully.

'Me? Oh, er . . .' The Lecturer in Recent Runes looked wildly at his colleagues, who were nodding frantically at him. 'Er . . . this would be a good time to catch up on my reading, obviously.'

'Right,' said Ridcully. 'Because we are *not*, and I want to make this very clear, we are not doing this in order to enjoy ourselves, is that understood?'

'What about the Senior Wrangler?' said the Dean nastily.

'Me? *Enjoy* it? There might even be *prawns* out there,' said the Senior Wrangler miserably.

Ridcully hesitated. The other wizards shrugged when he glanced at them. 'Look, old chap,' he said eventually, 'I think I understood about the clams, and I've got a *sort* of mental picture about your granny and the pineapple—'

'—my aunt—'

'—your aunt and the pineapple, but . . . What's deadly about prawns?'

'Hah, see how *you* like a crate of them dropping off the crane on to your head,' said the Senior Wrangler. 'My uncle didn't, I can tell you!'

'Okay, I think I understand. Important safety tip, everyone,' said Ridcully. 'Avoid all crates. Understood?

But we are *not* here on some kind of holiday! Do you all understand me?'

'Absolutely,' said the wizards in unison.

They all understood him.

Rincewind awoke with a scream, to get it over with.

Then he saw the man watching him.

He was sitting cross-legged against the dawn. He was black. Not brown, or blue-black, but black as space. This place baked people.

Rincewind pulled himself up and thought about reaching for his stick. And then he thought again. The man had a couple of spears stuck in the ground, and people here were good at spears, because if you didn't get efficient at hitting the things that moved fast you had to eat the things that moved slowly. He was also holding a boomerang, and it wasn't one of those toy ones that came back. This was one of the big, heavy, gently curved sort that didn't come back because it was sticking in something's ribcage. You could laugh at the idea of wooden weapons until you saw the kind of wood that grew here.

It had been painted with stripes of all colours, but it still looked like a business item.

Rincewind tried to seem harmless. It required little in the way of acting.

The watcher regarded him in that sucking silence that you just have to fill. And Rincewind came from a culture where, if there was nothing to say, you said something.

'Er . . .' said Rincewind. 'Me . . . big-fella . . . fella . . .

69

belong ... damn, what's the—' He gave up, and glanced at the blue sky. 'Turned out nice again,' he said.

The man seemed to sigh, stuck the boomerang into the strip of animal skin that was his belt and, in fact, the whole of his wardrobe, and stood up. Then he picked up a leathery sack, slung it over one shoulder, took the spears and, without a backward glance, ambled off around a rock.

This might have struck anyone else as rude, but Rincewind was always happy to see any heavily armed person walking away. He rubbed his eyes and contemplated the dismal task of subduing breakfast.

'You want some grub?' The voice was almost a whisper.

Rincewind looked around. A little way off was the hole from which last night's supper had been dug. Apart from that, there was nothing all the way to the infinite horizon but scrubby bushes and hot red rocks.

'I think I dug up most of them,' he said, weakly.

'Nah, mate. I got to tell you the secret of findin' tucker in the bush. There's always a beaut feed if you know where to look, mate.'

'How come you're speaking my language, mystery voice?' said Rincewind.

'I ain't,' said the voice. 'You're listenin' to mine. Got to feed you up proper. Gonna sing you into a real bush-tucker finder, true.'

'Lovely grub,' said Rincewind.

'Just you stand there and don't move.'

It sounded as though the unseen voice then began to chant very quietly through an unseen nose.

Rincewind was, after all, a wizard. Not a good one, but he was sensitive to magic. And the chant was doing strange things.

The hairs on the back of his hands tried to crawl up his arms, and the back of his neck began to sweat. His ears popped and, very gently, the landscape began to spin around him.

He looked down at the ground. There were his feet. Almost certainly his feet. And they were standing on the red earth and not moving at all. Things were moving round him. He wasn't dizzy but, by the look of it, the landscape was.

The chanting stopped. There was a sort of echo, which seemed to happen inside his head, as if the words had been merely the shadow of something more important.

Rincewind shut his eyes for a while, and then opened them again.

'Er . . . fine,' he said. 'Very . . . catchy.'

He couldn't see the speaker, so he spoke with that careful politeness you reserve for someone armed who is probably standing behind you.

He turned. 'I expect you . . . er . . . had to go somewhere, did you?' he said, to the empty air.

'Er . . . hello?'

Even the insects had gone quiet.

'Er . . . you haven't noticed a box walking around on legs, have you? By any chance?'

He tried to see if anyone could possibly be hiding behind a bush.

'It's not important, it's just that it's got my clean underwear in it.'

The boundless silence made an eloquent statement about the universe's views on clean underwear.

'So . . . er . . . I'm going to know how to find food in the bush, right?' he ventured. He glared at the nearest trees. They didn't look any more fruitful than before. He shrugged.

'What a strange person.'

He edged over to a flat stone and, with a stick raised in case of resistance from anything below, pulled it up.

There was a chicken sandwich underneath.

It tasted rather like chicken.

A little way away, behind the rocks near the water-hole, a drawing faded into the stone.

This was another desert, elsewhere. No matter where you were, this place would always be *elsewhere*. It was one of those places further than any conceivable journey, but possibly as close as the far side of a mirror, or just a breath away.

There was no sun in the sky here, unless the whole sky was sun – it glowed yellow. The desert underfoot was still red sand, but hot enough to burn.

A crude drawing of a man appeared on a rock. Gradually, layer by layer, it got more complex, as if the unseen hand was trying to draw bones and organs and a nervous system and a soul.

And he stepped on to the sand and put down his bag which, here, seemed a lot heavier. He stretched his arms and cracked his knuckles.

At least here he could talk normally. He daren't raise his voice down there in the shadow world, lest he raise mountains as well.

He said a word which, on the other side of the rock, would have shaken trees and created meadows. It meant, in the true language of things which the old man spoke, something like: Trickster. A creature like him appears in many belief systems, although the jolly name can be misleading. Tricksters have that robust sense of humour that puts a landmine under a seat cushion for a bit of a laugh.

A black and white bird appeared, and perched on his head.

'You know what to do,' said the old man.

'Him? What a wonga,' said the bird. 'I've been lookin' at him. He's not even heroic. He's just in the right place at the right time.'

The old man indicated that this was maybe the definition of a hero.

'All right, but why not go and get the thing yerself?' said the bird.

'You've gotta have heroes,' said the old man.

'And I suppose I'll have to help,' said the bird. It sniffed, which is quite hard to do through a beak.

'Yep. Off you go.'

The bird shrugged, which *is* easy to do if you have wings, and flew down off the old man's head. It didn't land on the rock but flew into it; for a moment there was a drawing of a bird, and then it faded.

Creators aren't gods. They make places, which is quite hard. It's men that make gods. This explains a lot.

The old man sat down and waited.

Confront a wizard with the concept of a bathing suit and he'll start to get nervous. Why does it have to be so skimpy? he'll ask. Where can I put the gold embroidery? How can you have any kind of costume without at least forty useful pockets? And occult symbols made out of sequins? There appears to be no place for them. And where, when you get right down to it, are the lapels?

There is also the concept of acreage. It is vitally important that as large an amount of wizard as possible is covered, so that timid people and horses are not frightened. There may be strapping young wizards with copper-coloured skins and muscles as solid as a plank, but not after sixty years of UU dinners. It gives senior wizards what they think is called *gravitas* but is more accurately called gravity.

Also, it takes heavy machinery to part a wizard from his pointy hat.

The Chair of Indefinite Studies looked sidelong at the Dean. They both wore a variety of garments, in which red and white stripes predominated.

'Last one into the water's a man standing all by himself on the beach!' he shouted.*

* Wizards also enjoy a bit of fun but never have much of a chance to develop the appropriate vocabulary.

Out on a point of rock, surf washing over his bare feet, Mustrum Ridcully lit his pipe and cast a line on the end of which was such a fearsome array of spinners and weights that any fish it didn't hook it might successfully bludgeon.

The change of scenery seemed to be working on the Librarian. Within a few minutes of being laid in the sunlight he'd sneezed himself back into his old shape, and he now sat on the beach with a blanket around him and a fern leaf on his head.

It was, indeed, a lovely day. It was warm, the sea murmured beautifully, the wind whispered in the trees. The Librarian knew he ought to be feeling better, but, instead, he was beginning to feel extremely uneasy.

He stared around him. The Lecturer in Recent Runes had gone to sleep with his book carefully shading his eyes. It had originally been entitled *Principles of Thaumic Propagation* but, because of the action of the sunlight and some specialized high-frequency vibrations from the sand granules on the beach, the words on the cover now read *The Omega Conspiracy.**

---

* This isn't magic. It is a simple universal law. People always expect to use a holiday in the sun as an opportunity to read those books they've always meant to read, but an alchemical combination of sun, quartz crystals and coconut oil will somehow metamorphose any improving book into a rather thicker one *with a name containing at least one Greek word or letter* (*The Gamma Imperative*, *The Delta Season*, *The Alpha Project* and, in the more extreme cases, even *The Mu Kau Pi Caper*). Sometimes a hammer and sickle turn up on the cover. This is probably caused by sunspot activity, since they are invariably the wrong way round. It's just as well for the Librarian that he sneezed when he did, or he might have ended up a thousand pages thick and crammed with weapons specifications.

In the middle distance was the window. It hung in the air, a simple square into a shadowy room. The Archchancellor hadn't trusted the window catch and had propped up the window with a piece of wood. A warning label pinned to it showed that some thought had gone into the wording: 'Do not remove this wood. Not even to see what happens. IMPORTANT!'

There appeared to be some forest behind the beach which rose a little way up the side of a small yet quite pointy mountain, certainly not tall enough to have snow on it.

Some of the trees lining the beach looked hauntingly familiar, and spoke to the Librarian of home. This was strange, because he had been born in Moon Pond Lane, Ankh-Morpork, next to the saddlemakers. But they spoke to the home in his bones. He had an urge to climb . . .

But there was something *wrong* with the trees. He looked down at the pretty shells on the beach. There was something wrong with them, too. Creepily, worryingly wrong.

A few birds wheeled overhead, and they were wrong. They were the right shape, as far as he knew, and they seemed to be making the right noises. But they were still *wrong*.

Oh, dear . . .

He tried to stop the sneeze as it gathered nasal momentum, but this is impossible for anyone who wants to continue to go through life with their eardrums.

There was a snort, a clattering sound, and the

Librarian changed into something suitable for the beach.

It is often said about desert environments that there is in fact a lot of nutritious food around, if only you know what to look for.

Rincewind mused on this as he pulled a plate of chocolate-covered sponge cakes from their burrow. They had dried coconut flakes on them.

He turned the plate cautiously.

Well, you couldn't argue with it. He was finding food in the desert. In fact, he was even finding dessert in the desert.

Perhaps it was some special talent hitherto undiscovered by the kind people who had occasionally shared their food with him in the last few months. They hadn't eaten this sort of thing. They'd ground up seeds and dug up skinny yams and eaten things with more eyeballs than the Watch had found after that business with Medley the Medical Kleptomaniac.

So something was going *right* for him. Out here in the red-hot wilderness something wanted him to stay *alive*. This was a worrying thought. No one ever wanted him alive for something *nice*.

This was Rincewind after several months: his wizardly robe was quite short now. Bits had been torn off or used as string or, after some particularly resistant *hors d'oeuvres*, as bandages. It showed his knees, and wizards are nowhere near championship standard at knees. They tend to appear, as the book might put it, a knobbly savage.

But he'd kept his hat. He'd woven a new wide brim for it, and he'd had to restore the crown once or twice with fresh bits of robe, and most of the sequins had been replaced with bits of shell stitched on with grass, but it was still his hat, the same old hat. A wizard without a hat was just a sad man with a suspicious taste in clothes. A wizard without a hat wasn't anyone.

Although this particular wizard had a hat, he didn't have keen enough eyes to see the drawing appear on a red rock half hidden in the scrub.

It started off like a bird. Then, without at any time being other than smears of ochre and charcoal that had been there for years, it began to change shape . . .

He set off towards the distant mountains. They'd been in view for several days. He hadn't the faintest idea if they represented a sensible direction but at least they *were* one.

The ground shivered underfoot. It had been doing that once or twice a day for a while, and that was another odd thing, because this didn't look like volcano country. This was the kind of country where, if you watched a large cliff for a few hundred years, you might see a rock drop off and you'd talk about it for ages. Everything about it said that it had got over all the more energetic geological exercises a long time ago and was a nice quiet country which, in other circumstances, a man might be at home in.

He became aware after a while that a kangaroo was watching him from the top of a small rock. He'd seen the things before, bounding away through the bushes.

They didn't usually hang around when there were humans about.

This one was stalking him. They were vegetarian, weren't they? It wasn't as though he was wearing green.

Finally it sprang out of the bushes and landed in front of him.

It brushed one ear with a paw, and gave Rincewind a meaningful look.

It brushed the other ear with the other paw, and wrinkled its nose.

'Yes, fine, good,' said Rincewind. He started to edge away, and then stopped. After all, it was just a big . . . well, rabbit, with a long tail and the kind of feet you normally see associated with red noses and baggy pants.

'I'm not frightened of you,' he said. 'Why should I be frightened of you?'

'Well,' said the kangaroo, 'I *could* kick your stomach out through your neck.'

'Ah. You can talk?'

'You're a quick one,' said the kangaroo. It rubbed an ear again.

'Something wrong?' said Rincewind.

'No, that's the kangaroo language. I'm trying it out.'

'What, one scratch for "yes", one for "no"? That sort of thing?'

The kangaroo scratched an ear, and then remembered itself. 'Yep,' it said. It wrinkled its nose.

'And that wrinkling?' said Rincewind.

'Oh, that means "Come quick, someone's fallen down a deep hole," ' said the kangaroo.

'That one gets used a lot?'

'You'd be amazed.'

'And . . . what's kangaroo for "You are needed for a quest of the utmost importance"?' said Rincewind, with guileful innocence.

'You know, it's funny you should ask that—'

The sandals barely moved. Rincewind rose from them like a man leaving the starting blocks, and when he landed his feet were already making running movements in the air.

After a while the kangaroo came alongside and accompanied him in a series of easy bounds.

'Why are you running away without even listening to what I have to say?'

'I've had long experience of being me,' panted Rincewind. 'I *know* what's going to happen. I'm going to be dragged into things that shouldn't concern me. And you're just a hallucination caused by rich food on an empty stomach, so don't you try to stop me!'

'Stop you?' said the kangaroo. 'When you're heading in the right direction?'

Rincewind tried to slow down, but his method of running was very efficiently based on the idea that stopping was the last thing he'd do. Legs still moving, he ran out over the empty air and plunged into the void.

The kangaroo looked down and, with a certain amount of satisfaction, wrinkled its nose.

'Archchancellor!'

Ridcully awoke, and sat up. The Lecturer in Recent Runes was hurrying up, out of breath.

'The Bursar and I went for a walk along the beach,' he said. 'And can you guess where we ended up?'

'In Kiddling Street, Quirm,' said Ridcully tartly, brushing an exploring beetle off his beard. 'That little bit by the teashop, with the trees in it.'

'That's astonishing, Archchancellor. Because, you know, in fact, we *didn't*. We wound up back here. We're on a tiny island. Were you having a rest?'

'A few moments' cogitating,' said Ridcully. 'Any idea where we are yet, Mister Stibbons?'

Ponder looked up from his notebook. 'I won't be able to work that out precisely until sundown, sir. But I think we're pretty close to the Rim.'

'And I think we found where the Professor of Cruel and Unusual Geography has been camping,' said the Lecturer in Recent Runes. He rummaged in a deep pocket. 'There was a camp, and a fireplace. Bamboo furniture and whatnot. Socks on a washing line. And this.'

He pulled out the remains of a small notebook. It was standard UU issue. Ridcully would never let anyone have a new one until they'd filled up every page on both sides.

'It was just lying there,' said the Lecturer in Recent Runes. 'I'm afraid ants have been eating it.'

Ridcully flicked it open and read the first page. '"Some interesting observations on Mono Island,"' he said. '"A most singular place."'

He flicked through the rest of the book. 'Just a list of plants and fishes,' he said. 'Doesn't look all that special to *me*, but then I ain't a geography man. Why's he callin' it Mono Island?'

'It means One Island,' said Ponder.

'Well, you've just told me it *is* one island,' said Ridcully. 'Anyway, I can see several more out there. Severe lack of imagination, I suggest.' He tucked the notebook into his robe. 'Right, then. No sign of the chap himself?'

'Strangely, no.'

'Probably went swimming and was eaten by a pineapple,' said Ridcully. 'How's the Librarian doing, Mister Stibbons? Comfortable, is he?'

'You should know, sir,' said Ponder. 'You've been sitting on him for three-quarters of an hour.'

Ridcully looked down at the deckchair. It was covered with red fur. 'This is—?'

'Yes, sir.'

'I thought perhaps our geography man had brought it with him.'

'Not, er, with the black toenails, sir.'

Ridcully peered further. 'Should I get up, do you think?'

'Well, he *is* a deckchair, sir. So being sat on is a perfectly normal activity for him, I suppose.'

'We must find a cure, Stibbons. This is too strange—'

'Coo-ee, gentlemen!'

There was activity in front of the window. It centred around a vision in pink, although admittedly the sort of vision associated with the more erratic kind of hallucinogen.

In theory there is no dignified way for a lady of a certain age to climb through a window, but nevertheless this one was attempting it. In fact she moved with more than dignity, which is something that is given away free with kings and bishops; what she had was respectability, which is home-made out of cast iron. However, at some point she would have to show a bit of ankle, and she was wedged awkwardly on the sill while trying to prevent this from happening.

The Senior Wrangler coughed. If he had been wearing a tie he would have straightened it.

'Ah,' said Ridcully. 'The inestimable Mrs Whitlow. Someone go and give her a hand, Stibbons.'

'I'll help,' said the Senior Wrangler, just a little faster than he meant.*

The University's housekeeper turned and spoke to someone unseen beyond the window and then turned back, her shouting-at-subordinates expression briefly visible before it was eclipsed by her much sunnier talking-to-wizards one.

The Chair of Indefinite Studies had once upset the Senior Wrangler by saying that the housekeeper had a face full of chins, but there *was* a glossiness about her that put some people in mind of a candle that had been kept in the warm for too long. There wasn't anything approaching a straight line anywhere on Mrs

---

* The Senior Wrangler had once walked past Mrs Whitlow's rooms when the door was open, and he'd caught sight of the bare, headless, armless dressmaker's dummy that she used to make all her own clothes. He'd had to go and lie down quietly after that and, ever since, had thought about Mrs Whitlow in a special way.

Whitlow, until she found that something hadn't been dusted properly, when you could use her lips as a ruler.

Most of the Faculty walked in dread of her. She had strange powers that they couldn't quite get a grip on, like the ability to get the beds made and the windows washed. A wizard who could wield a staff crackling with power against dreadful monsters from some ghastly region was nevertheless quite capable of picking up a feather duster by the wrong end and seriously injuring himself with it. At Mrs Whitlow's whim people's clothes got washed and socks got darned.* If anyone annoyed her, they found their study spring-cleaned more often than was good for them, and since to a wizard his room is as personal an item as his trouser pockets this was a terrible vengeance.

'Ai just thought you gentlemen would like a morning snack,' she said, as the wizards helped her down. 'So Ai took the liberty of getting the gels to put together a cold collation. Ai'll just go and fetch it . . .'

The Archchancellor stood up hastily. 'Well done, Mrs Whitlow.'

'Er . . . a morning snack?' said the Senior Wrangler. 'It looks like mid-afternoon to me . . .' His tone made it clear that if Mrs Whitlow wanted it to be the morning, he wasn't going to cause any trouble.

---

* Wizards lack the HW chromosome in their genes. Feminist researchers have isolated this as the one which allows people to see the washing-up in the sinks before the life forms growing there have actually invented the wheel. Or discovered slood.

'Speed of light crossing the Disc,' said Ponder. 'We *are* close to the Rim, I'm sure. I'm trying to remember how you tell the time by looking at the sun.'

'I should leave it for a while,' said the Senior Wrangler, squinting under his hand. 'It's too bright to see the numbers at the moment.'

Ridcully nodded happily. 'I'm sure we could all do with a snack,' he said. 'Something suitable for the beach, perhaps.'

'Cold pork and mustard,' said the Dean, waking up.

'Possibly some beer,' said the Senior Wrangler.

'And have we got any of those pies, you know, the ones with the egg inside them?' said the Lecturer in Recent Runes. 'Although I must say I've always thought that it was rather cruel to the chicken—'

There was a soft little sound, very similar to the one you get, aged around seven, when you stick your finger in your mouth and flick it out again quickly and think it is incredibly funny.

Ponder turned his head, dreading the sight he was about to see.

Mrs Whitlow had a tray of cutlery in one hand and was prodding ineffectually at the air with the stick that she held in the other.

'Ai only moved it to get things through,' she said. 'Now Ai can't seem to quate find where the silly thing is supposed to go.'

Where there had been a dark rectangle opening into the geographer's dingy study, there was now only waving palms and sunlit sand. Strictly speaking, it could be said to be an improvement. It depended on your point of view.

Rincewind surfaced, gasping for breath. He'd fallen into a waterhole.

It was in . . . well, it looked as though once there had been a cave, and the roof had collapsed. There was a big circle of blue right above him.

Rocks had fallen down here, and sand had blown in, and seeds had taken root. Cool, damp and green . . . the place was a little oasis, tucked away from the sun and the wind.

He pulled himself out of the water and looked around while he drained off. Vines had grown among the rocks. A few small trees had managed to take root in the crack. There was even a little bit of a beach. By the look of the stains on the rocks, the water had once been a lot higher.

And there . . . Rincewind sighed. Wasn't that just typical? You got some quiet little beauty spot miles from anywhere, and there was *always* some graffiti artist ready to spoil it. It was like that time when he was hiding out in the Morpork Mountains, and right in the back of one of the deepest caves some vandal had drawn loads of stupid bulls and antelopes. Rincewind had been so disgusted he'd wiped them off. *And* they'd left lots of old bones and junk lying around. Some people had no idea how to behave.

Here, they'd covered the rock walls with drawings in white, red and black. Animals again, Rincewind noticed. They didn't even look particularly realistic.

He stopped, water dripping off him, in front of one. Someone had probably wanted to draw a kangaroo. There were the ears and the tail and the clown feet. But they looked alien, and there were so many lines and cross-hatchings that the figure seemed . . . odd. It looked as though the artist hadn't just wanted to draw a kangaroo from the outside but had wanted to show the inside as well, and then had wanted to show the kangaroo last year and today and next week and also what it was thinking, all at the same time, and had set out to do the whole thing with some ochre and a stick of charcoal.

It seemed to move in his head.

He blinked, but it still hurt. His eyes seemed to want to wander off in different directions.

Rincewind hurried further along the cave, ignoring the rest of the paintings. The piled rubble of the collapsed ceiling reached nearly to the surface, but there was space on the other side, going on into darkness. It looked as though he was in a piece of tunnel that had collapsed.

'You walked right past it,' said the kangaroo.

He turned. It was standing on the little beach.

'I didn't see you get down here,' said Rincewind. 'How did you get down here?'

'Come on, I've got to show you something. You can call me Scrappy, if you like.'

'Why?'

'We're mates, ain't we? I'm here to *help* you.'

'Oh, dear.'

'Can't make it alone across this land, mate. How

d'you think you've survived so far? Water's bloody hard to find out here these days.'

'Oh, I don't know, I just keep falling into—'

Rincewind stopped.

'Yeah,' said the kangaroo. 'Strike you as odd, does it?'

'I thought I was just naturally lucky,' said Rincewind. He thought about what he'd just said. 'I must have been crazy.'

There weren't even flies down here. There was the occasional faint ripple on the water, and that wasn't comforting, since there wasn't apparently anything to stir the surface. Up above, the sun was torching the ground and the flies swarmed like, well, flies.

'Why isn't there anyone else here?' he said.

'Come and see,' said the kangaroo.

Rincewind raised his hands and backed away. 'Are we talking teeth and stings and fangs?'

'Just look at that painting there, mate.'

'What, the one of the kangaroo?'

'Which one's that, mate?'

Rincewind looked along the wall. The kangaroo picture wasn't where he remembered it.

'I could've sworn—'

'*That*'s the one I want you to look at, over there.'

Rincewind looked at the stone. What it showed, outlined in red ochre, were dozens of hands.

He sighed. 'Oh, right,' he said, wearily. 'I see the problem. Exactly the same thing happens to me.'

'What're you talking about, mister?'

'It's just the same with me when I try to take snaps

with an iconograph,' said Rincewind. 'You set up a nice picture, the demon paints away, and when you look at it, whoops, you had your thumb in the way. I must have got a dozen pictures of my thumb. No, I can see your lad there, doing his painting, in a bit of a hurry, got his brush all ready then, splosh, he'd forgotten to take his hand off the—'

'No. It's the painting *underneath* I'm talking about, mister.'

Rincewind looked closer. There *were* fainter lines there, which you'd think were just flaws in the rock if you weren't looking. Rincewind squinted. Other lines seemed to fit . . . Yes, someone had painted figures . . . They were . . .

He blew away some sand.

Yes, they were . . .

. . . curiously familiar . . .

'Yes,' said Scrappy, his voice apparently coming from a distance. 'Look a bit like you, don't they . . . ?'

'But they're—' he began. He straightened up. 'How long have these paintings been here?'

'Well, lessee,' said the kangaroo. 'Out of the sun and the weather, nothing to disturb 'em . . . Twenty thousand years?'

'That's not right!'

'Nah, true, prob'ly thirty thousand, in a nice sheltered spot like this.'

'But these are . . . That's my . . .'

'O' course, when I say thirty thousand years,' said the kangaroo, 'I mean it depends how you look at it. Even them hand paintings on the top've been there

five thousand years, see. And those faint ones . . . Oh,
yes, got to be pretty old, tens of thousands of years,
except—'

'Except what?'

'They weren't here last week, mate.'

'You're saying they've been here for ages . . . but not for
very long?'

'See? I knew you was clever.'

'And now you're going to tell me what the hell
you're talking about?'

'Right.'

'Excuse me, I'll just find something to eat.'

Rincewind lifted up a rock. There were a couple of
jam sandwiches underneath.

The wizards were civilized men of considerable
education and culture. When faced with being in-
advertently marooned on a desert island they
understood immediately that the first thing to do was
place the blame.

'It really was very clear!' shouted Ridcully, waving
his hand frantically in the air at the place where the
window had been. 'And I put a sign on it!'

'Yes, but you've got a "Do Not Disturb" sign nailed
to your study door,' said the Senior Wrangler, 'and you
still expect Mrs Whitlow to bring you your tea in the
mornings!'

'Gentlemen, please!' said Ponder Stibbons. 'We've
got to sort some things out right now!'

'Yes indeed!' roared the Dean. 'And it was *his* fault!
The sign wasn't large enough!'

'I mean we have to—'

'There are *ladies* present!' snapped the Senior Wrangler.

'La*dy*.' Mrs Whitlow uttered the word carefully and with deliberation, like a gambler putting down a winning hand. She stood primly watching them. Her expression said: I'm not worried, because with all these wizards around nothing bad can happen.

The wizards adjusted their attitudes.

'Ai *do* apologize if Ai've done something wrong,' she said.

'Oh, not, not *wrong*,' said Ridcully quickly. 'Not exactly *wrong*. As such.'

'Anyone could have done it,' said the Senior Wrangler. 'I could hardly read the lettering myself.'

'And, taking the broad view, it's certainly better to be stuck out here in the fresh air and sunshine than in that stuffy study,' Ridcully went on.

'That's quite a *broad* view, sir,' said Ponder doubtfully.

'And we'll be back home in two shakes of a lamb's tail,' said Ridcully, beaming.

'Unfortunately, this doesn't look a very agricultural sort of—' Ponder began.

'Figure of speech, Mister Stibbons, figure of speech.'

'The sun's going down, sir,' Ponder persisted. 'Which means it'll be night time soon.'

Ridcully looked nervously at Mrs Whitlow, and then at the sun.

'Is there a problem?' said Mrs Whitlow.

'Oh, good heavens, no!' said Ridcully hastily.

'Ai notice the little hole in the wall doesn't seem to have come back,' said Mrs Whitlow.

'We, er—'

'It's a little prank, is it?' the housekeeper went on. 'Ai'm sure you gentlemen will have your fun, and no mistake.'

'Yes, that's—'

'But Ai should be grateful if you would send me back now, Archchancellor. We're doing the laundry this afternoon, and Ai'm afraid we're having a lot of trouble with the Dean's sheets.'

The Dean suddenly knew how a mosquito feels in the beam of a searchlight.

'We'll sort this out directly, never fear, Mrs Whitlow,' said Ridcully, not taking his eyes off the wretched Dean. 'In the meantime, why don't you take a seat and enjoy the rather wonderful sheets, I mean sunshine?'

There was a clack as the deckchair folded itself up. Then it sneezed.

'Ah, back with us again, Librarian,' Ridcully went on, as the orang-utan sprawled in the sand. 'Help him up, please, Mister Stibbons. A word to the rest of you, please. If you'll excuse us a moment, Mrs Whitlow? Faculty meeting . . .'

The wizards went into a huddle.

'It was tomato sauce, all right?' said the Dean hurriedly. 'I just happened to be having a snack in bed and you know how that stuff stains!'

'I'm sure we're not at all interested in the state of your sheets, Dean,' said Ridcully.

'No, indeed,' said the Senior Wrangler brightly.

'Not us,' said the Lecturer in Recent Runes, slapping the Dean on the back.

'We have to get back,' said Ridcully. 'We can't spend the night alone with Mrs Whitlow. It wouldn't be decent.'

'I don't see why anyone should make a fuss about a bit of tomato sauce. I at least cleaned all the beans off—'

'Well, we're not actually alone, are we? Not as such,' said the Lecturer in Recent Runes. 'I mean, there's seven of us, not including the Librarian.'

'Yes, but we're all alone *together*,' said Ridcully urgently. 'There could be Talk.'

'What about?' said the Chair of Indefinite Studies, who sometimes lagged behind.

'*You* know,' said the Lecturer in Recent Runes. 'Seven men and one woman . . . It doesn't bear thinking about . . .'

'Well, I for one will certainly veto any suggestion about ordering another six women,' said the Chair firmly.

'Perhaps the hole will open again?' said the Senior Wrangler.

'I doubt it,' said Ridcully. 'Ponder says that our coming through probably altered the thaumostatic balance. What do you think, Dean?'

'Just tomato sauce,' said the Dean. 'It could have happened to anyone.'

'I meant about our being marooned on this island,' said Ridcully. 'Any ideas, anyone? We must tackle this as a team.'

'What shall we tell Mrs Whitlow?' whispered the Senior Wrangler. 'She thinks this is a *prank*.'

'Senior Wrangler, we are elderly, wise and experienced wizards,' said Ridcully. '*Students* are prankers.'

'Pranksters, possibly,' mumbled Ponder Stibbons.

'Whatever. *We* do not indulge in *pranks*.'

'With us it's a fully fledged gold-embossed cock-up or nothing,' said the Lecturer in Recent Runes.

'I don't see why people are making such a fuss about a bit of tomato sauce that hardly even shows up,' muttered the Dean.

'No one brought any suitable spells?' said Ridcully.

'At four in the morning? For the beach?' said the Lecturer in Recent Runes. 'Of course not.'

'Then we shall have to fall back on our own resources. There's bound to be a ship along sooner or later. The point *is*, gentlemen,' he added, 'that we are the product of a university education. I'm quite sure primitive people have no difficulties surviving in a place like this, and think of all the things we have that our rude forefathers lacked.'

'Mrs Whitlow, for a start,' said the Chair of Indefinite Studies.

'She wouldn't put up with rudeness of any sort,' the Senior Wrangler agreed.

'Do you know anything about boats, Dean? I believe you got a Brown for rowing when you were slimmer,' said Ridcully. 'Please note that this question did not raise the matter of sheets in any way.'

'Well, indeed, boat-building is not a difficult task,' said the Dean, surfacing. 'Even primitive people can build boats, and we *are* civilized men, after all.'

'Then you're head of the Boat-Building Committee,' said Ridcully. 'Senior Wrangler can help you. The rest of you fellows had better see if there's any fresh water. And food. Knock down a few coconuts. That sort of thing.'

'And what will you do, Archchancellor?' said the Senior Wrangler nastily.

'I shall be the Protein Acquisition Committee,' said Ridcully, waving his fishing rod.

'You going to stand here and fish again? What good's that going to do?'

'It might result in a fish dinner, Senior Wrangler.'

'Has anyone got any tobacco?' said the Dean. 'I'm dying for a smoke.'

The wizards went off about their tasks, complaining and blaming one another.

And just inside the forest, in the leafy debris, roots unfolded and a number of very small plants began to grow like hell . . .

'This is the last continent,' said Scrappy. 'It was . . . put together last, and . . . differently.'

'Looks pretty *old* to me,' said Rincewind. 'Ancient. Those hills look as old as the hills.'

'They were made thirty thousand years old,' said the kangaroo.

'Come on! They look *millions* of years old!'

'Yep. Thirty thousand years ago they were made a million years ago. Time here is,' the kangaroo shrugged, 'not the same. It was … glued together differently, right?'

'Search me,' said Rincewind. 'I'm a man sitting here listening to a kangaroo. I'm not arguing.'

'I'm trying to find words you might understand,' said the kangaroo reproachfully.

'Good, keep going, you'll get there. Want a jam sandwich? It's gooseberry.'

'No. Strictly herbivore, mate. Listen—'

'Unusual, gooseberry jam. I mean, you don't often see it. Raspberry and strawberry, yes, even blackcurrant. I shouldn't think more than one jar of jam in a hundred is gooseberry. Sorry, do go on.'

'You're taking this seriously, are you?'

'Am I smiling?'

'Have you ever noticed how time goes slower in big spaces?'

The sandwich stopped halfway to Rincewind's mouth. 'Actually, that *is* true. But it only *seems* slower.'

'So? When this place was made there wasn't much space and time left over to work with, see? He had to bodge them together to make them work harder. Time happens to space and space happens to time—'

'You know, I think there could be plum in it, too?' said Rincewind, with his mouth full. 'And maybe some rhubarb. You'd be amazed how often they do that sort of thing. You know, stuff cheaper fruit in. I met this man in an inn once, he worked for a jam-maker in Ankh-Morpork, and he said they put in any old rubbish and some red dye, and I said what about the raspberry pips, and he said they make them out of wood. Wood! He said they'd got a machine for stamping 'em out. Can you believe that?'

'Will you stop talking about jam and be sensible for a moment!'

Rincewind lowered the sandwich. 'Good grief, I hope not,' he said. 'I'm sitting in a cave in a country where everything bites you and it never rains and I'm talking, no offence, to a herbivore that smells of a carpet in a house where there are a lot of excitable puppies, and I've suddenly got this talent for finding jam sandwiches and inexplicable fairy cakes in unexpected places, and I've been shown something very odd in a picture on some old cave wall, and suddenly said kangaroo tells me time and space are all wrong and wants me to be *sensible*? What, when you get right down to it, is in it for me?'

'Look, this place wasn't finished, right? It wasn't fitted in . . . turned around . . .' The kangaroo looked at Rincewind as if reading his mind, which was the case. 'You know like with a jigsaw puzzle? The last piece is the right shape but you have to turn it round to fit? Right? Now think of the piece as a bloody big continent that's got to be turned around through about nine dimensions and you're home and . . .'

'Dry?' said Rincewind.

'Bloody right!'

'Er . . . I know this may seem like a foolish question,' said Rincewind, trying to dislodge a gooseberry pip from a tooth cavity, 'but why me?'

'It's your fault. You arrived here and suddenly things had always been wrong.'

Rincewind looked back towards the wall. The earth trembled again.

'Can you hop that past me again?' he said.

'Something went wrong in the past.'

The kangaroo looked at Rincewind's blank, jam-smeared expression, and tried again.

'Your arrival caused a wrong note,' it ventured.

'What in?'

The creature waved a paw vaguely.

'All this,' it said. 'You could call it a bloody multi-dimensional knuckle of localized phase space, or maybe you could just call it the song.'

Rincewind shrugged. 'I don't mind putting my hand up to killing a few spiders,' he said. 'But it was me or them. I mean some of those come at you at *head* height—'

'You changed history.'

'Oh, come *on*, a few spiders don't make that much difference, some of them were using their webs as *trampolines*, it was a case of "boing" and next moment—'

'No, not history from now on, history that's already happened,' said the kangaroo.

'I've changed things that already happened long ago?'

'Right.'

'By arriving here I changed what's *already happened*?'

'Yep. Look, time isn't as straightforward as you think—'

'I never thought it was,' said Rincewind. 'And I've been round it a few times . . .'

The kangaroo waved a paw expansively. 'It's not just that things in the future can affect things in the past,' he said. 'Things that didn't happen but might have happened can . . . affect things that really happened. Even things that happened and shouldn't have happened and were removed still have, oh, call 'em shadows in time, things left over which interfere with what's going on. Between you and me,' it went on, waggling its ears, 'it's all just held together by spit now. No one's ever got round to tidying it up. I'm always amazed when tomorrow follows today, and that's the truth.'

'Me too,' said Rincewind. 'Oh, me too.'

'Still, no worries, eh?'

'I think I'll lay off the jam,' said Rincewind. He put the sandwich down. 'Why me?'

The kangaroo scratched its nose. ''s got to be someone,' it said.

'And what'm I supposed to do?' said Rincewind.

'Wind it into the world.'

'There's a *key*?'

'Might be. Depends.'

Rincewind turned and looked at the rock pictures again, the pictures that hadn't been there a few weeks ago and then suddenly had always been there.

Figures holding long sticks. Figures in long robes. The artist had done a pretty good job of drawing something quite unfamiliar. And in case there was any doubt, you only had to look at what was on their heads.

'Yeah. We call them *The Pointy-Heads*,' said the kangaroo.

* * *

'He's started catching fish,' said the Senior Wrangler. 'That means he'll come over all smug and start asking what plans we've got for making a boat at any minute, you know what he's like.'

The Dean looked at some sketches he'd made on a rock.

'How hard can it be to build a boat?' he said. 'People with bones in their noses build boats. And we are the end product of thousands of years of enlightenment. Building a boat is *not* beyond men like us, Senior Wrangler.'

'Quite, Dean.'

'All we have to do is search this island until we find a book with a title like *Practical Boat-building for Beginners.*'

'Exactly. It'll be plain sailing after that, Dean. Ahaha.'

He glanced up, and swallowed hard. Mrs Whitlow was sitting on a log in the shade, fanning herself with a large leaf.

The sight stirred things in the Senior Wrangler. He was not at all sure what they were, but little details like the way something creaked when she moved twanged bits of the Senior Wrangler as well.

'You all right, Senior Wrangler? You look as if the heat is getting to you.'

'Just a little . . . warm, Dean.'

The Dean looked past him as he loosened his collar. 'Well, *they* haven't been long,' he said.

The other wizards were walking down the beach.

One advantage of a long wizarding robe is that it can be held like an apron, and the Chair of Indefinite Studies was bulging at the front even more than usual.

'Found anything to eat?' said the Senior Wrangler.

'Er . . . yes.'

'Fruit and nuts, I suppose,' grumbled the Dean.

'Er . . . yes, and then again, no,' said the Lecturer in Recent Runes. 'Um . . . it's rather odd . . .'

The Chair of Indefinite Studies let his burden spill out on to the sand. There were coconuts, other nuts of various sizes, and assorted hairy or knobbly vegetable things.

'All rather primitive,' said the Dean. 'And probably poisonous.'

'Well, the Bursar's been eating things like there's no tomorrow,' said the Lecturer in Recent Runes. The Bursar burped happily.

'That doesn't mean there will be,' said the Dean. 'What's up with you fellows? You keep looking at one another.'

'Er . . . we've tasted a few things too, Dean,' said the Lecturer in Recent Runes.

'Ah, I see the gatherers have returned!' roared Ridcully happily, walking towards them. He waved three fish on a string. 'Anything resembling potatoes in there, chaps?'

'You're not going to believe any of this,' mumbled the Lecturer in Recent Runes. 'You're going to accuse us of trickery.'

'What are you talking about?' said the Dean. 'They don't look very tricky to *me*.'

The Chair of Indefinite Studies gave a sigh. 'Have a coconut,' he said.

'Do they go off bang or something?'

'No, nothing like that at all.'

The Dean picked up a nut, gave it a suspicious look, and banged it on a stone. It fell into two exact halves.

There was no milk to spill out. Inside the husk was a brown inner shell, full of soft white fibres.

Ridcully picked up a bit of it and sniffed. 'I don't believe this,' he said. 'That's not natural.'

'So?' said the Dean. 'It's a coconut full of coconut. What's odd about that?'

The Archchancellor broke off a piece of the shell and handed it over. It was soft and slightly crumbly.

The Dean tasted it. 'Chocolate?' he said.

Ridcully nodded. 'Dairy milk, by the taste of it. With a creamy coconut filling.'

'Thaf's nod poffible,' said the Dean, his cheeks bulging.

'Spit it out, then.'

'I think I might perhaps try a *little* more,' said the Dean, swallowing. 'In a spirit of enquiry, you understand.'

The Senior Wrangler picked up a knobbly bluish nut about the size of a fist and tapped it experimentally. It shattered but was held together because of the gooey contents.

The smell was very familiar. A careful taste confirmed it. The wizards regarded the nut's innards in shocked silence.

'It's even got the blue veins,' said the Senior Wrangler.

'Yes, we know, we tried one,' said the Chair of Indefinite Studies weakly. 'And, after all, there *is* such a thing as a bread fruit—'

'I've heard of it,' said Ridcully. 'And I might believe there's such a thing as a nat'rally chocolate-covered coconut, because chocolate's a kind of potato—'

'A bean, possibly,' said Ponder Stibbons.

'Whatever. But I damn well don't believe there's such a thing as a mature Lancre Blue runny cheese nut!' He prodded the thing.

'But nature *does* come up with some very funny coincidences, Archchancellor,' said the Chair of Indefinite Studies. 'Why, I myself, as a child, once dug up a carrot which, ahaha, most amusingly looked just like a man with a—'

'Er . . .' said the Dean.

It was only a little sound, but it had a certain portentous quality. They turned to look at him.

He'd been peeling away the yellowing husk from something like a small bean pod. What he now held—

'Hah, yes, good joke,' said Ridcully. '*They* certainly don't grow on—'

'I didn't do anything! Look, it's still got bits of pith and stuff on it!' said the Dean, waving the thing wildly.

Ridcully took it, sniffed it, held it up to his ear and shook it, and then said quietly: 'Show me where you found it, will you?'

The bush was in a small clearing. Dozens of the little

green shoots hung down between its tiny leaves. Each was tipped by a flower, but the flowers were curling up and falling off. The crop was ripe.

Multi-coloured beetles zoomed away from the bush as the Dean selected a pod and peeled it open, revealing a slightly damp white cylinder. He examined it for a few seconds, then put one end in his mouth, took a box of matches from a pocket in his hat, and lit up.

'Quite a smooth smoke,' he said. His hand shook slightly as he took the cigarette out of his mouth and blew a smoke ring. 'Cork filter, too,' he said.

'Er ... well, both tobacco and cork are naturally occurring vegetable products,' quavered the Chair of Indefinite Studies.

'Chair?' said Ridcully.

'Yes, Archchancellor?'

'Shut up, will you?'

'Yes, Archchancellor.'

Ponder Stibbons broke open a cork tip. There was a tiny ring of what well might have been—

'Seeds,' he said. 'But that can't be right, because—'

The Dean, wreathed in blue smoke, had been staring at the nearby vines.

'Has it occurred to anyone else that those pods are remarkably rectangular?' he said.

'Go for it, Dean,' said Ridcully.

A brown outer husk was pulled aside.

'Ah,' said the Dean. 'Biscuits. Just the thing with cheese.'

'Er ...' said Ponder. He pointed.

Just beyond the bush a couple of boots lay on the ground.

Rincewind ran his fingers over the cave wall.

The ground shook again.

'What's causing that?' he said.

'Oh, some people say it's an earthquake, some say it's the country drying up, others say it's a giant snake rushing through the ground,' said Scrappy.

'Which is it?'

'The wrong sort of question.'

They definitely *looked* like wizards, thought Rincewind. They had that basic cone shape familiar to anyone who had been to Unseen University. They were holding staffs. Even with the crude materials available to them the ancient artists had managed to portray the knobs on the ends.

But UU hadn't even *existed* thirty thousand years ago . . .

Then he noticed, for the first time, the drawing right at the end of the cave. There were a lot of the ochre handprints on top of it, almost – and the thought expanded in his mind in a sneaky way – as though someone had thought that they could hold it down on to the rock, prevent it – this was a silly thought, he knew – prevent it from getting *out*.

He brushed away some dust.

'Oh, *no*,' he mumbled.

It was an oblong box. The artist hadn't got the hang of conventional perspective, but there was no doubt that he'd tried to paint hundreds of little legs.

'That's my Luggage!'

'Always the same, right?' said Scrappy, behind him. 'You arrive okay and your luggage ends up somewhere else.'

'Thousands of years in the past?'

'Could be a valuable antique.'

'It's got my clothes in it!'

'They'll probably be back in style, then.'

'You don't understand! It's a *magical* box! It's supposed to end up where I am!'

'It probably *is* where you are. Just not when.'

'What? Oh.'

'I told you time and space were all stirred up, didn't I? You wait till you're on your journey. There's places where there's several times happening at once and places where there's hardly any time at all, and times when there's hardly any place. You've got to sort it out, right?'

'What, like shuffling cards?' said Rincewind. He made a mental note about 'on your journey'.

'Yep.'

'That's impossible!'

'Y'know, I'd have said so too. But you *will* do it. Now, you'll have to concentrate about this bit, right?' Scrappy took a deep breath. 'I know you're going to do it because you've already done it.'

Rincewind put his head in his hands.

'I *told* you about time and space here being mixed up,' said the kangaroo.

'I've already saved the country, have I?'

'Yep.'

'Oh, good. Well, that wasn't so difficult. I don't want much – a medal, perhaps, the grateful thanks of the population, maybe a small pension and a ticket home . . .' He looked up. 'I'm not going to get any of that, though, am I?'

'No, because—'

'—I haven't already done it *yet*?'

'Exactly! You're getting the hang of it! You have to go and do what we know you're going to do because you've already done it. In fact, if you hadn't done it already I wouldn't be here to make sure it gets done. So you'd better do it.'

'Facing terrible dangers?'

The kangaroo waved a paw. 'Slightly terrible,' it said.

'And go for many miles over parched and trackless terrain?'

'Well, yeah. We haven't got any of the other sort.'

Rincewind brightened up slightly. 'And I'll meet comrades whose strengths and skills will be a great help to me?'

'Don't bet on it.'

'Any chance of a magic sword?'

'What would *you* do with a magic sword?'

'Fair enough. Fair enough. Forget the magic sword. But I've got to have *something*. Cloak of invisibility, potion of strength, something like that . . .'

'That stuff's for people who know how to use them, mister. You'll have to rely on your native wit.'

'I've got *nothing*? What sort of quest is that? Can't you give me any hints?'

'You may have to drink some beer,' said the

kangaroo. It cringed back for a moment, as if confident of facing a storm of objections.

Rincewind said: 'Oh. Right. Well, I know how to do that. What direction am I supposed to go?'

'Oh, you'll find it.'

'And when I get to where I'm going, what am I supposed to do?'

'It'll . . . be obvious, right?'

'And how will I know I've done it?'

'The Wet will come back.'

'The wet *what*?'

'It'll rain.'

'I thought it never rained here,' said Rincewind.

'See? I knew you were smart.'

The sun was setting. The rocks around the edge of the cave glowed red. Rincewind stared at them for a while, and reached a brave decision.

'I'm not the man to shirk when the fate of whole countries is in the balance,' he said. 'I will make a start at dawn to complete this task which I have already completed, by hoki, or my name isn't Rincewand!'

'Rincewind,' said the kangaroo.

'Indeed!'

'Well said, mate. Then I should get some sleep, if I were you. Could be a busy day tomorrow.'

'I've not been found wanting when duty calls,' said Rincewind. He reached into a hollow log and, after some rummaging around, pulled out a plate of egg and chips. 'See you at dawn, then.'

Ten minutes later he stretched out on the sand with

the log as his pillow, and looked up at the purple sky. Already a few stars were coming out.

Now, there was something . . . Oh, yes. The kangaroo was lying down on the other side of the waterhole.

Rincewind raised his head. 'You said something about when "he" created this place, and you talked about "him" . . .'

'Yep.'

'Only . . . I'm pretty sure I've met the Creator. Short bloke. Does all his own snowflakes.'

'Yeah? And when did *you* meet *him*?'

'When he was making the world, as a matter of fact.' Rincewind decided to refrain from mentioning that he'd dropped a sandwich into a rockpool at the time. People don't like to hear that they may have evolved from somebody's lunch. 'I get around quite a lot,' he added.

'Are you coming the raw prawn?'

'What? Oh, no. Certainly not. Coming a raw prawn? Not me. That's something I never do. Or even cooked prawns. Or crustaceans of any sort, especially in rock-pools. Not me. Er . . . what was it that you actually meant?'

'Well, he didn't create this place,' said Scrappy, ignoring him. 'This was done after.'

'Can that happen?'

'Why not?'

'Well, it's not like, you know, building on over the stables, is it?' said Rincewind. 'Someone just wanders along when a world's all finished and slings down an extra continent?'

'Happens all the time, mate,' said Scrappy. 'Bloody hell, yeah. Why not, anyway? If other creators go around leaving ruddy great empty oceans, someone's *bound* to fill 'em up, right? Does a world good, too, having a fresh look, new ideas, new ways.'

Rincewind stared up at the stars. He had a mental vision of someone walking from world to world, sneaking in extra lands when no one was looking.

'Yes indeed,' he said. 'I for one would not have thought of making all the snakes deadly, and all the spiders deadlier than the snakes. And putting pockets on everything? Great idea.'

'There you go, then,' said Scrappy. He was hardly visible now, as the dark filled up the cave.

'Made a lot of them, has he?'

'Yep.'

'Why?'

'So's maybe at least one of them won't get mucked up. Always puts kangaroos on 'em, too. Sort of a signature, you might say.'

'Does this Creator have a name?'

'Nope. He's just the man who carries the sack that contains the whole universe.'

'A leather sack?'

'Sounds like him,' the kangaroo agreed.

'The whole universe in one small sack?'

'Yep.'

Rincewind settled back. 'I'm glad I'm not religious,' he said. 'It must be very complicated.'

After another five minutes he began to snore. After half an hour he moved his head slightly.

The kangaroo didn't seem to be around.

With almost super-Rincewind speed he was upright and scrambling up the fallen rocks, over the lip of the cave and into the dark oven of the night.

He sighted on a random star and got into his stride, ignoring the bushes that lashed at his bare legs.

Hah!

He was not going to be found wanting when duty called. He did not intend to be found at all.

In the cave the water in the pool rippled under the starlight, the expanding circles lapping against the sand.

On the wall was an ancient drawing of a kangaroo, in white and red and yellow. The artist had tried to achieve on stone what might better have been attempted with eight dimensions and a large particle accelerator; he'd tried to include not just the kangaroo *now* but also the kangaroo in the past, and the kangaroo in the future and, in short, not what the kangaroo looked like but what the kangaroo *was*.

Among other things, as it faded, it was grinning.

Among the complexities that made up the intelligent biped known to the rest of the world as Mrs Whitlow was this: there was no such thing as an informal meal in Mrs Whitlow's world. If Mrs Whitlow made sandwiches even just for *herself* she would put a sprig of parsley on the top. She placed a napkin on her lap to drink a cup of tea. If the table could have a vase of flowers and a placemat with a tasteful view of something nice, so much the better.

It was unthinkable that she should eat a meal balanced on her knees. In fact it was unthinkable to think of Mrs Whitlow as having knees, although the Senior Wrangler had to fan himself with his hat occasionally. So the beach had been scoured to find enough bits of driftwood to make a very rough table, and some suitable rocks to use as seats.

The Senior Wrangler dusted one off with his hat. 'There we are, Mrs Whitlow . . .'

The housekeeper frowned. 'Ai'm really sure it's Not Done for the staff to eat with the gentlemen,' she said.

'Be our guest, Mrs Whitlow,' said Ridcully.

'Ai really can't. It does not Do to get ideas above one's station,' said Mrs Whitlow. 'Ai would never be able to look you in the face again, sir. Ai hope Ai know my Place.'

Ridcully looked blank for a moment, and then said quietly: 'Faculty meeting, gentlemen?'

The wizards went into another huddle a little way along the beach.

'What are we supposed to do about *that*?'

'I think it's very commendable of her. Her world is Below Stairs, after all.'

'Yes, very well, but it's not as if there're any stairs on this island.'

'Could we build some?'

'We can't let the poor woman sit off by herself somewhere, that is my point.'

'We spent *ages* on that table!'

'And did you notice something about the driftwood, Archchancellor?'

'Looked like perfectly ordinary wood to *me*, Stibbons. Branches, treetrunks and whatnot.'

'That's the strange thing, sir, because—'

'It's very simple, Ridcully. I hope that, as gentlemen, we know how to treat a woman—'

'La*dy*.'

'Let me just say that was unnecessarily sarcastic, Dean,' said Ridcully. 'Very well. If the Prophet Ossory won't go to the mountain, the mountain must go to the Prophet Ossory. As they say in Klatch.'

He paused. He knew his wizards.

'I believe, in fact, that it's in Omnia that—' Ponder began.

Ridcully waved a hand. 'Something like that, anyway.'

And that is why Mrs Whitlow dined alone at the table, while the wizards sat around the fire a little way away, except that very frequently one of them would lumber over to offer her some choice bit of nature's bounty.

It was obvious that starvation would not be a problem on this island, although dyspepsia and gout might be.

Fish was the main course. Frenzied searching had failed to locate a steak bush so far but *had* found, in addition to numerous more conventional fruits, a pasta bush, a sort of squash that contained something very much like custard and, to Ridcully's disgust, a pineapple-like plant the fruit of which was, when the husk had been stripped away, a large plum pudding.

'Obviously it's not *really* a plum pudding,' he

protested. 'We just think it's like a plum pudding because it tastes exactly like a . . . plum pudding . . .' His voice trailed off.

'It's got plums and currants in it,' said the Senior Wrangler. 'Pass the custard squash, will you?'

'My point is that we only *think* they look like currants and plums—'

'No, we also think they *taste* like currants and plums,' said the Senior Wrangler. 'Look, Archchancellor, there's no mystery. Obviously wizards have been here before. This is the result of perfectly ordinary magic. Perhaps our lost geographer did a bit of experimenting. Or it's sourcery, perhaps. Some of the things that got created in the old days, well, a cigarette bush is very small beer by comparison, eh?'

'Talking of small beer . . .' said the Dean, waving his hand, 'pass me the rum, will you?'

'Mrs Whitlow doesn't approve of strong liquor,' said the Senior Wrangler.

The Dean glanced at the housekeeper, who was daintily eating a banana, a feat which is quite hard to do.

He put down the coconut shell. 'Well, she . . . I am . . . I don't see . . . well, damn it all, that's all I've got to say.'

'Or bad language,' said the Lecturer in Recent Runes.

'I vote we take some of those bees back with us,' said the Chair of Indefinite Studies. 'Marvellous little creatures. No footling around being content with making boring honey. You just reach up and pick one of these handy little wax containers and bob's your uncle.'

'She takes all the peel off slowly before she eats it. Oh, dear . . .'

'Are you all right, Senior Wrangler? Is the heat getting to you?'

'What? Eh? Hmm? Oh, nothing. Yes. Bees. Wonderful things.'

They glanced up at a couple of the bees, who were busying themselves around a flowering bush in the last of the light. They were leaving little black smoke trails.

'Shooting around like little rockets,' said the Archchancellor. 'Amazing.'

'I'm still worried about those boots,' said the Senior Wrangler. 'You'd think the man had been pulled right out of them.'

'It's a tiny island, man,' said Ridcully. 'All we've seen is birds, a few little squeaky things and a load of insects. You don't get big fierce animals on islands you can practically throw a stone across. He must've just . . . felt a bit carefree. It's a bit hot for boots here, anyway.'

'So why haven't we seen him?'

'Hah! He's probably lying low,' said the Dean. 'Ashamed to face us. Keeping a nice sunny island in your study is against University rules.'

'Is it?' said Ponder. 'I've never seen it mentioned. How long has it been a rule?'

'Ever since I've had to sleep in a freezing bedroom,' said the Dean, darkly. 'Pass the bread-and-butter-pudding fruit, will you?'

'Ook,' said the Librarian.

'Ah, nice to see you your old shape, old chap,' said Ridcully. 'Try and keep it up for longer this time, eh?'

'Ook.'

The Librarian was sitting behind a pile of fruit. Normally he wouldn't question such a perfect piece of positioning, but now even the bananas were bothering him. There was the same sensation of *wrongness*. There were long yellow ones, and stubby ones, and red ones, and fat brown ones—

He stared at the remains of the fish. There was a big silver one, and a fat red one, and a small grey one, and a flat one a bit like a plaice—

'Obviously some sourcerer landed here and wanted to make the place more homely,' the Senior Wrangler was saying, but he sounded far off. The Librarian was counting.

The plum-pudding plant, the custard-squash vine, the chocolate coconut— He turned his head to look at the trees. And now he knew what he was looking for, he couldn't see it anywhere.

The Senior Wrangler stopped talking as the ape scrambled to his knuckles and sped back to the high-tide line. The wizards watched in silence as he scrabbled through the heaped-up seashells. He came back with a double handful, which he dropped triumphantly in front of the Archchancellor.

'Ook!'

'What's that, old chap?'

'*Ook!*'

'Yes, very pretty, but what's—'

'OOK!'

The Librarian seemed to remember what kind of intellects he was dealing with. He held up a finger and looked at Ridcully enquiringly. 'Ook?'

'Still not quite with you—'

Two fingers went up. 'Ook ook?'

'Not sure I fully—'

'Ook ook ook!'

Ponder Stibbons looked at the three fingers now raised. 'I think he's counting, sir.' The Librarian handed him a banana.

'Ah, the old "How Many Fingers Am I Holding Up?" game,' said the Dean. 'But usually we all have to have a bit more to drink first—'

The Librarian waved his hand at the fish, at the meal, at the shells and at the background of trees. One finger stabbed at the sky.

'Ook!'

'It's all one to you?' said Ridcully. 'It's one big place? It's one to remember?'

The Librarian opened his mouth again, and then sneezed.

A very large red seashell lay on the sand.

'Oh, dear,' said Ponder Stibbons.

'That's interesting,' said the Chair of Indefinite Studies. 'He's turned into quite a good specimen of the giant conch. You can get a marvellous sound out of one of them if you blow in the pointy end . . . '

'Volunteers?' said the Dean, almost under his breath.

'Oh, dear,' said Ponder again.

'What's up with you?' said the Dean.

'There's only one,' said Ponder. 'That's what he was trying to tell us.'

'One what?' said Ridcully.

'Of everything, sir. There's only one of everything.'

It was, he thought later, a good dramatic line. People ought to have looked at one another in growing and horrified realization and said things like, 'By George, you know, he's right!' But these were wizards, capable of thinking very big thoughts in very small chunks.

'Don't be daft, man,' said Ridcully. 'There's millions of the damn shells, for a start.'

'*Yes*, sir, but look, they're all *different,* sir. All the trees we found . . . there was only one of each sort, sir. Lots of banana trees, but they all produce different types of bananas. There was only one cigarette tree, wasn't there?'

'Lots of bees, though,' said Ridcully.

'But only one swarm,' said Ponder.

'*Millions* of beetles,' said the Dean.

'I don't think I've seen two *alike*, sir.'

'Well, that's *interesting*,' said Ridcully, 'but I don't see—'

'One of anything doesn't *work*, sir,' said Ponder. 'It can't breed.'

'Yes, but they're only *trees*, Stibbons.'

'Trees need males and females too, sir.'

'They do?'

'Yes, sir. Sometimes they're different bits of the same tree, sir.'

'*What?* You sure?'

'Yes, sir. My uncle grew nuts, sir.'

'Keep it down, boy, keep it down! Mrs Whitlow might hear you!'

Ponder was taken aback. 'What, sir? But . . . well . . . she is *Mrs* Whitlow, sir . . .'

'What's that got to do with the price of feet?'

'I mean . . . presumably there was a *Mr* Whitlow, sir?'

Ridcully's face went wooden for a moment and his lips moved as he tried out various responses. Finally he settled, weakly, for: 'That's as maybe, but it all sounds pretty *mucky* to me.'

'I'm afraid that's nature for you, sir.'

'I used to like walking through the woods on a nice spring morning, Stibbons. You mean to say the trees were at it like knives the whole time?'

Ponder's horticultural knowledge found itself a little exhausted at this point. He tried to remember what he could about his uncle, who'd spent most of his life up a ladder.

'I, er, think camel-hair brushes are sometimes involved—' he began, but Ridcully's expression told him that this wasn't a welcome fact, so he went on, 'Anyway, sir, ones don't work. And there's another thing, sir. Who smokes the cigarettes? I mean, if the bush just hopes that butts are going to be dropped around the place, who does it think is going to smoke them?'

'What?'

Ponder sighed. 'The point about fruit, sir, is that it's

a kind of lure. A bird'll eat the fruit and then, er, drop the seeds somewhere. It's the way the plant spreads its seeds around. But we've only seen birds and a few lizards on this island, so how—'

'Ah, I see what you mean,' said Ridcully. 'You're thinking: what kind of bird stops flyin' around for a quick smoke?'

'A puffin,' said the Bursar.

'Glad to see you're still with us, Bursar,' said Ridcully, without looking round.

'Birds don't smoke, sir. You've got to ask yourself what's in it for the bush, you see? If there were *people* here, well, I suppose you *might* get a sort of nicotine tree eventually, because they'd smoke the cigarettes – I mean,' he corrected himself, because he prided himself on his logical thought, 'these things that *look* like cigarettes, and stub them out around the place, thus spreading the seeds which are in the filter. Some seeds need heat to germinate, sir. But if there aren't any people, the bush doesn't make any sense.'

'*We're* people,' said the Dean. 'And I like a smoke after supper. Everyone knows that.'

'Yes, but with respect, sir, we've only been here a couple of hours and I doubt whether the news has spread all the way to small islands,' said Ponder patiently, and with, as it turned out, one hundred per cent inaccuracy. 'That's probably not long enough for one to evolve.'

'Are you tellin' me', said Ridcully, like a man with something on his mind, 'that you think when you eat an apple you're helping it to . . .' He stopped. 'It was bad enough about the trees.' He sniffed. 'I shall stick to eating fish. At least they make their own arrangements. At a decent distance, I understand. And you know what *I* think about evolution, Mister Stibbons. If it happens, and frankly I've always considered it a bit of a fairy story, it *has* to happen fast. Look at lemmings, for one thing.'

'Lemmings, sir?'

'Right. The little blighters keep chargin' over cliffs, right? And how many have ever changed into birds on the way down, eh? Eh?'

'Well, none, of cou—'

'There's my point,' said Ridcully triumphantly. 'And it's no good one of them on the way down thinking, "Hey, maybe I should waggle my claws a bit," is it? No, what it ought to do is decide really positively about growing some real wings.'

'What, in a couple of seconds? While they're plunging towards the rocks?'

'Best time.'

'But lemmings don't just turn into birds, sir!'

'Lucky for them if they could, though, eh?'

There was a roar, far off in the little jungle. It sounded rather like a foghorn.

'Are you *sure* there aren't any dangerous creatures on this island?' said the Dean.

'I think I saw some prawns,' said the Senior Wrangler nervously.

'No, the Archchancellor was right, it's far too small,' said Ponder, trying to dismiss the thought of flying lemmings. 'It couldn't possibly support anything that could hurt us, sir. After all, what would it eat?'

Now they could all hear something crashing through the trees.

'Us?' said the Dean hesitantly.

A creature blundered out on to the sunset sands. It was large and seemed to be mainly head – one huge, reptilian head that looked almost as big as the body below it. It walked on two long hind legs. There was a tail, but given the amount of teeth now showing at the other end the wizards weren't inclined to take in too much additional detail.

The creature sniffed the air and roared again.

'Ah,' said Ridcully. 'The solution to the mystery of the disappearing geographer, I suspect. Well done, Senior Wrangler.'

'I think I'll just—' the Dean began.

'Stay still, sir!' hissed Ponder. 'A lot of reptiles can't see you if you don't move!'

'I can assure you, at the speed *I* intend *nothing* is going to see me . . .'

The monster turned its head this way and that, and began to lumber forward.

'Can't see things that don't move?' said the Archchancellor. 'You mean we just have to wait for it to walk into a tree?'

'Mrs Whitlow's still sitting there!' said the Senior Wrangler.

She was in fact spreading some runny cheese on a biscuit in a ladylike fashion.

'I don't think she's seen it!'

Ridcully rolled up his sleeve. 'I think a round of fireballs, gentlemen,' he said.

'Hold on,' said Ponder. 'This may be an endangered species.'

'So is Mrs Whitlow.'

'But do we have the *right* to wipe out what—'

'Absolutely,' said Ridcully. 'If its creator had meant it to survive he would have given it a fireproof skin. That's your evolution for you, Stibbons.'

'But perhaps we ought to study it . . . ?'

The thing was beginning to get up speed now. It was amazing how fast it could move, considering how big it was.

'Er . . .' said Ponder nervously.

Ridcully raised his arm.

The creature stopped, jerked into the air, and then went flat, like a rubber ball that had been stepped on, and indeed when it sprang back into shape it was with a noise akin to the sound made when a bad conjuror is having trouble twisting the back legs on to the balloon animal. Insofar as it had an expression at all, it looked more astonished than hurt. Little flashes of lightning crackled around it. It went flat again, rolled up into a cylinder, twisted into a range of interesting but probably painful shapes, shrank to a ball the size of a grapefruit and then, with a final and rather sad little noise that might well have been spelled *prarp*, dropped back on to the sand.

'Now *that* was pretty good,' said Ridcully. 'Which of you fellows did that?'

The wizards looked at one another.

'Not us,' said the Dean. 'It was going to be fireballs all the way.'

Ridcully nudged Ponder. 'Go on, then,' he said. 'Study it.'

'Er . . .' Ponder looked at the bewildered creature on the sand. 'Er . . . the subject appears to have turned into a large chicken.'

'Good, well done,' said Ridcully, as if to wrap things up. 'Shame to waste this fireball, then.'

He hurled it.

It was a road.

At least, it was a long flat piece of desert with wheel ruts in it. Rincewind stared at it.

A road. Roads went somewhere. Sooner or later they went *everywhere*. And when you got there, you generally found walls, buildings, harbours . . . boats. And incidentally a shortage of talking kangaroos. That was practically one of the hallmarks of civilization.

It wasn't that he was *against* anyone saving the world, or whatever subset of it apparently wanted saving. He just felt that it didn't need saving by him.

Which way to go? He picked a direction at random and jogged along for a while, as the sun came up.

After a while there was a cloud of dust in the dawn, coming closer. Rincewind stood hopefully by the track.

What eventually appeared at the inverted apex of the cloud was a cart, pulled by a string of horses.

The horses were black. So was the cart. And it didn't seem to be slowing down.

Rincewind waved his hat in the air, just as the horses came past.

After a while the dust settled. He got back on to his feet and walked unsteadily through the bushes until he found the cart where it had come to rest. The horses watched him warily.

It wasn't a huge cart to be pulled by eight horses, but both they and the cart were covered with so much wood, leather and metal they probably didn't have much energy to spare. Spikes and studs covered every surface.

The reins led not to the usual seat, but into holes in the front of the cart itself. This was roofed over with more wood and ironmongery – bits of old stove, hammered-out body armour, saucepan lids, and tin cans that had been stamped flat and nailed on.

Above the slot where the reins went in was something like a piece of bent stovepipe, poking through the cart's roof. It had a watchful look.

'Er . . . hello?' said Rincewind. 'Sorry if I scared your horses . . .'

In the absence of any reply he climbed up an armoured wheel and looked at the top of the cart. There was a round lid that had been pushed open.

Rincewind didn't even consider looking inside. That'd mean his head would be outlined against the sky, a sure way of getting your body outlined against the dirt.

A twig cracked behind him.

He sighed, and got down slowly, taking great care not to turn around.

'I surrender totally,' he said, raising his hands.

'That's right,' said a level voice. 'This is a crossbow, mate. Let's have a look at your ugly mug.'

Rincewind turned. There was no one behind him.

Then he looked down.

The crossbow was almost vertical. If it were fired, the bolt would go right up his nose.

'A dwarf?' he said.

'You've got something against dwarfs?'

'Who, me? No! Some of my best friends would be dwarfs. If I had any friends, I mean. Er. I'm Rincewind.'

'Yeah? Well, I'm short-tempered,' said the dwarf. 'Most people call me Mad.'

'Just "Mad"? That's an . . . unusual name.'

'It ain't a name.'

Rincewind stared. There was no doubt that his captor *was* a dwarf. He didn't have the traditional beard or iron helmet, but there were other little ways that you could tell. There was the chin that you could break coconuts on, the fixed expression of ferocity, and the certain bullet-headedness that meant its owner could go through walls face first. And, of course, if all else failed, the fact that the top of it was about level with Rincewind's stomach was a clue. Mad wore a leather suit but, like the cart, it had metal riveted on to it wherever possible. Where there weren't rivets there was weaponry.

The word 'friend' jumped into the forefront of Rincewind's brain. There are many reasons for being friends with someone. The fact that he's pointing a deadly weapon at you is among the top four.

'Good description,' said Rincewind. 'Easy to remember.'

The dwarf cocked his head on one side and listened.

'Blast, they're catching me up.' He looked back up at Rincewind and said, 'Can you fire a crossbow?' in a way that indicated that answering 'no' was a good way to contract immediate sinus trouble.

'Absolutely,' said Rincewind.

'Get on the cart, then. Y'know, I've been travellin' this road for years and this is the first time anyone's ever dared to hitch a lift?'

'Amazing,' said Rincewind.

There was not much room under the hatch, and most of it was taken up by more weapons. Mad pushed Rincewind aside, grasped the reins, peered into the periscope stovepipe and urged the horses into motion.

Bushes scraped against the wheels and the horses dragged back on to the track and began to get up speed.

'Beaut, aren't they?' said Mad. 'They can outrun anything, even with the armour.'

'This is certainly a very ... *original* cart,' said Rincewind.

'Got a few modifications of my own,' said Mad. He grinned evilly. 'You a wizard, mister?'

'Broadly speaking, yes.'

'Any good?' Mad was loading another crossbow.

Rincewind hesitated. 'No,' he said.

'Lucky for you,' said Mad. 'I'd have killed you if you were. Can't stand wizards. Bunch of wowsers, right?'

He grasped the handles of the bent stovepipe and swivelled it around.

'Here they come,' he muttered.

Rincewind peered over the top of Mad's head. There was a piece of mirror in the bend of the pipe. It showed the road behind, and half a dozen dots under another cloud of red dust.

'Road gang,' said Mad. 'After my cargo. Steal anything, they will. All bastards are bastards, but some bastards is *bastards*.' He pulled a handful of nosebags from under the seat. 'Right, you get up on top with a couple of crossbows, and I'll fix the supercharger.'

'What? You want me to start *shooting* at people?'

'You want *me* to start shooting at people?' said Mad, pushing him up the ladder.

Rincewind crawled out on to the top of the cart. It was swaying and bouncing. Red dust choked him and the wind tried to blow his robe over his head.

He hated weapons, and not just because they'd so often been aimed at him. You got into *more* trouble if you had a weapon. People shot you instantly if they thought you were going to shoot them. But if you were unarmed, they often stopped to talk. Admittedly, they tended to say things like, 'You'll *never* guess what we're going to *do* to you, pal,' but that took *time*. And Rincewind could do a lot with a few seconds. He could use them to live longer in.

The dots in the distance were other carts, designed

for speed rather than cargo. Some had four wheels, some had two. One had ... just one, a huge one between narrow shafts, with a tiny saddle on top. The rider looked as though he'd bought his clothes in the scrapmetal yards of three continents and, where they wouldn't fit, had strapped on a chicken.

But not one as big as the chicken pulling his wheel. It was bigger than Rincewind and most of what wasn't leg was neck. It was covering the ground as fast as a horse.

'What the hell's *that*?' he yelled.

'Emu!' shouted Mad, who was now hanging among the harnesses. 'Try and pick it off, they're a good feed!'

The cart jolted. Rincewind's hat whirled away into the dust.

'Now I've lost my hat!'

'Good! Bloody awful hat!'

An arrow twanged off a metal plate by Rincewind's foot.

'And they're *shooting* at me!'

A cart rattled out of the dust. The man beside the driver whirled something around his head. A grapnel bit into the woodwork by Rincewind's other foot and ripped off a metal plate.

'And they're—' he began.

'You've got a bow, right?' yelled Mad, who was balancing on the back of one of the horses. 'And find something to hold onta, they're gonna go at any minute—'

The cart had been moving at the gallop, but now it suddenly shot forward and almost jolted Rincewind

right off. Smoke poured out of the axles. The landscape blurred.

'What the hell is that?'

'Supercharger!' shouted Mad, pulling himself on to
the cart inches from the frantically pounding hooves.
'Secret recipe! Now hold 'em off, right, 'cos someone's
gotta steer!'

The emu emerged from the dust cloud with a few of
the faster carts rattling behind it. An arrow buried
itself in the cart right between Rincewind's legs.

He flung himself flat on the swaying roof, held out
the crossbow, shut his eyes and fired.

In accordance with ancient narrative practice, the
shot ricocheted off someone's helmet and brought
down an innocent bird some distance away, whose only
role was to expire with a suitably humorous squawk.

The man driving the emu drew alongside. From
under a familiar hat with 'Wizzard' dimly visible in
the grime he gave Rincewind a grin. Every tooth
had been sharpened to a point, and the front six had
'Mother' engraved on them.

'G'day!' he shouted cheerfully. 'Hand over your
cargo and I promise you that you won't be killed all in
one go.'

'That's my hat! Give me back my hat!'

'You're a wizard, are you?' The man stood up on the
saddle, balancing easily as the wheel bounced over
the sand. He waved his hands over his head.

'Look at me, mates! I'm a bloody wizard! Magic,
magic, magic!'

A very heavy arrow, trailing a rope, smashed into

the back of the cart and stuck fast. There was a cheer from the riders.

'You give me back my hat or there'll be trouble!'

'Oh, there's gonna be trouble *anyway*,' said the rider, aiming his crossbow. 'Tell you what, why not turn me into somethin' *bad*? Oh, I'm all afrai—'

His face went green. He pitched backwards. The crossbow bolt hit the driver of the cart beside him, which veered wildly into the path of another, which swerved and crashed into a camel. That meant the carts behind were suddenly faced with a pile-up which, together with the absence of brakes on any vehicle, immediately got bigger. Part of it was kicking people as well.

Rincewind, hands over his head, watched until the last wheel had rolled away, and then walked unsteadily along the swaying cart to where Mad was leaning on the reins.

'Er, I think you can slow down now, Mr Mad,' he ventured.

'Yeah? Killed 'em all, didja?'

'Er . . . not all of them. Some of them just ran away.'

'You kiddin' me?' The dwarf looked round. 'Stone me, you ain't! Here, pull that lever as hard as you can!'

He waved at a long metal rod beside Rincewind, who tugged it obediently. Metal screamed as the brakes locked against the wheels.

'Why're they going so fast?'

'It's a mixture of oats and lizard glands!' shouted Mad, against the red-hot squealing. 'Gives 'em a big jolt!'

The cart had to circle for a few minutes until the adrenalin wore off, and then they went back along the track to look at the wreckage.

Mad swore again. 'What *happened*?'

'He shouldn't've stolen my hat,' Rincewind mumbled.

The dwarf jumped down and kicked a broken cartwheel.

'You did this to people because they stole your *hat*? What do you do if they spit in your eye, blow up the country?'

''s my hat,' said Rincewind sullenly. He wasn't at all sure what *had* happened. He wasn't any good at magic, that he knew. The only curses of his that stood a chance of working were on the lines of 'May you get rained on at some time in your life,' and 'May you lose some small item despite the fact that you put it there only a moment ago.' Going pale green . . . he looked down . . . oh, yes, and slightly yellow in blotches, now . . . was not the usual effect.

Mad wandered purposefully among the wreckage. He picked up a few weapons and tossed them aside.

'Want the camel?' he said. The creature was standing a little way off, eyeing him suspiciously. It looked quite unscathed, having been the cause of considerable scathe in other people.

'I'd really rather stick my foot in a bacon slicer,' said Rincewind.

'Sure? Well, hitch it onta the cart, it'll fetch a good price in Dijabringabeeralong,' said Mad. He looked at a home-made repeating crossbow, grunted and tossed it aside. Then he looked at another cart and his face brightened.

'Ah! *Now* we're cooking with charcoal!' he said. 'It's our lucky day, mate!'

'Oh. A bag of hay,' said Rincewind.

'Give us a hand to get it on the wagon, willya?' said Mad, unbolting the rear of his own cart.

'What's so special about hay?'

The cart opened. It was full of hay.

'Life or death out here, mate. There's people'd slit yew from here to breakfast for a bale of hay. Man without hay is a man without a horse, and out here a man without a horse is a corpse.'

'Sorry? I went through all that for a load of *hay*?'

Mad waggled his eyebrows conspiratorially. '*And* two sacks of oats in the secret compartment, mate.' He slapped Rincewind on the back. 'An' to think I thought yew was some back-stabbin' drongo I ort to toss over the rail! Turns out you're as mad as me!'

There are times when it does not pay to declare one's sanity, and Rincewind realized that he'd be mad to do so now. Anyway, he could talk to kangaroos and find cheese and chutney rolls in the desert. There were times when you had to look wobbly facts in the face.

'Mental as anything,' he said, with what he hoped was disarming modesty.

'Good bloke! Let's load up their weapons and grub and get goin'!'

'What do we want their weapons for?'

'Fetch a good price.'

'And what about the bodies?'

'Nah, worthless.'

While Mad was nailing salvaged bits of scrap metal to his cart, Rincewind sidled over to the green and yellow corpse . . . and, oh yes, large black areas now . . . and, using a stick, levered his hat from its head.

A small eight-legged ball of angry black fur sprang out and locked its fangs on to the stick, which began to smoulder. He put it down very carefully, grabbed the hat and ran.

Ponder sighed.

'I *wasn't* questioning your authority, Archchancellor,' he said. 'I just feel that if a huge monster evolves into a chicken right in front of you, the considered response should not be to eat the chicken.'

The Archchancellor licked his fingers. 'What would you have done, then?' he said.

'Well . . . studied it,' said Ponder.

'So did we. Post-mortem examination,' said the Dean.

'Minutely,' said the Chair of Indefinite Studies, happily. He belched. 'Pardon *me*, Mrs Whitlow. Will you have a little more br . . .' He caught Ridcully's steely glance, and went on, '. . . front part of the chicken, Mrs Whitlow?'

'And we've discovered that it'll no longer be any menace to visiting wizards,' said Ridcully.

'It's just that I think proper research should involve more than having a look to see if you can find a sage-and-onion bush,' said Ponder. 'You saw how quickly it changed, didn't you?'

'Well?' said the Dean.

'That can't be natural.'

'*You're* the one who says things naturally change into other things, Mister Stibbons.'

'But not *that* fast!'

'Have you ever *seen* any of this evolution happening?'

'Well, of course not, no one has ever—'

'There you are, then,' said Ridcully, in a closing-the-argument voice. 'That might be the normal speed. As I said, it makes perfect sense. There's no point in turning into a bird a bit at a time, is there? A feather here, a beak there . . . You'd see some damn stupid creatures wandering around, eh?' The other wizards laughed. 'Our monster probably simply thought, Oh, there's too many of them, perhaps I'd better turn into something they'd like.'

'Enjoy,' said the Dean.

'Sensible survival strategy,' said Ridcully. 'Up to a point.'

Ponder rolled his eyes. These things always sounded fine when he worked them out in his head. He'd read some of the old books, and sit and think for *ages*, and a little theory would put itself together in his head in a row of little shiny blocks, and then when he let it out it'd run straight into the Faculty and one of them, one of them, would always ask some bloody *stupid* question which he couldn't quite answer at the moment. How could you ever make any progress against minds like that? If some god somewhere had said, 'Let there be light,' they'd be the ones to say things like 'Why? The darkness has always been good enough for *us*.'

Old men, that was the trouble. Ponder was not totally enthusiastic about the old traditions, because he was well into his twenties and in a moderately important position and therefore, to some of the mere striplings in the University, a target. Or would have been, if they weren't getting that boiled eyeball feeling by sitting up all night tinkering with Hex.

He wasn't interested in promotion, anyway. He'd just be happy if people *listened* for five minutes, instead of saying, 'Well done, Mister Stibbons, but we tried that once and it doesn't work,' or, 'We probably haven't got the funding,' or, worst of all, 'You don't get proper fill-in-nouns these days – remember old "nickname" ancient-wizard-who-died-fifty-years-ago-who-Ponder-wouldn't-possibly-be-able-to-remember? Now *there* was a chap who knew his fill-in-nouns.'

Above Ponder, he felt, were a lot of dead men's shoes. And they had living men's feet in them, and were stamping down hard.

They never bothered to learn anything, they never bothered to remember anything apart from how much better things used to be, they bickered like a lot of children and the only one who ever said anything sensible said it in orang-utan.

He prodded the fire viciously.

The wizards had made Mrs Whitlow a polite rude hut out of branches and big woven leaves. She bade them goodnight and demurely pulled some leaves across the entrance behind her.

'A very respectable lady, Mrs Whitlow,' said Ridcully. 'I think I'll turn in myself, too.'

There were already one or two sets of snores building up around the fire.

'I think someone ought to stand guard,' said Ponder.

'Good man,' muttered Ridcully, turning over.

Ponder gritted his teeth and turned to the Librarian, who was temporarily back in the land of the bipedal and was sitting gloomily wrapped in a blanket.

'At least I expect this is a home from home for you, eh, sir?'

The Librarian shook his head.

'Would *you* be interested in hearing what else is odd about this place?' said Ponder.

'Ook?'

'The driftwood. No one listens to me, but it's *important*. We must have dragged loads of stuff for the fire, and it's all natural timber, do you notice that? No bits of plank, no old crates, no tatty old sandals. Just . . . ordinary wood.'

'Ook?'

'That means we must be a long way off the normal shipping . . . oh, no . . . don't . . .'

The Librarian wrinkled his nose desperately.

'Quickly! Concentrate on having arms and legs! I mean living ones!'

The Librarian nodded miserably, and sneezed.

'Awk?' he said, when his shape had settled down again.

'Well,' said Ponder sadly. 'At least you're animate. Possibly rather large for a penguin, though. I *think* it's your body's survival strategy. It keeps trying to find a stable shape that works.'

'Awk?'

'Funny it can't seem to do anything about the red hair . . .'

The Librarian glared at him, shuffled a little way along the beach, and sagged into a heap.

Ponder looked around the fire. *He* seemed to be the man on watch, if only because no one else intended to do it. Well, wasn't that a surprise.

Things twittered in the trees. Phosphorescence glimmered on the sea. The stars were coming out.

He looked up at the stars. At least you could depend—

And, suddenly, he saw what *else* was wrong.

'Archchancellor!'

So how long have you been mad? No, not a good start, really . . . It was quite hard to know how to open the conversation.

'So . . . I didn't expect dwarfs here,' Rincewind said.

'Oh, the family blew in from NoThingfjord when I was a kid,' said Mad. 'Meant to go down the coast a bit, storm got up, next thing we're shipwrecked and up to our knees in parrots. Best thing that could've happened. Back there I'd be down some freezing cold mine picking bits of rock out of the walls but, over here, a dwarf can stand tall.'

'Really,' said Rincewind, his face carefully blank.

'But not too bloody tall!' Mad went on.

'Certainly not.'

'So we settled down, and now my dad's got a chain of bakeries in Bugarup.'

'Dwarf bread?' said Rincewind.

'Too right! That's what kept us going across thousands of miles of shark-infested ocean,' said Mad. 'If we hadn't had that sack of dwarf bread we'd—'

'—never have been able to club the sharks to death?' said Rincewind.

'Ah, you're a man who knows your breads.'

'Big place, Bugarup? Has it got a harbour?'

'People say so. Never been back there. I like the out-door life.'

The ground trembled. The trees by the track shook, even though there was no wind.

'Sounds like a storm,' said Rincewind.

'What's one of them?'

'You know,' said Rincewind. 'Rain.'

'Aw, strain the flaming cows, you don't believe all *that* stuff, do you? My granddad used to go on about that when he'd been at the beer. It's just an old story. Water falling out of the sky? Do me a favour!'

'It never does that here?'

'Course not!'

'Happens quite a lot where I come from,' said Rincewind.

'Yeah? How's it get up into the sky, then? Water's heavy.'

'Oh, it ... it ... I think the sun sucks it up. Or something.'

'How?'

'I don't know. It just happens.'

'And then it drops out of the sky?'

'Yes!'

'For free?'

'Haven't you ever *seen* rain?'

'Look, *everyone* knows all the water's deep underground. That's only sense. It's heavy stuff, it leaks down. I never seen it floating around in the air, mate.'

'Well, how do you think it got on the ground in the first place?'

Mad looked astonished. 'How do mountains get on the ground?' he said.

'What? They're just there!'

'Oh, so *they* don't drop out of the sky?'

'Of course not! They're much heavier than air!'

'And water isn't? I've got a coupla drums of it under the cart and you'd sweat to lift 'em.'

'Aren't there any rivers here?'

'*Course* we've got rivers! This country's got everything, mate!'

'Well, how do you think the water gets into them?'

Mad looked genuinely puzzled. 'What'd we want water in the rivers for? What'd it do?'

'Flow out to sea—'

'Bloody waste! That's what you let it do where you come from, is it?'

'You don't *let* it, it . . . happens . . . it's what rivers do!'

Mad gave Rincewind a long hard look. 'Yep. And they call *me* mad,' he said.

Rincewind gave up. There wasn't a cloud in the sky. But the ground shook again.

Archchancellor Ridcully glared at the sky as if it was doing this to upset him personally.

'What, not *one*?' he said.

'Technically, not a single familiar constellation,' said the Chair of Indefinite Studies frantically. 'We've counted three thousand, one hundred and ninety-one constellations that *could* be called the Triangle, for example, but the Dean says some of them don't count because they use the same stars—'

'There's not a single star *I* recognize,' said the Senior Wrangler.

Ridcully waved his hands in the air. 'They change a *bit* all the time,' he said. 'The Turtle swims through space and—'

'Not this fast!' said the Dean.

The dishevelled wizards looked up at the rapidly crowding night.

Discworld constellations changed frequently as the world moved through the void, which meant that astrology was cutting-edge research rather than, as elsewhere, a clever way of avoiding a proper job. It was amazing how human traits and affairs could so reliably and continuously be guided by a succession of big balls of plasma billions of miles away, most of whom have never even heard of humanity.

'We're marooned on some other world!' moaned the Senior Wrangler.

'Er . . . I don't think so,' said Ponder.

'You've got a better suggestion, I suppose?'

'Er . . . you see that big patch of stars over there?'

The wizards looked at the large cluster twinkling near the horizon.

'Very pretty,' said Ridcully. 'Well?'

'I think it's what *we* call the Small Boring Group of Faint Stars. It's about the right shape,' said Ponder. 'And I know what you're going to say, sir, you're going to say, "But they're just a blob in the sky, not a patch on the blobs we used to get," sir, but, you see, that's what they might have looked like when Great A'Tuin was much closer to them, thousands of years ago. In other words, sir,' Ponder drew a deep breath, in dread of everything that was to come, 'I think we've travelled backwards in time. For thousands of years.'

And that was the other side of the odd thing about wizards. While they were quite capable of spending half an hour arguing that it could not possibly be Tuesday, they'd take the outrageous in their pointy-shoed stride. The Senior Wrangler even looked relieved.

'Oh, is *that* it?' he said.

'Bound to happen eventually,' said the Dean. 'It's not written down anywhere that these holes connect to the same time, after all.'

'Going to make gettin' back a bit tricky,' said Ridcully.

'Er . . .' Ponder began. 'It might not be so simple as that, Archchancellor.'

'You mean as simple as finding a way to move through time and space?'

'I mean there might not be any *there* to go back *to*,' said Ponder. He shut his eyes. This was going to be difficult, he *knew* it.

'Of course there is,' said Ridcully. 'We were there only this morn— Only yesterday. That is to say, yesterday thousands of years in the future, naturally.'

'But if we're not careful we might alter the future, you see,' said Ponder. 'The mere presence of us in the past might alter the future. We might *already* have altered history. It's vital that I tell you this.'

'He's got a point, Ridcully,' said the Dean. 'Was there any of that rum left, by the way?'

'Well, there isn't any history happening here,' said Ridcully. 'It's just an odd little island.'

'I'm afraid tiny actions anywhere in the world may have huge ramifications, sir,' said Ponder.

'We certainly don't want any ramifications. Well, what's your point? What do you advise?'

It had been going so well. They almost seemed up to speed. This may have been what caused Ponder to act like the man who, having so far fallen a hundred feet without any harm, believes that the last few inches to the ground will be a mere formality.

'To use the classic metaphor, the important thing is not to kill your own grandfather,' he said, and smacked into the bedrock.

'What the hell would I want to do that for?' said Ridcully. 'I quite liked the old boy.'

'No, of course, I mean accidentally,' said Ponder. 'But in any case—'

'Really? Well, as you know, I accidentally kill people every day,' said Ridcully. 'Anyway, I don't see him around—'

'It's just an illustration, sir. The problem is cause and effect, and the point is—'

'The point, Mister Stibbons, is that you suddenly seem to think everyone comes over all fratricidal when they go back in time. Now, if I'd met *my* grandfather I'd buy him a drink and tell him not to assume that snakes won't bite if you shout at them in a loud voice, information which he might come to thank me for in later life.'

'Why?' said Ponder.

'Because he would *have* some later life,' said Ridcully.

'No, sir, no! That'd be worse than shooting him!'

'It would?'

'Yes, sir!'

'I think there may be one or two steps in your logic that I have failed to grasp, Mister Stibbons,' said the Archchancellor coldly. 'I suppose you're not intending to shoot your own grandfather, by any chance?'

'Of course not!' snapped Ponder. 'I don't even know what he looked like. He died before I was born.'

'Ah-*hah*!'

'I didn't mean—'

'Look, we're a lot further back in time than that,'

said the Dean. 'Thousands of years, he says. No one's grandfather is alive.'

'That's a lucky escape for Mister Stibbons senior, then,' said Ridcully.

'*No*, sir,' said Ponder. 'Please! What I was trying to get across, sir, is that *anything* you do in the past changes the future. The tiniest little actions can have huge consequences. You might . . . tread on an ant now and it might entirely prevent someone from being born in the future!'

'Really?' said Ridcully.

'Yes, sir!'

Ridcully brightened up. 'That's not a bad wheeze. There's one or two people history could do without. Any idea how we can find the right ants?'

'No, sir!' Ponder struggled to find a crack in his Archchancellor's brain into which could be inserted the crowbar of understanding, and for a few vain seconds thought he had found one. 'Because . . . the ant you tread on might be your own, sir!'

'You mean . . . I might tread on an ant and this'd affect history and I wouldn't be born?'

'Yes! Yes! That's *it*! That's *right*, sir!'

'How?' Ridcully looked puzzled. 'I'm not descended from ants.'

'Because . . .' Ponder felt the sea of mutual incomprehension rising around him, but he refused to drown. 'Well . . . er . . . well, supposing it . . . bit a man's horse, and he fell off, and he was carrying a very important message, and because he didn't get there in time there was a terrible battle, and one of your ancestors got killed – no, sorry, I mean didn't get killed—'

'How did this ant get across the sea?' said Ridcully.

'Clung to a piece of driftwood,' said the Dean promptly. 'It's amazing what can get even on to remote islands by clinging to driftwood. Insects, lizards, even small mammals.'

'And then got up the beach and all the way to this battle?' said Ridcully.

'Bird's leg,' said the Dean. 'Read it in a book. Even fish eggs get transported from pond to pond on a bird's leg.'

'Pretty determined ant, then, really,' said Ridcully, stroking his beard. 'Still, I must admit stranger things have happened.'

'Practically every day,' said the Senior Wrangler.

Ponder beamed. They had successfully negotiated an extended metaphor.

'Only one thing I don't understand, though,' Ridcully added. '*Who'll tread on the ant?*'

'What?'

'Well, it's obvious, isn't it?' said the Archchancellor. 'If I tread on this ant, then *I* won't exist. But if I don't exist, then I can't have done it, so I won't, so I will. See?' He prodded Ponder with a large, good-natured finger. 'You've got some brains, Mister Stibbons, but sometimes I wonder if you really try to apply logical thought to the subject in hand. Things that happen stay happened. It stands to reason. Oh, don't look so downcast,' he said, mistaking – possibly innocently – Ponder's expression of futile rage for shameful dismay. 'If you get stuck with any of this compl'cated stuff, my door's always open.* I *am* your Archchancellor, after all.'

'Excuse me, *can* we tread on ants or not?' said the Senior Wrangler peevishly.

'If you like.' Ridcully swelled with generosity. 'Because, in fact, history already *depends* on your treading on any ants that you happen to step on. Any ants you tread on, you've already trodden on, so if you do it again it'll be for the first time, because you're doing it now because you did it then. Which is also now.'

'Really?'

'Yes indeed.'

'So we should have worn bigger boots?' said the Bursar.

'Try to keep up, Bursar.'

Ridcully stretched and yawned. 'Well, that seems to be it,' he said. 'Let's try to get back to sleep, shall we? It's been rather a long day.'

Someone *was* keeping up.

After the wizards got back to sleep, a faint light, like burning marsh gas, circled over them.

He was an omnipresent god, although only in a

---

* There's a certain type of manager who is known by his call of 'My door is always open' and it is probably a good idea to beat yourself to death with your own CV rather than work for him. In Ridcully's case, however, he meant, 'My door is always open because then, when I'm bored, I can fire my crossbow right across the hall and into the target just above the Bursar's desk.'

small area. And he was omnicognizant, but just enough to know that while he did indeed know everything it wasn't the *whole* Everything, just the part of it that applied to his island.

Damn! He'd *told* himself the cigarette tree would cause trouble. He should have stopped it the moment it started growing. He'd never meant it to get out of *hand* like this.

Of course, it had been a shame about the other ... pointy creature, but it hadn't been *his* fault, had it? Everything had to eat. Some of the things that were turning up on the island were surprising even him. And some of them never stayed stable for five minutes together.

Even so, he allowed himself a little smirk of pride. Two hours between the one called the Dean dying for a smoke and the bush evolving, growing and fruiting its first nicotine-laden crop. That was evolution in *action*.

Trouble was, now they'd start poking around and asking questions.

The god, almost alone among gods, thought questions were a good thing. He was in fact *committed* to people questioning assumptions, throwing aside old superstitions, breaking the shackles of irrational prejudice and, in short, exercising the brains their god had given them, except of course they hadn't been given them by any god, lord knows, so what they really ought to do was exercise those brains developed over millennia in response to the external stimuli and the need to control those hands with their opposable thumbs, another damn good idea that he was very proud of. Or would have been, of course, if he existed.

However, there were limits. Freethinkers were fine people, but they shouldn't go around thinking just *anything*.

The light vanished and reappeared, still circling, in the sacred cave on the mountain. Technically, he knew, it wasn't in fact sacred, since you needed believers to make a place sacred and this god didn't actually want believers.

Usually, a god with no believers was as powerful as a feather in a hurricane, but for some reason he'd not been able to fathom he was able to function quite happily without them. It may have been because he believed so fervently in himself. Well, obviously not in *himself*, because belief in gods was irrational. But he did believe in what he did.

He considered, rather guiltily, making a few more thunder lizards in the hope that they might eat the intruders before they got too nosey, but then dismissed the thought as being unworthy of a modern, forward-thinking deity.

There were racks and racks of seeds in this part of the cave. He selected one from among the pumpkin family, and picked up his tools.

These were unique. Absolutely no one else in the world had a screwdriver that small.

A green shoot speared up from the forest litter in response to the first light of dawn, unfolded into two leaves, and went on growing.

Down among the rich compost of fallen leaves, white shoots writhed like worms. This was no time for half-measures. Somewhere far down, a questing tap root found water.

After a few minutes, the bushes around the by now large and moving plant began to wilt.

The lead shoot dragged itself onwards, towards the sea. Tendrils just behind the advancing stem wound around handy branches. Larger trees were used as support, bushes were uprooted and tossed aside and a tap root sprouted to take possession of the newly vacated hole.

The god hadn't had much time for sophistication. The plant's instructions had been put together from bits and pieces lying around, things he knew would work.

At last the first shoot crossed the beach and reached the sea. Roots drove into the sand, leaves unfolded, and the plant sprouted one solitary female flower. Small male ones had already opened along the stem.

The god hadn't programmed this bit. The whole problem with evolution, he'd told himself, was that it wouldn't obey orders. Sometimes, matter thinks for itself.

A thin prehensile tendril bunched itself for a moment, then sprang up and lassoed a passing moth. It curved back, dipped the terrified insect waist deep in the pollen of a male flower, then coiled back with whiplash speed and slam-dunked it into the embracing petals of the female.

A few seconds later the flower dropped off and the

small green ball below it began to swell, just as the horizon began to blush with the dawn. *Argo nauticae uniquo* was ready to produce its first, and only, fruit.

There was a huge windmill, squeaking around on top of a metal tower. A sign attached to the tower read: 'Dijabringabeeralong: Check your Weapons.'

'Yep, still got all mine, no worries,' said Mad, urging the horses forward.

They crossed a wooden bridge, although Rincewind couldn't see why anyone had bothered to build it. It seemed a lot of effort just to cross a stretch of dry sand.

'Sand?' said Mad. 'That's the Lassitude River, that is!'

And, indeed, a small boat went past. It was being towed by a camel and was making quite good time on its four wide wheels.

'A boat,' said Rincewind.

'Never seen one before?'

'Not one being pedalled, no,' said Rincewind, as a tiny canoe went past.

'They'd hoist the sail if the wind was right.'

'But ... this might sound a strange question ... Why is it a boat shape?'

'It's the shape boats are.'

'Oh, right. I thought it'd be a *good* reason like that. How did the camels get here?'

'They cling to driftwood, people say. The currents wash a lot of stuff up, down on the coast.'

Dijabringabeeralong was coming into view. It was just as well there had been the sign, otherwise they might have ridden through it without noticing. The architecture was what is known professionally as 'vernacular', a word used in another field to mean 'swearing' and this was quite appropriate. But then, Rincewind thought, it's as hot as hell and it never rains – all you need a house for is to mark some kind of boundary between inside and outside.

'You said this was a big town,' he said.

'It's got a whole street. *And* a pub.'

'Oh, that's a *street*, is it? And that logpile is a pub?'

'You'll like it. It's run by Crocodile.'

'Why do they call him Crocodile?'

A night sleeping on the sand hadn't helped the Faculty very much. And the Archchancellor didn't help even more. He was an early-morning man *as well* as being, most unfairly, a late-night man. Sometimes he went from one to the other without sleeping in between.

'Wake up, you fellows! Who's game for a brisk trot around the island? There'll be a small prize for the winner, eh?'

'Oh, my gods,' moaned the Dean, rolling over. 'He's doing press-ups.'

'I certainly wouldn't want anyone to think I'm advocating a return to the bad old days,' said the Chair of Indefinite Studies, trying to dislodge some sand from his ear, 'but once upon a time we used to kill wizards like him.'

'Yes, but we also used to kill wizards like us, Chair,' said the Dean.

'Remember what we'd say in those days?' said the Senior Wrangler. ' "Never trust a wizard over sixty-five"? Whatever happened?'

'We got past the age of sixty-five, Senior Wrangler.'

'Ah, yes. And it turned out that we were trustworthy after all.'

'Good thing we found out in time, eh?'

'There's a crab climbing that tree,' said the Lecturer in Recent Runes, who was lying on his back and staring straight upwards. 'An actual crab.'

'Yes,' said the Senior Wrangler. 'They're called Tree-climbing Crabs.'

'Why?'

'I had this book when I was a little lad,' said the Chair of Indefinite Studies. 'It was about this man who was shipwrecked on an island such as this and he thought he was all alone and then one day he found a footprint in the sand. There was a woodcut,' he added.

'One footprint?' said the Dean, sitting up, clutching his head.

'Well . . . yes, and when he saw it he knew that he—'

'—was alone on an island with a crazed one-legged long-jump champion?' said the Dean. He was feeling testy.

'Well, *obviously* he found some other footprints later on . . .'

'I wish *I* was on a desert island all alone,' said the

Senior Wrangler gloomily, watching Ridcully running on the spot.

'Is it just me,' the Dean asked, 'or are we marooned thousands of miles and thousands of years from home?'

'Yes.'

'I thought so. Is there any breakfast?'

'Stibbons found some soft-boiled eggs.'

'What a useful young man he is,' the Dean groaned. 'Where did he find them?'

'On a tree.'

Bits of last night came back to the Dean.

'A soft-boiled-egg tree?'

'Yes,' said the Senior Wrangler. 'Nicely runny. They're quite good with breadfruit soldiers.'

'You'll be telling me next he found a spoon tree . . .'

'Of course not.'

'Good.'

'It's a bush.' The Senior Wrangler held up a small wooden spoon. It had a few small leaves still attached to it.

'A bush that fruits spoons . . .'

'Young Stibbons said it makes perfect sense, Dean. After all, he said, we'd picked them because they're useful, and then spoons are always getting lost. Then he burst into tears.'

'He's got a point, though. Honestly, this place is like Big Rock Candy Mountain.'

'I vote we leave it as soon as possible,' said the Chair of Indefinite Studies. 'We'd better have a serious look at this boat idea today. I don't want to meet another of those horrible lizards.'

'One of everything, remember?'

'Then probably there's a worse one.'

'Building some sort of boat can't be very hard,' said the Chair of Indefinite Studies. 'Even quite primitive people manage it.'

'Now *look*,' snapped the Dean, 'we've searched *everywhere* for a decent library on this island. There simply isn't one! It's ridiculous. How is anyone supposed to get anything done?'

'I suppose . . . we could . . . *try* things?' said the Senior Wrangler. 'You know . . . see what floats, that sort of thing.'

'Oh, well, if you want to be *crude* about it . . .'

The Chair of Indefinite Studies looked at the Dean's face and decided it was time to lighten the atmosphere.

'I was, aha, just wondering,' he said, 'as a little mental exercise . . . if you were marooned on a desert island, eh, Dean . . . what kind of music would you like to listen to, eh?'

The Dean's face clouded further. 'I think, Chair, that I would like to listen to the music in the Ankh-Morpork Opera House.'

'Ah. Oh? Yes. Well . . . very . . . very . . . very direct thinking there, Dean.'

Rincewind grinned glassily. 'So . . . you're a crocodile, then.'

'Thif worrying you?' said the barman.

'No! No! Don't they call you anything else, though?'

'Well . . . there'f a nickname they gave me . . .'

'Oh, yes?'

'Yeah. Crocodile Crocodile. But in here moft people call me Dongo.'

'And . . . er . . . this stuff? What do you call *this*?'

'We call it beer,' said the crocodile. 'What do *you* call it?'

The barman wore a grubby shirt and a pair of shorts, and until he'd seen a pair of shorts tailored for someone with very short legs and a very long tail Rincewind hadn't realized what a difficult job tailoring must be.

Rincewind held the beer glass up to the light. And that was the point. You could see light all the way through it. *Clear* beer. Ankh-Morpork beer was technically ale, that is to say, gravy made from hops. It had texture. It had flavour, even if you didn't always want to know what of. It had body. It had dregs. You could eat the last half-inch of it with a spoon.

This stuff was thin and sparkly and looked as though someone had already drunk it. Tasted all right, though. Didn't sit on your stomach the way the beer at home did. Weak stuff, of course, but it never did to insult someone else's beer.

'Pretty good,' he said.

'Where'd you blow in from?'

'Er . . . I floated here on a piece of driftwood.'

'Was there room with all the camels?'

'Er . . . yes.'

'Good on yer.'

Rincewind needed a map. Not a geographical map, although one of those would be a help, but one that

156

showed him where his head was at. You didn't usually get crocodiles serving behind a bar, but everyone else in this cavern of a place seemed to think it was perfectly normal. Mind you, the people in the bar included three sheep in overalls and a couple of kangaroos playing darts.

And they weren't *exactly* sheep. They looked more like, well . . . human sheep. Sticking-out ears, white curls, a definite sheepish look, but standing upright, with hands. And he was pretty sure that there was no way you could get a cross between a human and a sheep. If there was, people would definitely have found out by now, especially in the more isolated rural districts.

Something similar had happened with the kangaroos. There were the pointy ears and they definitely had snouts, but now they were leaning on the bar drinking this thin, strange beer. One of them was wearing a stained vest with the legend 'Wagga Hay – it's the Rye Grass!' just visible under the dirt.

In short, Rincewind had the feeling he wasn't looking at animals at all. He took another sip of the beer.

He couldn't raise the subject with Crocodile Dongo. There was a philosophical wrongness about drawing a crocodile's attention to the fact that there were a couple of kangaroos in the bar.

'Youse wanta nother beer?' said Dongo.

'Yeah, right,' said Rincewind.

He looked at the sign on the beer pump. It was a picture of a grinning kangaroo. The label said: Roo Beer.

He raised his eyes to a torn poster on the wall. It also advertised Roo Beer. There was the same kangaroo, holding a pint of said beer and wearing the same knowing grin.

It looked familiar, for some reason.

'I can't help nossisting . . .' He tried again. 'I can't help *noticing*', he said, 'that some people in this barrardifferentshap from other p'ple.'

'Well, old Hollowlog Joe over there'f put on a bit of weight lately,' said Dongo, polishing a glass.

Rincewind looked down at his legs. 'Whose legsare dese?'

'You okay, mifter?'

'Prob'ly been bitten by so'thing,' said Rincewind. A sudden urgent need gripped him.

'It'f out the back,' said Dongo.

'Out back in the outback,' said Rincewind, staggering forward. 'Hahahaha—'

He walked into an iron pillar, which picked him up in a fist and held him at arm's length. He looked along the arm to a large angry face and an expression that said a lot of beer was looking for a fight and the rest of the body was happy to go along with it.

Rincewind was muzzily aware that in his case a lot of beer wanted to run away. And at a time like this, it's always the beer talking.

'I bin *lisnin'* to you. Where're you from, mister?' said the giant's beer.

'Ankh-M'pork . . .' At a time like this, why lie?

The bar went quiet.

'An' you're gonna come here and make a lot of

cracks about us all drinkin' beer and fightin' and talkin' funny, right?'

Some of Rincewind's beer said, 'No worries.'

His captor pulled him so they were face to face. Rincewind had never seen such a huge nose.

'An' I expect you don't even know that we happen to produce some partic'ly fine wines, our Chardonnays bein' 'specially worthy of attention and compet'tively priced, not to mention the rich, firmly structur'd Rusted Dunny Valley Semillons, which are a tangily refreshin' discovery for the connesewer . . . *yew bastard?*'

'Jolly good, I'll have a pint of Chardonnay, please.'

'You takin' the piss?'

'No, I'd like to leave it here—'

'How about you putting my mate down?' said a voice.

Mad was in the doorway. There was a general scuffle to get out of the way.

'Oh, you looking for a fight too, stubby?' Rincewind was dropped as the huge creature turned to face the dwarf, fists clenching.

'I don't look for them. I just walk into pubs and there they are,' said Mad, pulling out a knife. 'Now, you going to leave him alone, Wally?'

'You call *that* a knife?' The giant unsheathed one that'd be called a sword if it had been held in a normal-sized hand. '*This* is what *I* call a knife!'

Mad looked at it. Then he reached his hand around behind his back, and it came back holding something.

'Really? No worries. *This*', he said, 'is what I call a crossbow.'

* * *

'It's a log,' said Ridcully, inspecting the boat-building committee's work to date.

'Rather more than a log—' the Dean began.

'Oh, you've made a mast and tied the Bursar's bathrobe to it, I can see that. It's a log, Dean. There's roots on one end and bits of branch at the other. You haven't even hollowed it out. It's a log.'

'It took us all *hours*,' said the Senior Wrangler.

'And it *does* float,' the Dean pointed out.

'I think the term is more like wallows,' said Ridcully. 'And we'd all get on it, would we?'

'This is the one-man version,' said the Dean. 'We thought we'd test it out and then try it with a lot of them together . . .'

'Like a raft, you mean?'

'I suppose so,' said the Dean, with considerable reluctance. He would have preferred a more dynamic name for it. 'Obviously these things take time.'

The Archchancellor nodded. He was impressed, in a strange way. The wizards had succeeded in recapitulating, in a mere day, a technological development that had probably taken mankind several hundred years. They might be up to coracles by Tuesday.

'Which of you is going to test it?' he said.

'We thought perhaps the Bursar could assist at this point in the development programme.'

'Volunteered, has he?'

'We're sure he will.'

In fact the Bursar was some distance away, wandering aimlessly but happily through the beetle-filled jungle.

The Bursar was, as he would probably be the first to admit, not the most mentally stable of people. He would probably be the first to admit that he was a tea-strainer.

But he was, as it were, only insane on the outside. He'd never been very interested in magic as a boy, but he had been good at numbers, and even somewhere like Unseen University needed someone who could add up. And he had indeed survived many otherwise exciting years by locking himself in a room somewhere and conscientiously adding up, while some very serious division and subtraction was going on outside.

Those were still the days when magical assassination was still a preferred and legal route to high office, but he'd been quite safe because no one had wanted to be a bursar.

Then Mustrum Ridcully had been appointed, and he'd put a stop to the whole business by being unkillable and had been, in his own strange way, a modernizer. And the senior wizards had gone along with him because he tended to shout at them if they didn't and it was, after some exhilarating times in the University's history, something of a relief to enjoy your dinner without having to watch someone else eat a bit of it first or having to check your shape the moment you got out of bed.

But it was hell for the Bursar. Everything about Mustrum Ridcully rasped across his nerves. If people were food, the Bursar would have been one of life's lightly poached eggs, but Mustrum Ridcully was a rich suet pudding with garlic gravy. He spoke as loudly as most people shouted. He stamped instead of walking. He roared around the place, and lost important bits of paper which he then denied he'd ever seen, and shot his crossbow at the wall when he was bored. He was aggressively cheerful. Never sick himself, he tended to the belief that sickness in other people was caused by sloppy thinking. And he had no sense of humour. And he told jokes.

It was odd that this affected the Bursar so much, since he did not have a sense of humour either. He was proud of it. He was not the kind of man to laugh. But he did know, in a mechanical sort of way, how jokes were supposed to go. Ridcully told jokes like a bullfrog did accountancy. They never added up.

So the Bursar found it much more satisfying to live inside his own head, where he didn't have to listen and where there were clouds and flowers. Even so, something must have filtered in from the world outside, because occasionally he'd jump up and down on an ant, just in case he was supposed to. Part of him rather hoped that one of the ants was, in some unimaginably distant way, related to Mustrum Ridcully.

It was while he was thus engaged in changing the future that he noticed what looked like a very thick green hosepipe on the ground.

'Hmm?'

It was slightly transparent and seemed to be pulsating rhythmically. When he put his ear to it he heard a sound like *gloop*.

Mildly deranged though he was, the Bursar had the

true wizard's instinct to amble aimlessly into dangerous places, so he followed the throbbing stem.

Rincewind awoke, because sleep was so hard with
someone kicking him in the ribs.

'Wzt?'

'You want I should pour a bucket of water on yez?'

Rincewind recognized the chatty tones. His eyes
unglued. 'Oh, not you! You're a figment of my
imagination!'

'I should kick you in the ribs again, then?' said
Scrappy.

Rincewind pulled himself upright. It was dawn, and
he was lying in some bushes out behind the pub.

Memory played its silent movie across the tattered
sheets of his eyelids.

'There was a fight . . . Mad shot that . . . that . . .
shot him with a *crossbow*!'

'Only through the foot so's he'd stand still to be hit.
Wombats can't hold their drink, that's their trouble.'

More recollections flickered across the smoky darkness of Rincewind's brain. 'That's right, there were
animals drinking in there!'

'Yes and no,' said the kangaroo. 'I *tried* to
explain . . .'

'I'm all ears,' said Rincewind. His eyes glazed for a
moment. 'No, I'm not, I'm all bladder. Back in a minute.'

The buzz of flies and a sort of universal smell drew
Rincewind into a nearby hut. Some people would
have liked to think of it as 'the bathroom', although
not after going inside.

He came out again, hopping up and down urgently. 'Er . . . there's a great big spider on the toilet seat . . .'

'What're you gonna do, wait till it's finished? Fan it with yer hat!'

It was odd, Rincewind thought as he shooed the spider out, that a human being would, er, use the bathroom behind a bush in the middle of a thousand miles of howling wilderness but would fight for a dunny if there was one available.

'And stay out,' he muttered, when he was confident the spider was out of earshot.

But the human brain often feels incapable of concentrating on the job in hand, and Rincewind found his gaze wandering. And here, as in private places everywhere, men had found the urge to draw on the walls.

Perhaps it was the way the light hit the ancient woodwork, but under the usual minutiae from people who needed people, and drawings done from over-heated hope rather than memory, was a deeply scored drawing of men in pointy hats.

He sidled out thoughtfully and edged away through the bushes.

'No worries,' said the kangaroo, so close to his ear that Rincewind was quite pleased that he'd already relieved himself.

'I don't believe it!'

'You'll see them everywhere. They're built in. They find their way into people's thoughts. You can't out-run your destiny, mate.'

Rincewind didn't even bother to argue.

'You're going to have to sort this out,' said Scrappy. 'You're the cause.'

'I'm not! Things happen to *me*, not the other way around!'

'I could disembowel you with a kick, you know. Would you like to see?'

'Er . . . no.'

'Haven't you noticed that by running away you end up in more trouble?'

'Yes, but, you see, you can run away from *that*, too,' said Rincewind. 'That's the beauty of the system. Dead is only for once, but running away is for ever.'

'Ah, but it is said that a coward dies a thousand deaths, while a hero dies only one.'

'Yes, but it's the *important* one.'

'Aren't you ashamed?'

'No. I'm going home. I'm going to find this city called Bugarup, find a boat, and go home.'

'Bugarup?'

'Don't tell me the place doesn't exist.'

'Oh, no. It's a big place. And that's where you're going?'

'And don't try to stop me!'

'I can see you've made up your mind,' said Scrappy.

'Read my lips!'

'Your moustache is in the way.'

'Read my beard, then!'

The kangaroo shrugged. 'In that case, I've got no choice but to carry on helping you, I suppose.'

Rincewind drew himself up. 'I'll find my own way,' he said.

'You don't *know* the way.'

'I'll ask someone!'

'What about food? You'll starve.'

'Ahah, that's where you're wrong!' Rincewind snapped. 'I've got this amazing power. Watch!'

He lifted up a nearby stone, extracted what was underneath, and flourished it.

'See? Impressed, eh?'

'Very.'

'Ahah!'

Scrappy nodded. 'I've never seen anyone do that with a scorpion before.'

The god was sitting high up in a tree working on a particularly promising beetle when the Bursar ambled past far below.

Well, at *last*. One of them had found it!

The god had spent some time watching the wizards' attempts at boat-building, although he had been unable to fathom out what it was they were trying to do. As far as he could tell, they were showing some interest in the fact that wood floated. Well, it did float, didn't it?

He threw the beetle into the air. It hummed into life at the top of the arc and flew away, a smear of iridescence among the treetops.

The god drifted out of his tree and followed the Bursar.

The god hadn't made up his mind about these creatures yet, but the island was, unfortunately and against all his careful planning, throwing up all sorts of odd things. These were obviously social creatures, with some of the individuals designed for specific tasks. The hairy red one was designed for climbing trees, and the dreamy ant-stamping one for walking into them. Possibly the reasons for this would become apparent.

'Ah, Bursar!' said the Dean heartily. 'How would you like a brief trip around the lagoon?'

The Bursar looked at the soaking log and sought for words. Sometimes, when he really needed to, it was possible to get Mr Brain and Mr Mouth all lined up together.

'I had a boat once,' he said.

'Well done! And here's another one, just for—'

'It was green.'

'Really? Well, we can—'

'I've found another green boat,' said the Bursar. 'It's floating in the water.'

'Yes, yes, I'm sure you have,' said Ridcully kindly. 'A big boat with lots of sails, I expect. Now then, Dean—'

'Just one sail,' said the Bursar. 'And a bare naked lady on the front.'

Hovering immanently, the god cursed. He'd never *intended* the figurehead. Sometimes, he really wanted to just break down and cry.

'Bare naked lady?' said the Dean.

'Settle down, Dean,' said the Senior Wrangler. 'He's probably just had too many dried frog pills.'

'It's going up and down in the water,' said the Bursar. 'Up and down, up and down.'

The Dean looked at their own creation. Contrary to

all expectations, *it* did not go up and down in the water. It stayed exactly where it was and the water went up and down over it.

'This *is* an island,' he said. 'I suppose someone could have sailed here, couldn't they? What kind of bare naked lady? A dusky one?'

'Really, Dean!'

'Spirit of enquiry, Senior Wrangler. Important bio-geographical information.'

The Bursar waited until his brain came around again. 'Green,' he volunteered.

'That is not a natural colour for a human being, clothed or not,' said the Senior Wrangler.

'She might be seasick,' said the Dean. There was only the vaguest of wistful longings in his head, but he did not want to let go of it.

'Going up and down,' said the Bursar.

'I suppose we could have a look,' said the Dean.

'What about Mrs Whitlow? She hasn't been out of her hut yet.'

'She can come too if she likes,' said the Dean.

'I don't think we can expect Mrs Whitlow to go looking at a bare naked lady, even if this one *is* green,' said the Senior Wrangler.

'Why not? She must have seen at least one. Not green, of course.'

The Senior Wrangler drew himself up. 'There's no call for that sort of imputation,' he said.

'What? Well, obviously she—'

The Dean stopped. The big leaves on Mrs Whitlow's hut were pushed aside, and she emerged.

It was probably the flower in her hair. That was certainly the crowning glory. But she'd also done things to her dress.

There was, for a start, less of it.

Since the word is derived from an island that did not exist on the Discworld, the wizards had never heard of a bikini. In any case, what Mrs Whitlow had sewn together out of her dress was a lot more substantial than a bikini. It was more a *newzealand* – two quite large respectable halves separated by a narrow channel. She'd also tied some of the spare cloth around her waist, sarong style.

In short, it was a very proper item of clothing. But it *looked* as if it wasn't. It was as if Mrs Whitlow was wearing a figleaf six feet square. It was still just a figleaf.

'Ai thought this might be a *leetle* more suitable for the heat,' she said. 'Of course, Ai wouldn't *dream* of wearing it in the University, but since we appear to be here for a little while Ai remembered a picture Ai saw of Queen Zazumba of Sumtri. Is there anywhere Ai could have a bath, do you think?'

'Mwaaa,' said the Senior Wrangler.

The Dean coughed. 'There's a little pool in the jungle.'

'With waterlilies in it,' said the Chair of Indefinite Studies. 'Pink ones.'

'Mwaaa,' said the Senior Wrangler.

'And there's a waterfall,' said the Dean.

'Mwaaa.'

'And a soap bush, as a matter of fact.'

They watched her walk away.

'Up and down, up and down,' said the Bursar.

'A fine figure of a woman,' said Ridcully. 'She walks differently without her shoes on, doesn't she? Are you all right, Senior Wrangler?'

'Mwaa?'

'I think the heat's getting to you. You've gone very red.'

'I'm a mwaa . . . I'm . . . gosh, it *is* hot, isn't it . . . ? I think perhaps I should have a dip too . . .'

'In the lagoon,' said Ridcully, meaningfully.

'Oh, the salt's very bad for the skin, Archchancellor.'

'Quite so. Nevertheless. Or you can go looking for the pool when Mrs Whitlow comes back.'

'I find it rather insulting, Archchancellor, that you should appear to think that—'

'Well done,' said Ridcully. 'Now, shall we go and look at this boat?'

Half an hour later all the wizards were assembled on the opposite shore.

It *was* green. And it bobbed up and down. It was clearly a ship, but built perhaps by someone who'd had a very detailed book of ship-building which nevertheless didn't have any pictures in it. There was a blurriness of the detail. The figurehead, for example, was certainly vaguely female, although to the Dean's disappointment it had the same detail as a half-sucked jellybaby.

It put the Senior Wrangler in mind of Mrs Whitlow, although currently rocks, trees, clouds and coconuts also reminded him of Mrs Whitlow.

And then there was the sail. It was, without a shadow of a doubt, a leaf. And once you realized that it *was* a leaf, then a certain marrow or pumpkin quality about the rest of the vessel began to creep over you.

Ponder coughed. 'There are some plants which rely for propagation on floating seeds,' he said, in a small voice. 'The common coconut, for example, has . . .'

'Does it have a figurehead?' said Ridcully.

'Er, one variety of mangrove fruit has a sort of keel which . . .'

'And a sail with what looks very much like rigging?' said Ridcully.

'Er . . . no . . .'

'And what are those flowers on the top?' Ridcully demanded. Where a crow's nest would be was a cluster of trumpet-shaped flowers, like green daffodils.

'Who cares?' said the Chair of Indefinite Studies. 'It's a ship, even if it *is* a giant pumpkin, and it looks as though there's room for all of us.' He brightened up. 'Even if it *is* a bit of a squash,' he added.

'It has appeared very fortuitously,' said Ridcully. 'I wonder why?'

'I said, "Even if it *is* a bit of a squash,"' said the Chair of Indefinite Studies. 'Because, a squash, you see, is another name for—'

'Yes, I know,' said Ridcully, looking thoughtfully at the bobbing vessel.

'I was only attempting to—'

'Thank you for sharing, Chair.'

'Actually it does look pretty roomy,' said the Dean, ignoring the Chair's pained expression. 'I vote we load up with provisions and go.'

'Where to?' said Ridcully.

'Somewhere where fearsome reptiles don't suddenly turn into birds!' the Dean snapped.

'You'd prefer it the other way around?' said Ridcully. He started to wade out into the water until, armpit deep, he was able to bang on the side of the hull with his staff.

'I think you are being a little obtuse, Mustrum,' said the Dean.

'Really? How many types of carnivorous plants are there, Mister Stibbons?'

'Dozens, sir.'

'And they eat prey up to——?'

'No upper limit in the case of the Sapu tree of Sumtri, sir. The Sledgehammer Plant of Bhangbhangduc takes the occasional human victim who doesn't see the mallet hidden in the greenery. There's quite a few that can take anything up to rat size. The Pyramid Strangler Vine really only preys on other more stupid plants, but——'

'I just think that there's something very odd about a boat-shaped plant turning up just when we want a boat,' said Ridcully. 'I mean, chocolate coconuts, *yes*, and even filter-tipped cigarettes, but a boat with a figurehead?'

'It's not a proper boat without a figurehead,' said the Senior Wrangler.

'Yes, but how does it know that?' said Ridcully,

wading ashore again. 'Well, I'm not falling for it. I want to know what's going on here.'

'*Damn!*'

They all heard the voice – thin, reedy and petulant. It came from everywhere around them.

Small soft white lights appeared in the air, spun around one another with increasing speed, and then imploded.

The god blinked, and rocked back and forth as he tried to steady himself.

'Oh, my goodness,' he said. 'What *do* I look like?'

He held up a hand in front of his face and flexed his fingers experimentally.

'Ah.'

The hand patted his face, his bald head, and lingered for a moment on the long white beard. He seemed puzzled.

'What's this?' he said.

'Er . . . a beard?' said Ponder.

The god looked down at his long white robe. 'Oh. Patriarchality? Oh, well . . . let me see, now . . .'

He seemed to pull himself together, focused his gaze on Ridcully, and his huge white eyebrows met like angry caterpillars.

'Begone from This Place Or I Will Smite Thee!' he commanded.

'Why?'

The god looked taken aback. 'Why? You can't ask why in this situation!'

'Why not?'

The god looked slightly panicky. 'Because . . . Thou

173

Must Go from This Place Lest I Visit Thee with Boils!'

'Really? Most people would bring a bottle of wine,' said Ridcully.

The god hesitated. 'What?' he said.

'Or cake,' said the Dean. 'Cake is a good present if you're visiting someone.'

'It depends on what *kind* of cake,' said the Senior Wrangler. 'Sponge cake, I've always thought, is a bit of an insult. Something with a bit of marzipan is to be preferred.'

'Begone from this place lest I visit you with cake?' said the god.

'It's better than boils,' said Ridcully.

'Provided it's not sponge,' said the Senior Wrangler.

The problem faced by the god was that, while he had never encountered wizards before, the wizards had in their student days met, more or less on a weekly basis, things that threatened them horribly as a matter of course. Boils didn't hold much of a menace when rogue demons had wanted to rip your head off and do terrible things down the hole.

'Listen,' said the god, 'I happen to be the god in these parts, do you understand? I am, in fact, omnipotent!'

'*I'd prefer that, what is it, you know, the cake with the pink and yellow squares*—' muttered the Senior Wrangler, because wizards tend to follow a thought all the way through.

'You're a bit small, then,' said the Dean.

'*And the sugary marzipan on the outside, marvellous stuff . . .*'

174

The god finally realized what else had been bothering him. Scale was always tricky in these matters. Being three feet high was not adding anything to his authority.

'Damn!' he said again. 'Why am I so small?'

'Size isn't everything,' said Ridcully. 'People always smirk when they say that. I can't think why.'

'You're absolutely right!' snapped the god, as if Ridcully had triggered an entirely new train of thought. 'Look at amoebas, except that of course you can't because they're so small. Adaptable, efficient and practically immortal. Wonderful things, amoebas.' His little eyes misted over. 'Best day's work I ever did.'

'Excuse me, sir, but exactly what *kind* of god are you?' said Ponder.

'And is there cake or not?' said the Senior Wrangler.

The god glared up at him. 'I beg your pardon?' he said.

'I meant, what is it that you're the god *of*?' said Ponder.

'I *said*, what about this cake you're supposed to have?' said the Senior Wrangler.

'Senior Wrangler?'

'Yes, Archchancellor?'

'Cake is not the issue here.'

'But he said—'

'Your comments have been taken on board, Senior Wrangler. And they will be thrown over the side as soon as we leave harbour. Do continue, god, please.'

For a moment the god looked in a thunderbolt mood, and then sagged. He sat down on a rock.

'All that smiting talk doesn't really work, does it?' he said gloomily. 'You don't have to be nice about it. I could tell. I *could* give you boils, you understand, it's just that I can't really see the point. They clear up after a while, anyway. And it *is* rather bullying people, isn't it? To tell you the truth, I'm something of an atheist.'

'Sorry?' said Ridcully. 'You are an *atheist* god?'

The god looked at their expressions. 'Yes, I know,' he said. 'It's a bit of a bottomer, isn't it?' He stroked his long white beard. 'Why exactly have I got this?'

'You didn't shave this morning?' said Ridcully.

'I mean, I simply tried to appear in front of you in a form that you recognize as godly,' said the god. 'A long beard and a nightshirt seem to be the thing, although the facial hair is a little puzzling.'

'It's a sign of wisdom,' said Ridcully.

'Said to be,' said Ponder, who'd never been able to grow one.

'Wisdom: insight, acumen, learning,' said the god thoughtfully. 'Ah. The length of the hair improves the operation of the cognitive functions? Some sort of cooling arrangement, perhaps?'

'Never really thought about it,' said Ridcully.

'The beard gets longer as more wisdom is acquired?' said the god.

'I'm not sure it's actually a case of cause and effect,' Ponder ventured.

'I'm afraid I don't get about as much as I should,' said the god sadly. 'To be frank, I find religion rather offensive.' He heaved a big sigh and seemed to look even smaller. 'Honest, I really do try but there are some days when life just gets me down . . . Oh, excuse me, liquid seems to be running out of my breathing tubes . . .'

'Would you like to blow your nose?' said Ponder.

The god looked panicky. 'Where to?'

'I mean, you sort of hold . . . Look, here's my handkerchief, you just sort of put it over your nose and sort of . . . well, snuffle into it.'

'Snuffle,' said the god. 'Interesting. And what a curiously white leaf.'

'No, it's a cotton handkerchief,' said Ponder. 'It's . . . made.' He stopped there. He knew that handkerchiefs *were* made, and cotton was involved, and he had some vague recollection of looms and things, but when you got right down to it you obtained handkerchiefs by going into a shop and saying, 'I'd like a dozen of the reinforced white ones, please, and how much do you charge for embroidering initials in the corners?'

'You mean . . . created?' said the god, suddenly very suspicious. 'Are you gods too?'

Beside his foot a small shoot pushed through the sand and began to grow rapidly.

'No, no,' said Ponder. 'Er . . . you just take some cotton and . . . hammer it flat, I think . . . and you get handkerchiefs.'

'Oh, then you're tool-using creatures,' said the god, relaxing a little. The shoot near his foot was already a plant now, and putting out leaves and a flowerbud.

He blew his nose loudly.

The wizards drew closer. They were not, of course, afraid of gods, but gods tended to have uncertain tempers and a wise man kept away from them. However, it's hard to be frightened of someone who's having a good blow.

'You're really the god in these parts?' said Ridcully.

The god sighed. 'Yes,' he said. 'I thought it would be so easy, you know. Just one small island. I could start all over again. Do it *properly*. But it's all going completely wrong.' Beside him the little plant opened a nondescript yellow flower.

'Start all over again?'

'Yes. You know . . . godliness.' The god waved a hand in the direction of the Hub.

'I used to work over there,' he said. 'Basic general godding. You know, making people out of clay, old toenails, and so on? And then sitting on mountain-tops and casting thunderbolts and all the rest of it. Although,' he leaned forward and lowered his voice, 'very few gods can actually do that, you know.'

'Really?' said Ridcully, fascinated.

'Very hard thing to steer, lightning. Mostly we waited until a thunderbolt happened to hit some poor soul and then spake in a voice of thunder and said it was his fault for being a sinner. I mean, they were bound to have done *something*, weren't they?' The god blew his nose again. 'Quite depressing, really. Anyway . . . I suppose the rot set in when I tried to see if it was possible to breed a more inflammable cow.'

He looked at the questioning expressions.

'Burnt offerings, you see. Cows don't actually burn all that well. They're naturally rather soggy creatures and frankly everyone was running out of wood.'

They carried on staring at him. He tried again.

'I really couldn't see the point of the whole business, to tell you the truth. Shouting, smiting, getting angry all the time . . . don't think anyone was getting anything out of it, really. But the worst part . . . You know the worst part? The worst part was that if you actually *stopped* the smiting, people wandered off and worshipped someone else. Hard to believe, isn't it? They'd say things like, "Things were a lot better when there was more smiting," and, "If there was more smiting, it'd be a lot safer to walk the streets." Especially since all that'd *really* happened was that some poor shepherd who just happened to be in the wrong place during a thunderstorm had caught a stray bolt. And then the priests would say, "Well, we all know about shepherds, don't we, and now the gods are angry and we could do with a much bigger temple, thank you."'

'Typical priestly behaviour,' sniffed the Dean.

'But they often *believed* it!' the god almost wailed. 'It was really *so* depressing. I think that before we made humanity, we broke the mould. There'd be a bad weather front, a few silly shepherds would happen to be in the wrong place at the wrong time, and next thing you know it was standing room only on the sacrificial stones and you couldn't see for the smoke.' He had another good blow on a piece of Ponder's handkerchief that had so far remained dry. 'I mean, I *tried*. God knows I tried, and since that's me, I know what I'm talking about. "Thou Shalt Lie Down Flat in Thundery Weather," I said. "Thou Shalt Site the

Midden a Long Way from the Well," I said. I even told them, "Thou Shalt Really Try to Get Along with One Another." '

'Did it work?'

'I can't say for sure. Everyone was slaughtered by the followers of the god in the next valley who told them to kill everyone who didn't believe in him. Ghastly fellow, I'm afraid.'

'And the flaming cows?' said Ridcully.

'The what?' said the god, sunk in misery.

'The more inflammable cow,' said Ponder.

'Oh, yes. Another good idea that didn't work. I just thought, you know, that if you could find the bit in, say, an oak tree which says "Be inflammable" and glue it into the bit of the cow which says "Be soggy" it'd save a lot of trouble. Unfortunately, that produced a sort of bush that made distressing noises and squirted milk, but I could see the *principle* was sound. And frankly, since my believers were all dead or living in the next valley by then I thought, to hell with it all, I'd come back here and get to grips with it and do it all more *sensibly*.' He brightened up a bit. 'You know, it's amazing what you get if you break even the common cow down into very small bits.'

'Soup,' said Ridcully.

'Because, sooner or later, *everything* is just a set of instructions,' the god went on, apparently not listening.

'That's just what I've always said!' said Ponder.

'Have you?' said the god, peering at him. 'Well, any-way . . . that's how it all began. I thought it would be a much better idea to create creatures that could change their own instructions when they needed to, you see . . .'

'Oh, you mean evolution,' said Ponder Stibbons.

'Do I?' The god looked thoughtful. ' "Changing over time . . ." Yes, that's actually quite a good word, isn't it? Evolution. Yes, I suppose that's what I do. Unfortunately, it doesn't seem to be working properly.'

Beside him, there was a pop. The little plant had fruited. Its pod had sprung open and there appeared to be, bunched up like a chrysanthemum, a fresh white hankie.

'You see?' he said. 'That's the sort of thing I'm up against. Everything is so completely *selfish* about it.' He took the handkerchief in an absentminded way, blew his nose on it, crumpled it up, and dropped it on the ground.

'I'm sorry about the boat,' he continued. 'It was a bit of a rush job, you see. I just didn't want anyone upsetting everything, but I really don't believe in smiting, so I thought that *since* you wanted to leave here I should help you do so as soon as possible. I think I did rather a good job, in the circumstances. It'll find new land automatically, I think. So why didn't you go?'

'The bare naked lady on the front was a bit of a giveaway,' said Ridcully.

'The what?' The god peered in the direction of the boat. 'These eyes are not particularly efficient . . . Oh, dear, yes. The figure. Morphic bloody resonance again. Will you *stop* doing that!'

The handkerchief plant had just put forth another fruit. The god narrowed his eyes, pointed his finger and incinerated it.

As one man the wizards stepped back.

'I stop concentrating for five minutes and everything loses any sense of discipline,' said the god. 'Everything wants to make itself damn *useful*! I can't think why!'

'Sorry? Am I getting this right? You're a *god* of *evolution*?' said Ponder.

'Er . . . is that wrong?' said the god anxiously.

'But it's been happening for ages, sir!'

'Has it? But I only started a few years ago! Do you mean someone else is doing it?'

'I'm afraid so, sir,' said Ponder. 'People breed dogs for fierceness and racehorses for speed and . . . well, even my uncle can do amazing things with his nuts, sir—'

'And everyone knows that you can cross a river with a bridge, ahaha,' said Ridcully.

'Can you?' said the god of evolution seriously. 'I'd have thought that you simply get some very soggy wood. Oh dear.'

Ridcully winked at Ponder Stibbons. Gods were often not good at humour, and this one was even worse than Ridcully.

'We're back in time, Mister Stibbons,' he said. 'It may not have happened already *yet*, eh?'

'Oh. Yes,' said Ponder.

'Anyway, two gods of evolution wouldn't be a bad thing, would they?' said Ridcully. 'Makes it a lot more interestin'. The one who's best at it would win.'

The god stared at him with his mouth open. Then he shut it just enough to mouth Ridcully's words to himself, snapped his fingers, and vanished in a puff of little white lights.

'*Now* you've done it,' said the Lecturer in Recent Runes.

'No cake for *you*,' said the Bursar.

'All I said was the one who's best at it would win,' said Ridcully.

'Actually, he didn't look upset,' said Ponder. 'He looked as if he'd suddenly realized something.'

Ridcully looked up at the small mountain in the centre of the island, and appeared to reach a decision.

'All right, we'll leave,' he said. 'The reason this island's so odd is that some rather daft god is messing around with it. That's a pretty good explanation as far as I'm concerned.'

'But, sir—' Ponder began.

'See that little vine just by the Senior Wrangler there? It's only been growing for the last ten minutes,' said the Dean.

It looked like a small cucumber vine, except that the fruits were yellow and oblong.

'Pass me your penknife, Mister Stibbons,' said Ridcully.

Ridcully sliced the fruit in half. It wasn't fully ripe yet, but the pattern of pink and yellow squares was clearly visible, surrounded by a layer of something sticky and sweet.

'But I only *thought* about that cake ten minutes ago!' said the Senior Wrangler.

'Seems perfectly logical to *me*,' said Ridcully, 'I mean, here we are, wizards, we move about, we want to leave the island . . . What will we take with us? Anyone?'

'Food, obviously,' said Ponder. 'But—'

'Right! If *I* was a vegetable, I'd want to make myself useful in a hurry, yes? No good hanging around for a thousand years just growing bigger seeds! No fear! All those other plants might come up with a better idea in the meantime! No, you see an opportunity and you *go* for it! There might not be another boat along for years!'

'Millennia,' said the Dean.

'Even longer,' Ridcully agreed. 'Survival of the fastest, eh? So I suggest we load up and go, gentlemen.'

'What, just like that?' said Ponder.

'Certainly. Why not?'

'But . . . but . . . but think of the things we could learn here!' said Ponder. 'The possibilities are breathtaking! At last there's a god who's actually got the right idea! At last we can get some answers to all the important questions! We could . . . we can . . . Look, we can't just *go*. I mean, not *go*! I mean . . . we're wizards, aren't we?'

He was aware that he had their full attention, something that wizards did not often give. Usually they defined 'listening' as a period in which you worked out what you were going to say next. It was disconcerting.

Then the spell broke. The Senior Wrangler shook his head. 'Curious way of looking at things,' he said, turning away. 'So . . . I vote we take plenty of those cheese nuts, Archchancellor.'

'Good provisioning is the essence of successful exploration,' said the Dean. 'Quite a roomy vessel, too, so we needn't stint.'

Ridcully pulled himself aboard via a trailing tendril, and sniffed.

'Smells rather like pumpkin,' he said. 'Always liked pumpkin. A very versatile vegetable.'

Ponder put a hand over his eyes. 'Oh, really?' he said, wearily. 'A group of Unseen University wizards are seriously considering putting to sea on an edible boat?'

'Fried, boiled, a good base for a soup stock and, of course, excellent in pies,' said the Archchancellor happily. 'Also the seeds are a tasty snack.'

'Good with butter,' said the Chair of Indefinite Studies. 'I suppose there isn't a butter plant anywhere, is there?'

'There will be soon,' said the Dean. 'Give us a hand up, will you, Archchancellor?'

Ponder exploded. 'I don't *believe* this!' he said. 'You're turning your back on an astonishing god-given opportunity—'

'Absolutely, Mister Stibbons,' said Ridcully, from above. 'No offence meant, of course, but if the choice is a trip on the briny deep or staying on a small island with someone trying to create a more inflammable cow then you can call me Salty Sam.'

'Is this the poop deck?' said the Dean.

'I hope not,' said Ridcully briskly. 'You see, Stibbons—'

'Are you sure?' said the Dean.

'I'm sure, Dean. You *see*, Stibbons, when you've had a little more experience in these matters you'll learn that there's nothing more dangerous than a god with too much time on his hands—'

'Except an enraged mother bear,' said the Senior Wrangler.

'No, they're far more dangerous.'

'Not when they're really close.'

'If it *was* the poop deck, how would we know?' said the Dean.

Ponder shook his head. There were times when the desire to climb the thaumaturgical ladder was seriously blunted, and one of them was when you saw what was on top.

'I . . . I just don't know what to say,' he said. 'I am frankly astonished.'

'Well done, lad. So run along and get some bananas, will you? Green ones will keep better. And don't look so upset. When it comes to gods, I have to say, you can give me one of the make-out-of-clay-and-smite-'em brigade any day of the week. That's the kind of god you can deal with.'

'The practically human sort,' said the Dean.

'Exactly.'

'Call me overly picky,' said the Chair of Indefinite Studies, 'but I'd prefer not to be around a god who might suddenly decide I'd run faster with three extra legs.'

'Exactly. Is there something wrong, Stibbons? Oh, he's gone. Oh well, no doubt he'll be back. And . . . Dean?'

'Yes, Archchancellor?'

'I can't help thinking you're working up to some sort of horrible joke about a poop deck. I'd prefer not, if it's all the same to you.'

'You all right, mate?'

No one in the world had ever been so pleased to see Crocodile Crocodile before.

Rincewind let himself be pulled upright. His hand, against all expectation, was *not* blue and three times its normal size.

'That bloody kangaroo . . .' he muttered, using the hand to wave away the eternal flies.

'What kangaroo waf that, mate?' said the crocodile, helping him back towards the pub.

Rincewind looked around. There were just the normal components of the local scenery – dry-looking bushes, red dirt and a million circling flies.

'The one I was talking to just now.'

'I was juft fweeping up and I faw you dancing around yellin', said Crocodile. 'I didn't fee no kangaroo.'

'It's probably a *magic* kangaroo,' said Rincewind wearily.

'Oh, *right*, a *magic* kangaroo,' said Crocodile. 'No worrieth. I think maybe I'd better make you up the cure for drinking too much beer, mate.'

'What's the cure?'

'More beer.'

'How much beer *did* I have last night, then?'

'Oh, about twenty pinth.'

'Don't be silly, no one can even *hold* that much beer!'

'Oh, you didn't hang on to much of it at all, mate. No worrieth. We like a man who can't hold hif beer.'

In the fetid fleapit of Rincewind's brain the projectionist of memory put on reel two. Recollection began to flicker. He shuddered.

'Was I . . . singing a song?' he said.

'Too right. You kept pointing to the Roo Beer pofter and finging . . .' Crocodile's huge jaws moved as he tried to remember, '"Tie my kangaroo up." Bloody good fong.'

'And then I . . . ?'

'Then you loft all your money playing Two Up with Daggy's shearing gang.'

'That's . . . I . . . there were these two coins, and the bloke'd toss them in the air, and you . . . had to bet on how they'd come down . . .'

'Right. And you kept bettin' they wouldn't come down at all. Faid it was bound to happen fooner or later. You got good odds, though.'

'I lost *all* the money Mad gave me?'

'Yep.'

'How was I paying for my beer, then?'

'Oh, the blokes were queueing up to buy it for you. They faid you were better than a day at the races.'

'And then I . . . there was something about sheep . . .' He looked horrified. 'Oh, no . . .'

'Oh, yeah. You faid, "Ftrain the fraying crones, a dollar a time for giving fheep a haircut? I could do a beaut foft job like that with my eyes fhut, too right no flaming worries by half bonza fhoot through ye gods this if good beer . . ."'

'Oh, gods. Did anyone hit me?'

'Nah, mate, they reckoned you were a good sport, 'specially when you wagered five hundred fquids that you could beat their best man at shearin'.'

'I couldn't've done that, I'm not a betting man!'

'Well, I am, and if you've been fhootin' a line I wouldn't give tuppence for your chances, Rinfo.'

'Rinso?' said Rincewind weakly. He looked at his beerglass. 'What's in this stuff?'

'Your mate Mad faid you were this big wizard and could kill people just by pointing at 'em and shoutin',' said Crocodile. 'I wouldn't mind feein' that.'

Rincewind looked up desperately and his eye caught the Roo Beer poster. It showed some of the damn silly trees they had here, and the arid red earth and – nothing else.

'Huh?'

'What's that?' said Crocodile.

'What happened to the kangaroo?' Rincewind said hoarsely.

'What kangaroo?'

'There was a kangaroo on that poster last night . . . wasn't there?'

Crocodile peered at the poster. 'I'm better at smell,' he admitted at last. 'But I got to admit, it smells like it's gorn.'

'Something very strange is going on here,' said Rincewind. 'This is a very strange country.'

'We've got an opera house,' Crocodile volunteered. 'That's *cultcher*.'

'And ninety-three words for being sick?'

'Yeah, well, we're a very . . . vocal people.'

'Did I really bet five hundred . . . What was it?'

'Squids.'

'. . . squids I haven't got?'

'Yup.'

'So I'll probably get killed if I lose, right?'

'No worries.'

'I wish people'd stop saying that—'

He caught sight of the poster again. 'That kangaroo's back!'

Crocodile turned around awkwardly, walked up to the poster and sniffed. 'Could be,' he said cautiously.

'And it's facing the wrong way!'

'Take it easy, mate!' said Crocodile Dongo, looking concerned.

Rincewind shuddered. 'You're right,' he said. 'It's the heat and the flies getting to me. It must be.'

Dongo poured him another beer. 'Ah well, beer's good for the heat,' he said. 'Can't do anythin' about the bloody flies, though.'

Rincewind started to nod, and stopped. He removed his hat and looked at it critically. Then he waved a hand up and down in front of his face, temporarily dislodging a few flies. Finally, he looked thoughtfully at a row of bottles.

'Got any string?' he said.

After a few experiments, and some mild con-
cussion, Dongo advanced the opinion that it'd be
better with just the corks.

The Luggage was lost. Usually, it could find its way
anywhere in time and space, but trying to do that now
was like a man trying to keep his footing on two
moving walkways heading in opposite directions, and
it simply couldn't cope. It knew it had been stuck
underground for a long time, but it *also* knew that it
had been stuck underground for about five minutes.

The Luggage had no brain as such, even though an
outsider might well get the impression that it could
think. What it *did* do was react, in quite complex ways,
to its environment. Usually this involved finding something to kick, as is the case with most sapient creatures.

Currently it was ambling along a dusty track.
Occasionally its lid would snap at flies, but without
much enthusiasm. Its opal coating glowed in the
sunlight.

'Oaaw! Isn't that *pretty*! Fetch it here, you two!'

It paid no attention to the brightly coloured cart
that stopped a little way along the track. It was
possibly aware at some level that people had got out
and were staring at it, but it didn't resist when they
appeared to reach a decision and lifted it on to the
cart. It didn't know where it had to go, and since it
also didn't know where this cart was going perhaps
it would take it there.

It waited a decent while after it had been put down,
and then took in its surroundings. It had been stacked

up by a lot of other boxes and suitcases, which was comforting. After five minutes spent being under-ground for millions of years the Luggage felt that it was due some quality time.

And it didn't even resist when someone opened its lid and filled it up with shoes. Quite large shoes, the Luggage noticed, and many of them with interesting heels and inventive ways with silk and sequins. They were clearly ladies' shoes. That was good, the Luggage thought (or emoted, or reacted). Ladies tended to lead quieter lives.

The purple cart rumbled off. Painted crudely on the back were the words: Petunia, The Desert Princess.

Rincewind looked hard at the shears that the head shearer was waving. They looked sharp.

'You know what we do to people who go back on a bet round here?' said Daggy, the gang boss.

'Er . . . but I was drunk.'

'So were we. So what?'

Rincewind looked out across the sheep pens. He knew what sheep were, of course, and had come into contact with them on many occasions, although normally in the company of mixed vegetables. He'd even had a toy stuffed lamb as a child. But there is something hugely unlovable about sheep, a kind of mad, eye-rolling brainlessness smelling of damp wool and panic. Many religions extol the virtues of the meek, but Rincewind had never trusted them. The meek could turn very nasty at times.

On the other hand . . . they were covered in wool,

and the shears looked pretty keen. How hard could it be? His radar told him that trying and failing was probably a lot less of a crime than not trying at all.

'Can I have a trial run?' he said.

A sheep was dragged out of the pens and flung down in front of him.

Rincewind gave Daggy what he hoped was the smile of one craftsman to another, but smiling at Daggy was like throwing meringues against a cliff.

'Er, can I have a chair and a towel and two mirrors and a comb?' he said.

Daggy's look of intense suspicion deepened. 'What's this? What d'you want all that for?'

'Got to do it properly, haven't I?'

Away out of sight at the back of the shearing shed, on the sun-bleached boards, the outline of a kangaroo began to form. And then, the white lines drifting across the wood like wisps of cloud across a clear sky, it began to change shape . . .

Rincewind hadn't had a proper haircut in a long time, but he knew how it was done.

'So . . . have you had your holidays this year, then?' he said, clipping away.

'Mnaaarrrhh!'

'What about this weather, eh?' Rincewind said, desperately.

'Mnaaarrrhh!'

The sheep wasn't even trying to struggle. It was an old one, with fewer teeth than feet, and even in the very limited depths of its extremely shallow mind it knew that this wasn't how shearing was supposed to go. Shearing was supposed to be a brief struggle followed by glorious cool freedom back in the paddock. It wasn't supposed to include searching questions about what it thought of this weather or enquiries as to whether it required something for the weekend, especially since the sheep had no concept of the connotations of the term 'weekend' or, if it came to that, of the word 'something' either. People weren't supposed to splash lavender water in its ear.

The shearers watched in silence. There was quite a crowd of them, because they'd gone and fetched everyone else on the station. They knew in their souls that here was something to tell their grandchildren.

Rincewind stood back, looked critically at his handiwork, and then showed the sheep the back of its head in the mirror, at which point the creature cracked, managed to get its feet under it and made a run for the paddock.

'Hey, wait till I take the curlers out!' Rincewind shouted after it.

He became aware of the shearers watching him. Finally one of them said, in a stunned voice, 'That's sheep-shearing where yew come from, is it?'

'Er . . . what did you think?' said Rincewind.

'It's a bit slow, innit?'

'How fast was I supposed to go?'

'Weell, Daggy here once did nearly fifty in an hour. That's what you've got to beat, see? None of that fancy rubbish. Just short back, front, top and sides.'

'Mind yew,' said one of the shearers, wistfully, 'that was a beautiful lookin' sheep.'

There was an outbreak of bleating from the sheep corrals.

'Ready to give it a *real* go, Rinso?' said Daggy.

'Ye gawds, what's *that*?' said one of his mates.

The fence shattered. A ram stood in the gap, shaking its head to dislodge bits of post from its horns. Steam rose from its nostrils.

Most of the things Rincewind had associated with sheep, apart from the gravy and mint sauce, had to do with . . . sheepishness. But this was a ram, and the word association was suddenly . . . *rampage*. It pawed the ground. It was a lot bigger than the average sheep. In fact, it seemed to fill Rincewind's entire future.

'That's not one of *mine*!' said the flock's owner.

Daggy placed his shears in Rincewind's other hand and patted him on the back.

'This one's yours, mate,' he said, and backed away. 'You're here to show us how it's done, eh, mate?'

Rincewind looked down at his feet. They weren't moving. They remained firmly fixed to the ground.

The ram advanced, snorting and looking Rincewind in the bloodshot eye.

'Okay,' it whispered, when it was very close. 'You just make with the shears and the sheep'll do the rest. No worries.'

'Is that *you*?' said Rincewind, glancing at the distant ring of watchers.

'Hah, good one. Ready? They'll do what I do. They're like sheep, okay?'

The shearers watched as wool fell like rain.

'That's somethin' you don't often see,' said one of them. 'Them standin' on their heads like that . . .'

'The cartwheels is good,' said another shearer, lighting his pipe. 'I mean, for sheep.'

Rincewind just hung on to the shears. They had a life of their own. The sheep flung themselves against the clippers as if in a real hurry to get into something more comfortable. Fleeces curled around his ankles, then around his knees, rose above his waist . . . and then the shears were slicing the air, and sizzling as they cooled down.

Several dozen dazed sheep were watching him very suspiciously. So were the sheep-shearers.

'Er . . . have we started the competition yet?' he said.

'You just sheared thirty sheep in two minutes!' roared Daggy.

'Is that good?'

'Good? No one takes two minutes for thirty sheep.'

'Well, I'm *sorry*, but I can't go any faster.'

The shearers went into a huddle. Rincewind looked around for the ram, but it didn't seem to be there any more.

Finally, something seemed to have been settled. The shearers approached him in the cautious, oblique way of men trying to hang back and walk forward at the same time.

Daggy stepped forward, but only comparatively; in fact, his mates had all, without discussion, taken one step backwards in the choreography of caution.

'G'day!' he said nervously.

Rincewind gave him a friendly wave, and it was only halfway through when he remembered that he was still holding the shears. Daggy hadn't forgotten about them.

'Er . . . we ain't got five hundred squids till we get paid—'

Rincewind wasn't certain how to deal with this. 'No worries,' he said. This covered most things.

'. . . so if yew're gonna be around . . .'

'I just want to get to Bugarup as soon as possible,' said Rincewind.

Daggy kept smiling but turned around and went into another huddle with the rest of the shearers. Then he turned back.

'. . . maybe we could sell a few things . . .'

'I'm not bothered about the money, actually,' said Rincewind loudly. 'Just point me in the direction of Bugarup. No worries.'

'Yew don't *want* the money?'

'No worries.'

There was another huddle. Rincewind heard hissed comments of 'Get him outta here right *now*.'

Daggy turned back. 'I got a horse you can have,' he said. 'It's worth a squid or two.'

'No worries.'

'And then you'll be able to ride away . . . ?'

'She'll be right. No worries.'

It was an amazing phrase. It was practically magical all by itself. It just . . . made things better. A shark's got your leg? No worries. You've been stung by a jellyfish?

197

No worries! You're dead? She'll be right! No worries! Oddly enough, it seemed to work.

'No worries,' he said again.

'Got to be worth a squid or two, that horse,' Daggy said again. 'Practically a bloody racehorse.'

There was some sniggering from the crowd.

'No worries?' said Rincewind.

Daggy looked for a moment as if he was entertaining the suggestion that maybe the horse was worth more than five hundred squid, but Rincewind was still dreamily holding on to the shears and he thought better of it.

'Get you to Bugarup in no time, that horse,' he said. 'No worries.'

A couple of minutes later it was obvious even to Rincewind's inexperienced eye that while you could race this horse, it wouldn't be sensible to race it against other horses. At least, ones that were alive. It was brown, stubby, mostly a thatch of mane, with hooves the size of soup bowls, and it had the shortest legs Rincewind had ever seen on anything with a saddle. The only way you could fall off would be to dig a hole in the ground first. It looked ideal. It was Rincewind's kind of horse.

'No worries,' he said. 'Actually ... one *small* worry.'

He dropped the shears. The shearers took a step back.

Rincewind went over to the corral and looked down at the ground, which was churned from the hoof-prints of the sheep. Then he looked at the back of the shearing shed. For a moment he was sure there was the outline of a kangaroo . . .

The shearers approached him cautiously as he banged on the sun-bleached planks, shouting, 'I know you're in there!'

'Er, that's what we call wood,' said Daggy. 'Woo-od,' he added, for the hard-of-thinking. 'Made into a wa-all.'

'Did you see a kangaroo walk into this wall?' Rincewind demanded.

'Not us, boss.'

'It was a sheep at the time!' Rincewind added. 'I mean, it's normally a kangaroo but I'll swear it turned into that sheep!'

The shearers shuffled uneasily.

'You're not going to say anything about woolly jumpers, are you?' said one, almost timorously.

'What? What's knitwear got to do with it?'

'That's a mercy, anyway,' the small shearer mumbled.

'You know, it's been doing that *all the time*,' said Rincewind. 'I *thought* there was something wrong with that beer poster!'

'Something wrong with the beer, too?'

'I'm not putting up with any more kangaroo nonsense. I'm off home,' said Rincewind. 'Where's that horse?'

It was standing where they'd left it. He waved a finger at it.

'And no talking!' he said, as he swung his leg over it. This simply resulted in him standing over the horse.

He was sure that somewhere under the overhanging mane something sniggered.

'Yew got to kinda sag down,' said Daggy. 'And then you kinda lift your legs kinda up.'

Rincewind did so. It was like sitting on an armchair.

'You *sure* this is a horse?'

'Won it in a game of Two Up from a bloke from Goolalah,' said Daggy. 'Got to be tough, coming from the mountains. They breeds 'em special to be sure-footed. He said it won't fall off *anything*.'

Rincewind nodded. His type of horse, all right. The quiet, dependable type.

'Which way's Bugarup?'

The men pointed.

'Right. Thank you. Giddyup . . . What's this horse called?'

Daggy seemed to think for a moment and then said, 'Snowy.'

'Why Snowy? That's an odd name for a horse.'

'I . . . used to have a dog called Snowy.'

'Oh, right. That makes sense. Sense for here, anyway. I suppose. Well . . . g'day, then.'

The shearers watched him go, which, at Snowy's pace, took some time.

'Had to get rid of him,' said Daggy. 'He could put us on the dole in a day.'

One of the men said, 'Why din't you tell him about the drop-bears over that way?'

'He's a wizard, ain't he? He'll find out.'

'Yeah, but only when they bloody drop on his head.'

'Quickest way,' said Daggy.

'Daggy?'

'Yup?'

'How long did you say you'd had that horse?'

'Ages. Won it off a bloke.'

'Right?'

'Right.'

'Right . . .'

'What?'

'Only . . . did yew always have it ages half an hour ago?'

Daggy's wide brow furrowed a little. He took off his hat and wiped his head with his arm. He looked at the disappearing horse, and then at the sheds, and then at the other men. Several times he started to speak, shut his mouth before he could get the first word out, and glared around him again.

'Yew all *know* I've had it for bloody ages, right?' he demanded.

''s right.'

'Ages.'

'Won it off'f a bloke.'

'Right. Yeah. Right. You must've done.'

Mrs Whitlow sat on a rock, combing her hair. A bush had sprouted several twigs with rows of blunt, closely set thorns just when she needed them.

Large, pink and very clean, she relaxed by the water like an amplified siren. Birds sang in the trees. Sparkling beetles hummed to and fro across the water.

If the Senior Wrangler had been present someone

could have scraped him up and carried him away in a bucket.

Mrs Whitlow did not feel in any danger. The wizards were around, after all. She was mildly worried that the maids would be getting lazy since she wasn't there, but she could look forward to making their lives a living hell when she got back. The possibility of not getting back never entered her head.

A lot of things never entered Mrs Whitlow's head. She'd decided a long time ago that the world was a lot nicer that way.

She had a very straightforward view of foreign parts, or at least those more distant than her sister's house in Quirm where she spent a week's holiday every year. They were inhabited by people who were more to be pitied than blamed because, really, they were like children.* And they acted like savages.†

On the other hand, the scenery was nice and the weather was warm and nothing smelled very bad. She was definitely feeling the benefit, as she'd put it.

Not to put too fine a point on it, Mrs Whitlow had left her corsets off.

The thing that the Senior Wrangler insisted on calling

---

* That is to say, she secretly considered them to be vicious, selfish and untrustworthy.

† Again, when people like Mrs Whitlow use this term they are not, for some inexplicable reason, trying to suggest that the subjects have a rich oral tradition, a complex system of tribal rights and a deep respect for the spirits of their ancestors. They are implying the kind of behaviour more generally associated, oddly enough, with people wearing a full suit of clothes, often with the same insignia.

the 'melon boat' was, even the Dean admitted, very impressive.

There was a big space below deck, dark and veined and lined with curved black boards, very like giant sunflower seeds.

'Boat seeds,' said the Archchancellor. 'Probably make good ballast. Senior Wrangler, don't eat the wall, please.'

'I thought perhaps we could do with more cabin space,' said the Senior Wrangler.

'Cabins possibly, staterooms no,' said Ridcully, heaving himself back on to the deck.

'Avast shipmate!' shouted the Dean, throwing a bunch of bananas on to the boat and climbing up behind them.

'Quite so. How do we sail this vegetable, Dean?'

'Oh, Ponder Stibbons knows all about that sort of thing.'

'And where is he?'

'Didn't he go off to fetch some bananas?'

They looked down at the beach, where the Bursar was stockpiling seaweed.

'He did seem a bit . . . upset,' said Ridcully.

'Can't imagine why.'

Ridcully glanced up at the central mountain, glowing in the afternoon sun.

'I suppose he wouldn't have done anything stupid, would he?' he said.

'Archchancellor, Ponder Stibbons is a fully trained wizard!' said the Dean.

'Thank you for that very concise and definite

answer, Dean,' said Ridcully. He leaned down into the cabin. 'Senior Wrangler! We're going to look for Stibbons. And we ought to go and fetch Mrs Whitlow, too.'

There was a shriek from below. 'Mrs Whitlow! How could we have forgotten her!'

'In your case, only by having a cold bath, Senior Wrangler.'

As horses went, this one went slowly. It moved in a stolid, I-can-do-this-all-day manner that clearly said the only way you get me to go faster will be to push me off a cliff. It had a curious gait, somewhere faster than a trot but slower than a canter. The effect was a jolting slightly out of synchronization with the moment of inertia in any known human organ, causing everything inside Rincewind to bounce off everything else. Also, if he forgot for a second and lowered his legs, Snowy went on without him, and this meant that he had to run ahead and stand there like a croquet hoop until he caught him up.

But Snowy didn't bite, buck, roll over or gallop insanely away, which were the traits Rincewind had hitherto associated with horses. When Rincewind stopped for the night the horse wandered off a little way and ate a bush covered with leaves the thickness, smell and apparent edibility of linoleum.

He camped beside what he had heard called a 'billy-bong', which was just an expanse of churned earth with a tiny puddle of water welling up in the middle. Little green and blue birds were clustered around it, cheeping happily in the late afternoon light. They scattered when Rincewind lay down to drink, and scolded him from the trees.

When he sat up, one of them landed on his finger.

'Who's a pretty boy, then?' said Rincewind.

The noise stopped. Up on the branches the birds looked at one another. There wasn't much room in their heads for a new idea, but one had just turned up.

The sun dropped towards the horizon. Rincewind poked very cautiously inside a hollow log and found a ham sandwich and a plate of cocktail sausages.

Up in the trees the budgerigars were in a huddle.

One of them said, very quietly, 'Wh . . . ?'

Rincewind lay back. Even the flies were merely annoying. Things began to sizzle in the bushes. Snowy went and drank from the tiny pool with a noise like an inefficient suction pump trying to deal with an unlucky turtle.

It was, nevertheless, very peaceful.

Rincewind sat bolt upright. He knew what was about to happen when things were peaceful.

Up in the darkening branches a bird muttered, '. . . pre'y b'y . . . ?'

He relaxed, but only a little.

'. . . 'sa prit' b'y . . . ?'

Suddenly the birds stopped.

A branch creaked.

The drop-bear . . . dropped.

It was a close relative of the koala, although this doesn't mean very much. After all, the closest relative of the common elephant is about the size and shape of a rabbit. The drop-bear's most notable feature was its posterior, thick and heavily padded to provide the maximum shock to the victim with the minimum shock to the bear. The initial blow rendered the prey unconscious, and then the bears could gather round to feed. It was a magnificent method of killing, since in other respects the bears were not very well built to be serious predators, and it was therefore particularly unfortunate for this bear that it chose, on this night, to drop on a man who might well have had 'Victim' written all over him but also had 'Wizzard' written on his hat, and that this hat, most significantly, came to a point.

Rincewind lumbered to his feet and ran into a few trees while he tried, with both hands on the brim, to lift his hat off his head. He managed it at last, stared in horror at the bear and its peculiarly confused expression, and shook it off and into the bushes. There were thumps around him as more bears, disoriented by this turn of events, hit the ground and bounced wildly.

In the trees the budgerigars woke up and, the simple message by now having had time to work its way into their brain cells, shrieked, 'Who's a pri'y boy, den?' A madly tumbling bear whirled past Rincewind's face.

Rincewind turned and ran towards Snowy, landing astride the horse's back, or where its back would have been had it been taller. Snowy obediently broke into his arrhythmical trot and headed into the darkness.

Rincewind looked down, swore and ran after his horse.

He held on tight as Snowy ran on like some small engine, leaving the bouncing bears behind, and didn't slow down until he was well away along the track and among bushes that were shorter than he was. Then he slid off.

What a bloody country!

There was a flurry of wings in the night and suddenly the bush was full of little birds.

'Wh'sa pri' boyden?'

Rincewind waved his hat at them and screamed a little, just to relieve his feelings. It didn't work. The budgerigars thought this was some sort of entertainment.

'Bug'roff!' they twittered.

Rincewind gave up, stamped on the ground a few times, and tried to sleep.

When he awoke, it was to a sound very much like a donkey being sawn in half. It was a kind of rhythmic scream of pain, anguished and forlorn, setting the teeth of the world on edge.

Rincewind raised his head cautiously over the scrub.

A windmill was spinning in the breeze, turning this way and that as stray gusts batted its tail fin.

Rincewind was seeing more of these, dotted across the landscape, and thought: If all the water's underground, that's a good idea . . .

There was a mob of sheep hanging around the base of this one. They didn't back off, but watched him carefully as he approached. He saw why. The trough below the pump was empty. The fan was spinning, grinding out its mournful squeak, but no water was coming out of the pipe.

The thirsty sheep looked up at him.

'Er ... don't look at me,' he mumbled. 'I'm a wizard. We're not supposed to be good at machinery.'

No, but we *are* supposed to be good at magic, said an accusing voice in his head.

'Maybe I can see if something's come loose, though. Or something,' he muttered.

Impelled by the vaguely accusing woolly stares, he clambered up the rickety tower and tried to look efficient. There didn't seem to be anything wrong, except that the metallic groaning was getting louder.

'Can't see any—'

Something that had finally been tortured beyond endurance broke, somewhere down in the tower. It shook, and the windmill spun free, dragging a broken rod which smashed heavily on the windmill's casing with every revolution.

Rincewind half fell, half slid back down to the ground.

'Seems to be a bit of a technical fault,' he mumbled. A lump of cast iron smashed into the sand by his feet. 'Probably needs to be seen to by a qualified artificer. Probably invalidates the warranty if I mess around—'

A cracking noise from overhead made him dive for cover, which in this case was a rather surprised sheep. When the racket had died away the windmill's fan was bowling over through the scrub. As for the rest of it, if there had ever been any user-serviceable parts inside they very clearly weren't in there any more.

Rincewind took off his hat to mop his brow, but he wasn't quick enough. A pink tongue rasped across his forehead like damp sandpaper.

'Ow! Good grief! You lot really are thirsty, aren't you . . . ?' He pulled the hat back on, right down to his ears just to be on the safe side. 'I could do with a drink myself, to tell the truth . . .'

He managed, after pushing a few sheep aside, to find a piece of broken windmill.

Wading with some difficulty through the press of silent bodies, he made his way to an area that was a little lower than the surrounding scrub, and contained a couple of trees whose leaves looked slightly fresher than the rest.

'Ow! G'd gr'f!' chattered the birds around him.

Two or three feet should do it, he thought as he shovelled the red soil aside. Amazing, really, all this water underground when it never rained at all. The whole place must be floating on water.

At three feet down the soil was barely damp. He sighed, and kept going.

He was more than chest deep before a trickle oozed out between his toes. The sheep fought for the damp soil as he threw it up to the surface. As he watched, the puddle sank into the ground.

'Hey, come back!'

'H'y, c'm bik!' screamed the birds in the bushes.

'Shut up!'

'Sh'tup! Wh'spr'boyden?'

He flailed at the ground with his makeshift shovel in an effort to catch up, and overtook the descending water after another few inches. He splashed on until he was knee deep, dragged his hat through the muddy liquid, pulled himself out of the hole and ran, water dribbling over his feet, until he could tip it into the trough.

The sheep clustered around it, struggling silently to get at the film of moisture.

Rincewind got two more hatfuls before the water sank out of sight.

He wrenched the ladder off the stricken windmill, threw it down the hole and jumped in after it. Damp soil fountained out as he dug, and each dripping lump attracted a mass of flies and small birds as soon as it hit the ground.

He managed another dozen or so hatfuls before the hole was deeper than the ladder. By now some cattle had lumbered up to the trough as well, and it was impossible to see the water for heads. The sound was that of a straw investigating the suds of the biggest milkshake in the world.

Rincewind took a final look down the hole, and as he did so the last drop of water winked out of sight.

'Weird country,' he muttered.

He wandered over to where Snowy was standing patiently in the sparse shade of a bush.

'You're not thirsty?' he said.

Snowy snorted and shook his mane.

'Oh, well. Maybe you've got a bit of camel in you. You certainly can't be all horse, I know that.'

Snowy moved aimlessly sideways and trod on Rincewind's foot.

By noon the track crossed another one, which was much wider. Hoofprints and wheel ruts suggested that it got a lot of traffic. Rincewind brightened up, and followed it through thickening trees, glad of the shade.

He passed another groaning windmill surrounded by a cluster of patiently waiting cattle.

There were more bushes and the land was rising into ancient, crumbling hills of orange rock. At least it gets the wind up here, he thought. Ye gods, is a drop of rain too much to ask? You can't never have any rain. *Everywhere* gets rained on sometimes. It has to drop out of the sky in order to get underground in the first place, doesn't it?

He stopped when he heard the sound of many hoofbeats on the track behind him.

A mob of riderless horses appeared round the bend at full gallop. As they swept past Rincewind he saw one horse out in front of the others, built on the sleekest lines he'd ever seen, a horse that moved as though it had a special arrangement with gravity. The pack divided and flowed around Rincewind as if he were a rock in a stream. Then they were just a disappearing noise in a cloud of red dust.

Snowy's nostrils flared, and the jolting increased as he speeded up.

'Oh, yes?' said Rincewind. 'Not a chance, mate. You can't play with the big boys. No worries.'

The cloud of dust had barely settled before there were more hoofbeats and a bunch of horsemen came around the curve. They galloped past without taking any notice of Rincewind, but a rider at the rear slowed down.

'You seen a mob of horses go by, mate?'

'Yes, mate. No worries, no worries, no worries.'

'A big brown colt leadin' 'em?'

'Yes, mate. No worries, no worries.'

'Old Remorse says he'll give a hundred squids to the man who catches him! No chance of that, it's canyon country ahead!'

'No worries?'

'What's that you're riding, an ironing board?'

'Er, excuse me,' Rincewind began, as the man set off in pursuit, 'but is this the right road to Bugar—?'

The dust swirled across the road.

'What happened to the well known Ecksian reputation for good-hearted friendliness, eh?' shouted Rincewind to empty air.

He heard shouts and the cracking of whips from the trees on the high slopes as he wound into the hills. At one point the wild horses burst out on to the track again, not even noticing him in their flight, and this time Snowy ambled off the track and followed the trail of broken bushes.

Rincewind had learned that hauling on the reins only had the effect of making his arms ache. The only way to stop the little horse when he didn't want to be stopped was probably to get off, run ahead, and dig a trench in front of him.

Once again the riders came up behind Rincewind and thudded past, foam streaming from the horses' mouths.

'Excuse me. Am I on the right road for—?'

And they were gone.

He caught up with them ten minutes later in a thicket of mountain ash, milling around uncertainly while their leader shouted at them.

'I say, can anyone tell me—' he ventured.

Then he saw why they had stopped. They'd run out of forwards. The ground fell away into a canyon, a few patches of grass and a handful of bushes clinging to the very nearly sheer drop.

Snowy's nostrils flared and, without even pausing, he continued down the slope.

He should have skidded, Rincewind saw. In fact he should have dropped. The slope was almost vertical. Even mountain goats would only try it roped together. Stones bounced around him and a few of the larger ones managed to hit him on the back of the neck, but Snowy trotted downwards at the same deceptive speed that he used on the flat. Rincewind settled for hanging on and screaming.

Halfway down, he saw the wild herd gallop along the canyon, skid around a rock and disappear between the cliffs.

Snowy reached the bottom in a shower of pebbles and paused for a moment.

Rincewind risked opening an eye. The little horse's nostrils flared again as it looked down the narrow canyon. It stamped a hoof uncertainly. Then it looked at the vertiginous far wall, only a few metres away.

'Oh, *no*,' moaned Rincewind. 'Please, no . . .' He tried to untangle his legs but they had met right under the horse's stomach and twisted their ankles together.

He *must* be able to do something to gravity, he told himself, as Snowy trotted up the cliff as though it wasn't a wall but merely a sort of vertical floor. The corks on his hat brim banged against his nose.

And ahead . . . *above* . . . was an overhang . . .

'No, *please*, no, please don't . . .'

He shut his eyes. He felt Snowy draw to a halt, and breathed a sigh of relief. He risked a look down, and the huge hooves were indeed standing on solid, flat rock.

There were no corks hanging in front of Rincewind's hat.

In dread and slowly mounting terror, he turned his eyes to what they'd always thought of as upwards.

There was solid rock above him, as well. Only it was a long way up, or down. And the corks were all hanging upwards, or downwards.

Snowy was standing on the underside of the overhang, apparently enjoying the view. He flared his nostrils again, and shook his mane.

He'll fall off, Rincewind thought. Any minute now he'll realize he's upside down and he'll fall off and from this height a horse'll *splat*. On *top* of me.

Snowy appeared to reach a decision, and set off again, around the curve of the overhang.

The corks swung back and hit Rincewind in the face but, hey, all the trees had the green bits pointing up, except that they were the grey bits.

Rincewind looked across the chasm at the horsemen.

'G'day!' he said, waving his hat in the air as Snowy set off again. 'I think I'm about to have a technicolour snake!' he added, and threw up.

''ere, mistah?' someone shouted back.

'Yes?'

'That was a chunder!'

'Right! No worries!'

It turned out that this piece of land was only a narrow spur between canyons. Another sheer drop loomed up, or down. But to Rincewind's relief the horse turned aside at the brink and trotted along the edge.

'Oh, no, please . . .'

A tree had fallen down and bridged the gulf. It was very narrow, but Snowy wheeled on to it without slowing.

Both ends of the tree drummed up and down on the lip of the cliff. Pebbles began to fall away. Snowy bounced across the gap like a small ball and stepped off on the far side just before the treetrunk teetered and dropped on to the rocks.

'Please, no . . .'

There wasn't a cliff here, just a long slope of loose rocks. Snowy landed among them, and flared his nostrils as the entire slope of scree began to move.

Rincewind saw the herd gallop past in the narrow canyon bottom, far below.

Large rocks bounded alongside him as the horse continued down in his own personal landslide. One or two jumped and bounced ahead, smashing on to the canyon floor just behind the last of the herd.

Numb with fear and the shaking, Rincewind looked further along the canyon. It was blind. The end was another cliff . . .

Stone piled into stone, building a rough wall across the canyon floor. As the last boulder slammed into place Snowy landed on top of it, almost daintily.

He looked down at the penned herd, milling in confusion, and flared his nostrils. Rincewind was pretty sure horses couldn't snigger, but this one radiated an air of sniggerruity.

It was ten minutes later that the horsemen rode up. By then the herd was almost docile.

They looked at the horses. They looked at Rincewind, who grinned horribly and said, 'No worries.'

Very slowly, he didn't fall off Snowy. He simply swivelled sideways, with his feet still twisted together, until his head banged gently on the ground.

'That was bloody great riding, mate!'

'Could someone separate my ankles, please? I fear they may have fused together.'

A couple of the riders dismounted and, after some effort, pulled him free.

The leader looked down at him. 'Name your price for that little battler, mate!' said Remorse.

'Er . . . three . . . er . . . squids?' said Rincewind, muzzily.

'What? For a wiry little devil like that? He's got to be worth a coupla hundred at least!'

'Three squids is all I've got . . .'

'I reckon a few of them rocks hit him on the head,' said one of the stockmen who were holding Rincewind up.

'I mean I'll *buy* him off 'f *you*, mister,' said Remorse, patiently. 'Tell you what – two hundred squids, a bag of tucker and we'll set you right on the road to . . . Where was it he wanted to go, Clancy?'

'Bugarup,' murmured Rincewind.

'Oh, you don't wanna go to Bugarup,' said Remorse. 'Nothing in Bugarup but a bunch of wowsers and pooftahs.'

''s okay, I *like* parrots,' mumbled Rincewind, who was just hoping that they would let him go so that he could hold on to the ground again. 'Er . . . what's Ecksian for going mad with terrified fatigue and collapsing in a boneless heap?'

The men looked at one another.

'Isn't that "snagged as a wombat's tonker"?'

'No, no, no, that's when you chuck a twister, isn't it?' said Clancy.

'What? Strewth, no. Chucking a twister's when . . . when you . . . yeah, it's when you . . . yeah, it's when your nose . . . Hang on, that's "bend a smartie" . . .'

'Er—' said Rincewind, clutching his head.

'What? "Bend a smartie" is when your ears get blocked underwater.' Clancy looked uncertain, and then seemed to reach a decision. 'Yeah, that's right!'

'Nah, that's "gonging like a possum's armpit", mate.'

'Excuse me—' said Rincewind.

'That ain't right. "Gonging like a possum's armpit"

is when you crack a crusty. When your ears are stuffed like a Mudjee's kettle after a week of Fridays, that's "stuck up like Morgan's mule".'

'No, you're referrin' to "happier than Morgan's mule in a choccy patch"—'

'You mean "as *fast* as Morgan's mule after it ate Ma's crow pie".'

'How fast was that? Exactly?' said Rincewind.

They all stared at him.

'Faster'n an eel in a snakepit, mate!' said Clancy. 'Don't you understand plain language?'

'Yeah,' said one of the men, 'he might be a fancy rider but I reckon he's dumber than a—'

'*Don't anyone say anything!*' shouted Rincewind. 'I'm feeling a lot better, all right? Just . . . all right, all right?' He straightened his ragged robe and adjusted his hat. 'Now, if you could just set me on the right road to Bugarup, I will not trespass further on your time. You may keep Snowy. He can bed down on a ceiling somewhere.'

'Oh, no, mister,' said Remorse. He reached into a shirt pocket, pulled out a bundle of notes and licked his thumb to count off twenty. 'I always pays me debts. You want to stay with us a while first? We could use another rider and it's tough going on the road by yourself. There's bush rangers about.'

Rincewind rubbed his head again. Now that his various bodily organs had wobbled their way back into their approximate positions he could get back to general low-key generalized dread.

'They won't have to worry about me,' he mumbled.

'I promise not to light fires or feed the animals. Well, I say *promise* – most of the time they're trying to feed off me.'

Remorse shrugged.

'Just so long as there's no more of those damn dropping bears,' said Rincewind.

The men laughed.

'Drop-bears? Who's been feedin' you a line about drop-bears?'

'What do you mean?'

'There's no such thing as drop-bears! Someone must've seen you coming, mate!'

'Huh? They've got . . . they went,' Rincewind waved his arm, 'boing . . . all over the place . . . great big teeth . . .'

'I reckon he madder'n Morgan's mule, mate!' said Clancy.

The group went silent.

'How mad is that, then?' said Rincewind.

Clancy leaned on his saddle and looked nervously at the other men. He licked his lips. 'Well, it's . . .'

'Yes?'

'Well, it's . . . it's . . .' His face twisted up. 'It's . . .'

'Ver' . . . ?' Rincewind hinted.

'Ver' . . .' Clancy mumbled, clutching the syllable like a lifeline.

'Hmm?'

'Ver . . . ry . . .'

'Keep going, keep going . . .'

'Ver . . . ry . . . mad?' said Clancy.

'Well done! See? So much easier,' said Rincewind.

'Someone mentioned something about food?'

Remorse nodded to one of the men, who handed Rincewind a sack.

'There's beer and veggies and stuff and, 'cos you're a good sport, we're giving you a tin of jam, too.'

'Gooseberry?'

'Yep.'

'And I'm wondering about your hat,' said Remorse. 'Why's there all corks round it?'

'Knocks the flies out,' said Rincewind.

'That works, does it?'

'Course not,' said Clancy. 'If'n it does, someone'd have thought of it by now.'

'Yes. Me,' said Rincewind. 'No worries.'

'Makes you look a bit of a drongo, mate,' said Clancy.

'Oh, good,' said Rincewind. 'Which way's Bugarup?'

'Just turn left at the bottom of the canyon, mate.'

'That's all?'

'You can ask again when you meet the bush rangers.'

'They've got some sort of cabin or station, have they?'

'They've . . . Well, just remember they'll find you if you get lost.'

'Really? Oh, well, I suppose that's part of their job. Good day to you.'

'G'day.'

'No worries.'

The men watched Rincewind until he was out of sight.

'Didn't seem very bothered, did he?'

'He's a bit gujeroo, if you ask me.'

'Clancy?'

'Yes, boss?'

'You made that one up, didn't you . . . ?'

'Well . . .'

'You bloody did, Clancy.'

Clancy looked embarrassed, but then rallied. 'All right, then,' he said hotly. 'What about that one you used yesterday, "as busy as a one-armed carpenter in Smackaroo"?'

'What about it?'

'I looked it up in the atlas and there's no such place, boss.'

'There damn well is!'

'There isn't. Anyway, no one'd employ a one-armed carpenter, would they? So he wouldn't be busy, would he?'

'Listen, Clancy—'

'He'd go fishing or something, wouldn't he?'

'Clancy, we're supposed to be carving a new language out of the wilderness here—'

'Probably'd need someone to help him bait the line, but—'

'Clancy, will you shut up and go and get the horses?'

It took twenty minutes to roll enough of the rocks away, and five minutes after that Clancy reported back.

'Can't find the little bastard, boss. And we looked underneath all the others.'

'It couldn't have got past us!'

'Yes it could, boss. You saw it goin' up those cliffs. Probably miles away by now. You want I should go after that bloke?'

Remorse thought about it, and spat. 'No, we got the colt back. That's worth the money.' He stared reflectively down the canyon.

'You all right, boss?'

'Clancy, after we get back to the station, go on into town and call in at the Pastoral Hotel and bring back as many corks as they've got, willya?'

'Think it'll work, boss? He was as weird as . . .' Clancy was pulled up by the look in his boss's eye. 'He was pretty weird,' hc said.

'Weird, yeah. But smart, too. No flies on him.'

Behind them, in the jumble of rocks and bushes at the end of the canyon, a drawing of a small horse became a drawing of a kangaroo and then faded into the stone.

The worst thing about losing your temper with Mustrum Ridcully was that he never noticed when you did.

Wizards, when faced with danger, would immediately stop and argue amongst themselves about exactly what kind of danger it was. By the time everyone in the party understood, either it had become the sort of danger where your options are so very, very clear that you instantly take one of them or die, or it had got bored and gone away. Even danger has its pride.

When he was a boy, Ponder Stibbons had imagined

that wizards would be powerful demi-gods able to change the whole world at the flick of a finger, and then he'd grown up and found that they were tiresome old men who worried about the state of their feet and, in harm's way, would even bicker about the origin of the phrase 'in harm's way'.

It had never struck him that evolution works in all kinds of ways. There were still quite deep scars in old buildings that showed what happened when you had the *other* kind of wizard.

His footsteps took him, almost without his being aware, along the gently winding path up the mountain. Strange creatures peered at him from the undergrowth on either side. Some of them looked like—

Wizards think in terms of books, and, now, one crept out from the shelves of Ponder's memory. It had been given to him when he was small. In fact, he'd still got it somewhere, filed away in a cardboard box.*

It had consisted of lots of small pages on a central spiral. Each one showed the head, body or tail of some bird, fish or animal. It was possible for the sufficiently bored to shuffle and turn them so that you got, say, a creature with the head of a horse, the body of a beetle

---

* Ponder had been that kind of child. He still had all the pieces for every game he'd ever been given. Ponder had been the kind of boy who carefully reads the label on every Hogswatch present before opening it, and notes down in a small book, who it is from, and has all the thank-you letters written by teatime. His parents had been impressed even then, realizing that they had given birth to a child who would achieve great things or, perhaps, be hunted down by a righteous citizenry by the time he was ten.

and the tail of a fish. The cover promised 'hours of fun' although, after the first three minutes, you couldn't help wondering what kind of person could make that kind of fun last for hours, and whether suffocating him as kindly as possible now would save the Serial Crimes Squad a lot of trouble in years to come. Ponder, however, had hours of fun.

Some of the creat— *things* in the undergrowth looked like the pages of that book. There were birds with beaks as long as their bodies. There were spiders the size of hands. Here and there the air shimmered like water. It resisted very gently as Ponder tried to walk through it, and then let him pass, but the birds and insects didn't seem inclined to follow him.

There were beetles everywhere.

Eventually, by easy stages, the winding path reached the top of the mountain. There was a tiny valley there, just below the peak. At the far end was a large cave mouth, lit by a blue glow within.

A large beetle sang past Ponder's ear.

The cave mouth opened into a cavern, filled with misty blue fog. There was a suggestion of complex shadows. And there were sounds – whistles, little zipping noises, the occasional thud or clang that suggested work going on somewhere in the mist.

Ponder brushed aside a beetle that had landed on his cheek and stared at the shape right in front of him.

It was the front half of an elephant.

The other half of the elephant, balancing against all probability on the two legs at the rear end, stood a few yards away. In between was . . . the rest of the elephant.

Ponder Stibbons told himself that if you cut an elephant in half and scooped out the middle, what you would get would be . . . well, mess. There wasn't much mess here. Pink and purple tubes had uncoiled neatly on to a workbench. A small stepladder led up into another complexity of tubes and bulky organs. There was a general feel of methodical work in progress. This wasn't the horror of an elephant in an explosive death. This was an elephant under construction.

Little clouds of white light spiralled in from all corners of the cavern, spun for a moment, and became the god of evolution, who was standing on the stepladder.

He blinked at Ponder. 'Oh, it's you,' he said. 'One of the pointy creatures. Can you tell me what happens when I do this?'

He reached inside the echoing depths of the front half. The elephant's ears flapped.

'The ears flapped,' squeaked Ponder.

The god emerged, beaming. 'It's amazing how difficult that is to achieve,' he said. 'Anyway . . . what do you think of it?'

Ponder swallowed. 'It's . . . very good,' he managed. He took a step back, bumped into something, and turned and looked into the gaping maw of a very large shark. It was in the middle of another . . . well, he had to think of it as a sort of biological scaffolding. It rolled an eye at him. Behind it, a much bigger whale was being assembled.

'It is, isn't it?' said the god.

Ponder tried to concentrate on the elephant. 'Although—' he said.

'Yes?'

'Are you sure about the wheels?'

The god looked concerned. 'You think they're too small? Not quite suitable for the veldt?'

'Er, probably not . . .'

'It's very hard to design an organic wheel, you know,' said the god reproachfully. 'They're little masterpieces.'

'You don't think just, you know, moving the legs about would be simpler?'

'Oh, we'd never get anywhere if I just copied earlier ideas,' said the god. 'Diversify and fill all niches, that's the ticket.'

'But is lying on your side in a mud hole with your wheels spinning a very *important* niche?' said Ponder.

The god looked at him, and then stared glumly at the half-completed elephant.

'Perhaps if I made the tyres bigger?' he said, hopefully yet in a hopeless voice.

'I don't think so,' said Ponder.

'Oh, you're probably right.' The little god's hands twitched. 'I don't know, I do *try* to diversify, but sometimes it's so difficult . . .'

Suddenly he ran across the crowded cave towards a huge pair of doors at the far end, and flung them open.

'I'm sorry, but I just have to do one,' said the god. 'They calm me down, you know.'

Ponder caught up. The cave beyond the doors was bigger than this one, and brilliantly lit. The air was full of small, bright things, hovering in their millions like beads on invisible strings.

'Beetles?' said Ponder.

'There's nothing like a beetle when you're feeling depressed!' said the god. He'd stopped by a large metal desk and was feverishly opening drawers and pulling out boxes. 'Can you pass me that box of antennae? It's just on the shelf there. Oh yes, you can't beat a beetle when you're feeling down. Sometimes I think it's what it's all about, you know.'

'What *all*?' said Ponder.

The god swept an arm in an expansive gesture. 'Everything,' he said cheerfully. 'The whole thing. Trees, grass, flowers . . . What did you think it was all for?'

'Well, I didn't think it was for beetles,' said Ponder. 'What about, well, what about the elephant, for a start?'

The god already had a half-finished beetle in one hand. It was green.

'Dung,' he said triumphantly. No head, when screwed on to a body, ought to make a sound like a cork being pushed into a bottle, but the beetle's did in the hands of the god.

'What?' said Ponder. 'That's rather a lot of trouble to go to just for dung, isn't it?'

'That's ecology for you, I'm afraid,' said the god.

'No, no, that can't be right, surely?' said Ponder. 'What about the higher lifeforms?'

'Higher?' said the god. 'You mean like . . . birds?'

'No, I mean like—' Ponder hesitated. The god had seemed remarkably incurious about the wizards, possibly because of their lack of resemblance to beetles, but he could see a certain amount of theological unpleasantness ahead.

'Like . . . apes,' he said.

'Apes? Oh, very amusing, certainly, and obviously the beetles have to have something to entertain them, but . . .' The god looked at him, and a celestial penny seemed to drop. 'Oh dear, you don't think *they're* the purpose of the whole business, do you?'

'I'd rather assumed—'

'Dear me, the purpose of the whole business, you see, is in fact to *be* the whole business. Although,' he sniffed, 'if we can do it all with beetles I shan't complain.'

'But surely the purpose of— I mean, wouldn't it be nice if you ended up with some creature that started to *think* about the universe—?'

'Good gravy, I don't want anything poking around!' said the god testily. 'There's enough patches and stitches in it as it is without some clever devil trying to find more, I can assure you. No, the gods on the mainland have got *that* right at least. Intelligence is like legs – too many and you trip yourself up. Six is about the right number, in my view.'

'But surely, ultimately, one creature might—'

The god let go of his latest creation. It whirred up and along the rows and rows of beetles and slotted itself in between two that were almost, but not exactly, quite like it.

'Worked that one out, have you?' he said. 'Well, of course you're right. I can see you have quite an efficient brain— Damn.'

There was a little sparkle in the air and a bird appeared alongside the god. It was clearly alive but entirely stationary, hanging in frozen flight. A flickering blue glow hovered around it.

The god sighed, reached into a pocket and pulled out the most complex-looking tool Ponder had ever seen. The bits that you could see suggested that there were other, even stranger bits that you couldn't and that this was probably just as well.

'However,' he said, slicing the bird's beak off, the blue glow simply closing over the hole, 'if I'm going to get any serious work done I'm really going to have to find some way of organizing the whole business. All I'm faced with these days is bills.'

'Yes, it must be quite expens—'

'Big bills, short bills, bills for winkling insects out of bark, bills for cracking nuts, bills for eating fruit,' the god went on. 'They're supposed to do their own evolving. I mean, that's the whole point. I shouldn't have to be running around *all* the time.' The god waved his hand in the air and a sort of display stand of beaks appeared beside him. He selected one that, to Ponder, hardly looked any different from the one he'd removed, and used the tool to attach it to the hanging bird. The blue glow covered it for a moment, and then the bird vanished. In the moment that it disappeared, Ponder thought he saw its wings begin to move.

And in that moment he knew that, despite the

apparent beetle fixation, *here* was where he'd always wanted to be, at the cutting edge of the envelope in the fast lane of the state of the art.

He'd become a wizard because he'd thought that wizards knew how the universe worked, and Unseen University had turned out to be stifling.

Take that business with the tame lightning. It had demonstrably *worked*. He made the Bursar's hair stand on end and sparks crackle out of his fingers, and that was by using only *one* cat and a couple of amber rods. His perfectly reasonable plan to use several thousand cats tied to a huge wheel that would rotate against hundreds of rods had been vetoed on the ridiculous grounds that it would be too noisy. His carefully worked out scheme to split the thaum, and thus provide endless supplies of cheap clean magic, had been quite unfairly sat upon because it was felt that it might make the place untidy. And that was even after he had presented figures to prove that the chances of the process completely destroying the entire world were no greater than being knocked down while crossing the street, and it wasn't his fault he said this just before the six-cart pile-up outside the University.

Here was a chance to do something that made sense. Besides, he thought he could see where the god was going wrong.

'Excuse me,' he said, 'but do you need an assistant?'

'Frankly, the whole thing is getting out of hand,' said the god, who was a wizard-class non-listener. 'It's really getting to the point where I need an—'

'I say, this is a pretty amazing place!'

Ponder rolled his eyes. You could say that for wizards. When they walked into a place that was pretty amazing, they'd *tell* you. Loudly.

'Ah,' said the god, turning around, 'this is the rest of your . . . swarm, isn't it?'

'I'd better go and stop them,' said Ponder as the wizards fanned out like small boys in an amusement arcade, ready to press anything in case there was a free game left. 'They poke things and then say, "What does this do?"'

'Don't they ask what things do *before* they poke them?'

'No, they say you'll never find out if you don't give them a poke,' said Ponder darkly.

'Then why do they ask?'

'They just do. And they bite things and then say, "I wonder if this is poisonous," with their mouths full. And you know the really annoying thing? It never is.'

'How odd. Laughing in the face of danger is not a survival strategy,' said the god.

'Oh, they don't laugh,' said Ponder gloomily. 'They say things like, "You call *that* dangerous? It's not a patch on the kind of danger you used to get when we were lads, eh, Senior Wrangler, what what? Remember when old 'Windows' McPlunder . . ."' He shrugged.

'When old "Windows" McPlunder what?' said the god.

'I don't know! Sometimes I think they make up the names! Dean, I really don't think you should do that!'

The Dean turned away from the shark, whose teeth he'd been examining.

'Why not, Stibbons?' he said. Behind him, the jaw snapped shut.

Only the Archchancellor's legs were visible in the exploded elephant. There were muffled noises from inside the whale; they sounded very much like the Lecturer in Recent Runes saying, 'Look at what happens when I twist this bit . . . See, that purple bit wobbles.'

'Amazin' piece of work,' said Ridcully, emerging from the elephant. 'Very good wheels. You paint these bits before assembly, do you?'

'It's not a kit, sir,' said Ponder, taking a kidney out of his hands and wedging it back in. 'It's a real elephant under construction!'

'Oh.'

'Being *made*, sir,' said Ponder, since Ridcully didn't seem to have got the message. 'Which is not *usual*.'

'Ah. How are they normally made, then?'

'By other elephants, sir.'

'Oh, yes . . .'

'Really? Are they?' said the god. 'How? Those trunks are pretty nimble, even if I say so myself, but not really very good for delicate work.'

'Oh, not made like that, sir, obviously. By . . . you know . . . sex . . .' said Ponder, feeling a blush start.

'Sex?'

Then Ponder thought: Mono Island. Oh *dear* . . .

'Er . . . males and females . . .' he ventured.

'What are they, then?' said the god. The wizards paused.

'Do go on, Mister Stibbons,' said the Archchancellor. 'We're all ears. Especially the elephant.'

'Well ...' Ponder knew he was going red. 'Er ... well, how do you get flowers and things at the moment?'

'I make them,' said the god. 'And then I keep an eye on them and see how they function and then when they wear out I make an improved version based on experimental results.' He frowned. 'Although the plants seem to be acting very oddly these days. What's the point of these seeds they keep making? I try to discourage it but they don't seem to listen.'

'I think ... er ... they're trying to invent sex, sir,' said Ponder. 'Er ... sex is how you can ... they can ... creatures can ... they can make the next ... creatures.'

'You mean ... elephants can make more elephants?'

'Yes, sir.'

'My word! Really?'

'Oh, yes.'

'How do they go about that? Calibrating the ear-waggling is particularly time-consuming. Do they use special tools?'

Ponder saw that the Dean was staring straight up at the ceiling, while the other wizards were also finding something apparently fascinating to look at that meant they could avoid one another's gaze.

'Um, in a way,' said Ponder. He knew that a sticky patch lay ahead and decided to give up. 'But really I don't know much about—'

'And workshops, presumably,' said the god. He took

a book from his pocket and a pencil from behind his ear. 'Do you mind if I make notes?'

'They . . . er . . . the female . . .' Ponder tried.

'Female,' said the god obediently, writing this down.

'Well, she . . . one popular way . . . she . . . sort of makes the next one . . . inside her.'

The god stopped writing. 'Now I *know* that's not right,' he said. 'You can't make an elephant inside an elephant—'

'Er . . . a smaller version . . .'

'Ah, once again I have to point out the flaw. After a few such constructions you'd end up with an elephant the size of a rabbit.'

'Er, it gets bigger later . . .'

'Really? How?'

'It sort of . . . builds itself . . . er . . . from the inside . . .'

'And the other one, the one that is not the, uh, female? What is its part in all this? Is your colleague ill?'

The Senior Wrangler hammered the Dean hard on the back.

'It's all right,' squeaked the Dean, '. . . often have . . . these . . . coughing fits . . .'

The god scribbled industriously for a few seconds, and then stopped and chewed the end of his pencil thoughtfully.

'And all this, er, this *sex* is done by unskilled labour?' he said.

'Oh, yes.'

'No quality control of any description?'

'Er, no.'

'How does *your* species go about it?' said the god. He looked questioningly at Ponder.

'It . . . er . . . we . . . er . . .' Ponder stuttered.

'We avoid it,' said Ridcully. 'Nasty cough you've got there, Dean.'

'Really?' said the god. 'That's very interesting. What do you do instead? Split down the middle? That works beautifully for amoebas, but giraffes find it extremely difficult, I do know that.'

'What? No, we concentrate on higher things,' said Ridcully. 'And take cold baths, healthy morning runs, that sort of thing.'

'My goodness, I'd better make a note of that,' said the god, patting his robe. 'How does the process work, exactly? Do the females accompany you? These higher things . . . How high, precisely? This is a *very* interesting concept. Presumably extra orifices are required?'

'What? Pardon?' said Ponder.

'Getting creatures to make themselves, eh? I thought this whole seed business was just high spirits but, yes, I can see that it would save a lot of work, a *lot* of work. Of course, there'd have to be some extra effort at the design stage, certainly, but afterwards I suppose it'd practically run itself . . .' The god's hand blurred as he wrote, and he went on, 'Hmm, drives and imperatives, they're going to be vital . . . er . . . How does it work with, say, trees?'

'You just need Ponder's uncle and a paintbrush,' said the Senior Wrangler.

'Sir!' said Ponder hotly.

The god gave them both a look of intelligent bewilderment, like a man who had just heard a joke told in a completely foreign language and isn't sure if the speaker has got to the punchline yet. Then he shrugged.

'The only thing I think I don't quite understand', he said, 'is why any creature would want to spend time on all this . . .' he peered at his notes, 'this *sex*, when they could be enjoying themselves . . . Oh dear, your associate seems to be choking this time, I'm afraid . . .'

'Dean!' shouted Ridcully.

'I can't help noticing', said the god, 'that when *sex* is being discussed your faces redden and you tend to shift uneasily from one foot to the other. Is this some sort of signal?'

'Erm . . .'

'If you could just tell me how it all works . . .'

Embarrassment filled the air, huge and pink. If it were rock, you could have carved great hidden rose-red cities in it.

Ridcully smiled a petrified smile. 'Excuse us,' he said. 'Faculty meeting, gentlemen?'

Ponder watched the wizards go into a huddle. He could hear a few phrases above the susurration.

'. . . *my father said, but of course I didn't believe . . . never raised its ugly head . . . Dean, will you shut up? We can't very well . . . cold showers, really . . .*'

Ridcully turned back and flashed the stony smile again. 'Sex is, er, not something we talk about,' he said.

'Much,' said the Dean.

'Oh, I see,' said the god. 'Well, a practical demonstration would be so much more comprehendable.'

'Er, we weren't, er . . . planning a . . .'

'Coo-eee! There you are, gentlemen!'

Mrs Whitlow entered the cave. The wizards went suddenly quiet, sensing in their wizardly minds that the introduction of Mrs Whitlow at this point was an electric fire in the swimming pool of life.

'Oh, another one of you,' said the god brightly. He focused. 'Or a different species, perhaps?'

Ponder felt that he had to say something. Mrs Whitlow was giving him a Look.

'Mrs, er, Whitlow is, er, a lady,' he said.

'Ah, I shall make a note of it,' said the god. 'And what sort of thing do *they* do?'

'They're, um, the same species as, er, us,' said Ponder, miserably. 'Um . . . the . . . um . . .'

'Weaker sex,' Ridcully supplied.

'Sorry, you've lost me there,' said the god.

'Er . . . she's, um, er, a . . . of the female persuasion,' said Ponder.

The god smiled happily. 'Oh, how very convenient,' he said.

'Excuse *me*,' said Mrs Whitlow, in as sharp a tone as she cared to use around the wizards, 'but will someone introduce this gentleman to me?'

'Oh, yes, of course,' said Ridcully. 'Do excuse me. God, this is Mrs Whitlow. Mrs Whitlow, this is God. A god. God of this island, in fact. Uh . . .'

'Charmed, Ai'm sure,' said Mrs Whitlow. In Mrs Whitlow's book, gods were socially very acceptable, at least if they had proper human heads and wore clothes; they rated above High Priests and occupied the same level as Dukes.

'Should Ai kneel?' she said.

'Mwaaa,' whimpered the Senior Wrangler.

'Genuflection of any sort is *not* required,' said the god.

'He means no,' said Ponder.

'Oh, as you wish,' said Mrs Whitlow. She extended a hand.

The god grasped it and waggled her thumb backwards and forwards.

'*Very* practical,' he said. 'Opposable, I see. I think I should make a note of this. Do you brachiate? Are you bipedal by habit? Oh, I notice your eyebrows go up, too. Is this a signal of some sort? I also note that you are a different shape from the others and don't have a beard. I assume that means you are less wise?'

Ponder saw Mrs Whitlow's eyes narrow and her nostrils flare.

'Is there some sort of problem, sirs?' she said. 'Ai followed your footprints to that funny boat, and this was the only other path, so—'

'We were discussing sex,' said the god enthusiastically. 'It sounds very exciting, don't you think?'

The wizards held their breath. This was going to make the Dean's sheets look very minor.

'It's *not* a subject on which Ai would venture an opinion,' said Mrs Whitlow carefully.

'Mwaa,' squeaked the Senior Wrangler.

'No one seems to want to *tell* me,' said the god

irritably. A spark leapt from his fingers and blew a very small crater in the floor, and that seemed to shock him as much as it did the wizards.

'Oh dear, what *can* you think of me? I'm so sorry!' he said. 'I'm afraid it's a sort of natural reaction if I get a bit, you know . . . testy.'

Everyone looked at the crater. The rock bubbled gently by Ponder's feet. He didn't dare move his sandal, just in case he fainted.

'That was just . . . testy, was it?' said Ridcully.

'Well, it may have been more . . . vexed, I suppose,' said the god. 'I can't really help it, it's a god-given reflex. I'm afraid as a . . . well, species, we're not good with, you know, defiance. I'm so sorry. So sorry.' He blew his nose, and sat down on a half-finished panda. 'Oh, dear. There I go again . . .' A tiny bolt of lightning flashed off his thumb and exploded. 'I hope it's not going to be the city of Quint all over again. Of course, you know what happened there . . .'

'I've never heard of the city of Quint,' said Ponder.

'Yes, I suppose you wouldn't have,' said the god. 'That's the whole point, really. It wasn't *much* of a city. It was mostly made of mud. Well, I *say* mud. Afterwards, of course, it was mainly ceramics.' He turned a wretched face to them. 'You know those days you get when you just snap at everyone?'

Out of the corner of his eye Ponder had noticed that the wizards, in a rare show of unanimity, were shuffling sideways, very slowly, towards the door.

A much bigger thunderbolt blew a hole in the floor near the cave entrance.

'Oh dear, where *can* I put my face?' said the god. 'It's all subconscious, I'm afraid.'

'Could you get treatment for premature incineration?'

'Dean! This is *not* the time!'

'Sorry, Archchancellor.'

'If only they hadn't turned up their noses at my inflammable cows,' said the god, sparks fizzing off his beard. 'All right, I would agree that on hot days, in certain rare circumstances, they would spontaneously combust and burn down the village, but is that any excuse for ingratitude?'

Mrs Whitlow had been giving the god a long, cool stare. 'What exactly is it you wish to know?' she said.

'Huh?' said Ridcully.

'Well, Ai mean no offence, but Ai for one would like to get out of here without mai hair on fire,' said the housekeeper.

The god looked up. 'This male and female concept seems really rather promising,' he said, sniffing. 'But no one seems to want to go into detail . . .'

'Oh, *that*,' said Mrs Whitlow. She glanced at the wizards, and then gently pulled the god to his feet. 'If you will excuse me for one moment, gentlemen . . .'

The wizards watched them in even more shock than had attended the lightning display, and then the Chair of Indefinite Studies pulled his hat over his eyes.

'I daren't look,' he said, and added, 'What are they doing?'

'Er . . . just talking . . .' said Ponder.

'Talking?'

'And she's . . . sort of . . . waving her hands about.'

'Mwaa!' said the Senior Wrangler.

'Quick, someone, give him some air,' said Ridcully. 'Now she's *laughing*, isn't she?'

Both the housekeeper and the god looked around at the wizards. Mrs Whitlow nodded her head as if to reassure him that what she'd just told him was true, and they both laughed.

'*That* looked more like a snigger,' said the Dean severely.

'I'm not sure I actually approve of this,' said Ridcully, haughtily. 'Gods and mortal women, you know. You hear stories.'

'Gods turning themselves into bulls,' said the Dean.

'Swans, too,' said the Chair of Indefinite Studies.

'Showers of gold,' said the Dean.

'Yes,' said the Chair. He paused for a second. 'You know, I've often wondered about that one—'

'What's she describing now?'

'I think I'd rather not know, quite frankly.'

'Oh, look, someone *please* do something for the Senior Wrangler, will you?' said Ridcully. 'Loosen his clothing or something!'

They heard the god shout, 'It *what?*' Mrs Whitlow glanced around at the wizards and appeared to lower her voice.

'Did anyone ever meet *Mr* Whitlow?' said the Archchancellor.

'Well . . . no,' said the Dean. 'Not that I remember. I suppose we've all assumed that he's dead.'

'Anyone know what he died of?' Ridcully went on.

'Ah, quieten down . . . they're coming back . . .'

The god nodded cheerfully at them as he approached.

'Well, *that*'s all sorted out,' he said, rubbing his hands together. 'I can't wait to see how it works in practice. You know, if I'd sat here for a hundred years I'd never have . . . well, really, no one could seriously believe . . . I mean . . .' He started to chuckle at their frozen faces. 'That bit where he . . . and then she . . . Really, I'm amazed that anyone stops laughing long enough to . . . Still, I can see how it could work, and it certainly opens the door to some very interesting possibilities indeed . . .'

Mrs Whitlow was looking intently at the ceiling. There was perhaps just a hint in her stance and the way her rather expressive bosom moved that she was trying not to laugh. It was disconcerting. Mrs Whitlow never usually laughed at anything.

'Ah? Oh?' said Ridcully, edging towards the door. 'Really? Well done, then. So, I expect you don't need us any more, eh? Only we've got a boat to catch . . .'

'Yes, certainly, don't let me hold you up,' said the god, waving a hand vaguely. 'You know, the more I think about it, the more I can see that "sex" will solve practically all my problems.'

'Not everyone can say that,' said Ridcully gravely. 'Are you, er . . . joining us, Mrs, er, Whitlow?'

'Certainly, Archchancellor.'

'Er . . . jolly good. Well done. Ahem. And you, of course, Mister Stibbons . . .'

The god had wandered over to a workbench and

was rummaging in boxes. The air glittered. Ponder looked up at the whale. It was clearly alive but . . . not at the moment. His gaze swept across the elephant-under-construction and past mysteriously organic-looking gantries, where shimmering blue light surrounded shapes as yet unrecognized, although one did appear to contain half a cow.

He carefully removed an exploring beetle from his ear. The point was, if he left now he'd always wonder . . .

'I think I'd like to stay,' he said.

'Good . . . er . . .' said the god, without looking around.

'Man,' said Ponder.

'Good man,' said the god.

'Are you *sure*?' said Ridcully.

'I don't think I've ever had a holiday,' said Ponder. 'I'd like to apply for time off to do research, sir.'

'But we're lost in the past, man!'

'Basic research, then,' said Ponder firmly. 'There's just so much to learn here, sir!'

'Really?'

'You've only got to look around, sir!'

'Well, I suppose I can't stop you if your mind's made up,' said the Archchancellor. 'We'll have to dock your pay, of course.'

'I don't think I've ever been paid, sir,' said Ponder.

The Dean nudged Ridcully and whispered in his ear.

'And we need to know how the boat works,' Ridcully went on.

'What? Oh, it shouldn't be a problem,' said the god, looking up from his bench. 'It'll find somewhere with a different biogeographical signature, you see. It's all automatic. No sense in coming back to where you started from!' He waved a beetle leg in the air. 'There's a new continent going up turnwise of here. The boat'll probably head straight for a landmass that size.'

'New?' said Ridcully.

'Oh, yes. I've never been interested in that sort of thing myself, but you can hear the construction noises all night. It's certainly causing a mess.'

'Stibbons, are you *sure* you want to stay?' the Dean demanded.

'Er, yes . . .'

'I'm sure Mister Stibbons will uphold the fine traditions of the University!' said Ridcully heartily.

Ponder, who knew all about the traditions of the University, nodded very slightly. His heart was pounding. He hadn't even felt like this when he'd first worked out how to program Hex.

At last he'd found his proper place in the world. The future beckoned.

Dawn was breaking when the wizards ambled back down the mountain.

'Not a bad god, I thought,' said the Senior Wrangler. 'As gods go.'

'That was good coffee he made us,' said the Chair of Indefinite Studies.

'And didn't he grow the bush fast, once we

explained what coffee was,' said the Lecturer in Recent Runes.

They strolled on. Mrs Whitlow was walking some way ahead, humming to herself. The wizards took care to remain at a respectful distance. They were aware that in some kind of obscure way she'd won, although they hadn't a clue what the game was.

'Funny of young Ponder to want to stay,' said the Senior Wrangler, desperately trying to think of anything except a vision in pink.

'The god seemed happy about it,' said the Lecturer in Recent Runes. 'He did say that designing sex was going to involve redesigning practically everything else.'

'I used to make snakes out of clay when I was a little boy,' said the Bursar happily.

'Well done, Bursar.'

'Doing the feet was the hard part.'

'I can't help thinking, though, that we may have . . . tinkered with the past, Archchancellor,' said the Senior Wrangler.

'I don't see how,' said Ridcully. 'After all, the past happened before we got here.'

'Yes, but now we're here, we've changed it.'

'Then we changed it before.'

And that, they felt, pretty well summed it up. It is very easy to get ridiculously confused about the tenses of time travel, but most things can be resolved by a sufficiently large ego.

'It's jolly impressive to think that a University man will be helping to create a whole new approach to designing lifeforms,' said the Chair of Indefinite Studies.

'Indeed, yes,' said the Dean. 'Who says education is a bad thing, eh?'

'I can't imagine,' said Ridcully. 'Who?'

'Well, if they did, we could point to Ponder Stibbons and say, look at him, worked hard at his studies, paid attention to his tutors, and now he's sitting on the right hand of a god.'

'Won't that make it rather difficult for—' the Lecturer in Recent Runes began, but the Dean got there first.

'That means on the right-hand *side* of the god, Runes,' he said. 'Which, I suspect, makes him an angel. Technically.'

'Surely not. He's scared of heights. Anyway, he's made of flesh and blood, and I'm sure angels have to be made of . . . light or something. He *could* be a saint, though, I suppose.'

'Can he do miracles, then?'

'I'm not sure. When we left they were talking about redesigning male baboons' behinds to make them more attractive.'

The wizards thought about this for a while.

'That'd be a miracle in *my* book, certainly,' said Ridcully.

'Can't say that's how I'd choose to spend an afternoon, though,' said the Senior Wrangler, in a thoughtful voice.

'According to the god it's all to do with making creatures *want* to have . . . to engage in . . . to get to grips with making a new generation, when they could otherwise be spending their time in more ... profitable activity. Apparently, a lot of animals will need a complete rebuild.'

'From the bottom up. Ahaha.'

'Thank you for your contribution, Dean.'

'So exactly how does it work, then?' said the Senior Wrangler. 'A female baboon sees a male baboon and says, "My word, that's a very colourful bottom and no mistake, let us engage in ... nuptial activity"?'

'I must say I've often wondered about that sort of thing myself,' said the Lecturer in Recent Runes. 'Take frogs. Now, if I was a lady frog looking for a husband, I'd want to know about, well, size of legs, competence at catching flies—'

'Length of tongue,' said Ridcully. 'Dean, will you *please* take something for that cough?'

'Quite so,' said the Lecturer in Recent Runes. 'Has he got a good pond, and so on. I can't say I'd base my choice on his ability to inflate his throat to the same size as his stomach and go *rabbit, rabbit.*'

'I believe it's *ribbit, ribbit*, Runes.'

'Are you sure?'

'I believe so, yes.'

'Which ones go *rabbit, rabbit*, then?'

'Rabbits, I believe.'

'Oh. Yes. Constantly, as I recall.'

'I've always thought sex was really a rather tasteless way of ensuring the continuity of the species,' said the Chair of Indefinite Studies, as they reached the beach. 'I'm sure there could be something better. It's all very

. . . old-fashioned, to my mind. And far too energetic.'

'Well, I'm generally in agreement, but what would you suggest instead?' said Ridcully.

'Bridge,' said the Chair of Indefinite Studies firmly.

'Really? Bridge?'

'You mean the game with cards?' said the Dean.

'I don't see why not. It can be extremely exciting, very sociable, and requires no special equipment.'

'But you do need *four* people,' Ridcully pointed out.

'Ah, yes. I had not considered that. Yes, I can see that there could be problems. All right, then. How about . . . croquet? You can do that with two. Indeed, I've often enjoyed a quiet knockabout all by myself.'

Ridcully let a little more space come between him and the Chair of Indefinite Studies.

'I fail to see how it could be utilized for the purpose of procreation,' he said carefully. 'Recreation, yes, I'll grant you that. But not procreation. I mean, how would it work?'

'*He*'s the god,' sniffed the Chair of Indefinite Studies. 'He's supposed to sort out the details, isn't he?'

'But you think women would really decide to spend their life with a man just because he can swing a big mallet?' said the Dean.

'I suppose, when you come to think about it, that's no more ridic—' Ridcully began, and then stopped. 'I think we should leave this subject,' he said.

'I played croquet with him only last week,' hissed the Dean to Ridcully, as the Chair wandered off. 'I shan't be happy now until I've had a good bath!'

'We'll lock up his mallets when we get back, depend upon it,' Ridcully whispered.

'He's got books and books about croquet in his room, did you know that? Some of them have got *coloured illustrations!*'

'What of?'

'Famous croquet strokes,' said the Dean. 'I think we ought to take his mallet away.'

'Close to what I was thinking, Dean. Close,' said Ridcully.

Once a moderately jolly wizard camped by a dried-up waterhole under the shade of a tree that he was completely unable to identify. And he swore as he hacked and hacked at a can of beer, saying, 'What kind of *idiots* put beer in *tins?*'

By the time he managed to make a hole with a sharp stone the beer came out as high-speed froth, but he fielded as much as he could.

Apart from the beer, though, things were looking up. He'd checked the trees for drop-bears and, best of all, there was no sign of Scrappy.

He managed to pierce another tin, more carefully this time, and sucked thoughtfully at the contents.

What a country! Nothing was exactly what it turned out to be, even the sparrows talked, or at least tried to say, 'Who's a pretty boy, then?' and it never ever rained. And all the water hid underground, so they had to pump it out with windmills.

He'd passed another one as he left the canyon country. This one was still managing a trickle of water, but it had dried up to an occasional drip even as he watched it.

Damn! He should've picked up some water to take away while he was there.

He looked at the food in the sack. There was a loaf of bread the size and weight of a cannonball, and some vegetables. But at least they were recognizable vegetables. There was even a potato.

He held it up against the sunset.

Rincewind had eaten in many countries on the Disc, and sometimes he'd been able to complete an entire meal before having to run away. And they'd always lacked something. Oh, people did great things with spices and olives and yams and rice and whatnot, but what he'd come to crave was the humble potato.

Time was when a plate of mash or chips would have been his for the asking. All he'd needed to do was wander down to the kitchens and ask. Food was always available for the asking at Unseen University, you could say that for the place, even if you said it with your mouth full. And, ridiculous though it sounded now, he'd hardly ever done that. The dish of potatoes'd come past at mealtimes and he'd probably have a spoonful but, sometimes, he wouldn't! He'd ... let ... the ... dish ... go ... by. He'd have rice instead. Rice! All very nutritious in its way, but basically only grown where potatoes would've floated to the surface.

He'd remember those times, sometimes, usually in his sleep, and wake up shouting, 'Will you pass the potatoes, please!'

Sometimes he remembered the melted butter. Those were the bad days.

He placed the potato reverentially on the ground and tipped out the rest of the bag. There was an onion and some carrots. A tin of . . . tea, by the smell of it, and a little box of salt.

A flash of inspiration struck him with all the force and brilliance that ideas have when they're travelling through beer.

Soup! Nutritious and simple! You just boiled everything up! And, yes, he could use one of the empty beer tins, and make a fire, and chop up the vegetables, and the damp patch over there suggested there was water . . .

He walked unsteadily over to have a look. There was a circular depression in the ground that looked as though it might have been some sort of pond once, and there was the usual cluster of slightly healthier than usual trees which you got in such places, but there was no sign of any water and he was too tired to dig.

Then another insight struck him at the speed of beer. Beer! It was only water, really, with stuff in it. Wasn't it? And most of what was in it was yeast, which was practically a medicine and definitely a food. In fact, when you thought about it, beer was only a kind of runny bread, in *fact*, it'd be *better* to use some of the beer in the soup! Beer soup! A few brain cells registered their doubt, but the rest of them grabbed them by the collar and said hoarsely, people cooked chicken in wine, didn't they?

It took him some time to hack one end off a tin, but eventually he had it standing in the fire with the chopped-up vegetables floating in the froth. A few more doubts assailed him at this point, but they were elbowed aside, especially when the smell that floated up made his mouth water and he'd opened another tin of beer as a pre-prandial appetizer.

After a while he poked the vegetables with a stick. They were still pretty hard, even though a lot of the beer seemed to have boiled away. Was there something else he hadn't done?

Salt! Yes, that was it! Salt, marvellous stuff. He'd read where you went totally up the pole if you didn't have any salt for a couple of weeks. That was probably why he was feeling so odd at the moment. He fumbled for the salt box and dropped a pinch in the tin.

It was a medicinal herb, salt. Good for wounds, wasn't it? And back in the really old days, hadn't soldiers been paid in salt? Wasn't that where the word *salary* came from? *Must*'ve been good, then. You went on a forced march all week, building your road as you went, then you fought the maddened blue-painted tribesmen of the Vexatii, and you force-marched all the way back home, and on Friday the centurion would turn up with a big sack and say, 'Well done, lads! Here's some salt!'

It was amazing how well his mind was working.

He peered at the salt box again, shrugged, and tipped it all in. When you thought about it like that, salt must really be an amazing food. And he hadn't had any for weeks, so that was probably why his eyesight was acting up and he couldn't feel his legs.

He topped up the beer, too.

He lay back with his head on a rock. Keep out of trouble and don't get involved, that was the important thing. Look at those stars up there, with nothing to do all the time but sit there and shine. No one ever told *them* what to do, the lucky bastards . . .

He woke up shivering. Something horrible had crawled into his mouth, and it was no great relief to find out that it was his tongue. It was chilly, and the horizon suggested dawn.

There was also a pathetic sucking noise.

Some sheep had invaded his camp during the night. One of them was trying to get its mouth around an empty beer tin. It stopped when it saw that he had woken up, and backed away a bit, but not too far, while fixing him with the penetrating gaze of a domesticated animal reminding its domesticator that they had a deal.

His head ached.

There had to be some water *somewhere*. He lurched to his feet and blinked at the horizon. There were . . . windmills and things, weren't there? He remembered the stricken windmills from yesterday. Well, there was bound to be some water around, no matter what anyone said. Ye gods, he was *thirsty*.

His gummed-up gaze fell upon last night's magnificent experiment in cookery. Yeasty vegetable soup, what a *wonderful* idea. Exactly the sort of idea that sounds really good around one o'clock in the morning when you've had too much to drink.

Now he remembered, with a shudder, some of the great wheezes he'd had on similar occasions. Spaghetti and custard, that'd been a good one. Deep-fried peas, that'd been another triumph. And then there'd been the time when it had seemed a really good idea to eat some flour and yeast and then drink some warm water, because he'd run out of bread and after all that was what the stomach *saw*, wasn't it? The thing about late-night cookery was that it *made sense at the time*. It always had some logic behind it. It just wasn't the kind of logic you'd use around midday.

Still, he'd have to eat *something* and the dark brown goo that half filled the tin was the only available food in this vicinity that didn't have at least six legs. He didn't even think about eating mutton. You couldn't, when it was looking at you so pathetically.

He poked the goo with the stick. It gripped the wood like glue.

'Gerroff!'

A blob eventually came loose. Rincewind tasted it, gingerly. It was just possible that if you mixed yeasty beer and vegetables together you'd get—

No, what you got was salty-tasting beery brown gunk.

Odd, though . . . It was kind of horrible, but nevertheless Rincewind found himself having another taste.

Oh, *gods*. Now he was *really* thirsty.

He picked up the tin and staggered off towards some trees. That's where you found water . . . you looked at where the trees were and, tired or not, you dug down.

It took him half an hour to squash an empty beer tin and use it to dig a hole waist deep. His toes felt damp.

Another half an hour took him to shoulder depth and a pair of wet ankles.

Say what you like – that brown muck was good stuff. It was the runny equivalent of dwarf bread. You didn't really believe what your mouth said you'd just tasted, so you had some more. Probably full of nourishing vitamins and minerals. Most things you couldn't believe the taste of generally were . . .

By the time he raised his head he was surrounded by sheep, eyeing him cautiously in between longing glances into the damp depths.

'It's no good you lot looking at me like that,' he said. They paid no attention. They carried on looking at him.

'It's not *my* fault,' Rincewind muttered. 'I don't care what any kangaroo says. I just arrived here. I'm not responsible for the *weather*, for heaven's sake.'

They went on looking. He cracked. Practically anyone will crack before a sheep cracks. A sheep hasn't got much that's crackable.

'Oh, hell, maybe I can rig up some kind of bucket and pulley arrangement,' he said. 'It's not as though I've got any appointments today.'

He was digging a bit further, in the hope of getting deep enough before the water ran away completely, when he heard someone whistling.

He looked up, through the legs of the sheep. A man was creeping down across the dried-up waterhole, whistling tunelessly between his teeth. He'd failed to notice Rincewind because his gaze was fixed so intently on the milling sheep. He dropped the pack he'd been carrying, pulled out a sack, sidled towards a sheep all by itself, and leapt. It barely had time to bleat.

As he was stuffing it into the sack a voice said: 'That probably belongs to someone, you know.'

The man looked around hurriedly. The voice was coming from a group of sheep.

'I reckon you could get into serious trouble, stealing sheep. You'll regret it later on, I'm sure. Probably someone really cares about that sheep. Come on, let it go.'

The man stared around wildly.

'I mean, think about it,' the voice went on. 'You've got this nice country here, parrots and everything, and you're going to spoil it all by stealing someone's sheep that they've worked so hard to grow. I bet you wouldn't like to be remembered as a sheep-stealer—Oh.'

The man had dropped the sack and was running away very fast.

'Well, you didn't have to waltz off like that, I was only trying to appeal to your better nature!' said Rincewind, pulling himself up out of the hole.

He cupped his hands. 'And you've forgotten your camping stuff!' he shouted, after the disappearing dust.

The sack baa-ed.

Rincewind picked it up, and a noise behind him made him look round. There was another man watching him from the back of a horse. He was glaring.

Behind him were three men wearing identical helmets and jerkins and humourless expressions that had 'watchman' written all over them in slow handwriting. And all three were pointing crossbows at him.

That bottomless feeling that he had once again wandered into something that didn't concern him and was going to find it hard to wander out again grew within Rincewind.

He tried to smile.

'G'day!' he said. 'No worries, eh? I must say I'm really glad to see you drongos and no two ways about it!'

Ponder Stibbons cleared his throat.

'Where would you like me to start?' he said. 'I could probably finish off the elephant . . .'

'How are you at slime?'

Ponder hadn't considered a future as a slime designer, but everyone had to start somewhere.

'Fine,' he said. 'Fine.'

'Of course, slime just splits down the middle,' said the god, as they walked along rows of glowing, life-filled cubes while beetles sizzled overhead. 'Not a lot of future in that, really. It works all right for lower life-forms but, frankly, it's a bit embarrassing for the more complicated creatures and positively lethal for horses. No, sex is going to be very, very useful, Ponder. It'll keep everything on its toes. And *that* will give us time to work on the *big* project.'

Ponder sighed. Ah . . . he *knew* there had to be a big project. *The* big project. A god wasn't going to do all this sort of thing just to make life better for inflammable cows.

'Could I help with that?' he said. 'I'm sure I could make a contribution.'

'Really? I thought perhaps animals and birds would be more up your . . . up your . . .' The god waved his hands vaguely. 'Up whatever you walk on. Where you live.'

'Well, yes, but they're a bit limited, aren't they?' said Ponder.

The god beamed. There's nothing like being near a happy god. It's like giving your brain a hot bath.

'Exactly!' he said. 'Limited! The very word! Each one stuck in some desert or jungle or mountain, relying on one or two foods, at the mercy of every vagary of the universe and wiped out by the merest change of climate. What a terrible waste!'

'That's right!' said Ponder. 'What you need is a creature that is resourceful and adaptable, am I right?'

'Oh, very well put, Ponder! I can see you've turned up at just the right time!' A pair of huge doors swung open in front of them, revealing a circular room with a shallow pyramid of steps in the centre. At the summit was another cloud of blue mist, in which occasional lights flared and died.

The future unrolled in front of Ponder Stibbons. His eyes were so bright that his glasses steamed, that he could probably scorch holes in thin paper. Oh, *right* ... what more could any natural philosopher dream of? He'd got the theories, now he could do the practice.

And this time it'd be done *properly*. To hell with messing up the future! That's what the future was *for*. Oh, he'd been against it, that was true, but it'd been ... well, when someone else was thinking of doing it. But now he'd got the ear of a god, and maybe some intelligence could be applied to the task of creating intelligence.

For a start, it ought to be possible to put together the human brain so that long beards *weren't* associated with wisdom, which would instead be seen to reside in those who were young and skinny and required glasses for close work.

'And ... you've finished this?' he said, as they climbed the steps.

'Broadly, yes,' said the god. 'My greatest achievement. Frankly, it makes the elephants look very flimsy by comparison. But there's plenty of fine detail left to do, if you think you're up to it.'

'It'd be an honour,' said Ponder.

The blue mist was right in front of him. By the look of the sparks, something very important was happening in there.

'Do you give them any instructions before you let them out?' he said, his breathing shallow.

'A few simple ones,' said the god. He waved a wrinkled hand, and the glowing ball began to contract. 'Mostly they work things out themselves.'

'Of course, of course,' said Ponder. 'And I suppose if they go wrong we could always put them right with a few commandments.'

'Not really necessary,' said the god, as the blue ball vanished and revealed the pinnacle of creation. 'I find very simple instructions are quite sufficient. You know . . . "Head for dark places," that sort of thing. There! Isn't it perfect? What a piece of work! The sun will burn out, the seas will dry up, but this chap will be there, you mark my— Hello? Ponder?'

The Dean wet a finger and held it up. 'We have the wind on our starboard beam,' he said.

'That's good, is it?' said the Senior Wrangler.

'Could be, could be. Let's hope it can take us to this continent he mentioned. I'm getting nervous of islands.'

Ridcully finished hacking through the stem of the boat and threw it overboard.

At the top of the green mast the trumpet-like blooms appeared to tremble in the wind. The leaf sail creaked slowly into a different position.

'I'd say this was a miracle of nature', said the Dean, 'if we hadn't just met the person who did it. Rather spoils it, that.'

While wizards were not generally adventurous, they did understand that a vital part of any great undertaking is the securing of adequate provisions, which is why the boat was noticeably heavier in the water.

The Dean selected a natural cigar, lit it, and made a face. 'Not the best,' he said. 'Rather green.'

'We'll just have to rough it,' said Ridcully. 'What *are* you doing, Senior Wrangler?'

'Just preparing a little tray for Mrs Whitlow. A few choice things.'

The wizards glanced towards the crude awning they'd erected towards the prow. It wasn't that she'd actually *asked* for it. It was simply that she'd made some remark about how hot the sun was, as anyone might, and suddenly wizards were getting in each other's way as they vied with one another to cut poles and weave palm leaves. Perhaps never has so much intellectual effort gone into building a sunshade, which might have accounted for the wobble.

'I thought it was *my* turn to do that,' said the Dean, coldly.

'No, Dean, you took her the fruit drink, if you remember,' said the Senior Wrangler, cutting a cheese nut into dainty segments.

'That was just one small drink!' the Dean snapped. 'You're doing a whole tray. Look, you've even done a flower arrangement in a coconut shell!'

'Mrs Whitlow likes that sort of thing,' said the Senior Wrangler calmly. 'But she did say it was still a bit warm, so possibly you can fan her with a palm leaf while I peel these grapes for her.'

'Once again it is left to me to point out the elementary unfairness,' said the Dean. 'Merely waving a leaf is a very menial activity compared to removing grape skins, and I happen to outrank you, Senior Wrangler.'

'Indeed, Dean? And exactly how do you work that out?'

'It's not my *opinion*, man, it's written into the Faculty structure!'

'Of where, precisely?'

'Have you gone totally Bursar? Unseen University, of course!'

'And where is that, exactly?' said the Senior Wrangler, carefully arranging some lilies in a pleasing design.

'Ye gods, man, it's . . . it's . . .' The Dean flapped a hand in the direction of the horizon, and his voice trailed off as certain facts of time and space bore in on him.

'I'll leave you to work it out, shall I?' said the Senior Wrangler, getting off his knees and raising the tray reverentially.

'I'll help!' shouted the Dean, lumbering to his feet.

'It's very light, I assure you—'

'No, no, I can't let you do it all by yourself!'

Each holding the tray with one hand, and trying to push the other man away with the spare hand, they lurched forward, leaving a trail of spilt coconut milk and petals.

Ridcully rolled his eyes. It must be the heat, he thought. He turned to the Chair of Indefinite Studies, who was trying to tie a short log to a long stick with a piece of creeper.

'I was just thinking', he said, 'that everyone's gone a little bit mad except me and you . . . Er, what are you doing there?'

'I was just wondering whether Mrs Whitlow might like a game of croquet,' said the Chair. He waggled his eyebrows conspiratorially.

The Archchancellor sighed and wandered off along the deck. The Librarian had gone back to being a deckchair as a suitable mode for shipboard life, and the Bursar had gone to sleep on him.

The big leaf moved slightly. Ridcully got the feeling that the green trumpets on the mast were *sniffing*.

The wizards were already a little way from shore, but he saw the column of dust come down the track. It stopped at the beach and became a dot, which plunged into the sea.

The sail creaked again, and flapped as the wind grew.

'Ahoy there!' shouted Ridcully.

The distant figure waved for a moment and then continued swimming.

Ridcully filled his pipe and watched with interest as Ponder Stibbons caught up with the boat.

'Very well swum, if I may say so,' he said.

'Permission to come aboard, sir?' said Ponder, treading water. 'Could you throw down a creeper?'

'Why, certainly.'

The Archchancellor puffed his pipe as the wizard climbed aboard. 'Possibly a record time over that distance, Mister Stibbons.'

'Thank you, sir,' said Ponder, dripping water on the deck.

'And may I congratulate you on being properly dressed. You are wearing your pointy hat, which is the *sine qua non* of a wizard in public.'

'Thank you, sir.'

'It is a good hat.'

'Thank you, sir.'

'They say a wizard without his hat is undressed, Mister Stibbons.'

'So I have heard, sir.'

'But in your case, I must point out, you are *with* your hat but you are still, in a very real sense, undressed.'

'I thought the robe would slow me down, sir.'

'And, while it is good to see you, Stibbons, albeit rather more of you than I would usually care to contemplate, I am moved to ask why you are, in fact, here.'

'I suddenly felt it would be unfair to deprive the University of my services, sir.'

'Really? A sudden rush of nostalgia for the old alma mater, eh?'

'You could say that, sir.'

Ridcully's eyes twinkled behind the smoke and, not for the first time, Ponder suspected that the man was sometimes rather cleverer than he appeared. It would not be hard.

The Archchancellor shrugged, removed his pipe, and poked around inside it to remove a particularly obstructive clinker.

'The Senior Wrangler's bathing costume is around somewhere,' he said. 'I should put it on, if I were you. I suspect that offending Mrs Whitlow at the moment will get you hanged. All right? And if there is anything you want to talk about, my door is always open.'

'Thank you, sir.'

'Right now, of course, I don't have a door.'

'Thank you, sir.'

'Imagine it as being open, nevertheless.'

'Thank you, sir.'

After all, Ponder thought as he slipped gratefully away, the wizards of UU were merely crazy. Not even the Bursar was *insane*.

Even now, if he closed his eyes, he could still see the God of Evolution beaming so happily as the cockroach stirred.

Rincewind rattled the bars. 'Don't I get a trial?' he shouted.

After a while a warder wandered along the corridor. 'Wha'd'yew want a trial for, mister?'

'What? Well, call me Mister Silly, but it might just prove that I wasn't trying to steal the damn sheep, mightn't it?' said Rincewind. 'I was in fact *rescuing* it. If only you people would track down the thief, he'd tell you!'

The warder leaned against the wall and stuck his hands in his belt.

'Yeah, well, it's a funny thing,' he said, 'but, y'know, we searched and searched and put up notices and everything but, funny thing, yew'll never believe this, the bastard hasn't had the decency to come forward? Makes yew despair of human nature, eh?'

'So what's going to happen to me?'

The warder scratched his nose. 'Gonna hang you by the neck until you're dead, mate. Tomorrow morno.'

'You couldn't perhaps just hang me by the neck until I'm sorry?'

'No, mate. Got to be dead.'

'Good grief, it was only a sheep when all's said and done!'

The warder grinned widely. 'Ah, a lot of men have gone to the gallows sayin' that in the past,' he said. ''s'matterofact, you're the first sheep-stealer we've had here for *years*. All our big heroes have been sheep-stealers. You're gonna get a big crowd.'

'Baah!'

'Maybe a flock, too,' said the warder.

'That's another thing,' said Rincewind. 'Why's this sheep in my cell?'

'Evidence, mate.'

Rincewind looked down at the sheep. 'Oh. Well, no worries, then.'

The warder wandered off. Rincewind sat down on the bunk.

Well, he could look on the bright side, couldn't he? This was *civilization*. He hadn't seen much of it, what with being tied across the back of a horse and everything, but what he'd been able to see was full of ruts and hoofprints and smelled pretty bad, which civilization often does. They were going to hang him in the morning. This building was the first one made of stone he'd seen in this country. They had watchmen, even. They were going to hang him in the morning. There were the sounds of carts and people filtering in through the high window. They were going to hang him in the morning.

He gazed around the cell. It looked as though whoever'd built it had unaccountably forgotten to include any useful trapdoors.

Trapdoors . . . Now there was a word he shouldn't think about.

He'd been in nastier places than this. Much, much nastier. And that made it worse, because he'd been up against nasty, weird and magical things which suddenly seemed a lot easier to contemplate than the fact that he was held in some stone box and in the morning some perfectly nice people who he might quite like if he met them in a bar were going to march him out and make him stand on a really unsafe floor in a very tight collar.

'Baah!'

'Shut up.'

'Baah?'

'Couldn't you have had a bath, or a dip or something? It's a bit agricultural in here.'

The wall, now his eyes had become accustomed to the gloom, was covered with scrawls, and in particular those little wicket gate tallies drawn by prisoners who were counting the days. They were going to hang him in the morning, so that was one chore he wouldn't have to . . . Shut up, shut up.

Now he came to look closer, most of the counts went up to one.

He lay back with his eyes closed. Of course he'd get rescued, he'd *always* got rescued. Although, come to think of it, always in circumstances that put him in such a lot more danger than a prison cell usually held.

Well, he'd been in enough cells. There were ways to handle these things. The important thing was to be direct. He got up and banged on the bars until the warder sauntered along the corridor.

'Yes, mate?'

'I just want to get things sorted out,' said Rincewind. 'It's not as though I've got time to waste, okay?'

'Yep?'

'Is there any chance that you're going to fall asleep in a chair opposite this cell with your keys fully exposed on a table in front of you?'

They looked at the empty corridor.

'I'd have to get someone to help me bring a table down here,' said the warder doubtfully. 'Can't see it happening, mister. Sorry.'

'Right. Okay.' Rincewind thought for a moment. 'All right . . . Is my dinner likely to be brought in by a young lady carrying, and this is important, *carrying a tray covered with a cloth*?'

'No, 'cos I do the cooking.'

'Right.'

'Bread and water is what I'm good at.'

'Right, just checking.'

''ere, that sticky brown stuff they brought in with you is top stuff on bread, mister.'

'Be my guest.'

'I can feel the vitamins and minerals doing me a power of good.'

'No worries. Now . . . ah, yes. Laundry. Are there any big laundry baskets around, which will happily get tipped down a chute to the outside world?'

'Sorry, mister. There's an old washerwoman comes in to collect it.'

'Really?' Rincewind brightened. 'Ah, a *washerwoman*. Big lady, bulky dress, possibly wears a hood which can be pulled down to cover a lot of her face?'

'Yep, pretty much.'

'Well then, is she due in—?'

'She's my mum,' said the warder.

'Right, fine . . .'

They looked at one another.

'I reckon that about covers it, then,' said Rincewind. 'I hope you didn't mind me asking.'

'Bless yew, no! No worries! Happy to help. Worked out what yew're gonna say on the gallows, have yer? Only some of the ballad-writers want to know, if yew wouldn't mind.'

'Ballads?'

'Oh, *yeah*. There's three so far and I reckon there'll be ten by tomorra.'

Rincewind rolled his eyes. 'How many of them have put "too-ra-la, too-ra-la addity" in the chorus?' he asked.

'All of them.'

'Oh, gods . . .'

'And yew wouldn't mind changin' your name, would yew? Only they're sayin' "Rincewind" is a bit tricky to turn a line on. "Concernin' of a bush ranger, Rincewind was his name . . ." 's got the wrong sort of sound . . .'

'Well, I'm sorry. Perhaps you'd better let me go, then?'

'Ha, nice one. Now, if you want my advice, you'll keep it short when yew're up on the gallows,' said the warder. 'The best Famous Last Words are the shortest. Something simple gen'rally works best. Go easy on the swearin'.'

'Look, all I did was steal a sheep! And I didn't even do that! What's everyone so *excited* about?' said Rincewind desperately.

'Oh, very notorious crime, sheep-stealing,' said the warder cheerfully. 'Strikes a chord. Little man battlin' against the forces of brutal authority. People like that. You'll be remembered in song 'n' story, 'specially if yew come up with some good Last Words, like I said.' The warder hitched up his belt. 'To tell you the truth, a lot of people these days haven't even *seen* a bloody sheep, but hearing that someone's stolen one makes 'em feel proper Ecksians. It even does *me* good to have a proper criminal in the cells for once, instead of all these bloody politicians.'

Rincewind sat down on the bunk again, with his head in his hands.

'O' course, a famous escape is nearly as good as gettin' hanged,' said the warder, in the manner of someone trying to keep up someone else's spirits.

'Really,' said Rincewind.

'Yew ain't asked if the little grille in the floor there leads into the sewers,' the warder prompted.

Rincewind peered between his fingers. 'Does it?'

'We ain't got any sewers.'

'Thank you. You've been very helpful.'

The warden strolled off again, whistling.

Rincewind lay back on the bunk and closed his eyes again.

'Baah!'

'Shut up.'

'scuse me, mister . . .'

Rincewind groaned and sat up again. This time the voice was coming from the high, small, barred window.

'Yes, what is it?'

'Yew know when you was caught?'

'Well? What about it?'

'Er . . . what kind of a tree were you under?'

Rincewind looked up at the narrow square of blue the prisoner calls the sky. 'What kind of question is that to ask me?'

'It's for the ballad, see? Only it'd help if it was a name with three syllables . . .'

'How do I know? I didn't stop for a bit of botany!'

'All right, all right, fair enough,' said the hidden speaker. 'But would you mind telling me what you was doing just before you stole the sheep?'

'I didn't steal the sheep!'

'Right, right, okay . . . What was you doing just before you didn't steal the sheep . . . ?'

'I don't know, I can't remember!'

'Were you boiling your billy, by any chance?'

'I'm not admitting to that! The way you people talk, that could mean *anything*!'

'Means cookin' something up in a tin.'

'Oh. Well, yes, I had been doing that, as it happens.'

'Good on yer!' Rincewind thought he heard the sound of scribbling. 'Shame you didn't die at the end, but you're gonna get hung so that's all right. Got a beaut tune for this one, you just can't stop whistling it . . . Well, of course *you* will, no worries.'

'Thank you for that.'

'Reckon you might be as famous as Tinhead Ned, mate.'

'Really.' Rincewind went and lay down on his bunk again.

'Yeah. They used to lock him up in that very cell you're in now, in fact. And he always escaped. No one knows how, 'cos that's a bloody good lock and he didn't bend any bars. He said they'd never build a jail that could hold him.'

'Thin fellow, was he?'

'Nope.'

'So he had a key or something.'

'Nope. Got to go now, mate. Oh, yeah, I remember. Er, do you think your ghost will be heard if people pass by the billybong, or not?'

'What?'

'It'd be helpful if it did. Makes a good last verse. Top stuff.'

'I don't know!'

'We-ell, I'll say it will, shall I? No one's gonna go back and check.'

'Don't let me stand in your way, then.'

'Bonza. I'll get these songsheets printed up

in time for the hanging, don't you worry about that.'

'I won't.'

Rincewind lay back. Tinhead Ned again. That was just a joke, he could spot it. It was some kind of torture, telling him that anyone had ever escaped from a cell like this. They wanted him to run around rattling bars and things, but even he could see they were well set in and very heavy and the lock was bigger than his head.

He was just lying back on the bunk again when the warder turned up.

There were a couple of men with him. Rincewind was pretty sure there weren't any trolls here, because it was probably too hot for them and anyway there wouldn't be enough room for them on the driftwood, what with all those camels, but these men definitely had the heavy-set look of men who occupy the kind of job where the entrance examination is 'What is your name?' and they scrape through on the third try.

The warder was wearing a big grin and carrying a tray. 'Got some dinnah for you,' he said.

'I won't tell you anything, no matter how much you feed me,' Rincewind warned.

'You'll like this,' the warder urged, pushing the tray forward. There was a covered bowl on it. 'I done it special for you. It's a regional speciality, mate.'

'I thought you said bread and water's what you're good at.'

'Well, yeah . . . but I had a bash at this anyway . . .'

Rincewind watched gloomily as the warder lifted the cover.*

It looked fairly inoffensive, but they often did. It looked, in fact, like—

'Pea soup?' he said.

'Yep.'

'The leguminous vegetable? Comes in pods?'

'Yep.'

'I thought I'd better check that point.'

'No worries.'

Rincewind looked down at the knobbly green surface. Was it just possible that someone had invented a regional speciality you could eat?

And then something rose out of the depths. For a moment Rincewind thought it was a very small shark. It bobbed to the surface and then settled back down, while the soup slopped over it.

'What was *that*?'

'Meat pie floater,' said the warder. 'Meat pie floating in pea soup. Best bloody supper on earth, mate.'

'Ah, *supper*,' said Rincewind, as realization dawned. 'This is another one of those late-night, after-the-pub foods, right? And what kind of meat is in it? No, forget I asked, it's a stupid question. I know this sort of food. If you have to ask "What kind of meat is in

---

* Any seasoned traveller soon learns to avoid anything wished on them as a 'regional speciality', because all the term means is that the dish is so unpleasant the people living everywhere else will bite off their own legs rather than eat it. But hosts still press it upon distant guests anyway: 'Go on, have the dog's head stuffed with macerated cabbage and pork noses – it's a regional speciality.'

it?" you're too sober. Ever tried spaghetti and custard?'

'Can you sprinkle coconut on top of it?'

'Probably.'

'Thanks, mate, I'll surely give it a go,' said the warder. 'Got some other good news for you, too.'

'You're letting me out?'

'Oh, you wouldn't want that, a hard-bitten larrikin like yourself. Nah, Greg and Vince here will be coming back later to put you in irons.'

He stepped aside. The wall-shaped men were holding a length of chain, several shackles and a small but very, very heavy-looking ball.

Rincewind sighed. One door closes, he thought, and another door slams shut. 'This is good, is it?' he said.

'Oh, yew'll get an extra verse for that, for sure,' said the warder. 'No one's been hung in irons since Tinhead Ned.'

'I thought there wasn't a prison cell that could hold him,' said Rincewind.

'Oh, he could get *out* of 'em,' said the warder. 'He just couldn't run very far.'

Rincewind eyed the metal ball. 'Oh, gods . . .'

'Vince says how much do you weigh, 'cos he has to add the chains to your weight to get the drop right,' said the warder.

'Does that matter?' said Rincewind in a hollow voice. 'I mean, I die anyway, don't I?'

'Yeah, no worries there, but if he gets it wrong, see, you either end up with a neck six feet long or, you'll laugh about this, your head flies off like a perishin' cork!'

'Oh, good.'

'With Larrikin Larry we had to search the roof all arvo!'

'Marvellous. All arvo, eh?' said Rincewind. 'Well, you won't have that problem with me. I shall be elsewhere when I'm being hanged.'

'That's what we like to hear!' said the warder, punching him jovially in the elbow. 'A battler to the end, eh?'

There was a rumbling from Mt Vince.

'And Vince says he'll be very privileged if you'd care to spit in his eye when he puts the rope aroun' your neck,' the warder went on. 'That'll be something to show his grandchildren—'

'Will you all please go away!' Rincewind shouted.

'Ah, you'll be wanting some time to plot your getaway,' said the warder knowingly. 'No worries. We'll be leavin' you alone, then.'

'Thank you.'

'Until about five a.m.'

'Good,' said Rincewind gloomily.

'Got any requests for your last breakfast?'

'Something that takes a really really long time to prepare?' said Rincewind.

'That's the spirit!'

'Go away!'

'No worries.'

The men walked off, but the warder strolled back after a while as if he had something on his mind.

'There *is* something that you ought to know about

the hanging, though,' he said. 'Might brighten up your night.'

'Yes?'

'We've got a special humanitarian tradition if the trapdoor sticks three times.'

'Yes?'

'Sounds a bit odd, but it's happened once or twice, believe it or not.'

A tiny green shoot rose from the blackened branches of hope.

'And what's the tradition?' said Rincewind.

'It's on account of it being heartless to have a man standing there more than three times, knowing that at any second his—'

'Yes, yes—'

'—and then all his—'

'Yes—'

'—and the worst part to my mind is where your—'

'Yes, I understand! And so . . . after the third time . . . ?'

'He's allowed back into his cell while we get a carpenter in to repair the trapdoor,' said the warder. 'We even give him his dinner, if it's gone on a long time.'

'And?'

'Well, when the carpenter's given it a good test, then we take him out again and hang him.' He saw Rincewind's expression. 'No need to look like that. 's better than having to stand around in the cold all morning, isn't it? That wouldn't be nice.'

When he'd gone, Rincewind sat and stared at the wall.

'Baa!'

'Shut up.'

So it was down to this, then. One brief night left, and then, if these clowns had anything to do with it, happy people would be wandering the streets to see where his head had come down. There was no justice!

G'DAY, MATE.

'Oh, no. *Please.*'

I JUST THOUGHT I SHOULD ENTER INTO THE SPIRIT OF THE THING. A VERY CONVIVIAL PEOPLE, AREN'T THEY? said Death. He was sitting beside Rincewind.

'You just can't wait, can you?' said Rincewind bitterly.

NO WORRIES.

'So this is really it, then. I was *supposed* to have saved this country, you know. And I'm going to really die.'

OH, YES. THIS IS CERTAIN, I'M AFRAID.

'It's the stupidity of it that gets me. I mean, think of all the times I've nearly died in the past. I could've been flamed by dragons, right? Or eaten by huge things with tentacles. Or even had every single particle of my body fly off in a different direction.'

YOU HAVE CERTAINLY HAD AN INTERESTING LIFE.

'Is it true that your life passes before your eyes before you die?'

YES.

'Ghastly thought, really.' Rincewind shuddered. 'Oh, *gods*, I've just had another one. Suppose I *am* just about to die and *this* is my whole life passing in front of my eyes?'

I THINK PERHAPS YOU DO NOT UNDERSTAND. PEOPLE'S WHOLE LIVES *DO* PASS IN FRONT OF THEIR EYES BEFORE THEY DIE. THE PROCESS IS CALLED 'LIVING'. WOULD YOU LIKE A PRAWN?

Rincewind looked down at the bucket on Death's lap.

'No, thank you. I really don't think so. They can be pretty deadly. And I must say it's a bit much of you to come here and gloat and eat prawns at me.'

I BEG YOUR PARDON?

'Just because I'm being hanged in the morning, I mean.'

ARE YOU? THEN I SHALL LOOK FORWARD TO HEARING HOW YOU ESCAPED. I'M DUE TO MEET A MAN IN . . . IN . . . Death's eyesockets glowed as he interrogated his memory. AH, YES . . . INSIDE A CROCODILE. SEVERAL HUNDRED MILES AWAY, I BELIEVE.

'What? Then why are you here?'

OH, I THOUGHT YOU MIGHT LIKE TO SEE A FRIENDLY FACE. AND NOW I THINK I HAD BETTER BE GOING. Death stood up. VERY PLEASANT CITY IN MANY RESPECTS. TRY TO SEE THE OPERA HOUSE WHILE YOU'RE HERE.

'Hang on . . . I mean, hold on, you told me I was certainly going to die!'

EVERYONE IS. EVENTUALLY.

The wall opened and closed around Death as if it wasn't there, which was, from his lengthy perspective, quite true.

'But *how?* I can't walk through—' Rincewind began.

He sat down again. The sheep cowered in the corner.

Rincewind looked at the untouched meat pie floater and gave the pie a prod. It sank slowly beneath the vivid green soup.

The sounds of the city filtered in.

After a while the pie rose again like a forgotten continent, sending a very small wave slopping against the edge of the bowl.

Rincewind lay back on the thin blanket and stared at the ceiling. Someone had even been writing on that, too. In fact . . .

Gdy mat. Look at the hinjis. Ned.

Slowly, as if being raised by invisible strings, Rincewind turned and looked at the door.

The hinges were massive. They weren't screwed into the doorframe so that some clever prisoner might unscrew them. They were huge iron hooks, hammered into the stone itself, so that two heavy rings welded on to the door could drop right down on them. What was the man talking about?

He walked over and examined the lock closely. It drove a huge metal rod into the frame on its side and looked quite unpickable.

Rincewind stared at the door for some time. Then he rubbed his hands together and, gritting his teeth, tried to lift the door on the hinge side. Yes, there was just enough play . . .

It was possible to lift the rings off the spikes.

Then, if you pulled slightly and took a knee-wobbling step *this* way, you could yank the lock's rod out of its hole and the entire door into the cell.

And then a man could walk through and carefully rehang the door again and quietly wander away.

And that, Rincewind thought as he carefully manoeuvred the door back on to the hinges, was exactly what a stupid person would do.

At moments like this cowardice was an exact science. There were times that called for mindless, terror-filled panic, and times that called for measured, considered, *thoughtful* panic. Right now he was in a place of safety. It was, admittedly, the death cell, but the point was that it was perhaps the one place in this country where nothing bad was going to happen for a little while. The Ecksians didn't look like the kind of people who went in for torture, although it was always possible they might make him eat some more of their food. So, for the moment, he had *time*. Time to plan ahead, to consider his next move, to apply his intellect to the problem at hand.

He stared at the wall for a moment, and then stood up and gripped the bars.

Right. That seemed to be about long enough. Now to run like hell.

The green deck of the melon boat had been divided into a male and female section, for the sake of decency. This meant that most of the deck was occupied by Mrs Whitlow, who spent a lot of the time sunbathing behind a screen. Her privacy was assured by the wizards themselves, since at least three of them would probably kill any of the others who ventured within ten feet of the palm leaves.

There was definitely what Ponder's aunt, who'd raised him, would have called An Atmosphere.

'I still think I ought to climb the mast,' he protested.

'Ah! A peeping tom, eh?' snarled the Senior Wrangler.

'No, I just think it would be a good idea to see where the boat is going,' said Ponder. 'There're some big black clouds ahead.'

'Good, we could do with the rain,' snapped the Chair of Indefinite Studies.

'In which case, I shall be honoured to make Mrs Whitlow a suitable shelter,' said the Dean.

Ponder walked back to the stern, where the Archchancellor was gloomily fishing.

'Honestly, you'd think Mrs Whitlow was the only woman in the world,' he said.

'Do you think she might be?' said Ridcully.

Ponder's mind raced, and hit some horrible speed bumps in his imagination. 'Surely not, sir!' he said.

'We don't *know*, Ponder. Still, look on the bright side. We may all be drowned.'

'Er . . . sir? Have you *looked* at the horizon?'

The everlasting storm was seven thousand miles long but only a mile wide, a great turning, boiling mass of enraged air circling the last continent like a family of foxes circling a henhouse.

The clouds were mounded up all the way to the edge of the atmosphere – and they were ancient clouds now, clouds that had rolled around their tortured circuit for years, building up personality and hatred and, above all, voltage.

It was not a storm, it was a battle. Mere gales, a few hundred miles long, fought amongst themselves within the cloud wall. Lightning forked from thunderhead to thunderhead, rain fell and flashed into steam half a mile from the ground.

The air glowed.

And below, emerging from the ocean of potentiality in a rainstorm so thunderous that it was no more than a descending sea, rose the last continent.

On the wall of the deserted cell in Bugarup Gaol, among the scratches and stick drawings and tallies of a man's last few days, a drawing of a sheep became a drawing of a kangaroo and then faded completely into the stone.

'So?' said the Dean. 'We're in for a bit of a blow?'

The grey line filled the immediate future like a dental appointment.

'I think it might be a lot worse,' said Ponder.

'Well, let's steer somewhere else, then.'

'There's no rudder, sir. And we don't know where anywhere else *is*. And we're low on water anyway.'

'Don't they say that a big bank of cloud means there's land ahead?' said the Dean.

'Bloody big land, then. EcksEcksEcksEcks, do you think?'

'I hope so, sir.' Above Ponder, the sail flapped and billowed. 'Wind's freshening, sir. I think the storm's sucking the air towards it. And . . . there's something else, I think. I wish I hadn't left my thaumometer on the beach, sir, because I think there's a very high level of background magic in this area.'

'What makes you say this, boy?' said the Dean.

'Well, for one thing everyone seems to be getting a bit tense, and wizards tend to get stro— to get touchy in the presence of large amounts of magic,' said Ponder. 'But my suspicions were first aroused when the Bursar developed planets.'

There were two of them, orbiting his head at a height of a few inches. As was so often the case with magical phenomena, they possessed virtual unreality and passed unscathed through him and one another. They were slightly transparent.

'Oh dear, Mugroop's Syndrome,' said Ridcully. 'Cerebral manifestation. Better than a canary down a coalmine, a sign like that.'

A little sub-routine in Ponder's head began a short countdown.

'Remember old "Dicky" Bird?' said the Chair of Indefinite Studies. 'He—'

'Three! No, I don't, as a matter of fact. Do tell!' Ponder heard himself bark, louder than he would have done even if he *had* meant to vocalize his thoughts.

'Indeed I shall, Mister Stibbons,' said the Chair calmly. 'He was very susceptible to high magical fields, and if his mind wandered, as it might do when he was dozing off, sometimes around his head there'd be, hehehe, there'd be these little—'

'Yes, certainly,' said Ponder, quickly. 'We'll have to be very careful to keep an eye open for unusual behaviour.'

'Among wizards?' said Ridcully. 'Mister Stibbons, unusual behaviour is perfectly ordinary for wizards.'

'People acting out of character, then!' Ponder shouted. 'Talking sense for two minutes together, perhaps! Acting like normal civilized people instead of a herd of self-regarding village idiots!'

'Stibbons, it's not like you to take *that* tone,' said Ridcully.

'That's what I mean!'

'Now then, Mustrum, go easy on him, we're all under a lot of stress,' said the Dean.

'Now *he's* doing it!' Ponder yelled, pointing a shaking finger. 'The Dean is normally *never* nice! Now he's being aggressively reasonable!'

Historians have pointed out that it is in times of plenty that people feel like going to war. In times of famine they're simply trying to find enough to eat. When they've just enough to go round they tend to be polite. But when a banquet is spread before them, it's time to argue over the place settings.*

And Unseen University, as even wizards realized at somewhere just below the top level of their minds,

---

* In fact it's the view of the more thoughtful historians, particularly those who have spent time in the same bar as the theoretical physicists, that the entirety of human history can be considered as a sort of blooper reel. All those wars, all those famines caused by malign stupidity, all that determined, mindless repetition of the same old errors, are in the great cosmic scheme of things only equivalent to Mr Spock's ears falling off.

existed not to further magic but, in a very creative way, to suppress it. The world had seen what happened when wizards got their hands on enormous amounts of magical power. It had happened a long time ago and there were still some areas where you didn't go, if you wanted to walk out on the same kind of feet that you'd had when you went in.

Once upon a time the plural of 'wizard' was 'war'.

But the great, open ingenious purpose of UU was to be the weight on the arm of magic, causing it to swing with grave majesty like a pendulum rather than spin with deadly purpose like a morningstar. Instead of hurling fireballs at one another from fortified towers the wizards learned to snipe at their colleagues over the interpretation of Faculty Council minutes, and long ago were amazed to find that they got just as much vicious fun out of it. They consumed big dinners, and after a really good meal and a fine cigar even the most rabid Dark Lord is inclined to put his feet up and feel amicable towards the world, especially if it's offering him another brandy. And slowly, and by degrees, they absorbed the most important magical power of all, which is the one that persuades you to stop using all the others.

The trouble is that it's easy to abstain from sweets when you're not standing knee deep in treacle and it's raining sugar.

'There does indeed seem to be a certain . . . tang in the air,' said the Lecturer in Recent Runes. Magic tastes like tin.

'Hold on a moment,' said Ridcully. He reached up,

pulled open one of the many drawers in his wizarding hat, and removed a cube of greenish glass.

'Here we are,' he said, handing it to Ponder.

Ponder took the thaumometer and peered into it.

'Never used it myself,' Ridcully said. 'Wetting a finger and holding it up has always been good enough for me.'

'It's not working!' said Ponder, tapping the thaumometer as the ship rocked under them. 'The needle's . . . Oow!'

He dropped the cube, which was molten by the time it hit the deck.

'That's impossible!' he said. 'These things are good up to a million thaums!'

Ridcully licked his finger and held it up. It sprouted a halo of purple and octarine.

'Yep, that's about right,' he said.

'There's not that much magic anywhere any more!' shouted Ponder.

There was a gale behind the boat now. Ahead, the wall of storm was widening and seemed to be a lot blacker.

'How much magic does it take to create a continent?' said Ridcully.

They looked up at the clouds. And further up.

'We'd better batten down the hatches,' said the Dean.

'We don't have any hatches.'

'Batten down Mrs Whitlow at least. Get the Bursar and the Librarian somewhere safe—'

They hit the storm.

* * *

Rincewind dropped into an alley and reflected that he'd been in far worse prisons. The Ecksians were a friendly lot, when not drunk or trying to kill you or both. What Rincewind looked for in a good gaol were guards who, instead of ruining everyone's night by prowling around the corridors, got together in one room with a few tins and a pack of cards and relaxed. It made it so much more . . . friendly. And, of course, easier to walk past.

He turned – and there *was* the kangaroo, huge and bright and outlined against the sky. Rincewind shrank back for a moment and then realized that it was nothing but an advertising sign on the roof of a building some way off and further down the hill. Someone had rigged up lamps and mirrors below it.

It had a hat on, with some stupid holes for its ears to stick out, and it wore a vest as well, but it was certainly *the* kangaroo. No other kangaroo could possibly smirk like that. And it was holding a tin of beer.

'Where did you drift in from, curly?' said a voice behind him.

It was a very familiar voice. It had a sort of complaining wheedle in it. It was a voice that kept looking out of the corners of its eyes and was always ready to dodge. It was a voice you could have used to open a bottle of whine.

He turned. And the figure in front of him, except for a few details, was as familiar as the voice.

'You *can't* be called Dibbler,' said Rincewind.

'Why not?'

'Because— Well, how did you get *here*?'

'What? I just came up Berk Street,' said the figure. It had a large hat, and large shorts, and large boots, but in every other respect it was the double of the man who, in Ankh-Morpork, was always there after the pubs shut to sell you one of his very special meat pies. Rincewind had a theory that there was a Dibbler everywhere.

Suspended from the neck of this one was a tray. On the front of the tray was written 'Dibbler's Café de Feet.'

'I reckoned I'd better get up to the gaol early for a good pitch,' said Dibbler. 'Always gives the crowd an appetite, a good hanging. Can I interest you in anything, mate?'

Rincewind looked at the end of the alley. The streets were quite busy. As he watched, a couple of guards strolled by.

'Such as what?' he said suspiciously, drawing back into the shadows.

'Got some good broadsheet ballads about the notorious outlaw they're gonna top . . . ?'

'No, thank you.'

'Souvenir piece of the rope they're gonna hang him with? Authentic!'

Rincewind looked at the short length of thick string being dangled hopefully in front of him. 'Some people might say that had a hint of clothesline about it,' he said.

Dibbler gave the string a look of extreme interest.

'Obviously we had to unravel it a bit, mate,' he said.

'And some people might pick holes in the suggestion that you could, philosophically speaking, sell lengths of the rope *before* the hanging?'

Dibbler paused, his smile not moving. Then he said, 'It's the rope, right? Three-quarter-inch hemp, the usual stuff. Authentic. Probably even from the same ropemaker. Come on, all I'm looking for here is a fair go. Probably it's a pure fluke this ain't the actual bit that's gonna go round his neck—'

'That's only half an inch thick. Look, I can *see* the label, it says "Hill's Clothesline Co."'

'Does it?'

Once again Dibbler appeared to be looking at his product for the first time. But the traditions of the Dibbler clan would never let a mere disastrous fact get in the way of a spiel.

'It's still rope,' he averred. 'Authentic rope. No? No worries. How about some authentic native art?'

He rummaged in his crowded tray and held up a square of cardboard. Rincewind gave it an appraising look.

He'd seen something like this out in the red country, although he'd not been certain that it was art in the way Ankh-Morpork understood it. It was more like a map, a history book and a menu all rolled together. Back home, people tied a knot in their handkerchief to remind them of things. Out in the hot country there weren't any handkerchiefs, so people tied a knot in their thoughts.

They didn't paint very many pictures of a string of sausages.

''s called *Sausage and Chips Dreaming*,' said Dibbler.

'I don't think I've seen one like that,' said Rincewind. 'Not with the sauce bottle in it as well.'

'So what?' said Dibbler. 'Still native. Genuine picture of traditional city tucker, done by a native. A fair go, that's all I ask.'

'Ah, suddenly I think I understand. The native in this case, perhaps, being you?' said Rincewind.

'Yep. Authentic. You arguing?'

'Oh, come *on*.'

'What? I was born over there in Treacle Street, Bludgeree, and so was my dad. And my granddad. And his dad. I didn't just step off the driftwood like some people I might mention.' His ratty little face darkened. 'Coming over here, taking our jobs ... What about the little man, eh? All I'm askin' for is a fair go.'

For a moment Rincewind contemplated handing himself over to the Watch.

'Nice to hear someone siding with the rights of the indigenous population,' he muttered, checking the street again.

'Indigenous? What do they know about a day's work? Nah, they can go back where they came from too,' said Dibbler. 'They don't *want* to work.'

'Good thing for you, though, I can see that,' said Rincewind. 'Otherwise they'd be taking your job, right?'

'The way I see it, I'm more indigenous than them,'

said Fair Go, pointing an indignant thumb at himself. 'I *earned* my indigenuity, I did.'

Rincewind sighed. Logic could take you only so far, then you had to get out and hop. 'A fair go, that's what you want,' he said. 'Am I right?'

'Yep!'

'So . . . is there anyone who you don't want to go back where they came from?'

Fair Go Dibbler gave this some deep consideration. 'Well, me, *obviously*,' he said. 'And my mate Duncan, 'cos Duncan's me mate. And Mrs Dibbler, of course. And some of the blokes down at the fish and chip shop. Lots of people, really.'

'Well, I'll tell you what,' said Rincewind. 'I *definitely* want to go back where I came from.'

'Good on yer!'

'Your socio-political analysis is certainly working on me.'

'Beaut!'

'And maybe you can show me how? Like, where the docks are?'

'Well, I *would*,' said Dibbler, obviously torn. 'Only there's going to be this hanging in a few hours and I want to get the meat pies warmed up.'

'As a matter of fact, I heard the hanging had been cancelled,' said Rincewind, conspiratorially. 'The bloke escaped.'

'Never!'

'He certainly did!' said Rincewind. 'I'm not pulling your raw prawn.'

'Did he have any last words?'

' "Goodbye," I think.'

'You mean he wasn't in a famous last-stand shoot-out with the Watch?'

'Apparently not.'

'What kind of escape is that?' said Fair Go. 'That's no way to behave. I didn't have to come up here, I gave up a good spot at the Galah for this. 's not a good hanging without a meat pie.' He leaned closer and gave a furtive look both ways before continuing: 'Say what you like, the Galah's good for business. Their money's the same as anyone else's, that's what I say.'

'Well . . . yes. Obviously. Otherwise it'd be . . . different money,' said Rincewind. 'So, since your night's ruined, why not just show me where the docks are?'

There was still some uncertainty in Dibbler's stance. Rincewind swallowed. He'd faced spiders, angry men with spears and bears that dropped on you out of trees, but now the continent was presenting him with its most dangerous challenge.

'Tell you what,' he said, 'I'll . . . I'll even . . . *buy* . . . something off you?'

'The rope?'

'Not the rope. Not the rope. Um . . . I know this may seem a somewhat esoteric question, but what's in the meat pies?'

'Meat.'

'And what kind of meat?'

'Ah, you want one of the *gourmet* meat pies, then?'

'Oh, I *see*. That's where you say what's in them?'

'Yup.'

'Before or after the customers have bitten into them?'

'Are you suggesting that my pies ain't right?'

'Let us say I'm inching my way to the possibility that they might be, shall we? All right, I'll try a *gourmet* pie.'

'Good on yer.' Dibbler removed a pie from the little heated section of his tray.

'Now . . . what's the meat? Cat?'

'Do you mind? Mutton's cheaper'n cat,' said Dibbler, upending the pie into a dish.

'Well, that's—' Rincewind's face screwed up. 'Oh, no, you're pouring pea soup all over it too. Why does everyone always pour pea soup over it!'

'No worries, mate. Puts a lining on your stomach,' said Dibbler, producing a red bottle.

'And what's *that*?'

'The *cut de grass*, mate.'

'You're tipping a meat pie into a dish of pea soup and now you want me to eat it with . . . with tomato sauce on it?'

'Pretty colours, ain't they?' said Fair Go, handing Rincewind a spoon.

Rincewind prodded the pie. It rebounded gently off the side of the dish.

Well, now . . . He'd eaten Cut-Me-Own-Throat Dibbler's sausages-in-a-bun, and Disembowel-Meself-Honourably Dibhala's funny-coloured antique eggs. And he'd survived, although there had been a few minutes when he'd hoped he wouldn't.

He'd eaten Al-Jiblah's highly suspicious cous-cous, drunk the terrible yak-butter tea made by May-I-Never-Achieve-Enlightenment Dhiblang, forced down the topless, bottomless smorgasbord of Dib Diblossonson and tried not to chew the lumps of unmentionable blubber purveyed by May-I-Be-Kicked-In-My-Own-Ice-Hole Dibooki (his stomach heaved at the memory of that – after all, it was one thing to butcher dead beached whales and quite another just to leave them there until they exploded into bite sized chunks of their own accord). As for the green beer made by Swallow-Me-Own-Blowdart Dlang-Dlang . . .

He'd drunk and eaten all these things. Everywhere in the world, someone turned up out of some strange primal mould to sell him a really dreadful regional delicacy. And this was just a pie, after all. How bad could it be? No, put it another way . . . *How much worse* could it be?

He swallowed a mouthful.

'Good, eh?' said Fair Go.

'My gods,' said Rincewind.

'They're not just any mushy peas,' said Fair Go, slightly disconcerted by the fact that Rincewind was staring wildly at nothing. 'They're mushed by a champion pea musher.'

'Good *grief* . . .' said Rincewind.

'Are you all right, mister?'

'It's . . . everything I expected . . .' said Rincewind.

'Now, mister, it ain't that bad—'

'You're certainly a Dibbler.'

'What kind of thing is that to say?'

'You put pies upside down in runny peas and then put sauce on them. Someone actually sat down one day, after midnight if I'm any judge, and thought that would be a good idea. No one will ever believe *this* one.' Rincewind looked at the submerged pie. 'That's going to make the story about the land of the giant walking plum puddings look *very* tame, I don't mind telling you. No wonder you people drink so much beer . . .'*

He stepped out into the flickering lamplight of the street, shaking his head.

'You actually *eat* the pies here,' he said mournfully, and looked up into the face of the warder. There were several watchmen behind him.

'That's him!'

Rincewind nodded cheerfully. 'G'day!' he said.

Two little thuds were his home-made sandals bouncing on the street.

The sea steamed and crackling balls of lightning

---

* There is no such thing as an edible, nay delicious, meat pie floater, its mushy peas of just the right consistency, its tomato sauce piquant in its cheekiness, its pie filling tending even towards named parts of the animal. There are platonic burgers made of beef instead of cow lips and hooves. There are fish 'n' chips where the fish is more than just a white goo lurking at the bottom of a batter casing and you can't use the chips to shave with. There are hot dog fillings which have more in common with meat than mere pinkness, whose lucky consumers don't apply mustard because that would spoil the taste. It's just that people can be trained to prefer the other sort, and seek it out. It's as if Machiavelli had written a cookery book.

Even so, there is no excuse for putting pineapple on pizza.

zipped across its surface like drops of water on a hotplate.

The waves were too big to be waves, but about the right size for mountains. Ponder looked up from the deck only once, just as the boat began to slide down a trough that gaped like a canyon.

Next to him, and gripping his leg, the Dean groaned.

'You know about this sort of thing, Ponder,' he growled, as they hit the trough and then began the stomach-twisting climb to the next crest. 'Are we going to die?'

'I . . . don't think so, Dean . . .'

'Pity . . .'

Rincewind heard whistles blowing behind him by the time he reached the corner, but he never let that sort of thing worry him.

This was a city! Cities were so much easier. He was a creature of cities. There were so many places to—

Whistles started blowing up ahead as well.

The crowds were thicker here, and most people were heading in the same direction. But Rincewind *liked* crowds to run through. As the pursued, he had novelty on his side and could shoulder his way past the unsuspecting, who *then* turned around and milled about and complained and were definitely not in the right frame of mind to greet the people following him. Rincewind could run through a crowd like a ball on a bagatelle board, and always got an extra go.

Downhill was best. That's where they generally put docks, so as to have them close to the water.

Dodging and ducking across the streets brought him, suddenly, to the waterside. There were a few boats there. They were on the small side for a stow-away, but—

There were running footsteps in the dark!

These watchmen were too good!

This wasn't how it was supposed to go!

They weren't supposed to double-back. They weren't supposed to *think*.

He ran in the only direction left, along the waterfront.

There was a building there. At least, it . . . well, it had to be a building. No one could have left an open box of tissues that big.

Rincewind felt that a building should be a box with a pointed lid on it, basically, and it should be the approximate colour of whatever the local mud was. On the other hand, as the philosopher Ly Tin Wheedle once remarked, it is never wise to object to the decor of a hidey-hole.

He bounded up the steps and circled around the strange white building. It seemed to be some kind of music hall. Opera, by the sound of it, although it was a damn funny place to sing opera, you couldn't imagine ladies with horns in a building that looked about to set sail, but no time to wonder about that, there was a door with some rubbish bins outside it and here was the door *open* . . .

'You from the agency, mate?'

Rincewind peered into the steam.

'An' I hope you can do puddings, 'cos cheffy's banging his head on the wall,' went on a figure emerging from the wisps. It was wearing a tall white hat.

'No worries,' said Rincewind, hopefully. 'Ah, this is a *kitchen*, is it?'

'You pullin' my leg?'

'Only I thought it was some kind of opera house or something—'

'Best bloody opera house in the world, mate. Come on, this way . . .'

It wasn't a very big kitchen and, like most of the ones Rincewind had been in, it was full of men working very hard at cross purposes.

'The boss upstairs only decided to throw a big dinner for the prima donna,' said the cook, forcing his way through the throng. 'And all of a sudden Charley sees the pudding staring him in the face.'

'Ah, right,' said Rincewind, on the basis that sooner or later he'd be given a clue.

'Boss says, you can do the pudding for her, Charley.'

'Just like that, eh?'

'He sez, it ought to be the best one yet, Charley.'

'No worries?'

'He sez, the great Nunco invented the Strawberry Sackville for Dame Wendy Sackville, and the famous chef Imposo created the Apple Glazier for Dame Margyreen Glazier, and your own father, Charley, honoured Dame Janeen Ormulu with the Orange Ormulu and tonight, Charley, it's your big chance.' The cook shook his head as he reached a table where a small man in a white uniform was sobbing un-controllably into his hands. There was a stack of empty beer cans in front of him. 'Poor bastard's been on the beer ever since, and we thought we'd better get someone in. I'm a steak and prawns man, myself.'

'So, you want me to make a pudding? Named after an opera singer?' said Rincewind. 'That's the tradition, is it?'

'Yeah, and you'd better not let Charley down, mate. It's not *his* fault.'

'Oh, well . . .' Rincewind thought about puddings. Basically it was just fruit and cream and custard, wasn't it? And cakes and stuff. He couldn't see where the problem lay.

'No worries,' he said. 'I think I can knock up some-thing right away.'

The kitchen became silent as the scurrying cooks stopped to watch him.

'First,' said Rincewind, 'what fruit have we got?'

'Peaches was all we could find at this time of night.'

'No worries. And we've got some cream?'

'Yep. Of course.'

'Fine, fine. Then all I need to know is the name of the lady in question . . .'

He felt the silence open up.

'She's a beaut singer, mind you,' said a cook, in a defensive tone of voice.

'Good. And her name?' said Rincewind.

'Er . . . that's the trouble, see,' said another cook.

'Why?'

* * *

Ponder opened his eyes. The water was calm, or at least calmer than it had been. There were even patches of blue sky above, although cloud banks were criss-crossing the air as if each were in possession of its own bag of wind.

His mouth tasted as though he'd been sucking a tin spoon.

Around him, some of the wizards managed to push themselves to their knees. The Dean frowned, removed his hat, and pulled out a small crab.

''s a good boat,' he murmured.

The green mast stem still stood, although the leaf sail looked ragged. Nevertheless, the boat was tacking nicely against the wind off—

—the continent. It was a red wall, glowing under the thunder light.

Ridcully got uncertainly to his feet and pointed to it. 'Not far now!' he said.

The Dean actually growled. 'I've just about had enough of that insufferable cheerfulness,' he said. 'So just shut up, will you?'

'Enough of that. I am your Archchancellor, Dean,' said Ridcully.

'Well, let's just talk about that, shall we?' said the Dean, and Ponder saw the nasty gleam in his eye.

'This is hardly the time, Dean!'

'Exactly on what basis are you giving orders, Ridcully? You're the Archchancellor of what, precisely? Unseen University doesn't even *exist*! Tell him, Senior Wrangler!'

'I don't have to if I don't want to,' sniffed the Senior Wrangler.

'What? What?' snapped the Dean.

'I don't believe I have to take orders from you, Dean!'

When the Bursar climbed up on deck a minute later the boat was already rocking. It was hard to say how many factions there were, since a wizard is capable of being a faction all by himself, but there were broadly two sides, both liaisons being as stable as an egg on a seesaw.

What amazed Ponder Stibbons, when he thought about it later, was that no one had yet resorted to using magic. The wizards had spent a lot of time in an atmosphere where a cutting remark did more damage than a magic sword and, for sheer malign pleasure, a well structured memo could do more real damage than a fireball every time. Besides, no one had their staff, and no one had any spells handy, and in those circumstances it's easier to hit someone, although in the case of wizards non-magical fighting usually means flailing ineffectually at the opponent while trying to keep out of his way.

The Bursar's fixed smile faded a little.

'I got three per cent more than you in my finals!'

'Oh, and how do you know that, Dean?'

'I looked up the paper when you were appointed Archchancellor!'

'What? After forty years?'

'An examination is an examination!'

'Er . . .' the Bursar began.

'Ye gods, that's petty! That's just the sort of thing I'd expect from a student who even had a separate pen for red ink!'

'Hah! At least I didn't spend all my time drinking and betting and staying out at all hours!'

'Hah! *I* bloody well did, yes, and I learned the ways of the world and I still got nearly as many marks as you in spite of a prize-winning hangover, you puffed-up barrel of lard!'

'Oh? Oh? It's personal remarks now, is it?'

'Absolutely, Two-chairs! Let's have some personal remarks! We always said that walking behind you made people seasick!'

'I wonder if at this point . . .' said the Bursar.

The air crackled around the wizards. A wizard in a foul temper attracts magic like overripe fruit gets flies.

'You think I'd make a better Archchancellor, don't you, Bursar?' said the Dean.

The Bursar blinked his watery eyes. 'I, er, the two of you . . . er . . . many good points . . . er . . . perhaps this is the time to, er, make a common cause . . .'

They spent just a moment considering this.

'Well said,' said the Dean.

'Got a point,' said Ridcully.

'Because, you know, I've *never* liked the Lecturer in Recent Runes very much . . .'

'Smirks all the time,' Ridcully agreed. 'Not a member of the team.'

'Oh, really?' The Lecturer in Recent Runes put on a particularly evil smirk. 'At least I got higher marks than you and am noticeably thinner than the Dean!

Although a great many things are! Tell them, Stibbons!'

'That's *Mister* Stibbons, fatman!' Ponder heard the voice. He knew it was his. He felt as though he was hypnotized. He could stop any time he liked, it was just that he didn't quite feel like it.

'Could I just, er, say . . .' the Bursar tried.

'Shut up, Bursar!' roared Ridcully.

'Sorry, sorry. Sorry . . .'

Ridcully waved a finger at the Dean. 'Now you listen to me . . .'

A crimson spark leapt off his hand, left a trail of smoke past the Dean's ear, and hit the mast, which exploded.

The Dean took a deep breath, and when the Dean took a deep breath appreciably less air was left in the atmosphere. It was let out with a roar.

'*You dare fire magic at me?*'

Ridcully was staring at his hand. 'But I . . . I . . .'

Ponder finally managed to force the words out between teeth that were trying to clamp together.

'Er agic's egecting ug!'

'What? What are you gurgling about, man?' said the Lecturer in Recent Runes.

'I'll show you *magic*, you pompous clown!' screamed the Dean, raising both hands.

'It's the magic talking!' Ponder managed, grabbing one arm. 'You don't want to blow the Archchancellor to little pieces, Dean!'

'Yes, I damn well do!'

'Excuse me, Ai don't wish to intrude . . .' Mrs Whitlow's head appeared at the hatchway.

'What is it, Mrs Whitlow?' yelled Ponder, as a blast from the Dean's hand sizzled over his head.

'Ai know you are engaged on University business, but should there be all these cracks? The water is coming in.'

Ponder looked down. The deck creaked under his feet.

'We're sinking . . .' he said. 'You *stupid old*—' He bit down on the words. 'The boat is cracking up as fast as we are! Look, it's going yellow!'

The green was leaching from the deck like sunlight from a stormy sky.

'It's *his* fault!' the Dean screamed.

Ponder raced to the side. There were crackling noises all around him.

The important thing was to settle his mind and be calm and, possibly, think of nice things like blue skies and kittens. Preferably ones which weren't about to drown.

'Listen,' he said, 'if we don't sink our differences they'll sink us, understand? The boat's . . . ripening or something. And we're a long way from land, do you *understand*? And there could be sharks down there.'

He looked down. He looked up.

'*There's sharks down there!*' he shouted.

The boat tilted as the wizards joined him.

'*Are* they sharks, do you think?' said Ridcully.

'Could be tuna,' said the Dean. Behind them the remains of the sail fell away.

'How can you reliably tell the difference?' said the Senior Wrangler.

'You could count their teeth on the way down,' sighed Ponder. But at least no one was throwing magic around any more. You could take the wizards out of Unseen University, but you couldn't take the University out of the wizards.

The boat listed still further as Mrs Whitlow looked over the side.

'What happens if we fall in the water?' she said.

'We must devise a plan,' said Ridcully. 'Dean, form a working party to consider our survival in unknown, shark-infested waters, will you?'

'Should we swim for the shore?' said Mrs Whitlow. 'Ai was good at swimming as a gel.'

Ridcully gave her a warm smile. 'All in good time, Mrs Whitlow,' he said. 'But your suggestion has been taken aboard.'

'It's going to be the only thing that is, in a minute,' said Ponder.

'And what exactly will *your* role be, Archchancellor?' the Dean snarled.

'I have defined your objectives,' said Ridcully. 'It is up to you to consider the options.'

'In that case,' said the Dean, 'I move that we abandon ship.'

'What for?' said the Chair of Indefinite Studies. 'The sharks?'

'That is a secondary problem,' said the Dean.

'That's right,' said Ponder, 'we can always vote to abandon shark.'

The ship lurched suddenly. The Senior Wrangler struck a heroic pose.

'I will save you, Mrs Whitlow!' he cried, and swept her off her feet. Or, at least, made the effort. But the Senior Wrangler was lightly built for a wizard and Mrs Whitlow was a fine figure of a woman and, furthermore, the wizard's grip was limited by the fact that there were very few areas of Mrs Whitlow that he dared actually touch. He did his best with some out-lying regions and managed to lift her slightly. All this did was transfer the entire weight of wizard *and* housekeeper to the Senior Wrangler's quite small feet, which went through the deck like a steel bar.

The boat, dry as tinder now, soft as wood punk, fell apart very gently.

The water was extremely cold. Spray filled the air as they struggled. A piece of wreckage hit Ponder on the head and pushed him under, into a blue world where his ears went *gloing-gloing*.

When he struggled to the surface again this noise turned out to be an argument. Once again, the sheer magic of Unseen University triumphed. When tread-ing water in a circle of sharks, a wizard will always consider other wizards to be the most immediate danger.

'Don't blame *me*! He was . . . well, I think he was asleep!'

'You *think*?'

'He was a mattress. A red one!'

'He's the only Librarian we've got! How could you be so thoughtless!' shouted Ridcully. He took a deep breath, and dived.

'Abandon sea!' shouted the Bursar cheerfully.

Ponder shuddered as something big and black and streamlined rose out of the water in front of him. It sank back into the foam and flopped over.

Other shapes were bobbing to the surface all around the frantically treading wizards. The Dean tapped one.

'Well, these sharks don't seem anything like as dangerous as I expected,' he said.

'They're the seeds out of the boat!' said Ponder. 'Get on top of them, quickly!'

He was sure that something had brushed his leg. In those circumstances, a man finds unexpected agility. Even the Dean managed to get aboard a board, after a revolving, foamy period when man and seed fought for supremacy.

Ridcully surfaced in a shower of spray. 'It's no good!' he spluttered. 'I went down as far as I could. There's no sign of him!'

'Try and get on a seed, Archchancellor, do,' said the Senior Wrangler.

Ridcully flailed at a passing shark. 'They won't attack you if you make a lot of noise and splash around,' he said.

'I thought that's when they *will* attack you, sir,' Ponder called out.

'Ah, an interesting practical experiment,' said the Dean, craning to watch.

Ridcully hauled himself on to one of the seeds. 'What a mess. I suppose we can float to land, though,' he said. 'Er . . . where's Mrs Whitlow, gentlemen?'

They looked around.

'Oh, no . . .' the Senior Wrangler moaned. 'She's swimming for the shore . . .'

They followed his gaze, and could just see a hairdo moving jerkily yet determinedly towards the shore in what Ridcully would probably have referred to as a chest stroke.

'I don't call *that* very practical,' said the Dean. 'What about the sharks?'

'Well, they're swimming around under *us*, in fact,' said the Senior Wrangler, as the seeds rocked.

Ponder looked down. 'They appear to be leaving now that we're not dangling our legs in the water,' he said. 'They're heading . . . for the shore, too. '

'Well, she knew the risks when she got the job,' said the Dean.

'What?' said the Senior Wrangler. 'Are you saying that before you apply for the job of housekeeper of a university you should seriously consider being eaten by sharks on the shores of some mysterious continent thousands of years before you are born?'

'She didn't ask many questions at the interview, I know that.'

'Actually, we are worrying unduly,' said the Chair of Indefinite Studies. 'Sharks have a very undeserved reputation as man-eaters. There is not a single authenticated case of a shark attacking anyone, despite what you may have heard. They are sophisticated and peaceful creatures with a rich family life and, far from being ominous harbingers of doom, have reputedly even befriended the occasional lost traveller. As hunters they are of course very efficient, and a full-grown shark can bring down even a moose with . . . er . . .'

He looked at their faces.

'Er . . . I think I might perhaps have got them confused with wolves,' he mumbled. 'I have, haven't I?'

They nodded, in unison.

'Er . . . sharks are the other ones, aren't they?' he went on. 'The vicious and merciless killers of the sea that don't even stop to chew?'

They nodded again.

'Oh dear. Where can I put my face . . . ?'

'Some distance from a shark,' said Ridcully briskly. 'Come on, gentlemen. That's our housekeeper! Do you wish to make your own beds in future? Fireballs again, I think.'

'She's gone too far away—'

A red shape rocketed out of the sea beside Ridcully, curled through the air and slid below the surface again like a razorblade cutting into silk.

'What was that? Who of you did that?' he said.

A bow wave ripped its way to the cluster of tri-angular fins like a bowling ball heading down an alley. Then the water erupted.

'Ye gods, look at the way it's going at those sharks!'

'Is it a monster?'

'It's a dolphin, surely . . .'

'With red hair?'

'Surely it's not—'

A stricken shark barrelled past the Senior Wrangler. Behind it the water exploded again into the big red grin of the only dolphin ever to have a leathery face and orange hair all over its body.

'Eek?' said the Librarian.

'Well done, old chap!' shouted Ridcully across the water. 'I said you wouldn't let us down!'

'No, actually you didn't, sir, you said you thought—' Ponder began.

'Good choice of shape, too,' Ridcully continued loudly. 'Now, if you can sort of nudge us all together, then perhaps you could push us towards the shore? Are we all still here? Where's the Bursar?'

The Bursar was a small dot away on the right, paddling dreamily along.

'Well, he'll get there,' said Ridcully. 'Come on, let's get on to dry land.'

'That sea,' said the Senior Wrangler nervously, staring ahead as the seeds were jockeyed towards the shore like a string of overloaded barges, 'that sea . . . Does it look as though it's *girting* to you?'

'Certainly a very *big* sea,' said the Lecturer in Recent Runes. 'You know, I don't think it's just the rain that's making the roaring. There may be a spot of surf.'

'A few waves won't do us any harm,' said Ridcully. 'At least water is soft.'

Ponder felt the board underneath him rise and fall as a long swell passed. An odd shape for a seed, he had to admit. Of course, nature paid a lot of attention to seeds, equipping them with little wings and sails and flotation chambers and other devices necessary to give them an edge over all the other seeds. *These* were just flattish versions of the Librarian's current shape, which

311

was obviously intended for moving through water very fast.

'Er . . .' he said, to the universe in general. It meant: I wonder if we've really *thought* about this.

'Can't see any rocks ahead,' the Dean observed.

'Girting,' mused the Senior Wrangler, as if the word was nagging at him. 'That's a very *definite* sort of word, isn't it? Has a certain martial sort of sound.'

It occurred to Ponder that water is not *exactly* soft. He'd never been much of a one for sports when he was a boy, but he remembered playing with the other local lads and joining in all their games, such as Push Poncy Stibbons Into the Nettles or Tie Up Stibbo and Go Home for Tea, and there had been the time at the old swimming hole when they'd thrown him in off the top of the cliff. And it had *hurt*.

The flotilla gradually caught up with Mrs Whitlow, who was holding on to a floating tree and treading water. The tree already had its fair share of occupants – birds, lizards and, for some reason, a small camel trying to make itself comfortable in the branches.

The swell was heavier now. There was a deep, continuous booming underlying the noise of the rain.

'Ah, Mrs Whitlow,' said the Senior Wrangler. 'And what a nice tree. Even got leaves on, look.'

'We've come to save you,' said the Dean, in the face of the evidence.

'I think it might be a good idea if Mrs Whitlow hung on to a seed,' said Ponder. 'I really think that really might be a really good idea. I think the waves might be . . . slightly big . . .'

'Girting,' said the Senior Wrangler, morosely.

He looked towards the beach, and it wasn't ahead of them any more.

It was *down there*. It was at the bottom of a green hill. And the green was made of water. And, for some reason, it was getting taller.

'Look,' said Rincewind. 'Why can't you tell me her name? Presumably lots of people know it. I mean, it must be put on the posters and so on. It's only a name, isn't it? I don't see the problem.'

The cooks looked at one another. Then one coughed and said, 'She's . . . her name's . . . Dame Nellie . . . Butt.'

'But what?'

'Her name *is* Butt.'

Rincewind's lips moved silently. 'Oh,' he said.

The cooks nodded.

'Has Charley drunk all the beer, do you think?' Rincewind said, sitting down.

'Maybe we can find some bananas, Ron,' said another cook.

Rincewind's eyes unfocused and his lips moved again. 'Did you tell Charley that?' he said at last.

'Yep. Just before he broke down.'

There was the sound of running feet outside. One of the cooks looked out of the window.

'It's just the Watch. Probably after some poor bastard . . .'

Rincewind moved back slightly so that he was not obvious from the window.

Ron shuffled his feet. 'I reckon if we went and saw Idle Ahmed and got him to open up his shop we might get some—'

'Strawberries?' said Rincewind. The cooks shuddered. There was another sob from Charley.

'All his life he's been waiting for this,' said a cook. 'I call it bloody unfair. Remember when that little soprano left to marry that drover? He was miserable all week.'

'Yeah. Lisa Delight,' said Ron. 'A bit wobbly in mid-range but definitely showin' promise.'

'He was really pinning his hopes on her. He said a name like that'd even work with rhubarb.'

Charley howled.

'I think . . .' said Rincewind, slowly and thought-fully.

'Yes?'

'I think I can see a way.'

'You *can*?' Even Charley raised his head.

'Well, you know how it is, the outsider sees most of the game . . . Let's go with the peaches, the cream, a bit of ice cream if you can make it, maybe a dash of brandy . . . Let's see, now . . .'

'Coconut flakes?' said Charley, looking up.

'Yes, why not?'

'Er . . . some tomato sauce, maybe?'

'I think not.'

'You'd better get a move on, they're halfway through the last act,' said Ron.

'She'll be right,' said Rincewind. 'Okay . . . halve the peaches, put them in a bowl with the other things, and then add the brandy and *voilà*.'

'That some kind of foreign stuff?' said Charley. 'I don't think we've got any of that wollah.'

'Just add twice as much brandy, then,' said Rincewind. 'And there it *is*.'

'Yeah, but what's it *called*?' said Ron.

'I'm coming to that,' said Rincewind. 'Bowl, please, Charley. Thank you.' He held it aloft. 'Gentlemen . . . I give you . . . the Peach *Nellie*.'

A saucepan bubbled on a stove. Apart from that insistent little noise, and the distant strains of the opera, the room fell silent.

'What do you think?' said Rincewind brightly.

'It's . . . different . . .' said Charley. 'I'll grant you that.'

'But it's not exactly *commemorative*, is it?' said Ron. 'The world is full of Nellies.'

'On the other hand, would you prefer it if everyone remembered the alternative?' said Rincewind. 'Do you want to be associated in any way with the Peach Bu—'

There was a howl as Charley burst into tears again.

'Put like that, it doesn't sound too bad,' said Ron. 'Peach Nellie . . . yeah.'

'You could use bananas,' said Rincewind.

Ron's lips moved silently. 'Nah,' he said. 'Let's go with the peaches.'

Rincewind brushed himself off. 'Glad to be of service,' he said. 'Tell me. How many ways are there out of here?'

'Busy night for everyone, what with the Galah and everything,' said Ron. 'Not my taste, of course, but it does bring in the visitors.'

'Yeah, and the hanging in the morning,' said Charley.

'I was planning to miss that,' said Rincewind. 'Now, if you'll just—'

'I for one hope he escapes,' said Charley.

'I'm with you on that,' said Rincewind. Heavy boots walked past the door and stopped. He could hear distant voices.

'They say he fought a dozen policemen,' said Ron.

'Three,' said Rincewind. 'It was three. I heard. Someone told me. Not a dozen. Three.'

'Oh, gotta be more than three, gotta be a *lot* more than three for a bold bush ranger like that one. Rinso, they call him.'

'I heard where this bloke arrived from Dijabringabeeralong and said Rinso sheared a hundred sheep in five minutes.'

'I don't believe that,' said Rincewind.

'They *say* he's a wizard but that can't be true 'cos you never catch one of them doin' a proper job of work.'

'Well, in fact—'

'All right, but a bloke who works up at the gaol says he'd got this strange brown stuff which gives him enormous strength!'

'It was only beer soup!' shouted Rincewind. 'I mean,' he added, 'that's what I heard.'

Ron gave him a lopsided look. 'You look a *bit* like a wizard,' he said.

Someone knocked heavily on the door.

'You're wearing those dresses they wear,' Ron went

on, without taking his eyes off Rincewind. 'Go and open the door, Sid.'

Rincewind backed away, reached behind him to a table laden with knives, and found his fingers closing on a handle.

Yes, he hated the idea of weapons. They always, always, upped the ante. But they did impress people.

The door opened. Several men peered in, and one of them was the gaoler.

'That's him!'

'I warn you, I'm a desperate man,' Rincewind said, bringing his hand around. Most of the cooks dived for cover.

'That's a ladle, mate,' said a watchman, kindly. 'But bloody plucky, all the same. Good on yer. What do you think, Charley?'

'I reckon it's never going to be said that a bold larrikin like him was run to earth in a kitchen of mine,' said Charley. He picked up a cleaver in one hand and the dish of Peach Nellie in the other. 'You nip out the other door, Rinso, and we'll talk to these policemen.'

'Suits us,' said the watchman. ''s not a proper last stand, just having a punch-up in a kitchen . . . We'll give you a count to ten, all right?'

Once again Rincewind felt that he hadn't been given the same script as everyone else.

'You mean you've got me cornered and you aren't going to arrest me?' he said.

'We-ell, it wouldn't look good in the ballad, would it?' said the guard. 'You've got to think about these things.' He leaned on the doorway. 'Now, there's the old Post Office in Grurt Street. I reckon a man could hold out for two, maybe three days there, no worries. Then you could run out, we shoot you full of arrows, you utter some famous last words ... kids'll be learnin' about you in school in a hundred years' time, I'll bet. And look at yourself, willya?' He stepped forward, ignoring the deadly ladle, and prodded Rincewind's robe. 'How many arrows is that going to stop, eh?'

'You're all mad!'

Charley shook his head. 'Everyone likes a battler, mister. That's the Ecksian way. Go down fighting, that's the ticket.'

'We heard about you takin' on that road gang,' said the guard. 'Bloody good job. Man who'd do a job like that ain't gonna be hanged, he gonna want to make a famous last stand.'

The men had all entered the kitchen now. The doorway was clear.

'Has anyone ever had a Famous Last Run?' said Rincewind.

'No. What's one of them?'

'G'day!'

As he sped away along the darkened waterfront he heard the shout behind him.

'That's the ticket! We'll count to ten!'

He glanced up as he ran and saw that the big sign over the brewery seemed to be dark. And then he realized that something was hopping along just behind him.

'Oh, no! Not *you*!'

'G'day,' said Scrappy, drawing level.

'Look at the mess you've got me into!'

'Mess? You were gonna be hanged! Now you're enjoying the healthy fresh air in a god's own country!'

'And I'm going to be shot full of arrows!'

'So? You can *dodge* arrows. This place needs a hero. Champion shearer, road warrior, bush ranger, sheep-stealer, horse rider . . . all you need now is to be good at some damn silly bat and ball game that no one's invented yet and maybe build a few tall buildings with borrowed money and you'd have a full house. They ain't gonna kill *you* in a hurry.'

'That's not much comfort! Anyway, I didn't do any of that stuff— Well, I mean I *did*, but—'

'It's what people think that matters. Now they believe you waltzed out of a locked cell.'

'All I did was—'

'Doesn't matter! The number of gaolers who want to shake you by the hand, well, I reckon they wouldn't get around to hanging you by lunchtime!'

'Listen, you giant jumping rat, I've made it to the docks, okay? I can outrun them! I can lie low! I know how to stow away, throw up, get discovered, be thrown over the side, stay afloat for two days by clinging on to an old barrel and eating plankton sieved through my beard, carefully negotiate the treacherous coral reef surrounding an atoll and survive by eating yams!'

'That's a very special talent you got there,' said the kangaroo, bounding over a ship's hawser. 'How many

Ecksian ships have you ever seen in Ankh-Morpork? Busiest port in the world, ain't it?'

Rincewind slowed. 'Well . . .'

'It's the currents, mate. Get more'n ten miles off'f the coast here and there ain't one captain in a hundred who can stop his ship going right over the Rim. They stick very close inshore.'

Rincewind stopped. 'You mean this whole place is a *prison*?'

'Yep. But the Ecksians say this is the best bloody place in the world, so there's no point in going anywhere else anyway.'

There were shouts behind him. The guards here didn't take so long counting to ten as most guards did.

'What're you going to do now?' said Rincewind.

The kangaroo had gone.

He ducked down a side street and found his way completely blocked. Carts filled the street from edge to edge. Gaily decorated carts.

Rincewind paused. He had always been the foremost exponent of the *from* rather than the *to* of running. He could have *written* 'The From of Running'. But just occasionally a certain subtle sense told him that the *to* was important.

For one thing, a lot of the people standing and chatting around the carts were wearing leather.

You could make a lot of arguments in favour of leather. It was long-lasting, practical and hard-wearing. People like Cohen the Barbarian found it so hard-wearing and long-lasting that their old loincloths had to be removed by a blacksmith. But the people here didn't look as if these were the qualities that they'd been looking for in the boutique. They'd asked questions like: How many studs has it got? How shiny is it? Has it got holes cut out in unusual places?

But still, one of the most basic rules for survival on any planet is never to upset someone wearing black leather.* Rincewind sidled politely past them, giving them a friendly nod and a wave whenever he saw one looking in his direction. For some reason, this caused more of them to take an interest in him.

There were groups of ladies, too, and there was no doubt that if EcksEcksEcksEcks was where a man could stand tall, so could a woman. Some of them were nevertheless very pretty, in an overstated kind of way, although the occasional moustache looked out of place, but Rincewind had been to foreign parts and knew that things could be a bit lush in the more rural regions.

There were more sequins than you usually saw. More feathers, too.

Then it dawned on him in a great rush of relief.

'Oh, this is a *carnival*, right?' he said aloud. 'This is the Galah they keep talking about.'

'Pardon you?' said a lady in a spangly blue dress, who was changing the wheel on a large purple cart.

'These are carnival floats, aren't they?' said Rincewind.

The woman gritted her teeth, rammed the new

---

* This is why protesters against the wearing of animal skins by humans unaccountably fail to throw their paint over Hell's Angels.

wheel into place and then released the axle. The cart bounced down on to the cobbles.

'Damn, I think I broke a nail on that,' she said. She glanced at Rincewind. 'Yeah, this is *the* carnival. That dress has seen better days, hasn't it? Nice moustache, shame about the beard. It'd look good with a tint.'

Rincewind glanced back down the street. The floats and the press of people were hiding him from view, but this wouldn't last long.

'Er . . . could you help me, madam?' he said. 'Er . . . the Watch are after me.'

'They can be so tiresome like that.'

'There was a misunderstanding over a sheep.'

'There so often is, mate.' She looked Rincewind up and down. 'You don't look like a country boy, I must say.'

'Me? I get nervous when I see a blade of grass, miss.'

She stared at him. 'You . . . haven't been here very long, have you, Mister . . . ?'

'Rincewind, ma'am.'

'Well, get on the cart, Mister Rincewind. My name's Letitia.' She held out a rather large hand. He shook it, and then tried surreptitiously to massage some blood back into his fingers as he scrambled up.

The purple cart had been decorated with huge swathes of pink and lavender, and what looked like roses made out of paper. Boxes, also covered in cloth, had been set up in the centre to give a sort of raised dais.

'What d'you think?' said Letitia. 'The girls worked all arvo.'

The scheme was a bit too feminine for Rincewind's taste, but he'd been brought up to be polite. He snuggled down, as far out of view as possible.

'Very nice,' he said. 'Very gay.'

'Glad you think so.'

Up ahead somewhere a band started to play. There was a stirring as people got on to the floats or formed up to march. A couple of women climbed up into the purple cart, all sequins and long gloves, and stared at Rincewind.

'What the—' one began.

'Darleen – we have to talk,' said Letitia, from the front of the cart.

Rincewind watched them go into a huddle. Occasionally one of them would raise her head and give him an odd look, as if she was reassuring herself that he was here.

Fine big girls they had here, though. He wondered where they got their shoes from.

Rincewind was not intensively familiar with women. Quite a lot of his life that hadn't been spent at high speed had been passed within the walls of Unseen University, where women were broadly put in the same category as wallpaper or musical instruments – interesting in their way, and no doubt a small but important part of the proper structure of civilization but not, when you got right down to it, essential.

On these occasions when he had spent some time in the intimate company of a woman, it was generally when she was trying to either cut his head off or persuade him to a course of action that would probably get someone else to do it. When it came to women he was not, as it were, capable of much fine-tuning. A few neglected instincts were telling him that something was out of place, but he couldn't work out what it was.

The one addressed as Darleen strode down the cart with a decisive and rather aggressive air. Rincewind pulled his hat off respectfully.

'Are you coming the raw prawn?' she demanded.

'Me? Certainly not, miss. No prawns at all. If I can just lie low until we're a few streets away, that's all I ask—'

'You know what this is, don't you?'

'Yes, miss. The carnival.' Rincewind swallowed. 'No worries there. Everyone likes dressing up, don't they?'

'But are you tellin' me you really think . . . I mean we . . . What are you staring at my hair for?'

'Er . . . I was wondering how you get it so sparkly. Are you on the stage at all?'

'We're moving, girls,' Letitia called back. 'Remember . . . pretty smiles. Leave him alone, Darleen, you don't know where he's been.'

The third woman, the one the others had called Neilette, was watching him curiously, and Rincewind felt that there was something not right about her. Her hair *wasn't* drab, but it certainly appeared to be when compared with that of her colleagues. She didn't seem to have enough make-up. She seemed, in short, slightly out of place.

Then he caught sight of a watchman ahead, and flung himself below the edge of the cart. A gap in the boards gave him a view, as the cart turned the corner, of the waiting crowds.

He'd been to quite a number of carnivals, although not usually on purpose. He'd even attended Fat Lunchtime in Genua, generally regarded as the biggest in the world, although he vaguely recalled that he'd been hanging upside down under one of the floats in order to escape pursuers, but right now he couldn't quite remember why he'd been chased and it was never wise to stop and ask. Although Rincewind had covered quite a lot of the Disc in his life, most of his recollections were like that – a blur. Not through forgetfulness, but because of speed.

This looked like the usual audience. A real carnival procession should only take place after the pubs have been open for a good long time. It adds to the spontaneity. There were cheers, whistles, jeers and catcalls. Up ahead, people were blowing horns. Dancers whirled past Rincewind's peephole.

He sat back and pulled a swathe of taffeta over his head. This sort of thing always took up a lot of Watch time, what with pickpockets and so on. He'd wait until they were in whatever bit of wasteground these things always ended up in, and drop quietly out of sight.

He glanced down.

These ladies were certainly into shoes in a big way. They had *hundreds*.

Hundreds of shoes, all lined up, peeking out from under a heap of women's clothing. Rincewind looked away. There was probably something morally wrong about staring at women's clothes without women in them.

His head turned back and looked at the shoes again. He was sure that several of them had moved—

A bottle shattered near his head. Glass showered around him. Up above, Darleen uttered a word he'd never have expected on the lips of a lady.

Rincewind raised his head cautiously and another bottle bounced off his hat.

'Some hoonies having a bit of fun,' said Darleen, through gritted teeth. 'There's always some joker— *oh really?*'

'Give us a kiss, mister?' said a young man who'd leapt on to the edge of the cart, waving a beer can happily.

Rincewind had seen some serious fighters in action, but no one had ever swung a punch like Darleen. Her eyes narrowed, her fist seemed to travel in a complete circle, it met the man's chin about halfway round and when he disappeared from the wizard's view he was still rising.

'Will you look at that?' Darleen demanded, waving her hand at Rincewind. 'Ripped! These evening gloves cost a fortune, the bastard!' A beer can sailed past her ear. 'Didja see who threw that? Didja? I saw yer, yer mazza! I'll stick my hand down yer throat and pull yer trousers up!'

The crowd roared their appreciation and derision at the same time. Rincewind caught sight of watchmen's helmets heading purposefully towards them.

'Er . . .' he said.

'Hey, that's him! That's Rinso the bush ranger!' someone yelled, pointing.

'It wasn't bushes, it was just a sheep!'

Rincewind wondered who'd said that, and realized it was him. And there was no escape. And the watchmen were looking up at him. And there was *really* no escape. The street was packed. There was another fight further up the procession. There were no nearby alleyways, the fugitive's friend. And the watchmen were fighting their way through the throng, with great difficulty. And the crowd were having the time of their lives. And the huge kangaroo beer sign gleamed overhead.

This was it, then. Time for a Famous Last Stand.

'What?' he said aloud. 'It's *never* time for a Famous Last Stand!'

He turned to Letitia. 'I should just like to thank you for trying to help me,' he said. 'It's a pleasure to meet some real ladies for once.'

They looked at one another.

'The pleasure's all ours,' said Letitia. 'Such a change to meet a real gentleman, isn't it, girls?'

Darleen kicked a fishnet leg at a man trying to climb on the cart, causing with a stiletto heel what bromide in your tea is reputed to take several weeks to achieve.

'Too bloody true,' she said.

Rincewind leapt from the cart, landed on someone's shoulder, jumped again very briefly on to someone's head. It worked. Provided you kept moving, it really worked. A few hands grabbed at him and one or two cans were thrown, but there were also plenty of cries of 'Good on yer!' and 'That's the way!'

At last there was an alley. He jumped down from the last obliging shoulder and changed leg gear, and then found that the best way to describe the alley was as a cul-de-sac. The worst way was as an alley with three or four watchmen in it, who'd ducked in for a smoke.

They gave him that look of harassed policemen everywhere which said that, as an unwelcome intruder into their brief smoko, he was *definitely* going to be guilty of something. And then light dawned in the face of their sergeant.

'That's him!'

Out in the street people started yelling and screaming. These were not the beery shouts of the carnival. People were in real pain out there. They were also pressing in so tightly that there was no way out.

'I can explain everything,' said Rincewind, half aware of the growing noise. 'Well . . . most things. Some things, certainly. A few things. Look, about this sheep—'

Something brilliant passed over his head and landed on the cobbles between him and the guards.

It looked rather like a table wearing an evening dress, and it had hundreds of little feet.

They were wearing high heels.

Rincewind rolled into a ball and put his hands over his head, trying to block his ears until the noise had died away.

* * *

At the very edge of the sea, the surf bubbled and sucked at the sand. As the wavelet drew back it flowed around the splintered bulk of a tree.

The drifting wood's cargo of crabs and sand fleas waited for their moment and slid off cautiously, scuttling ashore ahead of the next wave.

The rain banged into the beach, running in miniature canyons of crumbling sand on its way to the sea. The crabs surged across these like a home-steaders' stampede, rushing to mark out territory on the endless, virgin beach.

They followed the salty tideline of weed and shells, scrambling over one another in their search for a space where a crab can proudly stand sideways and start a new life and eat the heady sand of freedom.

A few of them investigated a grey, sodden pointy hat that was tangled in seaweed, and then ran on to a more promising heap of soaked cloth which offered even more interesting holes and crevices.

One of them tried to climb into Ponder Stibbons's nose, and was snorted out again.

Ponder opened an eye. When he moved his head, the water filling his ears made a ringing noise.

The history of the last few minutes was compli-cated. He could remember rushing along a tube of green water, if such a thing were possible, and there had been several periods where the air and the sea and Ponder himself had been very closely entwined. Now he felt as though someone had, with great precision, hit every part of his body with a hammer.

'Get off, will you!'

Ponder reached up and pulled another crab out of his ear, and realized that he had lost his glasses. They were probably rolling at the bottom of the sea by now, frightening lobsters. So here he was, on an alien shore, and he'd be able to see everything really clearly provided everything was meant to be a blur.

'Am I dead this time?' It was the Dean's voice, from a little further away along the beach.

'No, you're *still* alive, sir,' said Ponder.

'Damn. Are you sure?'

There were other groans as bits of tidal debris turned out to be wizards mixed with seaweed.

'Are we all here?' said Ridcully, trying to get to his feet.

'I'm sure I'm not,' moaned the Dean.

'I don't see . . . Mrs Whitlow,' said Ridcully. 'Or the Bursar . . .'

Ponder sat up.

'There's . . . oh, dear . . . well, there's the Bursar . . .'

Out at sea a huge wave was building up. It towered higher and higher. And the Bursar was on top of it.

'Bursar!' Ridcully screamed.

The distant figure stood up on the seed and waved.

'He's standing up,' said Ridcully. 'Is he supposed to stand up on those things? He's not supposed to stand up, is he? I'm sure he shouldn't be standing up. YOU'RE NOT SUPPOSED TO STAND UP, BURSAAAR! How . . . That's not supposed to happen, is it?'

The wave curled, but the Bursar seemed to be skimming down the side of it, skidding along the huge green wet wall like a man on one ski.

Ridcully turned to the other wizards. 'He can't do that, can he? He's walking up and down on it. Can he do that? The wave's curling over and he's just sliding gently along the . . . Oh, no . . .'

The foaming crest curled over the speeding wizard.

'That's it, then,' said Ridcully.

'Er . . . no . . .' said Ponder.

The Bursar reappeared further along the beach, expelled from the collapsing tube of water like an arrow from a bow. The wave crashed over behind him, striking the shore as if it had just offended it.

The seed changed direction, cruised gently over the backwash and crunched to a halt on the sand.

The Bursar stepped off. 'Hooray,' he said. 'My feet are wet. What a nice forest. Time for tea.'

He picked up the seed and rammed it point first in the sand. Then he wandered away up the beach.

'How did he do that?' said Ridcully. 'I mean, the man's crazier than a ferret! Damn good Bursar, of course.'

'Possibly the lack of mental balance means there's nothing to impede physical stability?' said Ponder wearily.

'You think so?'

'Not really, sir. I just said it for something to say.' Ponder tried to massage some life back into his legs, and started to count under his breath.

'Is there anything to *eat* here?' said the Chair of Indefinite Studies.

'Four,' said Ponder.

'I beg your pardon?'

'What? Oh, it was just some counting I was doing, sir. No, sir. There's probably fish and lobsters in the sea, but the land looks pretty bare to me.'

It did. Reddish sand stretched away through the greyish drizzle to bluish mountains. The only greenishness was the Dean's face and, suddenly, the shoots winding out of the Bursar's surfing seed. Leaves unfolded in the rain, tiny flowers opened with little plopping noises.

'Well, at least we'll have another boat,' said the Senior Wrangler.

'I doubt it, sir,' said Ponder. 'The god wasn't very good at breeding things.' And, indeed, the swelling fruit was not looking very boat-shaped.

'You know, I still think it would help if we thought of all this as a valuable opportunity,' said Ridcully.

'That's true,' said the Dean, sitting up. 'It's not many times in your life you get the chance to die of hunger on some bleak continent thousands of years before you're born. We should make the most of it.'

'I meant that pitting ourselves against the elements will bring out the best in us and forge us into a go-getting and hard-hitting team,' said Ridcully. This view got no takers.

'I'm *sure* there must be *something* to eat,' mumbled the Chair of Indefinite Studies, looking around aimlessly. 'There usually is.'

'After all, nothing is beyond men like us,' said Ridcully.

'That's true,' said Ponder. 'Oh gods, yes. That's true.'

'And at least a wizard can always make a decent fire.'

Ponder's eyes opened wide. He rose in one movement aimed at Ridcully, but was still airborne when the Archchancellor tossed a small fireball at a heap of driftwood. By the time the glowing ball was halfway to the wood Ponder had hit Ridcully in the back, so that both of them were sprawled on the wet sand when the world went *whooph*.

When they looked up the heap of driftwood was a blackened crater.

'Well, thank you,' said the Dean, behind them. 'I feel lovely and dry now, and I never did like my eyebrows all that much.'

'High thaumic field, sir,' Ponder panted. 'I *did* say.'

Ridcully stared at his hands. 'I was going to light my pipe with one . . .' he muttered. He held the hand away from him. 'It was only a Number Ten,' he said.

The Dean stood up, brushing away some tufts of burnt beard.

'I'm not sure I believe what I just saw,' he said, and pointed a finger at a nearby rock.

'No, sir, I don't think you—'

Most of the rock was lifted off the ground and landed a hundred yards away. The rest of it sizzled in a red-hot puddle.

'Can I have a go?' said the Senior Wrangler.

'Sir, I really think—'

'Oh, well done, Senior Wrangler,' said the Dean, as another rock fractured into fragments.

'Ye gods, you were *right*, Stibbons,' said Ridcully. 'The magic field here is *huge*!'

'Yes, sir, but I really don't think we should be using it, sir!' Ponder shrieked.

'We're wizards, young man. Using magic is what wizarding is all about.'

'No, sir! *Not* using magic is what wizarding is all about!'

Ridcully hesitated.

'This is fossil magic, sir!' said Ponder, speaking fast. 'It's what's being used to create this place! We could do untold damage if we're not careful!'

'All right, all right, no one do anything for a moment,' said Ridcully. 'Now . . . what are you talking about, Mister Stibbons?'

'I don't think the place is properly, well, *finished*, sir. I mean, there're no plants or animals, are there?'

'Nonsense. I saw a camel a little while ago.'

'Yes, sir, but that came with us. And there's seaweed and crabs on the beach and they got washed up too. But where are the trees and bushes and grasses?'

'Interesting,' said Ridcully. 'Place is as bald as a baby's bottom.'

'Still under construction, sir. The god *did* say it was being built.'

'Unbelievable, really,' said Ridcully. 'A whole continent being created out of nothing?'

'Exactly, sir.'

'Gazillions of thaums of magic pouring into the world.'

'You've got it, sir.'

'Whole mountains and cliffs and beaches where once there was nothing, style of thing.'

'That's right, sir.'

'Bit of a miracle, you could say.'

'I certainly would, sir.'

'Unimaginably vast amounts of magic doing their stuff.'

'Astonishing, sir.'

'So I expect no one will miss a little bit, eh?'

'*No!* That's not how it works, sir! If we use it, it's like ... like treading on ants, sir! This isn't like ... finding an old staff in a cupboard and using up the magic that's left. This is the real primal energy! *Anything* we do might well have an effect.'

The Dean tapped him on the shoulder. 'Then here we are, young Stibbons, stuck on this forsaken shore. What do you suggest? We're thousands of years from home. Perhaps we should just sit and wait? That Rincewind fellow's bound to be along in a few millennia?'

'Er, Dean ...' said the Senior Wrangler.

'Yes?'

'Are you standing behind Stibbons there, or are you sitting on this rock over here?'

The Dean looked at himself, sitting on the rock.

'Oh, blast,' he muttered. 'Temporal discontinuity again.'

'Again?' said Ponder.

'We had a patch of it in Room 5b once,' said the Senior Wrangler. 'Ridiculous. You had to cough before you went in, in case you were already there. Anyway, *you* shouldn't be surprised, young man. Enough magic distorts all physical la—'

The Senior Wrangler vanished, leaving only a pile of clothes.

'Took a while to take hold,' said Ridcully. 'I remember when—'

His voice suddenly rose in pitch. Ponder spun around and saw a small heap of clothing with a pointed hat on top of it.

He raised the hat gingerly. A pink face under a mop of curls looked up at him.

'Bugger!' squeaked Ridcully. 'How old am I, mister?'

'Er . . . you look about six, sir,' said Ponder. His back twinged.

The small worried face crinkled up. 'I want my mum!' The little nose sniffed. 'Was that me who just said that?'

'Er, yes . . .'

'You can keep on top of it if you concentrate,' the Archchancellor squeaked. 'It resets the tempor— I wanna sweetie! – it resets the temporal gl— I wanna sweetie, oh, you wait till I get me home, I'll give me such a smack – it resets the body's clo— where's Mr Pootle? – it resets the body's clock – wanna wanna Mr Pootle! – don't worry, I think I've got the hang of it—'

The wail behind Ponder made him turn around. There were more piles of clothing where the wizards had been. He pulled aside the Dean's hat just as a faint *bloop* suggested that Mustrum Ridcully had managed to regain full possession of his years again.

'That the Dean, Stibbons?'

'Could be, sir. Er . . . some of them have *gone*, sir!'

Ridcully looked unflustered. 'Temporal gland acting up in the high field,' he said. 'Probably decided that since it's thousands of years ago they're not here. Don't worry, they'll come back when it works it out . . .'

Ponder suddenly felt breathless. 'And . . . hwee . . . think this one's the Lecturer in Recent Runes . . . hwee . . . of course . . . hwee . . . all babies look the . . . hwee . . . same.'

There was another wail from under the Senior Wrangler's hat.

'Bit of a . . . hwee . . . kindergarten here, sir,' Ponder wheezed. His back creaked when he tried to stand upright.

'Oh, they'll probably come back if they don't get fed,' said Ridcully. 'It's you that'll be the problem, lad. I mean, *sir.*'

Ponder held his hands up in front of him. He could see the veins through the pale skin. He could nearly see the bones.

Around him the piles of clothing rose again as the wizards clambered back to their proper age.

'How . . . old . . . hwee . . . I . . . ha . . . look?' he panted. 'Like someone who shouldn't . . . hwee . . . start reading a long book?'

'A long sentence,' said Ridcully cheerfully, holding him up. 'How old do you feel? In yourself?'

'I . . . hwee . . . ought to feel . . . hwee . . . about twenty-four, sir,' Ponder groaned. 'I actually . . . hwee . . . feel like a twenty-four-year-old who has been hit by eighty years travelling at . . . hwee . . . high speed.'

'Hold on to that thought. Your temporal gland knows how old you are.'

Ponder tried to concentrate, but it was hard. Part of him wanted to go to sleep. Part of him wanted to say, 'Hah, you call *this* a temporal disturbance? You should've seen the temporal disturbances we will have been used to be going to get in *my* day.' A pressing part of him was threatening that if he didn't find a toilet it would make its own arrangements.

'You've kept your hair,' said the Senior Wrangler, encouragingly.

Ponder heard himself say, 'Remember old "Cruddy" Trusset? Now *there* was a wizard who had . . . good . . . hair . . .' He tried to get a grip. 'He's still alive, isn't he?' he wheezed. 'He's the same age as me. Oh, *no* . . . now I'm remembering only yesterday as if it was . . . hwee . . . seventy years ago!'

'You can get over it,' said Ridcully. 'You've got to make it clear you're not accepting it, you see. The important thing is not to panic.'

'I *am* panicking,' squeaked Ponder. 'I'm just doing it very slowly! Why've I got this horrible feeling that I'm . . . hwee . . . falling forward all the . . . hwee . . . time?'

'Oh, that's just apprehensions of mortality,' said Ridcully. 'Everyone gets that.'

'And . . . hwee . . . now I think my memory's going . . .'

'What makes you think that?'

'Think what? Speak up, you . . . hwee . . . man . . .'

Something exploded somewhere behind Ponder's

eyeballs and lifted him off the ground. For a moment he felt he had jumped into icy water.

The blood flowed back to his hands.

'Well done, lad,' said Ridcully. 'Your hair's going brown again, too.'

'Ow . . .' Ponder slumped to his knees. 'It was like wearing a lead suit! I never want to go through *that* again!'

'Suicide's your best bet, then,' said Ridcully.

'Is this going to happen *again*?'

'Probably. At least once, anyway.'

Ponder got to his feet with a steely look in his eyes. 'Then let's find whoever's building this place and ask them to send us home,' he growled.

'They might not want to listen,' said Ridcully. 'Deities can be touchy.'

Ponder shook his sleeves to leave his hands free. For a wizard, this was equivalent to checking the functioning of a pump-action shotgun.

'Then we'll insist,' he said.

'Really, Stibbons? What about protection of the magical ecology?'

Ponder turned on him a look that would have opened a strongroom. Ridcully was in his seventies and spry even for wizards, who tended to live well into their second century if they survived their first fifty years. Ponder wasn't sure how old *he'd* been, but he'd definitely thought he could hear a blade being sharpened. It was one thing to know you were on a journey, and quite, quite another to see your destination on the horizon.

'It can get stuffed,' he said.*

'Well thought out, Mister Stibbons! I can see we'll make a wizard of you yet. Ah, the Dean's . . . oh . . .'

The Dean's clothes billowed up but did not, as it were, inflate to their old size. The hat in particular was big enough to rock on the Dean's ears, which were redder and stuck out more than Ponder remembered.

Ridcully raised the hat.

'Push off, granddad,' said the Dean.

'Ah,' said the Archchancellor. 'Thirteen years old, I'd say. Which explains a lot. Well, Dean, help us with the others, will you?'

'Why should I?' The adolescent Dean cracked his knuckles. 'Hah! I'm young again and soon you'll be *dead*! I've got my whole life ahead of me!'

'Firstly, you'll spend it here, and secondly, Dean, *you* think it's going to be jolly good fun being the Dean in a thirteen-year-old body, don't you, but within a minute or two you'll start forgetting it all, you see? The old temporal gland can't allow you to remember being fourteen when you're not even thirteen yet, you follow me? You'd know this stuff, Dean, if you weren't forgetting. You'll have to go through it *all* over again, Dean . . . ah . . .'

The brain has far less control over the body than the body does over the brain. And adolescence is not a

---

* It would be nice to say that this experience taught Ponder a valuable lesson and that he was a lot more considerate towards old people afterwards, and this was true for about five minutes.

good time. Nor is old age, for that matter, but at least the spots have cleared up, some of the more troublesome glands have settled down and you're allowed to take a nap in the afternoons and twinkle at young women. In any case, the Dean's body hadn't experienced too much old age yet, whereas every junior spot, ache and twinge was firmly embossed on the morphic memory. Once, it decided, was enough.

The Dean expanded. Ponder noticed that his head in particular swelled up to fit his ears.

The Dean rubbed his spot-free face. 'Five minutes wouldn't have been bad,' he complained. 'What was *that* all about?'

'Temporal uncertainty,' said Ridcully. 'You've seen it before, didn't you realize? What were you thinking of?'

'Sex.'

'Oh, yes, of course ... silly of me, really.' Ridcully looked along the deserted beach. 'Mister Stibbons thinks we can—' he began. 'Ye gods! There *are* people here!'

A young woman was walking towards them. Swaying, anyway.

'My word,' said the Dean. 'I suppose this isn't Slakki, by any chance?'

'I thought they wore grass skirts ...' said Ridcully. 'What's she wearing, Stibbons?'

'A sarong.'

'Looks right enough to me, haha,' said the Dean.

'Certainly makes a man wish he was fifty years younger,' said the Chair of Indefinite Studies.

'Five minutes younger would do for me,' said the Dean. 'Incidentally, did any of you notice that rather clever inadvertent joke just then? Stibbons said it was "a sarong" and I—'

'What's that she's carrying?' said Ridcully.

'—no, listen, you see, I misheard him, in fact, and I—'

'Looks like ... coconuts ...' said Ponder, shading his eyes.

'This is a bit more *like* it,' said the Senior Wrangler.

'—because actually I *thought* he said, "It's wrong," you see—'

'Certainly *a* coconut,' said Ridcully. 'I'm not complaining, of course, but aren't these sultry maids generally black-haired? Red doesn't seem very typical.'

'—so *I* said—'

'I *suppose* you'd get coconuts here?' said the Lecturer in Recent Runes. 'They float, don't they?'

'—and, listen, when Stibbons said "sarong", I thought he—'

'Something familiar about her,' Ridcully mused.

'Did you see that nut in the Museum of Quite Unusual Things?' said the Senior Wrangler. 'Called the coco-de-mer and ...' he permitted himself '... ha, very curious shape, you know, you'll never guess who it used to put me in mind of ...'

'It *can't* be Mrs Whitlow, can it?' said Ponder.

'As a matter of fact, I must admit that it—'

'Well, *I* thought it was mildly amusing, anyway,' said the Dean.

'It *is* Mrs Whitlow,' said Ridcully.

'More of a nut, really, but—'

It dawned on the Senior Wrangler that the sky was a different colour on his personal planet. He turned around, looked, said, 'Mwaaa . . .' and fell gently to the sand.

'Ai don't quate know what's happened to Mister Librarian,' said Mrs Whitlow, in a voice that made the Senior Wrangler twitch even in his swoon.

The coconut opened its eyes. It looked as if it had just seen something truly horrific, but this is a normal expression for baby orang-utans and in any case it was looking at the Dean.

'Eek!' it said.

Ridcully coughed. 'Well, at least he's the right shape,' he said. 'And, er, you, Mrs Whitlow? How do you feel?'

'Mwaa . . .' said the Senior Wrangler.

'Very well indeed, thank you,' said Mrs Whitlow. 'This country agrees with me. I don't know whether it was the swim, but Ai haven't felt quate so buoyant in years. But Ai looked around and there was this dear little ape just sitting there.'

'Ponder, would you mind just throwing the Senior Wrangler in the sea for a moment?' said Ridcully. 'Nowhere too deep. Don't worry if it steams.' He took Mrs Whitlow's spare hand.

'I don't want to worry you, dear Mrs Whitlow,' he said, 'but I think something is shortly going to come as a big shock to you. First of all, and please don't misunderstand me, it might be a good idea to loosen your clothing.' He swallowed. 'Slightly.'

* * *

The Bursar had experienced some changes of age as he wandered through the wet but barren land, but to a man capable of being a vase of flowers for an entire afternoon this was barely a mild distraction.

What had caught his eye was a fire. It was burning bits of driftwood, and the flames were edged with blue from the salt.

Close to it was a sack made of some sort of animal skins.

The damp earth beside the Bursar stirred and a tree erupted, growing so fast that the rain steamed off the unfolding leaves. This did not surprise him. Few things did. Besides, he'd never seen a tree growing before, so he did not know how fast it was supposed to go.

Then several more trees exploded around him. One grew so fast that it went all the way from sapling to half-rotten trunk in a few seconds.

And it seemed to the Bursar that there were other people here. He couldn't see them or hear them, but something in his bones sensed them. However, the Bursar was also quite accustomed to the presence of people who couldn't be seen or heard by anyone else, and had spent many a pleasant hour in conversation with historical figures and, sometimes, the wall.

All in all the Bursar was, depending on your outlook, the most or least suitable person to encounter deity on a first-hand basis.

An old man walked around a rock and was halfway to the fire before he noticed the wizard.

Like Rincewind, the Bursar had no room in his head for racism. As a skin colour black came as quite a relief compared to some of the colours he'd seen, although he'd never seen anyone quite so black as the man now staring at him. At least, the Bursar assumed he was staring. The eyes were so deep set that he couldn't be sure.

The Bursar, who had been properly brought up, said, 'Hooray, there's a rosebush?'

The old man gave him a rather puzzled nod. He walked over to the dead tree and pulled off a branch, which he pushed into the fire. Then he sat down and watched it as though watching wood char was the most engrossing thing in the world.

The Bursar sat down on a rock and waited. If the game was patience, then two could play at it.

The old man kept glancing up at him. The Bursar kept smiling. Once or twice he gave the man a little wave.

Finally the burning branch was pulled out of the fire. The old man picked up the leather sack in his other hand and walked off among the rocks. The Bursar followed him.

There was an overhang here under a small cliff, shielding a stretch of vertical rock from the rain. It was the kind of tempting surface that would, in Ankh-Morpork, have already been covered so thickly with so many posters, signs and graffiti that if you'd removed the wall the general accretion would still have stood up.

Someone had drawn a tree. It was the simplest

drawing of a tree the Bursar had ever seen since he'd been old enough to read books that weren't mainly pictures, but it was also in some strange way the most accurate. It was simple because something complex had been rolled up small; as if someone had drawn trees, and started with the normal green cloud on a stick, and refined it, and refined it some more, and looked for the little twists in a line that said *tree* and refined *those* until there was just one line that said TREE.

And now when you looked at it you could hear the wind in the branches.

The old man reached down beside him and took up a flat stone with some white paste on it. He drew another line on the rock, slightly like a flattened V, and smeared it with mud.

The Bursar burst out laughing as the wings emerged from the painting and whirred past him.

And again he was aware of a strange effect in the air. It reminded him of . . . yes . . . old 'Rubber' Houser, that was his name, dead now, of course, but remembered by many of his contemporaries as the inventor of the Graphical Device.

The Bursar had joined the University when likely wizards started their training early, somewhere after the point where they learned to walk but before they started to push over girls in the playground. The writing of lines in detention class was a familiar punishment and the Bursar, like everyone else, toyed with the usual practice of tying several pens to a ruler in a group attempt to write lines in threes. But

Houser, a reflective sort of boy, had scrounged some bits of wood and stripped a mattress of its springs and devised the four-, sixteen- and eventually the thirty-two-line writing machine. It had got so popular that boys were actually breaking rules in order to have a go on it, at threepence a time to use it and a penny to help wind it up. Of course, more time was spent setting it up than was ever saved by using it, but this is the case in many similar fields and is a sign of Progress. The experiments tragically came to an end when someone opened a door at the wrong moment and the entire pent-up force of Houser's experimental prototype 256-line machine propelled him backwards out of a fourth-floor window.

Except for the absence of screams, the hand tracing its infinitely simple lines on the rock brought back memories of Houser. There was a sense of something small being done that was making something happen that was huge.

He sat and watched. It was, he remembered later whenever he was in a state to remember anything, one of the happiest times of his life.

When Rincewind lifted his head a watchman's helmet was spinning gently on the ground.

To his amazement the men themselves were still there, although they were lying around in various attitudes of unconsciousness or at least, if they had sense, *feigned* unconsciousness. The Luggage had a cat's tendency to lose interest in things that didn't fight back even after you'd kicked them a few times.

Shoes littered the ground, too. The Luggage was limping around in a circle.

Rincewind sighed, and stood up. 'Take the shoes off. They don't suit you,' he said.

The Luggage stood still for a moment, and then the rest of the shoes clattered against the wall.

'And the dress. What would those nice ladies think if they saw you dressing up like this?'

The Luggage shrugged off the few sequinned tatters that remained.

'Turn around, I want to see your handles. No, I said turn around. Turn around *properly*, please. Ah, I thought so . . . I said turn *around*. Those earrings . . . they don't do anything for you at all, you know.' He leaned closer. 'Is that a stud? Have you had your lid pierced?'

The Luggage backed away. Its manner indicated very clearly that while it might give in on the shoes, the dress and even the earrings, the battle over the stud would go to the finish.

'Well . . . all right. Now give me my clean underwear, you could make shelves out of the stuff I'm wearing.'

The Luggage opened its lid.

'Good, now I— Is that my underwear? Would I be seen *dead* in something like that? Yes, as a matter of fact I suspect I would. *My* underwear, please. It's got my name inside, although I must admit I can't quite remember why I thought that was necessary.'

The lid shut. The lid opened.

'Thank you.'

It was no use wondering how it was done, or for

that matter why the laundry returned freshly ironed.

The watchmen were still very wisely remaining unconscious, but out of habit Rincewind went behind a stack of old boxes to change. He was the sort of person who'd go behind a tree to change if he was on a desert island all alone.

'You noticed something odd about this alley?' he said, over the top of the boxes. 'There're no drain-pipes. There're no gutters. They've never heard of rain here. I suppose you are the Luggage, aren't you, and not some kangaroo in disguise? Why am I asking? Ye gods, these feel good. Right, let's go—'

The Luggage opened its lid again, and a young woman looked up at Rincewind.

'Who are—? Oh, you're the blind man,' she said.

'I beg your pardon?'

'Sorry . . . Darleen said you must be blind. Well, actually she said you must be bloody blind. Can you give me a hand out?'

It dawned on Rincewind that the girl clambering out of the Luggage was Neilette, the third member of Letitia's crew and the one who'd seemed quite plain compared to the others and certainly a lot less . . . well, noisy wasn't quite the word. Probably the word was 'expansive'. They filled the space around them to capacity. Take Darleen, a lady he'd last seen holding a man daintily by the collar so that she could punch him in the face. When she walked into a room, there'd be no one in it unaware that she had done so.

Neilette was just . . . ordinary. She brushed some dirt off her dress, and sighed.

'I could see there was going to be another fight so I hid in Trunkie,' she said.

'Trunkie, eh?' said Rincewind. The Luggage had the decency to look embarrassed.

'Sooner or later there's always a fight where Darleen goes,' said Neilette. 'You'd be amazed the things she can do with a stiletto heel.'

'I think I've seen one of them,' said Rincewind. 'Don't tell me the others. Um, can I help you? Only me and Trunkie here' – he gave the Luggage a kick – 'were heading off, weren't we, *Trunkie*?'

'Oh, don't kick her, she's been so useful,' said Neilette.

'Really?' said Rincewind. The Luggage turned around slowly so that he couldn't see the expression on its lock.

'Oh, yes. I reckon the miners in Cangoolie would've . . . been very unpleasant to Letitia if Trunkie hadn't stepped in.'

'Stepped on, I expect.'

'How did you know that?'

'Oh, the L— Trunkie is mine. We got separated.'

Neilette tried to arrange her hair. 'It's all right for the others,' she said. 'They just have to change wigs. Beer might be a good shampoo, but not when it's still in the tinnie.' She sighed. 'Oh, well. I suppose I'll have to find a way home, now.'

'Where do you live?'

'Worralorrasurfa. It's Rimwards.' She sighed again. 'Back to life in the banana-bending factory. So much for showbusiness!'

Then she burst into tears and sat down heavily on the Luggage.

Rincewind didn't know whether he should go into the 'pat, pat, there, there' routine. If she was like Darleen, he might lose an arm. He made what he hoped was a soothing yet non-aggressive mumble.

'I mean, I know I can't sing very well and I can't dance but, frankly, neither can Letitia and Darleen. When Darleen sings "Prancing Queen" you could slice bread with it. Not that they've been unkind,' she added quickly, polite even in the throes of woe, 'but really there's got to be more to life than getting beer thrown at you every night and being chased out of town.'

Rincewind felt confident enough to venture a 'there, there'. He didn't risk a 'pat, pat'.

'Really I only did it because of Noelene dropping out,' Neilette sobbed. 'And I'm about the same height and Letitia couldn't find anyone else in time and I needed the money and she said it would be okay provided people didn't notice my hands were so small . . .'

'Noelene being—?'

'My brother. I *told* him, trying for the surf championship is fine, and ballgowns are fine, but both together? I don't think so. Did you know what a nasty rash you can get from being rolled across coral? And next morning Letitia had this tour organized and, well, it seemed a good idea at the time.'

'Noelene . . .' Rincewind mused. 'That's an unusual name for a . . .'

'Darleen said you wouldn't understand.' Neilette stared into the middle distance. 'I think my brother worked in the factory too long,' she mused. 'He always was very impressionable. Anyway, I—'

'Oh, I get it, he's a *female impersonator*,' said Rincewind. 'Oh, I know about *those*. Old pantomime tradition. A couple of balloons, a straw wig and a few grubby jokes. Why, when I was a student, at Hogswatch parties old Farter Carter and Really Pants would put on a turn where—'

He was aware that she was giving him one of those long, slow looks.

'Tell me,' she said. 'Do you get about much?'

'You'd be amazed,' said Rincewind.

'And you meet all kinds of people?'

'Generally the nastier kind, I have to admit.'

'Well, some men . . .' Neilette stopped. 'Really Pants? That was someone's *name*?'

'Not exactly. He was called Ronald Pants, so of course when anyone heard that they said—'

'Oh, is that all?' said Neilette. She stood up and blew her nose. 'I told the others I'd leave when we got to the Galah, so they'll understand. Being a . . . female impersonator is no job for a woman, which is what I am, incidentally. I'd hoped it was obvious, but in your case I thought I'd better mention it. Can you get us out of here, Trunkie?'

The Luggage wandered over to the wall at the end of the alley and kicked it until there was a decent-sized hole. On the way back it clogged a watchman who was unwise enough to stir.

'Er, I call him the Luggage,' said Rincewind helplessly.

'Really? We call her Trunkie.'

The wall opened up into a dark room. Crates were packed against the walls, covered with cobwebs.

'Oh, we're in the old brewery,' said Neilette. 'Well, the new one, really. Let's find a door.'

'Good idea,' said Rincewind, eyeing the spiderwebs. '*New* brewery? Looks pretty old to me . . .'

Neilette rattled a door. 'Locked,' she said. 'Come on, we'll find another one. Look, it's the new brewery because we built it to replace the one over the river. But it never worked. The beer went flat, or something. They all said it was haunted. *Everyone* knows that, don't they? We went back to the old brewery. My dad lost nearly all his money.'

'Why?'

'He owned it. Just about broke his heart, that did. He left it to me,' she tried another door, 'because, well, he never got on with Noelene, what with the, well, you know, or rather, obviously you don't . . . but it ruined the business, really. And Roo Beer used to be the best there was.'

'Can't you sell it? The site, I mean.'

'Here? A place where beer goes flat within five seconds? Can't give it away.'

Rincewind peered up at the big metal vats. 'Perhaps it was built on some old religious site,' he said. 'That sort of thing can happen, you know. Back home there was this fish restaurant that got built on a—'

Neilette rattled another unbudging door. 'That's

what everyone thought,' she said. 'But apparently Dad asked all the local tribes and they said it wasn't. They said it wasn't any kind of sacred site. They said it was an unsacred site. Some chief went to prison to see the prime minister and said, "Mate, your mob can dig it all up and drop it over the edge of the world, no worries." '

'Why did he have to go to prison?'

'We put all our politicians in prison as soon as they're elected. Don't you?'

'Why?'

'It saves time.' She tried an unrelenting handle. 'Damn! And the windows are too high . . .'

The ground trembled. Metal jangled, somewhere in the darkness. Dust moved in strange little waves across the floor.

'Oh, not *again*,' said Neilette.

Now not only the dust moved. Tiny shapes scuttled across it, flowed around Rincewind's feet and sped under the locked door.

'The spiders are leaving!' said Neilette.

'Fine by me!' said Rincewind.

This time the tremor made the wall creak.

'It's never been this bad,' Neilette muttered. 'Find a ladder, we'll give the windows a go.'

Above them a ladder parted company from the wall and folded itself into a metal puzzle on the floor.

'This may not seem a good time to ask,' said Rincewind, 'but are you a kangaroo, by any chance?'

Far above them metal creaked and went on creaking, in a long-drawn wail of inorganic pain. Rincewind looked up, and saw the dome of the brewery gently dissolve into a hundred falling pieces of glass.

And, dropping through the middle of it, some of its lamps still burning, the grinning shape of the Roo Beer kangaroo.

'Trunkie! Open up!' Neilette yelled.

'No—' Rincewind began, but she grabbed him and dragged him and in front of him was an opening lid . . .

The world went dark.

There was wood underneath him. He tapped it, very carefully. And wood in front of him. And w—

'Excuse *me*.'

'We're *inside* the Luggage?'

'Why not? That's how we got out of Cangoolie last week! Y'know, I think it may be a *magic* box.'

'Do you *know* some of the things that have been inside it?'

'Letitia kept her gin in it, I know that.'

Rincewind felt upwards, gingerly.

Maybe the Luggage had more than one inside. He'd suspected as much. Maybe it was like one of those conjuror's boxes where, after you'd put a penny in, the drawer miraculously slid around and it had gone. Rincewind had been given one of those as a toy when he was a kid. He'd lost almost two dollars before he gave up and threw the thing away . . .

His fingers touched what might have been a lid, and he pushed upwards.

They were still in the brewery. This came as some relief, considering where you might end up if you got into the Luggage. There was still the bowel-disturbing rumble, punctuated by clangs and tinkles as bits of rusted metal crashed down with lethal intent.

The big kangaroo sign was well alight.

In the smoke that rose from it were some pointy hats.

That is, the curls swirling and billowing around holes in the air looked very much like the three-dimensional silhouettes of a group of wizards.

Rincewind stepped out of the Luggage. 'Oh, no, no, no,' he mumbled. 'I only got here a couple of months ago. It's not my fault!'

'They look like ghosts,' said Neilette. 'Do you *know* them?'

'No! But they're all mixed up with these earthquakes! And something called The Wet, whatever that was!'

'That's just some old story, isn't it? Anyway, Mister Wizard, it might have escaped your notice that the place is filling up with smoke! Which way did we come in?'

Rincewind looked around desperately. Smoke obscured everything.

'Has this place got cellars?' he said.

'Yeah! I used to play Mothers and Mothers with Noelene in them when we were kids. Look for hatches in the floor!'

And it was three minutes later that the ancient wooden hatchcover in the alley finally gave way under the Luggage's insistent pounding. Several rats poured out, followed by Rincewind and Neilette.

No one paid them any attention. A column of smoke was rising over the city. Watchmen and citizens were already forming a bucket chain and men with a battering ram were trying to break open the brewery's main doors.

'We're well out of that,' Rincewind observed. 'Oh, boy, yes.'

'Hey, what's going on? Where's the bloody water gone?'

The cry came from a man working the handle of a pump out on the street, just as the pump gave a groan and the handle went limp. A watchman grabbed his arm.

'There's another one in the yard over there! Get a wiggle on, mate!'

A couple of men tried the other pump. It made a choking noise, spat out a few drops of water and some damp rust, and gave up.

Rincewind swallowed. 'I think the water's gone,' he said, flatly.

'What do you mean, *gone*?' said Neilette. 'There's *always* water. Huge great seas of it underground!'

'Yes, but . . . it doesn't get filled up much, does it? It doesn't rain here.'

'There you go aga—' She stopped. 'What's it you know? You're looking shifty, Mister Wizard.'

Rincewind stared glumly up at the tower of smoke. There were twirling, tumbling sparks in it, rising in the heat and showering down over the city. Everything will be bone dry, he thought. It doesn't rain here. It— Hang on . . .

'How do you know I'm a wizard?' he said.

'It's written on your hat,' she said. 'Badly.'

'You know what a wizard *is*? This is a serious question. I'm not pushing a prawn.'

'Everyone knows what a wizard is! We've got a university full of the useless mongrels!'

'And you can show me where this is, can you?'

'Find it yourself!' She tried to stride off through the milling crowd. He ran after her.

'Please don't go! I need someone like you! As an interpreter!'

'What do you mean? We speak the same language!'

'Really? Stubbies here are really short shorts or small beer bottles. How often do newcomers confuse the two?'

Neilette actually smiled. 'Not more than once.'

'Just take me to this university of yours, will you?' said Rincewind. 'I think I can feel a Famous Last Stand coming on.'

There was a brief scream of metal overhead and a windmill fan crashed down into the street.

'And we'd better be quick,' he added. 'Otherwise all there'll be to drink is beer.'

The Bursar laughed again as a series of little charcoal dots extended their legs, formed up and marched down the stone and across the sand in front of him. Behind him the trees were already loud with birdsong—

And then, sadly, with wizards as well.

He could hear the voices in the distance and, while

wizards are always questioning the universe, they mainly direct the questions at other wizards and don't bother to listen to the answers.

'—*certainly saw no trees when we arrived.*'

'*Probably we didn't see them because of the rain, and the Senior Wrangler didn't see them because of Mrs Whitlow. And get a grip on yourself, will you, Dean? I'm sure you're getting young again! No one's impressed!*'

'*I think I must just be naturally youthful, Archchancellor.*'

'*Nothing to be proud of there! And please, someone, stop the Senior Wrangler getting a grip on hims— Oh, looks like someone's had a picnic . . .*'

The painter seemed engrossed in his work, and paid them no attention at all.

'*I'm sure the Bursar went this way—*'

A little red mud coloured a complex curve and there, as if it had always been there, was a creature with the body of a giant rabbit, the expression of a camel and a tail that a lizard would be proud of. The wizards appeared around the rock just in time to see it scratch its ears.

'Ye gods, what's *that*?'

'Some sort of rat?' said the Chair of Indefinite Studies.

'Hey, look, Bursar's found one of the locals . . .' The Dean ambled across to the painter, who was watching the wizards with his mouth open. 'Good morning, fellow. What's that thing called?'

The painter followed the pointing finger. 'Kangaroo?' he said. The voice was a whisper, on the very cusp of hearing, but the ground trembled.

'Kangaroo, eh?'

'That might not be what it's called, sir,' said Ponder. 'He might just be saying, "I don't know."'

'Can't see why not. He looks the sort of chap you find in this sort of place,' said the Dean. 'Deep tan. Shortage of trousers. The sort of fellow who'd know what the wildlife is called, certainly.'

'He just drew it,' said the Bursar.

'Oh, did he? Very good artists, some of these chaps.'

'He's not Rincewind, is he?' said Ridcully, who seldom bothered to remember faces. 'I know he's a bit on the dark side, but a few months in the sun'd bake anyone.'

The other wizards drew together and looked around for any nearby sign of mobile rectangularity.

'No hat,' said Ponder, and that was that.

The Dean peered at the rock wall. 'Quite good drawings for native art,' he said. 'Interesting . . . lines.'

The Bursar nodded. As far as he could see, the drawings were simply alive. They might be coloured earth on rock, but they were as alive as the kangaroo that'd just hopped away.

The old man was drawing a snake now. One wiggly line.

'I remember seeing some of those palaces the Tezumen built in the jungle,' said the Dean, watching him. 'Not an ounce of mortar in the whole place and the stones fit together so well you couldn't stick a knife between them. Hah, they were about the only things the Tezumen *didn't* stick a knife between,' he added. 'Odd people, really. Very big on wholesale human sacrifice and cocoa. Not an obvious combination, to my mind. Kill fifty thousand people and then relax with a nice cup of hot chocolate. Excuse me, I used to be quite good at this.'

To the horror even of Ridcully the Dean took the piece of frayed twig out of the painter's hand and dabbed it gently on the rock.

'See? A dot for the eye,' said the Dean, handing it back.

The painter gave him a sort of smile. That is, he showed his teeth. Like many other beings on astral planes of all kinds, he was puzzled by the wizards. They were people with the family-sized self-confidence that seems to be able to get away with anything. They generated an unconscious field which said that *of course* they should be there, but no one was to worry or fuss around tidying up the place on their account and just get on with what they were doing. The more impressionable victims were left with the feeling that they had clipboards and were awarding marks.

Behind the Dean a snake wriggled away.

'Anyone feel anything odd?' said the Lecturer in Recent Runes. 'My fingers tingled. Did any of you do any magic just then?'

The Dean picked up a burnt twig. The painter's mouth dropped open as the wizard drew a scratching line on the stone.

'I think you might be offending him,' said Ponder.

'Nonsense! A good artist is always prepared to

361

learn,' said the Dean. 'Interesting thing, these fellows never seem to get the idea of perspective—'

The Bursar thought, or received the thought: that's because perspective is a lie. If I know a pond is round then why should I draw it oval? I will draw it round because round is true. Why should my brush lie to you just because my eye lies to me?

It sounded like quite an angry thought.

'What's that you're drawing, Dean?' said the Senior Wrangler.

'What does it look like? A bird, of course.'

The voice in the Bursar's head thought: but a bird must fly. Where are the wings?

'This one's standing on the ground. You don't see the wings,' said the Dean, and then looked puzzled at having answered a question no one had asked. 'Blast! You know, it's harder than it looks, drawing on a rock . . .'

I *always* see the wings, thought the voice in the Bursar's head. The Bursar fumbled for his dried frog pill bottle. The voices were never usually this *precise*.

'Very *flat* bird,' said Ridcully. 'Come on, Dean, our friend here isn't very happy. Let's go and work out a really good boat spell . . .'

'Looks more like a weasel to me,' said the Senior Wrangler. 'You've got the tail wrong.'

'The stick slipped.'

'A duck's fatter than that,' said the Chair of Indefinite Studies. 'You shouldn't try to show off, Dean. When was the last time you saw a duck that didn't have peas round it?'

'Last week, actually!'

'Yes, we had crispy duck. With plum sauce, I now recall. Here, let me have a go . . .'

'Now you've given it three legs!'

'I did *ask* for the stick! You snatched it away!'

'Now look,' said Ridcully. 'I'm a man who knows his ducks, and what you've got there is laughable. Give me that . . . thank *you*. You do a beak like *this* . . .'

'That's on the wrong end and it's too big.'

'You think *that's* a beak?'

'Look, all three of you are barking up the wrong tree here. Give me that stick . . .'

'Ah, but, you see, ducks don't bark! Hah! There's no need to snatch like that—'

Unseen University was built of stone – so built out of stone that in fact there were many places where it was hard to tell where wild rock ended and domesticated stone began.

It was hard to imagine what else you could build a university out of. If Rincewind had set out to list possible materials he wouldn't have included corrugated iron sheets.

In response to some sort of wizardly ancestral memory, though, the sheets around the gates had been quite expertly bent and hammered into the shape of a stone arch. Over it, burned into the thin metal, were the words: NULLUS ANXIETAS.

'I shouldn't be surprised, should I?' he said. 'No worries.'

The gates, which were also made of corrugated iron

nailed to bits of wood by a man using second-hand nails, were firmly shut. A crowd of people were hammering on them.

'Looks like a lot of other people have the same idea,' said Neilette.

'There'll be another way in,' said Rincewind, walking away. 'There'll be an alley . . . Ah, there it is. Now, these aren't stone walls, so there won't be removable bricks, which means . . .' He prodded at the tin sheets, and one of them wobbled. 'Ah, yes. A loose sheet which swings aside so you can get back in after hours.'

'How did you know that?'

'This is a university, isn't it? Come on.'

A message had been chalked beside the loose sheet.

' "*Nulli Sheilae sanguineae,*"' Rincewind read aloud. 'But your name's not Sheila, so we're probably okay.'

'If it means what I think it means, it means they don't allow women,' said Neilette. 'You should've brought Darleen.'

'Sorry?'

'Forget I mentioned it.'

Somewhat to Rincewind's surprise there was a short, pleasant lawn on the other side of the fence, illuminated by the light from a large low building. *All* the buildings were low but had big wide roofs, giving the effect you might get if someone stepped on a lot of square mushrooms. If they had been painted, it had been an historical event, probably coming somewhere between Fire and the Invention of the Wheel.

There *was* a tower. It was about twenty feet high.

'I don't call *this* much of a university,' said

Rincewind. He allowed himself a touch of smugness. 'Twenty feet high? I could pi— I could spit from the top of it. Oh well . . .'

He made for the doorway, just as the light grew a lot brighter and was tinted with octarine, the eighth colour that was intimately associated with magic. The doors themselves were shut fast.

He banged on them, making them rattle. 'Fraternal greetings, brothers!' he shouted. 'I bring you— Good grie—'

The world simply changed. One moment he was standing in front of a rusting door and the next he was in a circle with half a dozen wizards watching him.

He caught his balance.

'Well, full marks for effort,' he managed. 'Where I come from, and you can call me Mister Boring if you like, we just open the door.'

'Stone the crows, but we're getting good at this,' said a wizard.

And they *were* wizards. Rincewind was in no doubt of it. They had proper pointy hats, although the brims were larger than anything he'd seen without flying buttresses. Their robes weren't much more than waist length, and below them they wore shorts, long grey socks, and big leather sandals. A lot of this was not the typical wizarding outfit as he'd grown up to understand it, but they were still wizards. They had that unmistakable hot-air-balloon-about-to-take-off look.

The apparent leader of the group nodded at Rincewind.

'Good evening, Mister Boring. I must say you got here a lot quicker than we expected.'

Rincewind felt intuitively that saying 'I was just outside the door' was not a good idea.

'Er, I had an assisted passage,' he said.

'He doesn't look very demonic,' said a wizard. 'Remember that last one we called up? Six eyes and three—'

'The really good ones can disguise themselves, Dean.'

'Then this one must be a bloody genius, Archchancellor.'

'Thank you very much,' said Rincewind.

The Archchancellor nodded at him. He was, of course, elderly, with a face that looked as though it had been screwed up and then smoothed out, and a short, greying beard. There was something oddly *familiar* that Rincewind couldn't quite place.

'We've called you up, Boring,' said the man, 'because we want to know what's happened to the water.'

'It's all gone, has it?' said Rincewind. 'Thought so.'

'It can't *go*,' said the Dean. 'It's *water*. There's always water, if you go down deep enough.'

'But if we go any deeper we're going to give an elephant a bloody nasty shock,' said the Archchancellor. 'So we—'

There was a clang as the doors hit the floor. The wizards backed away.

'What the hell's *that*?' said one of them.

'Oh, that's my Luggage,' said Rincewind. 'It's made out of—'

'Not the box on legs! Isn't that a *woman*?'

'Don't ask him, he's not very quick at that sort of thing,' said Neilette, stepping in behind the Luggage. 'Sorry, but Trunkie got impatient.'

'We can't have women in the University!' shouted the Dean. 'They'll want to drink *sherry*!'

'No worries,' said the Archchancellor, waving a hand irritably. 'What's happened to the water, Boring?'

'It's all been used up, I suppose,' said Rincewind.

'So how can we get some more?'

'Why does everyone ask me? Don't you have some rainmaking spells or something?'

'There's that word again,' said the Dean. 'Water sprinkling out of the sky, eh? I'll believe that when I see it!'

'We tried making one of these – what were they called? Big white bags of water? The things some of the sailors say they see in the sky?'

'Clouds.'

'Right. They don't stay up, Boring. We threw one off the tower last week and it hit the Dean.'

'I've never believed those old stories,' said the Dean. 'And I reckon you mongrels waited till I was walking past.'

'You don't have to make them, they just happen,' said Rincewind. 'Look, I don't know how to make it rain. I thought any halfway decent wizard knew how to do a rainmaking spell,' he added, as someone who wouldn't know where to start.

'Really?' said the Archchancellor, with dangerous brightness.

'No offence meant,' said Rincewind hurriedly. 'I'm sure this is a very good university, considering. Obviously it's not a *real* one, but it's amazingly good in the circumstances.'

'What's wrong with it?' said the Archchancellor.

'Well . . . your tower's a little bit on the small side, isn't it? I mean, even compared to the buildings around here? Not that there's—'

'I think we ought to show Mister Boring our tower,' said the Archchancellor. 'I don't think he's taking us seriously.'

'I've seen it,' said Rincewind.

'From the top?'

'No, obviously not from the top—'

'We haven't got time for this, Archchancellor,' said a small wizard. 'Let's send this wozza back to Hell and find something better.'

'Excuse *me*?' said Rincewind. 'By "Hell" do you mean some hot red place?'

'Yes!'

'Really? How do Ecksians know when they've got there? The beer's warmer?'

'No more arguing. This one turned up very fast when we did the summoning, so this is the one we need,' said the Archchancellor. 'Come along, Boring. This won't take a minute.'

Ponder shook his head and wandered over to the fire. Mrs Whitlow was sitting demurely on a rock. In front of her, getting as close to the fire as possible, was the Librarian. He was still extremely small. Maybe his temporal gland had to take longer to work itself out, Ponder thought.

'What are the gentlemen doing?' said Mrs Whitlow. She had to raise her voice above the argument, but Mrs Whitlow would still have said, 'Is there some difficulty?' if she saw the wizards out on the lawn throwing fireballs at the monsters from the Dungeon Dimensions. She liked to be told these things.

'They've found a man drawing the most *alive*-looking pictures I've ever seen,' said Ponder. 'So now they're trying to teach him Art. By committee.'

'The gentlemen always take an interest,' said Mrs Whitlow.

'They always interfere,' said Ponder. 'I don't know what it is about wizards, they can't just *watch*. So far they're arguing about how to draw a duck and frankly I don't think a duck has four legs, which is what it's got so far. Honestly, Mrs Whitlow, they're like kittens in a feather-plucking shed . . . What's that?'

The Librarian had tipped up the leather bag lying by the fire and was testing the contents for taste, in the way of young mammals everywhere.

He picked up a flat, bent piece of wood, painted in lines of many colours – far more pigments than the old man had been using to paint, and Ponder wondered why. He tested it for palatability, banged it on the ground in a vaguely hopeful way, and threw it away. Then he pulled out a flat oval of wood on a piece of string, and tried chewing the string.

'Is that a yo-yo?' said Mrs Whitlow.

'We used to call them bullroarers when I was a kid,'

said Ponder. 'You whirl it around over your head to make a funny noise.' He waved his hand vaguely in the air.

'Eeek?'

'Ooh, isn't that sweet? He's trying to do what you do!'

The Librarian tried to whirl the string, wrapped it round his face and hit himself on the back of the head.

'Oh, the poor little thing! Take it off him, Mister Stibbons, do.'

The Librarian bared some small fangs as Ponder unwound the string.

'I hope he's going to grow up soon,' he said. 'Otherwise the Library will be filled up with cardboard books about bunnies . . .'

It really *was* a very stubby tower. The base was stonework, but about halfway the builders had got fed up and resorted to rusted tin sheets nailed on to a wooden framework. One rickety ladder led up.

'Very impressive,' sighed Rincewind.

'The view's even better from the top. Go on up.'

The ladder shook under Rincewind's weight until he pulled himself up on to the planks, where he lay down and panted. Must be the beer and the excitement, he told himself. One short ladder shouldn't do this to me.

'Bracing air up here, isn't it?' said the Archchancellor, walking to the edge and waving a hand towards the city.

'Oh, certainly,' said Rincewind, tottering towards

the corrugated battlements. 'Why, I expect you can see all the way to the gr— Aaargh!'

The Archchancellor grabbed him and pulled him back.

'That's— It's—' Rincewind gasped.

'Want to go back down again?'

Rincewind glared at the wizard and inched his way carefully back to the stairs. He looked down, ready at an instant's notice to draw his head back, and carefully counted the steps.

Then he walked back gingerly to the parapet and risked looking over the edge.

There was the fiery speck of the burning brewery. There was Bugarup, and its harbour . . .

Rincewind raised his gaze.

There was the red desert, glittering under the moonlight.

'How high is this?' he croaked.

'On the outside? About half a mile, we think,' said the Archchancellor.

'And on the inside?'

'You climbed it. Two storeys.'

'You're trying to tell me you've got a tower that's taller at the top than it is at the *bottom*?'

'Good, isn't it?' said the Archchancellor happily.

'That's . . . very clever,' said Rincewind.

'We're a clever country—'

'Rincewind!'

The voice came from below. Rincewind looked very carefully down the steps. It was one of the wizards.

'Yes?' he said.

'Not you,' snapped the wizard. 'I want the Archchancellor!'

'I'm Rincewind,' said Rincewind.

The Archchancellor tapped him on the shoulder. 'That's a coincidence,' he said. 'So am I.'

Ponder very carefully handed the bullroarer back to the little Librarian.

'There, you can have it,' he said. 'I'm giving it to *you* and, in return, perhaps *you* can take your teeth out of my leg.'

From the other side of the rock came the voice of reason: 'There's no need to fight, gentlemen. Let's vote on it: now, all those who think a duck has webbed feet, raise your hands . . .'

The Librarian swung the thing a few more times.

'Doesn't seem to be a very good one,' said Ponder. 'Not much of a noise . . . honestly, how much longer are they going to be?'

. . . *whum* . . .

'Eek!'

'Yes, yes, very good . . .'

. . . *whum* . . . *whum* . . . *whUUMMMMM* . . .

Ponder looked up as yellow light spread across the plain.

There was a circle of blue sky opening above. The rain was stopping.

'Eek?'

It occurred to Ponder to wonder what a little old man was doing painting pictures in a bare landscape on a whole new continent . . .

And then there was darkness.

The old man smiled with something like satisfaction, and turned away from the drawing he'd just completed. It had a lot of pointy hats in it, and it had faded right into the rock.

And he was as happy as anything, and had drawn all the spiders and several possums before he found out what was missing.

He never even knew about the very strange and unhappy duck-billed creature that slid silently into the river a little way off.

'Got to be at least some kind of cousins,' said the Archchancellor. 'It's not a common name. Have another beer.'

'I had a look through the Unseen records once,' said Rincewind morosely. 'They never had a Rincewind before.' He upended the can of beer and finished the dregs. 'Never had a *relative* before, come to that. Never ever.' He pulled the top off another can. 'No one to do all those little things relatives are s'posed to do, like ... like ... like send you some horrible cardigan at Hogswatch, stuff like that.'

'You got a first name? Mine's Bill.'

''s a good name, Bill Rincewind. Dunno if I've even *got* a first name.'

'What do people usually call you, mate?'

'Well, they usually say, "Stop him!"' said Rincewind, and took a deep draught of beer. 'Of course, that's just a nickname. When they want to be formal they shout "Don't let him get away!"'

He squinted at the can. "'s much better than that other stuff,' he said. 'What's this say? "Funnelweb"? 's a funny name for a beer.'

'You're reading the list of ingredients,' said Bill.

'Really?' mumbled Rincewind. 'Where was I?'

'Pointy hats. Water running out. Talking kangaroos. Pictures coming alive.'

'That's right,' said the Dean. 'If that's what you're like sober, we want to see what effect the beer has.'

'Y'see, when the sun's up,' said Archchancellor Bill, 'I've got to go down to the prison and see the prime minister and explain why we don't know what's happened to the water. Anything you can do to assist would be very useful. Give him another tinnie, Dean. People're already banging on the gates. Once the beer runs out, we're in strife.'

Rincewind felt that he was in a warm amber haze. He was among wizards. You could tell by the way they bickered all the time. And, somehow, the beer made it easier to think.

A wizard leaned over his shoulder and put an open book in front of him.

'This is a copy of a cave painting from Cangoolie,' he said. 'We've often wondered what the blobs are above the figures . . .'

'That's rain,' said Rincewind, after a glance.

'You mentioned this before,' said Bill. 'Little drops of water flying through the air, right?'

'Dropping,' Rincewind corrected him.

'And it doesn't hurt?'

'Nope.'

'Water's heavy. Can't say the idea of big white bags of the stuff floating around over our heads appeals.'

Rincewind had never studied meteorology, although he had been an end-user all his life.

He waved his hands vaguely. 'They're like . . . steam,' he said, and hiccuped. ''s right. Lovely fluffy steam.'

'They're *boiling*?'

'No, no. Nono. Ver' cold, clouds. Sometimes they come down ver' low, they even touch the ground.'

The wizards looked at one another.

'Y'know, we're making some bloody good beer these days,' said Bill.

'Clouds sound bloody dangerous to me,' said the Dean. 'We don't want them knocking over trees and buildings, do we?'

'Ah, but. But. They're *soft*, see? Like smoke.'

'But you said they weren't hot!'

Rincewind suddenly saw the perfect explanation.

'Have you ever huffed on a cold mirror?' he said, beaming.

'Not on a regular basis, but I know what you mean.'

'Well, basically, that's clouds! Can I have another beer? It's amazing, it doesn't feem to have any essect on me, no matter how much I dnirk. Helps me think clearerer.'

Archchancellor Rincewind drummed his fingers on the table. 'You and this rain stuff – you've got to be connected, yes? We've run out of water and you turn up . . .'

Rincewind burped. 'Got to put something right, too,' he said. 'Pointy hats, all floating in the air . . .'

'Where did you last see them?'

'In the brewery with no beer in it. Said it's haunted, haha. Pointy hat haunting, hahah . . .'

Bill stared at him. '*Right*,' he said. He looked at the forlorn figure of his distant cousin, now very close up. 'Let's get down there.' He glanced at Rincewind again and seemed to think for a moment.

'And we'll take some beer,' he added.

Ponder Stibbons tried to think, but his thoughts seemed to be going very slowly. Everything was dark and he couldn't move but, somehow, it wasn't too bad. It felt like those treasured moments in bed when you're just awake enough to know that you're still nicely asleep.

It's amazing how time passes.

There was a huge bucket chain now, stretching all the way from the harbour to the brewery. Despite the tangily refreshing oak spiciness of their Chardonnays, the Ecksians weren't the kind of people to let a brewery burn. It didn't matter that there was no beer in it. There was a principle at stake.

The wizards marched through the crowd to a chorus of mutters and the occasional jeer from someone safely tucked away at the back.

Smoke and steam came out of the main doorway, which had been burst open by a battering ram.

Archchancellor Rincewind stepped inside, dragging his happily smiling relative with him.

The smouldering Roo Beer sign, reduced to a

metal skeleton, still lay in the middle of the floor.

'He kept waving at it and going on about pointy hats,' Neilette volunteered.

'Test it for magic, Dean,' said Archchancellor Rincewind.

The Dean waved a hand. Sparks flew up. 'Nothing there,' he said. 'I said we—'

For a moment some pointed shapes hung in the air, and then vanished.

'That's not *magic*,' said one of the wizards. 'That's ghosts.'

'Everyone *knows* this place is haunted. Evil spirits, they say.'

'Should've stuck to beer,' said Archchancellor Rincewind.

Neilette pointed to the trapdoor. 'But it doesn't go anywhere,' she said. 'There's a hatch to the outside and some storerooms and that's about it.'

The wizards looked down.

Below was utter darkness. Something small skittered away on what sounded very much like more than four legs. There was the smell of very old, very stale beer.

'No worries,' said Rincewind, waving a tin expansively. 'I'll go down first, shall I?'

This was *fun*.

There was a rusted ladder bolted to the wall below him. It creaked under his weight, and gave way when he was a few feet from the cellar floor, dropping him on to the stones. The wizards heard him laugh.

Then he called up: 'Do any of you know someone called Dibbler?'

'What – old Fair Go?' said Bill.

''s right. He'll be outside selling stuff to the crowd, right?'

'Very likely.'

'Can someone go and get me one of his floating meat pies with extra tomato sauce? I could really do with one.'

The Dean looked at Archchancellor Rincewind. 'How much beer did he drink?'

'Three or four tinnies. He must be allergic, poor bastard.'

'I reckon I could even eat two,' Rincewind called up.

'*Two?*'

'No worries. Anyone got a torch? It's dark down here.'

'Do you want the gourmet pies or the ordinary?' said the Dean.

'Oh, the ordinary will do me. No swank, eh?'

'Poor bastard,' said Bill, and sorted through his small change.

It was indeed dark in the cellars, but enough dim light filtered through the trapdoor for Rincewind to make out huge pipes in the gloom.

It was obvious that some time after the brewery had been closed, but before people had got around to securely locking every entrance, the cellars had been employed by young people as such places are when you live with your parents, the house is too small, and no one has got around to inventing the motorcar.

In short, they'd written on the walls. Rincewind could make out careful inscriptions telling posterity that, for example, B. Smoth Is A Pozza. While he didn't know what a pozza was, he was quite, quite sure that B. Smoth didn't want to be called one. It was amazing how slang seemed to radiate its meaning even in another language.

There was a thump behind him as the Luggage landed on the stone floor.

'Me old mate Trunkie,' said Rincewind. 'No worries!'

Another ladder was eased down and the wizards, with some care, joined him. Archchancellor Rincewind was holding a staff with a glowing end.

'Found anything?' he said.

'Well, yes. I wouldn't shake hands with anyone called B. Smoth,' said Rincewind.

'Oh, the Dean's not a bad bloke when you get to know him—What's up?'

Rincewind pointed to the far end of the room.

There, on a door, someone had drawn some pointy hats, in red. They glistened in the light.

'My word. Blood,' said Rincewind.

His cousin ran a finger over it. 'It's ochre,' he said. 'Clay . . .'

The door led to another cellar. There were a few empty barrels, some broken crates, and nothing else except musty darkness.

Dust whirled up on the floor from the draught of their movement, in a series of tiny, inverted whirlwinds. Pointy hats again.

'Hmm, solid walls all round,' said Bill. 'Better pick a direction, mate.'

Rincewind had a drink, shut his eyes and pointed a finger at random.

'That way!'

The Luggage plunged forward and struck the brickwork, which fell away to reveal a dark space beyond.

Rincewind stuck his head through. All the builders had done was wall up and square off a part of a cave. From the feel of the air, it was quite a large one.

Neilette and the wizards climbed through behind him.

'I'm sure this place wasn't here when the brewery was built!' said Neilette.

'It's big,' said the Dean. 'How'd it get made?'

'Water,' said Rincewind.

'You what? Water makes great big holes in rock?'

'Yes. Don't ask me why— What was that?'

'What?'

'Did you hear something?'

'You said, "What was that?"'

Rincewind sighed. The cold air was sobering him up.

'You really are wizards, aren't you?' he said. 'Real honest-to-goodness wizards. You've got hats that're more brim than point, the whole university's made of tin, you've got a tiny tower which is, I must admit, good grief, a lot taller on the outside, but you're wizards all right, and will you now, please, *shut up*?'

In the silence there was, very faintly, a *plink*.

Rincewind stared into the depths of the cave. The

light from the staffs only made them worse. It cast shadows. Darkness was just darkness, but *anything* could be hiding in shadows.

'These caves must've been explored,' he said. It was a hope rather than a statement. History here was rather a rubbery thing.

'Never heard of 'em,' said the Dean.

'Points again, look,' said Bill, as they advanced.

'Just stalactites and stalagmites,' said Rincewind. 'I don't know how it works, but water drips on stuff and leaves piles of stuff. Takes thousands of years. Perfectly ordinary.'

'Is this the same kind of water that floats through the sky *and* gouges out big caves in rocks?' said the Dean.

'Er . . . yes . . . er, obviously,' said Rincewind.

'It's good luck for us we only have the drinking and washing sort, then.'

'Had,' said Rincewind.

There were hurrying feet behind them and a junior wizard ran up, holding a plate covered with a lid.

'Got the last one!' he said. 'It's a *gourmet* pie, too.'

He lifted the lid. Rincewind stared, and swallowed. 'Oh dear . . .'

'What's up?'

'Have you got some more of that beer? I think I might be losing . . . concentration . . .'

His cousin stepped forward, ripping the top off a can of Funnelweb.

'Cartwright, you cover that pie up and keep it warm. Rincewind, you drink this.'

They watched him drain the tin.

'Right, mate,' said the Archchancellor. 'How about a nice meat pie upside down in a big bowl of mushy green peas covered with tomato sauce?'

He looked at the colour change on Rincewind's face, and nodded.

'You need another tin,' he said firmly.

They watched him drink this.

'Okay,' said the Archchancellor after a while. 'Now, Rincewind, how about a nice one of Fair Go's pie floaters, eh? Meat pie in pea soup and tomato sauce?'

Rincewind's face twitched a bit as amber blessings shut down vital protective systems.

'Sounds . . . good,' he said. 'Maybe with some coconut on the top?'

The wizards relaxed.

'So now we know,' said Archchancellor Rincewind. 'We've got to keep you just drunk enough so that Dibbler's pies sound tasty, but not so drunk that it causes lasting brain damage.'

'That's a very narrow window we've got there,' said the Dean.

Bill looked up at the roof, where the shadows danced among the stalactites, unless they were stalagmites.

'This is right under the city,' he said. 'How come we've never heard of it?'

'Good question,' said the Dean. 'The men who built the cellar must've seen it.'

Rincewind tried to think. 'It wasn't here then,' he said.

'You said these stalag things took thousands of—'

'They probably weren't here last month but now they've been here for thousands of years,' said Rincewind. He hiccuped. 'It's like your tower,' he said. 'Taller onna outside.'

'Huh?'

'Prob'ly only works here,' said Rincewind. 'The more geography you've got, the less hist'ry, ever notice that? More space, less time. I bet it only took a second or two for this place to be here for thousands of years, see? Shorter on the *outside*. Makes serfect pense.'

'I don't think I've drunk enough beer to understand that,' said the Dean.

Something nudged him in the back of the legs. He looked down at the Luggage. It was one of its habits to come up so close behind people that, when they looked down, they felt seriously over-feeted.

'Or this,' he added.

The wizards grew quieter as Rincewind led them onward. He wasn't sure who was leading him. Still, no worries.

Contrary to the usual procedures it began to grow lighter, although the proliferation of luminous fungi or iridescent crystals in deep caves where the torchlessly improvident hero needs to *see* is one of the most obvious intrusions of narrative causality into the physical universe. In this case, the rocks were glowing, not from some mysterious inner light but simply as though the sun were shining on them, just after dawn.

There are other imperatives that operate on the human brain. One says: the bigger the space, the softer the voice, and refers to the natural tendency to speak very, very quietly when stepping into somewhere huge. So when Archchancellor Rincewind stepped out into the *big* cave he said, 'Strewth, it's bloody big!' in a low whisper.

The Dean, however, shouted, 'Coo-eee!' because there's always one.

Stalactites crowded the cave here, too, and in the very centre a gigantic stalactite had almost touched its mirror-image stalagmite. The air was chokingly hot.

'This isn't right—' said Rincewind.

Plink.

They spotted the source of the noise eventually. A tiny trickle was making its way down the side of the stalactite and forming droplets that fell a few feet to the stalagmite.

Another drop formed while they watched, and hung there.

One of the wizards clambered up the dry slope and peered at it.

'It's not moving,' he said. 'The trickle's drying up. I think . . . it's evaporating.'

The Archchancellor turned to Rincewind. 'Well, we've followed you this far, mate,' he said. 'What now?'

'I think I could do with another b—'

'There's none left, mate.'

Rincewind looked desperately around the cave, and then at the huge translucent mass of limestone in front of him.

It was definitely pointy. It was also in the centre of the cave. It had a certain *inevitability* about it.

Odd, really, that something like this would form down here, shining away like a pearl in an oyster. The ground trembled again. Up there, people would already be getting thirsty, cursing the windmills as only an Ecksian could curse. The water was gone and that was very bad, and when the beer ran out people would *really* get angry . . .

The wizards were all waiting for him to *do* something.

All right, start with the rock. What did he know about rocks and caves in these parts?

There was a curious freedom at a time like this. He was going to be in real trouble whatever he did, so he might as well give this a try . . .

'I need some paint,' he said.

'What for?'

'For what I need,' said Rincewind.

'There's young Salid,' said the Dean. 'He's a bit of an arty blager. Let's go and kick his door down.'

'And bring some more beer!' Rincewind called after them.

Neilette patted Rincewind on the shoulder. 'Are you going to do some magic?' she said.

'I don't know if it counts as magic here,' said Rincewind. 'If it doesn't work, stand well back.'

'Is it going to be dangerous, then?'

'No, I might have to start running without looking where I'm going. But . . . this rock's warm. Have you noticed?'

She touched it. 'I see what you mean . . .'

'I was just thinking . . . Supposing someone was in

a country who shouldn't be there? What would it do?'

'Oh, the Watch would catch him, I expect.'

'No, no, not the people. What would the *land* do? I think I need another drink, it made more sense then . . .'

'Okay, here we are, we couldn't find much, but there's some whitewash and some red paint and a tin of stuff which might be black paint or it could be tar oil.' The wizards hurried up. 'Not much in the way of brushes, though.'

Rincewind picked up a brush that looked as though it had once been used to whitewash a very rough wall and then to clean the teeth of some large creature, possibly a crocodile.

He'd never been any good at art, and this is a distinction quite hard to achieve in many education systems. Basic artistic skills and a familiarity with occult calligraphy are part of a wizard's early training, yet in Rincewind's fingers chalk broke and pencils shattered. It was probably due to a deep distrust of getting things down on paper when they were doing all right where they were.

Neilette handed him a tin of Funnelweb. Rincewind drank deeply and then dipped the brush in what might have been black paint and essayed a few upturned Vs on the rock, and some circles under the lines, with three dots in a V and a friendly little curve in each one.

He took another deep draught of the beer and saw what he was doing wrong. It was no good trying to be strictly true to life here; what he had to go for was an *impression*.

He sloshed wildly at the stone, humming madly under his breath.

'Anyone guess what it is yet?' he said, over his shoulder.

'Looks a bit modern to me,' said the Dean.

But Rincewind was into the swing of it now. Any fool could just copy what he saw, except possibly Rincewind, but surely the whole point was to try to paint a picture that moved, that definitely expressed the, the, the—

Definitely expressed it, anyway. You went the way the paint and the colour wanted you to go.

'You know,' said Neilette, 'the way the light falls on it and everything . . . it could be a group of wizards . . .'

Rincewind half closed his eyes. Perhaps it *was* the way that the shadows moved, but he had to admit he'd done a really good job. He slapped some more paint on.

'Looks like they're almost coming out of the stone,' said someone behind him, but the voice sounded muffled.

He felt as though he was falling into a hole. He'd had the sensation before, although usually it *was* when he was falling into a hole. The walls were fuzzy, as though they were streaking past him at a tremendous rate. The ground shook.

'Are we moving?' he said.

'Feels like it, doesn't it?' said Archchancellor Rincewind. 'But we're standing still!'

'Moving while standing still,' muttered Rincewind,

and giggled. 'That's a good one!' He squinted happily at the beer can. 'Y'know,' he said, 'I can't stomach more than a pint or two of the ale we have at home but this stuff is like drinking lemonade! Has anyone got that meat pie—'

As loudly as a thunderstorm under the bed but as softly as two soufflés colliding, past and present ran into one another.

They contained a lot of people.

'What's this?'

'Dean?'

'Yes?'

'You're not the Dean!'

'How dare you say that! Who are you!'

'Ook!'

'Stone the cows, there's a *monkey* in here!'

'No! No! *I* didn't say that! *He* said that!'

'Archchancellor?'

'Yes?'

'Yes?'

'What? How many of you are there?'

The darkness became a deep purple, shading to violet.

'*Will you all stop shouting and listen to me!*'

To Rincewind's amazement, they did.

'Look, the walls are getting closer! This place is trying not to exist!'

And, having done his duty to the community, he turned and ran over the shaking rock floor.

After a couple of seconds the Luggage passed him, which was always a bad sign.

He heard the voices behind him. Wizards had a hard job accepting the term 'clear and present danger'. They liked the kind you could argue about. But there is something about a rapidly descending ceiling that intrudes into the awareness of even the most quarrelsome.

'I'll save you, Mrs Whitlow!'

'Up the tunnel!'

'How fast are those walls closing in, would you say?'

'Shut up and run!'

Now Rincewind was passed by a large red, furry kangaroo. The Librarian's erratic morphism, having briefly turned him into a red stalactite as an obviously successful shape for surviving in caves, had finally taken on board the fact that it would make for a terminally lengthy survival in a cave that was rapidly getting smaller, and had flipped into a local morphic field built for speed.

Man, Luggage and kangaroo piled through the hole into the cellar and ended in a heap against the opposite side.

There was a rumbling behind them and wizards and women were fired out into the cellar with some speed, several of them landing on Rincewind. Behind the wall, the rock groaned and creaked, expelling these alien things in what, Rincewind thought, was a geological chunder.

Something flew out of the hole and hit him on the ear, but this was only a minor problem compared to the meat pie, which came out trailing mushy peas and tomato sauce and hit him in the mouth.

It wasn't, actually, all that bad.

*   *   *

The ability to ask questions like 'Where am I and who is the "I" that is asking?' is one of the things that distinguishes mankind from, say, cuttlefish.*

The wizards from Unseen University, being perhaps the intellectual cream or certainly the cerebral yoghurt of their generation, passed through this stage within minutes. Wizards are very adept at certain ideas. One minute you're arguing over the shape of a duck's head and the next there are people telling you you've been inside a rock for thousands of years because time goes slower on the inside. This presents no great problem for a man who has found his way to the lavatory at Unseen University.†

There were more important questions as they sat round the table in BU.

'Is there anything to eat?' said Ridcully.

'It's the middle of the night, sir.'

'You mean we missed *dinner*?'

'Thousands of years of dinners, Archchancellor.'

'Really? Better start catching up, then, Mister Stibbons. Still . . . nice little place you've got here . . . archchancellor.'

Ridcully pronounced the word very carefully in order to accentuate the lower case 'a'.

Archchancellor Rincewind gave him a fraternal nod. 'Thank you.'

---

* Although of course it's not the most obvious thing and there are, in fact, some beguiling similarities, particularly the tendency to try to hide behind a big cloud of ink in difficult situations.
† The one on the first floor, with the curious gravitational anomaly.

'For a colony, of course. I daresay you do your best.'

'Why, thank you, Mustrum. I'd be happy to show you our tower later on.'

'It does look rather small.'

'So people say.'

'Rincewind, Rincewind . . . name rings a faint bell . . .' said Ridcully.

'We came looking for Rincewind, Archchancellor,' said Ponder, patiently.

'Is he? Done well for himself, then. Fresh air made a man of him, I see.'

'No, sir. Ours is the skinny one with the bad beard and the floppy hat, sir. You remember? The one sitting over there.'

Rincewind raised a hand diffidently. 'Er. Me,' he said.

Ridcully sniffed. 'Fair enough. What's that thing you're playing with, man?'

Rincewind held up the bullroarer. 'It came with you out of the cave,' he said. 'What were you doing with it?'

'Oh, some toy the Librarian found,' said Ponder.

'All sorted out, then,' said Ridcully. 'I say, this beer's good, isn't it? Very drinkable. Yes, I'm sure there's a lot we can learn from one another, archchancellor. You from us rather more than us from you, of course. Perhaps we could set up a student exchange, that sort of thing?'

'Good idea.'

'You can have six of mine in exchange for a decent lawnmower. Ours has broken.'

'The Arch— the *arch*chancellor is trying to say that getting back might be rather hard, sir,' said Ponder. 'Apparently things ought to have changed now we're here. But they haven't.'

'Your Rincewind seemed to think that bringing you blokes here would make it rain,' said Bill. 'But it hasn't.'

. . . whumm . . .

'Oh, do stop playing with that thing, Rincewind,' said Ridcully. 'Well . . . Bill, it's obvious, isn't it? As more experienced wizards than you, we naturally know plenty of ways of making it rain. No problem there.'

. . . whumm . . .

'Look, lad, take that thing outside, will you?'

The Librarian was sitting at the top of the tin tower, with a leaf over his head.

'Something odd, see?' said Rincewind, dangling the bullroarer from its string. 'I've only got to wiggle my hand a bit and it swings right round.'

'. . . ook . . .'

The Librarian sneezed.

'. . . awk . . .'

'Er . . . now you're some sort of large bird . . .' said Rincewind. 'You *are* in a bad way, aren't you? Still, once I tell them your name . . .'

The Librarian changed shape and moved fast. There was a very short period of time in which a lot happened.

'Ah,' said Rincewind calmly when it seemed to be

over. 'Well, let us start with what we know. I can't see. The reason I can't see is that my robe is hanging over my eyes. From this I can deduce that I am upside down. You are gripping my ankles. Correction, one ankle, so obviously you are holding me upside down. We are at the top of the tower. This means . . .'

He fell silent.

'All right, let's start again,' he said. 'Let's start by me not telling anyone your name.'

The Librarian let go.

Rincewind dropped a few inches on to the planks of the tower.

'You know, that was a really mean trick you just did,' he said.

'Ook.'

'We'll say no more about it, shall we?'

Rincewind looked up at the big, empty sky. It *ought* to be raining. He'd done everything he was supposed to do, hadn't he? And all that had happened was that the Faculty of UU was down there being condescending about everything. It wasn't even as if they could *do* a rainmaking spell. For one of those to work you needed some rain around to start with. In fact, it was prudent to make sure that some heavy-looking clouds were being blown in your direction.

And if it wasn't raining then probably those terrible currents they talked about were still around, too.

It wasn't a *bad* country. They were big on hats. They were big on *big* hats. He could save up and buy a farm on the Never-Never and watch sheep. After all, they fed themselves and they made more sheep. All you had to do was pick the wool off occasionally. The Luggage'd probably settle down to being a sheepdog.

Except . . . that there wasn't any more water. No more sheep, no more farms. Mad, and Crocodile Crocodile, the lovely ladies Darleen and Letitia, Remorse and his horses, all those people who'd shown him how to find the things you could eat without throwing up too often . . . all drying up, and blowing away . . .

Him, too.

G'DAY.

'Ook?'

'Oh, *no* . . .' Rincewind moaned.

THROAT A BIT PARCHED?

'Look, you're not supposed to—'

IT'S ALL RIGHT, I HAVE AN APPOINTMENT DOWN IN THE CITY. THERE'S BEEN A FIGHT OVER THE LAST BOTTLE OF BEER. HOWEVER, LET ME ASSURE YOU OF MY PERSONAL ATTENTION AT ALL TIMES.

'Well, thank you. When it's time to stop living, I will certainly make Death my number one choice!'

Death faded.

'The cheek of him, turning up like that! We're not dead yet,' shouted Rincewind to the burning sky. 'There's lots we could do! If we could get to the Hub we could cut loose a big iceberg and tow it here and that'd give us plenty of water . . . if we could get to the Hub! Where there's hope there's life, I'll have you know! I'll find a way! Somewhere there's a way of making rain!'

Death had gone.

Rincewind swung the bullroarer menacingly. 'And don't come back!'

'Ook!'

The Librarian gripped Rincewind's arm, and sniffed the air.

Then Rincewind caught the smell too.

Rincewind spoke a fairly primitive language, and it had no word for 'that smell you get after rain' other than 'that smell you get after rain'. Anyone trying to describe the smell would have to flounder among words like moisture, heat, vapour and, with a following wind, exhalation.

Nevertheless, there was the smell you get after rain. In this burning land, it was like a brief jewel in the air.

Rincewind whirled the piece of wood again. It made noise out of all proportion to the movement, and there was that smell again.

He turned it over. It was still just a wooden oval. There weren't any markings on it.

He gripped the end of the string and whirled the thing experimentally a few more times.

'Did you notice that when it did this—' he began.

It wouldn't stop. He couldn't lower his arm.

'Er . . . I think it wants to be spun,' he said.

'Ook!'

'You think I should?'

'Ook!'

'That's very helpful. Oooh—'

The Librarian ducked.

Rincewind spun. He couldn't see the wood now because the string was getting longer with each turn. A blur curved through the air some way from the tower, getting further away with each spin.

The sound of it was a long-drawn-out drone.

When it was well out over the city it exploded in a thunderclap. But something still whirled on the end of the line, like a tight silver cloud, throwing out a trail of white particles that made a spiral that sped out wider and wider.

The Librarian was flat on his face with his hands over his head.

Air roared up the side of the tower, carrying dust, wind, heat and budgerigars. Rincewind's robe flapped around his chin.

Letting go was unthinkable. He wasn't even sure if he could, until it wanted him to.

Thin as smoke now, the spiral drifted out into the heat haze.

(. . . and out over the red desert and the unheeding kangaroos, and as the tail of it flew out over the coast and into the wall of storms the warring airs melted peacefully together . . . the clouds stopped their stately spin around the last continent, boiled up in confusion and thunderheads, reversed their direction and began to fall *inwards* . . .)

And the string whipped out of Rincewind's hand, stinging his fingers. The bullroarer flew away, and he didn't see it fall.

This may have been because he was still pirouetting, but at last gravity overcame momentum and he fell full length on the boards.

'I think my feet have caught fire,' he muttered.

* * *

The dead heat hung on the land like a shroud. Clancy the stockman wiped the sweat off his brow very thoroughly, and wrung out the rag into an empty jam tin. The way things were going, he'd be glad of it. Then, carrying the tin with care, he climbed back down the windmill's ladder.

'The bore's fine, boss, there's just no bloody water,' he said.

Remorse shook his head. 'Look at them horses,' he said. 'Look at the way they're lying down, willya? That's not good. This is it, Clancy. We've battled through thick and thin, and this is too thick altogether by half. We may as well cut their poor bloody throats for the meat that's on 'em—'

A gust of wind took his hat off for him, and blew a lash of scent across the wilted mulga bushes. A horse raised his head.

Clouds were pouring across the sky, rolling and boiling across each other like waves on a beach, so black that in the middle they were blue, lit by occasional flashes.

'What the hell's *that*?' said Clancy.

The horse stood up awkwardly and stumbled to the rusted trough under the windmill.

Under the clouds, dragging across the land, the air shimmered silver.

Something hit Remorse's head.

He looked down. Something went 'plut' in the red dust by his boot, leaving a little crater.

'That is *water*, Clancy,' he said. 'It's bloody *water* dropping out of the bloody *sky*!'

They stared at one another with their mouths open as, around them, the storm hit and the animals stirred and the red dust turned into mud which spattered them up to their waists.

This was no ordinary rainstorm. This was The Wet.

As Clancy said later, the second best bloody thing that happened that day was that they were near high ground.

The *best* bloody thing was that, with all the corks on their hats, they were able to find the bloody things later on.

There'd been debate about having this year's regatta in Dijabringabeeralong, given the drought. But it was a tradition. A lot of people came into town for it. Besides, the organizers had discussed it long and hard all the previous evening in the bar of the Pastoral Hotel and had concluded that, no worries, she'll be right.

There were classes for boats pulled by camels, boats optimistically propelled by sails and, a high spot of the event, skiffs propelled by the simple expedient of the crew cutting the bottoms out, gripping the sides and running like hell. It always got a good laugh.

It was while two teams were trotting upriver in the semi-final that the spectators noticed the black cloud pouring over Semaphore Hill like boiling jam.

'Bushfire,' said someone.

'Bushfire'd be white. Come on . . .'

That was the thing about fire. If you saw one, everyone went to put it out. Fire spread like wildfire.

But as they turned away there was a scream from the riverbed.

The teams rounded the bend neck and neck, carrying their boats at a record-breaking speed. They reached the slipway, collided in their efforts to get up it, made it to the top locked together, and collapsed in splinters and screams.

'Stop the regatta!' panted one of the coxes. 'The river . . . the river . . .'

But by then everyone could see it. Around the bend, travelling slowly because it was pushing in front of it a huge logjam of bushes, carts, rocks and trees, was the flood.

It thundered past and the mobile dam slid on, scything the river bottom free of all obstruction. Behind it foaming water filled the river from bank to bank.

They cancelled the regatta. A river full of water made a mockery of the whole idea.

The university's gates had burst open and now the angry mob was in the grounds and hammering on the walls.

Above the din, the wizards searched feverishly through the books.

'Well, have you got something like Maxwell's Impressive Separator?' said Ridcully.

'What's that do?' said Archchancellor Rincewind.

'Unmixes two things, like . . . sugar and sand, for example. Uses nanny's demons.'

'Nano-demons, possibly,' murmured Ponder wearily.

'Oh, like Bonza Charlie's Beaut Sieve? Yeah, we've got that.'

'Ah, parallel evolution. Fine. Dig it out, man.'

Archchancellor Rincewind nodded at one of the wizards, and then broke into a grin.

'Are you thinking about it working on salt?' he said.

'Exactly! One spell, one bucket of seawater, no more problem . . .'

'Er, that's not *exactly* true,' said Ponder Stibbons.

'Sounds perfect to me, man!'

'It takes a great deal of magic, sir. And the demons take about a fortnight per pint, sir.'

'Ah. A significant point, Mister Stibbons.'

'Yes, sir.'

'However, just because it wouldn't work does not mean it was a *bad* idea – I wish they'd stop that shouting!'

The shouting outside stopped.

'Perhaps they heard you, sir,' said Ponder.

Pang. Pang, pang . . .

'Are they throwing stuff on to the roof?' said Archchancellor Rincewind.

'No, that's probably just rain,' said Ridcully. 'Now, I suppose you've tried evaporating—'

He realized that no one was listening. Everyone was looking up.

Now the individual thuds had merged into a steady hammering and from outside came the sound of wild cheering.

The wizards struggled in the doorway and finally fought their way outside, where water was pouring off the roof in a solid sheet and cutting a channel in the lawn.

Archchancellor Rincewind stopped abruptly and reached out to the water like a man not sure if the stove is hot.

'Out of the sky?' he said. He pushed his way out through the liquid curtain. Then he took off his hat and held it upside down to catch the rain.

The crowd had filled the university grounds and spilled out into the surrounding streets. Every face was turned upwards.

'And those dark things?' Archchancellor Rincewind called out.

'They *are* the clouds, archchancellor.'

'There's a hell of a lot of them!'

There were. They piled up over the tower in an enormous, spreading black thunderhead.

A couple of people looked down long enough to see the group of soaked wizards, and there were some cheers. And suddenly they were the new centre of attention, and being picked up and carried shoulder high.

'They think we did it!' shouted Archchancellor Rincewind, as he was borne aloft.

'Who's to say we didn't?' shouted Ridcully, tapping the side of his nose conspiratorially.

'Er . . .' someone began.

Ridcully didn't even look round. 'Shut up, Mister Stibbons,' he said.

'Shutting up, sir.'

'Can you hear that thunder?' said Ridcully, as a

rumble rolled across the city. 'We'd better take cover ...'

The clouds above the tower were rising like water against a dam. Ponder said afterwards the fact that the BU tower was very short and extremely tall at the same time might have been the problem, since the storm was trying to go around it, over it and through it, all at the same time.

From the ground the clouds seemed to open up slowly, leaving a glowing, spreading chimney filled with the blue haze of electrical discharges ...

... and pounced. One solid blue bolt hit the tower at every height all at once, which is technically impossible. Pieces of wood and corrugated iron roared into the air and rained down across the city.

Then there was just a sizzling, and the rushing of the rain.

The crowd stood up again, cautiously, but the fireworks were over.

'And that's what we call lightning,' said Ridcully.

Archchancellor Rincewind got up and tried to brush mud off his robe, then found out why you cannot do this.

'It's not usually as big as that, though,' Ridcully went on.

'Oh. Good.'

There was a clank from the steaming debris where the tower had stood, and a sheet of metal was pushed aside. Slowly, with much mutual aid and many false starts, two blackened figures emerged. One of them was still wearing a hat, which was on fire although the rain was putting out the flames.

Leaning against one another, weaving from side to side, they approached the wizards.

One of them said, 'Ook,' very quietly and fell backwards.

The other one looked blearily at the two arch-chancellors, and saluted. This caused a spark to leap from its fingers and burn its ear.

'Er, Rincewind,' it said.

'And what have *you* been up to while we've been doing all this hard work, pray?' said Ridcully.

Rincewind looked around, very slowly. Occasional little blue streaks crackled in his beard.

'Well, that all seemed to go pretty well, really. All things considered,' he said, and fell full length into a puddle.

It rained. After that, it rained. Then it rained some more. The clouds were stacked like impatient charter flights over the coast, low on fuel, jockeying for position, and raining. Above all, raining.

Floodwater roared down the rocks and scoured out the ancient muddy waterholes. A species of tiny shrimps whose world for thousands of years had been one small hole under a stone were picked up and carried wholesale into a lake that was spreading faster than a man could run. There had been fewer than a thousand of them. There were a *lot* more next day. Even if the shrimps had been able to count how many, they were far too busy to bother.

In the new estuaries, rich in sudden silt and

unexpected food, a few fish began the experiment of a salt-free diet. The mangroves started their stop-motion conquests of the new mudbanks.

It went on raining.

Then it rained some more.

After that, it rained.

It was some days later.

The ship rose and fell gently by the dock. The water around it was red with suspended silt in which a few leaves and twigs floated.

'A week or two to NoThingfjord and we're practically home,' said Ridcully.

'Practically on the same continent, anyway,' said the Dean.

'Quite an int'resting long vacation, really,' said the Lecturer in Recent Runes.

'Probably the longest ever,' said Ponder. 'Did Mrs Whitlow like her stateroom?'

'I for one will quite enjoy bunking down in the hold,' said the Senior Wrangler loyally.

'The bilges, actually,' said Ponder. 'The hold's full. Of opals, beer, sheep, wool and bananas.'

'Where's the Librarian?' said Ridcully.

'In the hold, sir.'

'Yes, I suppose it was silly of me to ask. Still, nice to see him his old self again.'

'I think it may have been the lightning, sir. He's certainly very lively now.'

And Rincewind sat on the Luggage, down on the dock.

Somehow, he felt, something should be happening. The worst time in your life was when nothing much was going on, because that meant that something bad was about to hit you. For some strange reason.

He could be back in the University Library in a month or so, and then ho! for a life of stacking books. One dull day after another, with occasional periods of boredom. He could hardly wait. Every minute not being a minute wasted was, well, a minute wasted. Excitement? That could happen to other people.

He'd watched the merchants loading the ship. It was pretty low in the water, because there would be so many Ecksian things the rest of the world wanted. Of course, it'd come back light, because it was hard to think of any bloody thing it could bloody import that was better than any bloody thing in EcksEcksEcksEcks.

There were even a few more passengers willing to see the world, and most of them were young.

'Hey, aren't you one of the foreign wizards?'

The speaker was a young man carrying a very large knapsack topped by a bedroll. He seemed to be the impromptu leader of a small group of similarly over-loaded people, with wide, open faces and slightly worried expressions.

'You can tell, can't you?' said Rincewind. 'Er . . . you wanted something?'

'D'yew think we can buy a cart in this place NoThingfjord?'

'Yes, I should think so.'

'Only me and Clive and Shirl and Gerleen were

thinkin' of picking one up and driving to—' He looked around.

'Ankh-Morpork,' said Shirl.

'Right, and then selling it, and gettin' a job for a while, having a look round, y'know . . . for a while. That'd be right?'

Rincewind glanced at the others trooping up the gangplank. Since the invention of the dung beetle, which had in fact happened not too far away, it was probable that no creature had ever carried so much weight.

'I can see it catching on,' he said.

'No worries!'

'But . . . er . . .'

'Yes, mate?'

'Do you mind not humming that tune? It was only a sheep, and I didn't even steal it . . .'

Someone tapped him on the shoulder. It was Neilette. Letitia and Darleen were standing behind her, grinning. It was ten in the morning. They were wearing sequinned evening gowns.

'Budge up,' she said, and settled down beside him. 'We just thought . . . well, we've come to say, you know, thanks and everything. Letitia and Darleen are coming in with me and we're going to open up the brewery again.'

Rincewind glanced up at the ladies.

'I've had enough beer thrown at me, I ought to know something about it,' said Letitia. 'Although I do think we could make it a more attractive colour. It's so . . .' she waved a large, be-ringed hand irritably, '. . . aggressively *masculine*.'

'Pink would be nice,' said Rincewind. 'And you could put in a pickled onion on a stick, perhaps.'

'Bloody good suggestion!' said Darleen, slapping him so hard on the back that his hat fell over his eyes.

'You wouldn't like to stay?' said Neilette. 'You look like someone with ideas.'

Rincewind considered this attractive proposition, and then shook his head.

'It's a nice offer, but I think I ought to stick to what I do best,' he said.

'But everyone says you're no good at magic!' said Neilette.

'Er . . . yes, well, being no good at magic *is* what I do best,' said Rincewind. 'Thanks all the same.'

'At least let me give you a big wet sloppy kiss,' said Darleen, grabbing his shoulders. Out of the corner of his eye Rincewind saw Neilette's foot stamp down.

'All right, all right!' said Darleen, letting go and hopping away. 'It wasn't as if I was going to bite him, miss!'

Neilette gave Rincewind a peck on the cheek.

'Well, drop in whenever you're passing,' she said.

'Certainly will!' said Rincewind. 'I'll look for the pubs with the mauve umbrellas outside, shall I?'

Neilette gave him a wave and Darleen made an amusing gesture as they walked away, almost bumping into a group of men in white. One of them shouted, 'Hey, there he is . . . Sorry, ladies . . .'

'Oh, hello, Charley . . . Ron . . .' said Rincewind, as the chefs bore down on him.

'Heard you wuzzas was leavin',' said Ron. 'Wouldn't be fair to let you go without shaking you by the hand, Charley said.'

'The Peach Nellie went down a treat,' said Charley, beaming broadly.

'Glad to hear it,' said Rincewind. 'Good to see you looking so cheerful.'

'It gets better!' said Ron. 'There's a new soprano just been taken on and she's a winner if I'm any judge and . . . no, Charley, *you* tell him her name . . .'

'Germaine Trifle,' said Charley. A wider grin would have resulted in the top of his head slipping off.

'I'm very happy for you,' said Rincewind. 'Start whipping that cream right now, y'hear?'

Ron patted him on the shoulder. 'We could always do with another hand in the kitchens,' he said. 'Just say the word, mate.'

'Well, it's very kind of you, and when I pull another tissue out of a box I'll always remember you blokes at the Opera House, but—'

'There he is!'

The gaoler and the captain of the guard were jogging along the quay. The gaoler was waving encouragingly at him.

'Nah, nah, it's all right, you don't have to run!' he shouted. 'We've got a pardon for you!'

'Pardon?' said Rincewind.

'That's right!' The gaoler reached him, and fought for breath. 'Signed . . . by . . . the prime minister,' he managed. 'Says you're a . . . good bloke and we're not to . . . hang you . . .' He straightened up. 'Mind you, we wouldn't do that anyway, not now. Best bloody escape we've ever bloody had since Tinhead Ned!'

Rincewind looked down at the writing on the official lined prison notepaper.

'Oh. Good,' he said weakly. 'At least someone thinks I didn't steal the damn thing.'

'Oh, everyone *knows* you stole it,' said the gaoler happily. 'But after that escape, we-ell ... and that chase, eh? Bluey here says he's never seen anyone run like you, and that's a fact!'

The guard punched Rincewind playfully on the arm. 'Good on yer, mate,' he said, grinning. 'But we'll catch yer next time!'

Rincewind looked blankly at the pardon. 'You mean I'm getting this for being a good sport?'

'No worries!' said the gaoler. 'And there's a queue of farmers sayin' if you want to steal one of *their* sheep next time that'd be bonza, just so long as they get a verse in the ballad.'

Rincewind gave up. 'What can I say?' he said. 'You keep one of the best condemned cells I've ever stayed in, and I've been in a few.' He looked at the glow of admiration in their faces and decided that, since fortune had been kind, it was time to give something back. 'Er ... I'd take it kindly, though, if you'd never ever redecorate that cell.'

'No worries. Here, I thought we ought to give you this,' said the gaoler, handing him a little giftwrapped package. 'Got no use for it now, eh?'

Rincewind unwrapped the hempen rope.

'I'm lost for words,' he said. 'How thoughtful. I'm

bound to find lots of uses for it. And what's this . . . *sandwiches*?'

'Y'know that sticky brown stuff you made? Well, all the lads tried it and they all went "yukk" and then they all wanted some more, so we tried cooking up a batch,' said the gaoler. 'I was thinking of going into business. You don't mind, do you?'

'No worries. Be my guest.'

'Good on yer!'

Someone else wandered up as he watched them hurry away.

'I heard you were going back,' said Bill Rincewind. 'Want to stay on here? I had a word with your Dean. He gave you a bloody good reference.'

'Did he? What did he say?'

'He said if I could get you to do any work for me I'd be lucky,' said Bill.

Rincewind looked around at the city, glistening under the rain.

'It's a nice offer,' he said. 'But . . . oh, I dunno . . . all this sun, sea, surf and sand wouldn't be good for me. Thanks all the same.'

'You sure?'

'Yes.'

Bill Rincewind held out his hand. 'No worries,' he said. 'I'll send you a card at Hogswatch, and some bit of clothing that doesn't fit properly. I'd better get back to the university now, I've got all the staff up on the roof mending the leaks . . .'

And that was it.

Rincewind sat for a while watching the last of the

passengers get aboard, and took a final look around the rain-soaked harbour. Then he stood up.

'Come on, then,' he said.

The Luggage followed him up the gangplank, and they went home.

It rained.

The flood gurgled along ancient creek beds and overflowed, spreading out in a lacework of gullies and rivulets.

Further rain ensued.

Near the centre of the last continent, where waterfalls streamed down the flanks of a great red rock that steamed with the heat of a ten-thousand-year summer, a small naked boy sat in the branches of a tree along with three bears, several possums, innumerable parrots and a camel.

Apart from the rock, the world was a sea.

And someone was wading through it. He was an old man, carrying a leather bag on his back.

He stopped, waist deep in swirling water, and looked up at the sky.

Something was coming. The clouds were twisting, spinning, leaving a silvery hole all the way up to the blue sky, and there was a sound that you might get if you took a roll of thunder and stretched it out thin.

A dot appeared, growing bigger. The man raised a skinny arm and, suddenly, it was holding an oval of wood that trailed a cord, which hit his hand with a *slap*.

The rain stopped.

The last few drops hammered out a little rhythm

that said: now we know where you are, we'll be coming back . . .

The boy laughed.

The old man looked up, caught sight of him, and grinned. He tucked the bullroarer into the string around his waist and took up a boomerang painted in more colours than the boy had ever seen in one place together.

The man tossed it up and caught it a couple of times and then, glancing sideways to make sure his audience was watching him, he hurled it.

It rose into the sky and went on climbing, long past the point where any normal thing should have started to fall back. It grew bigger, too. The clouds parted to let it through. And then it stopped, as if suddenly nailed to the sky.

Like sheep which, having been driven to a pasture, can now spread out at their leisure, the clouds began to drift. Afternoon sunlight sliced through into the still waters. The boomerang hung in the sky, and the boy thought he would have to find a new word for the way the colours glowed.

In the meantime, he looked down at the water and tried out the word he'd been taught by his grandfather, who'd been taught it by *his* grandfather, and which had been kept for thousands of years for when it would be needed.

It meant *the smell after rain*.

It had, he thought, been well worth waiting for.

THE END

THE DISCWORLD NOVELS

The Discworld novels can be read in any order,
but here they are in the order they were published

1. The Colour of Magic ★
2. The Light Fantastic ★
3. Equal Rites 🧙
4. Mort ⧖
5. Sourcery ★
6. Wyrd Sisters 🧙
7. Pyramids ●
8. Guards! Guards! †
9. Eric ★
10. Moving Pictures ●
11. Reaper Man ⧖
12. Witches Abroad 🧙
13. Small Gods ●
14. Lords and Ladies 🧙
15. Men at Arms †
16. Soul Music ⧖
17. Interesting Times ★
18. Maskerade 🧙
19. Feet of Clay †
20. Hogfather ⧖
21. Jingo †
22. The Last Continent ★
23. Carpe Jugulum 🧙
24. The Fifth Elephant †
25. The Truth ●
26. Thief of Time ⧖
27. The Last Hero ●
28. Night Watch †
29. Monstrous Regiment ●
30. Going Postal ⚙
31. Thud! †
32. Making Money ⚙
33. Unseen Academicals ★
34. Snuff †
35. Raising Steam ⚙

Key:
🧙 Witches
† City Watch
★ Wizards
⧖ Death
⚙ Industrial Revolution
● Standalones

A complete list of Terry Pratchett books – including shorter writing, children's books, illustrated titles, graphic novels, comics and plays – can be found at terrypratchettbooks.com

Unseen Academicals
Discworld: A Wizards Novel

*'We play and are played and the best we can hope
for is to do it with style.'*

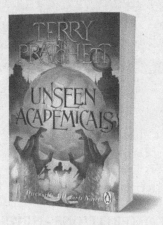

Football has come to the ancient city of Ankh-Morpork.
And now the wizards of Unseen University must win a football
match without using magic . . . so they're in the mood
for trying everything else.

To do so, they recruit an unlikely group of players: Trev,
a street urchin with a talent for kicking a tin can; Glenda, the night
chef who makes a mean pie; Juliet, the kitchen hand turned world's
greatest fashion model; and the mysterious Mr Nutt, who has
something powerful, and dark, locked away inside him . . .

And the thing about football – the *important* thing about
football – is that it is not just about football. Here we go,
here we go, here we go!

Unseen Academicals is the seventh book in the Wizards series

**Available in paperback, ebook
and unabridged audiobook read by Colin Morgan**

Find out more about
Terry Pratchett and the
Discworld novels at
terrypratchettbooks.com

**COMPETITIONS • NEWS
EXTRACTS • FAN FORUM • QUIZZES
AUDIO CLIPS • CHARACTERS
TRIVIA • QUOTES**

Follow at:

🐦 @terryandrob

📘 /Pratchett

📷 /TerryPratchettBooks

And sign up for the monthly newsletter at
terrypratchettbooks.com/newsletter